The Curator of Broken Things

Trilogy

Book 1

From Smyrna to Paris

A novel by Corine Gantz

ISBN-13: 978-0-9834366-5-2
ISBN-10: 0-9834366-5-7

To David and Nathan

TABLE OF CONTENTS

CHAPTER 1

Move-in Day

All around, Cassie saw men. But it seemed that that ship had sailed for her. Fathers or sons, young or old, the percentage who paid her any attention was exactly zero.

It was liberating, this new-found invisibility. These days Cassie dressed strictly for comfort, her black curls had reverted to their natural unruliness, and the money she economized on makeup was spent liberally and without guilt on chocolate.

It was liberating, yes, but also depressing, if she dwelled on the thought too long.

She was sitting on a plastic chair between a pool table and a vending machine and pretending to be immensely occupied with her cellphone. What she was doing, though, was observing without being seen, one of the rare perks of impending middle age.

Freshmen of every race, shape, culture, nationality, and gender – some whose race or gender she could not identify – entered and exited the building carrying suitcases, boxes, rolled-up memory foam mattresses, clothes on hangers, toasters, and computers, while their parents fretted. Move-in Day, Cassie understood, was a flirt-fest on an epic scale. The boys and girls were checking each other out, ready as they were for the parentally orchestrated and financed independence that awaited them.

It should have been a consolation that she wasn't the only one struggling. Around Cassie, other hapless, apologetic-looking parents carried objects up and down stairwells in a heart-wrenching attempt at being relevant one last time. Meanwhile, the freshmen, consciously or not, counted the minutes until that last hug, when the gates would at last close behind their lives as children.

It dawned on her that up until today she had had a function. The function of mother of twins. But Alexander and Jeanne had come in like a tornado, transformed her life into a seventeen-year-long hurricane, and in a matter of hours would be out of the house and into college, both of them on the very same day. In the chaos and excitement of organizing them for college, Cassie had not prepared herself for becoming extraneous to their lives overnight.

Whom would she take care of now?

Who would take care of *her*?

Move-in Day for both kids being on the same weekend, they had divided the task. Peter, her ex-husband, was in New York with Alex, while Cassie was in Miami with Jeanne. Alexander and Jeanne had come out of her womb with distinct outlooks on life. Jeanne would be studying acting at the University of Miami, the only school willing to overlook her 2.0 GPA. Cassie and Peter had the strong suspicion that Peter's status as the most sought-after screenwriter in Hollywood had weighed heavily on the admission committee's decision. They regardless breathed a huge sigh of relief and Peter gladly signed the exorbitant tuition check. Meanwhile, Alexander, surprising no one, had been accepted to several Ivy Leagues and had opted for the full ride at Columbia.

Cassie tucked herself in a corner of the hall to do what people do when they already feel immensely crappy about their lives and called her ex-husband.

She dialed his cell, almost hoping to land on voicemail but Peter picked up on the first ring.

"What's going on in New York?" she asked.

"I'm at the campus's Starbucks," Peter said, "treating myself to a delicious tres leches iced macchiado. I asked the barista if it was vegan but she did not know."

"Why vegan?"

"Jessica wants me to give it a shot," Peter said.

"Tres leches means three milks in Spanish," Cassie pointed out.

"Oh well, I already syphoned half of it anyway."

"You're with Alex?"

"No, by myself."

Cassie sat back in her plastic chair and rolled her eyes, "Sheesh, Peter."

"What?"

"You won't be seeing your son until Thanksgiving and you're spending those last precious minutes alone at Starbucks?"

Peter had known her for eighteen years and had spent the first twelve married to her. He could tell when she was upset. "How are you feeling?" he asked.

"They still haven't come up with an adjective to describe what I'm feeling," she said.

"Here is what you're feeling," Peter said. "Proud, excited, and a little sad."

"Children pried away from their parents and vice versa. I can't understand what there is to rejoice about."

"French kids go to college too," Peter said. "I'm sure they have Move-in Day there as well. It's all part of life."

Cassie had grown up in France and gone to school there. Her conception of American university life was second-hand or fictionalized: *Legally Blonde*, *Animal House*, Peter droning on about his alma mater, brochures depicting intellectually and genetically gifted youth, rape on campus statistics – and what in the world was a sorority rush? "I'll have you know that the rest of the world's schools aren't filled with cheerleaders, marching bands, and keg parties," she said.

Peter did not respond, as was his new technique when she was unjustifiably aggressive. Had he done just that when they were married, had he just waited for the storm to pass as he now did so well, they might still be together today.

Peter was a good guy, great father, and a friend. The worst of Peter, not to mention Cassie's worst, had found free and creative ways to express itself in their marriage. Five years after their separation Peter seemed at last capable of being happily married, although to someone else.

"I hate that I'm not with you and Jeanne today," Peter said. "I hate it every time I need to be two places at once. It just tears me up inside."

What other time was there? Cassie briefly wondered. "Damn. That lump in my throat is back," she said, "I don't want Jeanne to see me in tears when she comes back."

"Where is she?"

"I got sick of following her around like a love-struck puppy. I'm sitting in the reception area while she organizes her room. I don't want to be one of those pathetic mothers who makes her daughter's bed and arranges her closet."

Now, of course, that was precisely what she wanted to do.

"You know this is a sanctioned day for parents to be pathetic," Peter said. "We're all in the same boat. A little humiliation is part of the separation process."

Cassie considered that before replying. "Only my situation is a little shittier than yours." She stopped herself. She didn't want to look any more pitiful than was necessary.

"I know what you mean," Peter said conciliatorily.

"No, you don't."

Peter knew not to go there. After dropping off Alex, he would be returning to Los Angeles; to his crisp, new, shiny life; to Jessica, his young wife whom Cassie called Jessica Rabbit – although never to her face – because of her cartoon-like figure and determination to be with child every eighteen months or so, who was pregnant at the moment with their third boy in five years. Whereas tomorrow Cassie would fly back to Los Angeles and return to an empty house.

Peter knew all too well that tomorrow Cassie was back to square one.

****

Later, in the cafeteria, Cassie and Jeanne were having lunch. Cassie stared at the stringy meat on her plate, the pale mushrooms that floated in industrial-strength gravy. In the cafeteria line, students stood next to their parents, the kids wishing their parents could just disappear, and the parents just as aware of being unwanted. All were piling up bland food on their plastic trays. Cassie wondered what was worse, not to be wanted, or not to be needed?

"What are you going to do now, mom?" Jeanne asked.

Cassie looked at Jeanne. If someone could become a Hollywood star, it was her daughter. Not for the acting – although she was terrific at drama and was, after all, here to learn all about it since they were investing two hundred thousand dollars into it – but for her loveliness, her sleek auburn hair, her eyes a rare shade of green, her porcelain skin, her slender neck, and her long body. The question took Cassie by surprise. It wasn't like Jeanne to corner her like this. "I'll go on living if that is what you're wondering."

"I'm just imagining you being all alone in Los Angeles. I bet Alex is thinking about it too."

"Yet you both spent the last two years planning an East Coast education."

"You could have told us not to apply out of state."

"The last thing you need is to worry about where it leaves me," Cassie said.

Jeanne picked at the lone tomato slice in her salad. "But I do."

Cassie's heart melted. It was hard to remember the hell Jeanne had put her through over the last few years. "Please don't worry about me," she said. "See, you made it to college! Isn't that incredible? You are starting your life, my love. My job here is done." Jeanne's eyes flooded with tears, and the green of her pupils turned gorgeously near-fluorescent. Cassie bit her lip. She too had greenish eyes, although hers were more on the amber side, but all she'd get out of tears would be puffy eyes and a red nose. "I'll be fine, mon ange. I'll garden. You know. I've been looking forward to gardening for years."

"Mom, you know you're never going to garden."

"And there are so many things I look forward to doing now. Reading uninterrupted, going to the movies, spending time with friends, writing for myself for once."

Jeanne shook her head. "First of all, what friends? The only people you spend time with are Dad and us."

"I have friends," Cassie protested. "Friends are overrated. People are, in general."

"I can't picture you working from home with Dad every day. It's kind of creepy."

"Why creepy? Your father and I have been working together for almost two decades."

"I don't know … Alex and I won't be around. It'll be weird, the old home, the ex-husband, no kids. Will Jessica be creeped out by that?"

"Honey, Jessica Rabbit and I are not in competition. You just enjoy school. What your mother does from here on out is none of your beeswax."

Jeanne rolled her eyes. "Oh Mom, stop saying that. You can't even say it right."

"How do you say it?"

"Without a French accent."

"I look forward to my accent not being mocked." Cassie added, "Motherhood is about adapting to your children's needs and changes. Right now, your need is that I get out of the way so that you and your brother can become adults. I left my country and started over with a new language when I was barely older than you are. I think I've demonstrated my capacity to adapt. The whole world is open to you. Your job is to start soaring."

"Hello, Mother! Don't act like you have a foot in the grave. You're 39. Most of my friends' moms are much older than you are. That's the good part of having us when you were twenty."

"The bad part is that I was a child when I had children and did not know myself at all. Don't make the same mistake, I'm begging you."

"My point is, you better find something exciting to do. You know how you are. You get restless. And you have potential too, for soaring and stuff."

"I'm not like you and Alex, honey. I've had a very different set of circumstances."

"French parents, I know."

"That's right."

"That great Potential-Crusher."

"Exactement."

Jeanne bit into a French fry and said, "There are people with worse childhoods than yours that end up doing all kinds of cool stuff."

"And for this I applaud them." Cassie looked at her beautiful daughter and tried to sear this moment into her memory. "Promise me just one thing," she pleaded.

Jeanne looked at her wearily. "What?"

"Call your brother occasionally."

Jeanne twisted her lip. "You know Alex has no desire to speak to me."

"Then email him. You don't have to say personal things. Maybe send him a funny link, or, I don't know, like his Facebook status."

"We're not even friends on social media, mom. He hates me."

"The two of you are just going through a phase."

"He can't stand that I got into a college in the end and that I enjoyed high school. I didn't have to kill myself the way he did."

Cassie did not respond. How could she have responded? This was the truth. She had experienced a similar reaction from Alex when she had made the same request before he left. Her son was more laconic, less inclined to volunteering information, but he was sweet and gentle, except when it came to his sister. "The only reason they admitted her," he had said, "is that they saw Dad's name on her application."

"I'm sure it was a factor," Cassie had to admit.

"Remind me again? How much are you forking out for her acting education?"

"This is the first time your sister is motivated to do something."

"As if she wasn't self-indulgent enough. You realize she'll never make a living that way?"

"What are we going to do, Alex? Disown her because you're a workhorse and a math genius? And had you not gotten the scholarship, we would have paid for your education too."

"But I *did* get the scholarship. And you won't have to pay for my education."

"Alex, we are so proud of you. And yes, we hope that your sister will rise to the occasion. But parenting is not a meritocracy. We love you both for your strengths, your weaknesses, and everything in between. I know it's hard to comprehend that we can love you for being so accomplished while at the same time love her for –"

"– being a fuck-up?" Alex asked.

"Please just try to call her once in a while."

"She'll be much too busy posting videos of herself applying makeup. And you know she hates me."

"She doesn't. It's just that she might feel a bit insecure around you."

"Same difference."

On the plane back to Los Angeles, Cassie felt numb, as though none of this was happening to her. She told herself that if anything, this was good material. When you're a writer and life kicks you in the jaw, you always have that consolation.

CHAPTER 2

The Ottoman Boy

1912. Smyrna, in the ailing Ottoman Empire. Above, only blue sky. It is the hottest time of the day on the hottest day of the year. Everywhere: dirt, rocks, boulders, some as tall as houses. A half dozen petrified-looking goats stunned into stillness by the terrible heat. The sharp scent of wild sage. The crackling hum of flying insects. And then something peculiar in the distance: a lone dark silhouette is climbing agilely through the barren earth and jagged rocks. On closer observation, it is a boy, perhaps ten years old, dressed entirely in black in the traditional garment of rabbinical students, in a heavy cloak and a wide-brimmed hat. The boy hops from rock to rock, light-footed despite the cumbersome clothes, and suddenly he is gone: disappeared into thin air.

****

For the last two years, Albano never took the same path twice so that his footsteps did not form a trail. He wiped his brow, leaned against the pulsating heat of the stone and, for a minute, took in his deserted surroundings. Satisfied that no one was there who could have seen him, he plunged under the seemingly impenetrable thorny bushes at the base of the rock, into the narrow opening only he knew about. On his hands and feet, he crawled into the pitch-black cavity in the rocks and felt for the matches he had placed there. He sat down on the cool dirt and lit the oil lamp.

When the cave illuminated, Albano was always gripped with the same feeling. A miracle had brought him here.

The cave was a cool and damp world of echoing silence and looked the way all of Earth must have at the beginning of time. A minuscule spring trickled from a crack in the rock and pooled in one corner to disappear a few meters further down a subterranean path. A bit of light found its way through a crack high above, and so things grew there: nothing much, moss and a few tender ferns, but enough to transform the cave into an otherworldly wonder. It was about twenty by fifteen feet wide and tall enough for a man to stand. A palace.

Albano wasted no time in removing his clothes. His cave was furnished with only what he had managed to hide under his clothes, bits of useful objects which might make a person comfortable: an oil lamp, a rug, even a small reserve of food and water. He removed his leather slippers, breeches, and black linen stockings and placed them neatly on a rock.

He wished that he could remain this way eternally, feel the cool air on his bare skin, the freedom of it. The feeling of being undressed transported him to the time when his mother used to let him and his brothers splash around in the sea half naked. He knelt on a rug next to the spring, cupped his hand, and drank the cold water. For a while, he sat by the water, breathed in the dampness, and listened to the bubbling brook that echoed against the smooth stone of the cavern. For a fleeting moment, he experienced a sense of deep connectedness with a beauty and power he could not name.

Two years ago, the cholera pandemic had left absolute loss in its trail. Days after it happened, he was torn away from his village and everything he knew and was brought to Smyrna's Jewish quarter to live with his cousins and Uncle Joshua and Aunt Sadie – the only relatives able to take in an eight-year-old orphan.

He had discovered the cave by accident, on a day when he had hoped to die. But the cave had welcomed him like a loving mother, made him feel protected, made him feel safe. It was in this cave that Albano had taken refuge and cursed Adonai for taking his mother, father, brothers, and sisters and sparing him for no reason he could understand. It was in the cave that he was able to bury his face into his arms and sob in secret. It was in the cave that he had later on resigned himself to his aunt and uncle's decision that he should take on rabbinical studies.

But in the last few days, he had met Uncle Moshe, and then Hagop and Xandra. Now everything had changed, and perhaps his whole life and destiny along with it.

Albano carefully folded his tallis, brought his lips to it, and said a prayer of his composition. Adonai would not approve of what he was about to do. He reached inside a narrow crevice between two rocks and felt for the leather satchel. He opened it. The money was still there.

Albano unfolded the white linen djellaba, the loose breeches, and the sandals his friend Hagop had given him. Hagop. Yes, Albano now had a friend. A friend who was not Jewish!

When he was dressed, Albano slung the satchel over his thin body. He combed his payots behind his ears the way Hagop had taught him, which was no easy feat, and then secured them in place with a red fez. "You don't want to look like a Jew," Hagop had told him. "No one in Smyrna trusts a Jew. Not the Turks, not the Greeks, not the Armenians, not even the Jews themselves." This was not true, of course. Jews did trust Jews. Although Hagop's comment had made Albano angry at the time, he could not deceive himself entirely. Wasn't he, at this very moment, being untrustworthy to his people?

Up on the highest ridge inside the cave, set upright against the stone, in a spot where they caught the best light of the single ray of sun that made its way inside the cave, his family's finials seemed to look down at him with reproach. The two Torah ornaments destined to top a Torah case were shaped like tiny, intricate gold and silver crowns, each only large enough for a squirrel's head. His father, a Kohen descendant of Aaron, brother of Moses, and high priest by birth, had demanded of him, on his deathbed, to hide the finials. They were sacred, although Albano didn't know what made them so. They had belonged to his father and his grandfather, and his great-grandfather before that. Albano only needed to know that, like all things that were ancient, precious, and sacred, they had to be kept a secret. One day, Albano would take on the responsibility of Kohanim, which was an everlasting covenant, although he was unsure what the words Kohanim, everlasting, and covenant meant.

His mother used to love to tell the tale of how, when he was born, the village's rabbi had scrutinized him for disqualifying traits. Albano had been born with both hands and feet; he wasn't blind, his eyebrows weren't too thick, his limbs were in good proportion and his testicles in good order, and therefore the rabbi had proclaimed him suitable. But because he was a Kohen, Albano was not allowed to take part in his family burials. Those were the kinds of rules that God made. Albano carried the weight of that responsibility and also the burden of what they meant regarding his obligation to God.

When he exited the cave later, Albano looked very different. He was dressed in white and wore a fez. He looked just like a Muslim boy. He walked down the rocky sides of Mount Pagus, trying not to think too much about the Kohanim, and kept a nervous hand in his trouser pocket into which he had tucked a portion of yesterday's earnings. This was just enough akçes for today's business. The bulk of his and Hagop's profit would remain hidden in the cave for now. Albano felt great anguish at the responsibility of keeping his new friend's share of their earnings, but Hagop slept with four nosy sisters in a small room above his parent's bakery and so did not possess a good hiding place of his own.

But wasn't Hagop contradicting himself? Hagop had an agile mind, and Albano often became confused when his friend spoke to him a mile a minute in a mixture of Arabic, Armenian, and Hebrew, but this time, Albano had a solid argument. By trusting him to hold on to the money, wasn't Hagop the precise example of an Armenian boy trusting a Jew? Albano smiled at the idea and began to rehearse in his mind their future conversation on the subject.

Albano descended the hill feeling light at last in clothes so much better suited for walking in the sun than the clothes meant to toil over the word of God. He thought of Moshe, the extraordinary uncle he had just met, who had arrived in Smyrna and within a week's time had managed to turn Albano's life upside down. Uncle Moshe was scandalous; that was what the women in the Jewish quarter said. But in what way? This, Albano could not figure out. When he asked, there were eye rolls and giggles, and that was that. Did Albano's time spent with his new friend Hagop make him scandalous as well, he wondered?

As he reached the main road, deserted mountains turned into the city's suburb. There were many people in the streets. Houses sprouted one after another, and the temperature eased with each step. A faint sea breeze swept lightly through the air, and the arid landscape made way for palm trees and masses of bougainvillea against whitewashed walls. The pungent aroma of wild oregano soon mingled with the scents of jasmine emanating from the houses' courtyards. Albano followed the dirt road where it made its turn around the mountain and, as it happened every time without fail, he was overcome with awe at the beauty before him. There, magnificent, dark blue against the turquoise sky, was the vast expanse of the Aegean Sea cradled by the glorious bay of Smyrna and, further into the horizon, his wide-open future.

CHAPTER 3

Empty Nester

Cassie faced the jungle that was her garden. She and the plants knew that this had nothing to do with gardening. This was war. The bougainvillea, which was tangled into the Italian Cypress almost all the way up, had won the minute it began to grow thorns the size of butcher's knives. She narrowed her eyes at the mass of giant echiums and their foot-long cone-shaped flowers. No, not them either. Their silver leaves stuck to everything like Velcro: hair, clothes, even mysteriously the inside of her bra. And forget about the pampas grass, so feather-like and innocent-looking but mercenary with blades sharp as razors, or the blue trumpet vines, which she had planted fifteen years before: three saucer-size flowers on a strand of vine wrapped daintily around a two-foot tall bamboo. Since then each flower had popped bullet-like seeds that rudely planted themselves and multiplied like the broom in *Fantasia*. They had overtaken the garden, and Cassie was allergic to them on contact. This much she had learned in her nearly two decades of gardening in Southern California: here a plant either withered and died within a week or became invasive and wanted to kill you.

Cassie threw down her hedge trimmers and went inside the house. Jeanne had been spot-on. Nearly eight months later, Cassie wasn't having such a great time enjoying her new found quiet after all. She had waited from September to Christmas for the twins to come for winter break, but as soon as they were back home, they had resumed their teenage habits and disappeared to hang out with old friends, only coming home to sleep, and did not wake up until noon while she paced. Had she not been a horrible cook she would have fed them delicious meals, but even this was out of her reach. Her microwave chocolate cake in a mug only went so far to lure in her children.

In the last eight months, Peter and Jessica had produced another spawn, Jeanne and Alex had gone through almost two semesters of college, and all Cassie had to show for it were rose thorn scratches and cracked fingernails. Christmas and all its trimmings had been consummated at Peter's house. Jessica Rabbit (who was a won-der-ful! cook) had prepared the whole meal while handling two toddlers and a newborn with Mary Poppins-like magic.

Cassie had tried so hard to *act* relaxed that her body, clenched to the breaking point, had thrown in the towel the next day with the mother of all sciaticas, and she had spent January unable to stand straight.

Inside the house, she placed the last of the boxes of her cleaning spree by the entryway. Her efforts were single-minded, more akin to the Great Purge than to spring cleaning. Everything had to go. Why she wasn't sure. This last box was filled with old shoes, boots, sandals, and that pair of one-size-too-small Christian Louboutin stilettos that Peter had given her on some occasion. That book she had read recently on the evils of a cluttered life had legitimized her craving for something, and she had decided that what she craved was minimalism. It was progress, she told herself, to crave something. But if she was honest with herself, she had made too little progress where it mattered the most: when it came to the one major goal she had set for herself, which was to let go of Peter, Cassie had not made a dent.

She went down the staircase to her bedroom and unearthed from the depth of the closet the last item she had planned to add to the giveaway pile: an old suitcase, monstrous-looking with a green and pink zebra pattern, a rusty zipper, and wobbly wheels. She dragged it up the stairs. The main part of the house stood at street level and was jaw-dropping with glossy wood floors, white walls, and a soaring ceiling. A first impression that blinds you to details that will, down the line, ruin your life – i.e. the two rooms per floor, the laundry room located at the lowest level, and the millions of steps this quirk implies. Because of this oversight, you will spend the next eighteen years climbing and descending steps, which will give you, along with buns and thighs of steel, a major laundry chip on your shoulder. The floor plan that had seemed eccentric and so Los Angeles, not to mention all that Cassie and Peter could afford at the time, had soon turned into a massive annoyance to them both. From day one (maybe to be allowed to argue about something safe), Cassie had made herself the house's staunch advocate and Peter its relentless detractor. He had wanted to move. She had wanted to stay. Everyone had dug in their heels.

She parked the suitcase next to the pile of boxes. She had timed this just right. The Salvation Army truck would be here any moment, and Peter was arriving at one. The boxes had better be gone before he got here or she would never hear the end of it. She looked at the nice pile. Mission accomplished!

But what she heard coming from the street below was not the sounds of the Salvation Army truck making its way up the hill, but the groan of Peter's Porsche.

Merde! She thought.

A minute later Peter was letting himself in. "You're early!" she said as Peter made a beeline for the pile of boxes.

"Jessica's car is at the shop," he said. "She had to drop me off on her way to taking the boys to their Glockenspiel class. What's all this?"

"What in the world is a Glockenspiel class?"

Peter was digging into the boxes already. "Beats me," he said.

"By the way, she better not just let herself in when she picks you up."

Peter shrugged, "Then lock the front door."

"I want her to learn to knock first, and then wait for me to open the door, whether the door is open or not."

"Cassie, I can't tell Jess that. She won't understand. She'll think you're mad at her."

"Well, I am."

"You know she adores you. She looks up to you."

"Oh yes, because I'm what to her? A mother figure?"

"She considers you a friend."

"My friends don't barge in unannounced. They sensibly knock and wait for me to let them in."

"How's gardening treating you?" Peter asked. He was taking things out of the cardboard boxes, examining them.

"Terribly," she admitted.

A handsome, masculine specimen at age forty-five, Peter filled any room with his massive presence. Six-foot-three, 250 pounds, all banter and charm. Peter never shortchanged anyone of his attention, his warmth, even his hugs. Even now, even divorced, if she asked him for a hug, he would take her in his arms and make her feel safe. Now that Jessica groomed him, he wore designer jeans and shirts and pointy shoes that didn't suit him at all. Cassie preferred him in sneakers, cargo shorts, and generic T-shirts, the kind of clothes a man who loves his steak and beer could function in. She liked him all-American, not in that metrosexual look Jessica had cooked up for him.

As he bent down over the cardboard boxes, his too-tight shirt popped out of his too-tight jeans. "What is this?" he yelped, brandishing a framed photo. "You're not giving Alexander's baseball portrait away are you?"

"We already have all those pictures," she mumbled, feeling caught. "Digitally."

"If you don't want a picture, burn it!"

"It felt wrong to destroy it."

"Giving your own children's framed photographs to charity? Who does this?"

"Oh, come on, this was just one picture. Of course, with my luck, that's the first thing you find."

"What else is in there?" Peter started opening more boxes and digging through them.

"This is my stuff! I can do whatever I want with it. Unless you want it all, but I don't imagine our family memorabilia will sit well with Jessica Rabbit."

"Stop calling her that," he said, his head deeper into the box. He came out of it waving a baseball trophy. "You can't throw those things out! You just can't. And what do you have against baseball?" Peter shook his head in disbelief as he handled an old plaid shirt of his, a lampshade, a ping pong racket and then dropped them back into the box and foraged for more damning evidence. He would tire of this and stop, she hoped. Peter had the attention span of a hamster. She hoped he would stop before getting to the bottom boxes where the real sentimental stuff was: posters they had bought together, mixed tapes, letters they had exchanged, lingerie from their honeymoon.

"I'm doing it for the twins," she said. "That way, after I'm dead, they won't have to feel guilty throwing away objects that I was too weak to part with."

"Who's dying? You haven't had a cold in years. You'll be a centenarian, giving everyone a pain in the ass for generations to come."

"I'm facing my mortality, thinking about a future without me."

"While methodically destroying the past!"

You're the one who destroyed the past, buddy, Cassie thought. "If you had it your way, this house would remain a mausoleum to your old life, and I would be the keeper of all the shit you moved on from. This would be the museum of your old family, and I would be its curator."

"I'm talking about the *past* past. It's your pattern," Peter said, opening an old tin can, finding it empty, sniffing it, and tossing it back into the cardboard box. "Your childhood. Your parents. Trashing all our stuff is more of what you've been doing all along: brushing your somber family antecedents under the rug."

"I'd love to sweep things under the rug, but you keep pulling it from under me."

Peter stopped in mid-dig and lifted his head. "That's good. That's a fun line. Let's use it in the screenplay." He pulled something out and, brandishing it, said, "This is still good! A perfectly usable bathroom mat."

"Take it. You can ask Jessica to weave winter booties out if it."

"What's this?" he asked, holding a small gilded frame. Inside the frame was an old key on display atop black velvet. The glass was cracked in places.

"Some junk from Alex's room."

"Oh yeah, your father gave this to him the last time we went to France as a family," Peter said. "We were at their house, remember?"

"Nope."

"Alex found it in a drawer, and your father said he could have it. That's as close to a gift as our children ever received from that disgruntled geezer." Peter pointed to the zebra suitcase. "This, however, you can trash."

"How about you keep all this. Jessica will be thrilled to find a place for it in that tower of cold metal you call a house."

"She's a minimalist," Peter said.

"You sure compartmentalize. Little shrines all over my house devoted to your old family, while your new house is all about the new wife, the minimalism, the babies."

"I don't have a new and an old family, Cassie," he said. "You are all my family. And don't forget that I'm not the one who threw our life upside down." As expected, Peter lost interest in the boxes and went into the kitchen to inspect the cupboard for Oreos. The indignity was that now that the kids were gone, Cassie bought processed snacks for her ex-husband. There was something reassuring in the act of filling a grocery cart with comfort food her family liked. Peter opened a package and stuffed the whole cookie into his mouth. "You chaid you were micherable," he said, chewing. "You kicked me out and into a hotel room when I had done noching. Noching!" He opened the refrigerator. "Wheh ich my lactoche-free milk?"

She went to the fridge, took out his milk, and set it on the kitchen table, their preferred workplace, in the bright light, within arm's reach of the coffee maker. The kitchen had been the object of an expensive and soul-crushing remodel and, per Peter's modernistic taste, was all open shelves, frosted glass cupboards, polished concrete countertop, and a gleaming six-burner range that remained gleaming due to Cassie's utter incompetence as a cook. Why could everything not be prepared in a microwave, and in a mug? Cassie did not care about food much. As long as she had ketchup to pour on whatever was served, she ate it. "I asked for time to evaluate my life for a few weeks, and you find yourself some chick," she said.

"See how you rewrite history? Six months is not a few weeks. We were separated. And Jessica isn't some chick," Peter said as he set his laptop at the kitchen table. "Stay with the anger, by the way. Your character is supposed to be a bitch."

"Must every strong woman be a bitch?"

"This one is."

"Is that how you see her? That's not how I want the audience to feel about her."

"Don't worry," Peter said, "we're Hollywood. We'll tell them how they're supposed to feel."

As they had done daily for the better part of two decades, Cassie flipped the switch on the coffee maker, and they sat across from each other in front of their respective laptops. As the smell of coffee mingled with the jasmine scent that flowed in through the open window, they dug into their screenplay *Women in Black, Before There Was Space*, the prequel to *Women in Black–An Intergalactic Dramedy*, their blockbuster of two summers ago. The film had grossed 250 million dollars internationally and had been hailed by some critics as a wild romp through space, time, and the fear of women, and by others as a wretched film that epitomized everything that's wrong with America and the movie business. Meanwhile, the sequel, *Women in Black, Part Two*, was about to open on screens worldwide the following week, helped by a stratospheric advertising budget.

Sitting across from each other, a mug of steaming coffee in hand, they began writing, each typing on a shared document. Peter usually wrote one character's lines and Cassie another's, and they went back and forth, analyzing each word, trimming and pumping up the emotional resonance in each scene, crafting dialogues until they gave the illusion of sounding natural. Screenwriting was to words what food photography was to actual, edible food. A lot of artifice, glycerin, and spray paint went into making that burger look juicy and piping hot.

Peter was fresh out of film school when he and Cassie got married. His first job was that of a quasi-slave and whipping boy for the prolific writer of a now-defunct soap opera. Peter's job was to edit the screenplays. The pay was laughable. The screenplays began coming at Peter at ever-increasing speed by courier – this was before the internet – at first one per week, then two, then one or two per day. Cassie and Peter accepted that this was the way the game was played. He had to pay his dues. It was how people entered what is referred to in Los Angeles as The Business. But Peter couldn't cope with the volume of work, so Cassie began to help. English was not her first language, and she had no training, but she caught on fast. They divided the task. The courier would arrive. Cassie would open the envelopes and read the scripts. She would explain the plots to Peter, and they would brainstorm ideas, find ways out of impasses, polish dialogue by acting them out. It was a fun time. Through this process, she absorbed all kinds of writing techniques and at the same time perfected her English. Soon Peter was asked to write for the soap opera, and he was officially in The Business. A year later he was hired to write for a new sitcom. When it came to writing, Cassie turned out to be fast, efficient, indefatigable, and she had one attribute Peter lacked: concentration. Peter was the one who had gone to film school, the one with the TV credit and Emmy under his belt. Also, he was a fantastic salesperson. Hollywood loves a man with both skills and an affable personality.

All this paid very well. When *Rescue Hour*, their first feature film screenplay, written on specs, was made into a movie and became a box office smash, Peter's career was launched for good.

The divorce papers had come with a work contract stipulating that Peter wanted to continue their work relationship. It even specified how much he would pay Cassie to do what she had previously done for free, and it gave her a writing credit on all the work they would collaborate on in the future, something she never had in the past.

Cassie got a lot out of the divorce. She also stopped being Cassandra Carawell, Peter's last name (when she introduced herself in Los Angeles. people often asked, "Carawell? The one from *Women in Black*?" and she answered, "No, only his wife") and went back to signing her checks Cassandra Lombard. She now was paid considerable money to do something she enjoyed. She got custody of the children. The house was hers. What else could she ask for? Peter's enveloping hands on her? No, this she could not have anymore.

Peter did well in the deal too. By buying a nearby house, he got to keep the twins close at hand. He kept his work relationship with her and got to start a whole new family with a girl with big boobs. Jessica was sweet. Very sweet. There was nothing for which Cassie could reproach Jessica. Aside from stealing her man and destroying her family.

Peter could afford the wife, the ex-wife, both houses, and all the children. He was, according to Newsweek, the most sought-after screenwriter in Hollywood. And Cassie was the most sought-after screenwriter in Hollywood's secret weapon. She alone could read Peter's mind and transform it into one hundred and twenty pages of twists, turns, snappy dialogue, wit, and drama. Working together for so many years came with its share of conflicts. They argued the most about which screenplay ideas to pitch. Peter felt that their bread and butter was high concept comedies and thrillers. She said there was never a cliché he didn't embrace, and she was ready to write something more substantial. When the studios bought only his ideas, she accused him of not pitching hers.

"You think you can become an A-list screenwriter because you can write?" Peter had said one day in one of his rants when she had threatened to stop helping him. "Screenwriting isn't about writing, Cassie. It never was about writing. If your ambition is to produce great writing, write a novel. Screenwriting is about timing. It's about connections. It's about your alma mater and how much you can out-drink the boys at parties. It's about golf more than it is about movies. It's about luck."

The best thing about the divorce was an understanding when it came to a contentious point that had polluted their marriage. Cassie now had a *credit.* Yep, Hollywood couples have something to fight about that is unknown to the general population. A particular disease. A unique form of mutual torture. For years, Cassie and Peter had fought about proprietorship of the screenplays they worked on together over the course of their marriage, including six screenplays optioned, and four made into blockbuster movies. It was not a money thing. It was an ego thing. "So, you really think you can fly solo?" Peter had said. "Go for it. Write a screenplay and try to get someone to read it – anyone. Good luck with that. Without my connections, your beautiful screenplay will languish in some asshole's drawer because he will be too busy meeting with me, reading my screenplays, and having cocktails with me." And the sad truth was that Peter was right.

According to their contract, Cassie could not reveal her contribution to past screenplays. Peter was the one with a mile-long list of credits on IMDb. It would have been a logistic nightmare to go back in time, paperwork, expenses, Peter had explained, and she suspected a bit of humiliation too, so she let it go. For all past work done together, she was a ghostwriter in the strictest of sense. No one would ever know about her involvement. From her standpoint, she had something better. During their entire marriage, Peter had never admitted to anyone, least of all himself, that he needed Cassie to write, and it was finally right there, printed on a legal document. It was sad that when that validation arrived at last, it was via lawyers and for all the wrong reasons.

This was an excellent arrangement for everyone, a symbiotic relationship – hopefully symbiotic and not parasitic, as she had pointed out to him many times.

****

Cassie and Peter were engrossed in their work, giggling and snarling dialogue lines at each other when the telephone rang. They looked at the phone. The rule was not to pick up unless it was family. Peter frowned at the lengthy set of digits displayed, but Cassie recognized the number, pounced out of her chair, her face flushed, and said "Allô?" in French. She did not need to tell Peter why she was picking up. This was a call from France. No other phone call put her in that kind of state.

"Cassandra?" asked a woman's voice.

"Oui," Cassie answered, switching to French. Only four people in the world called her Cassandra, all of them French, all of them related to her. It was Sabine, her younger sister. The fact that Sabine called at all, let alone in the middle of the night in France, was cause for worry. Sabine's speech was always cautious, deliberate, as though she weighed the power of every syllable and was reluctant to use any more words than necessary. "C'est Papa," she said. "Il est à l'hôpital."

"My dad is in the hospital," she responded mezza voce to Peter's interrogative stare. "What happened?" she asked Sabine.

"He went in four days ago to replace a valve in his heart."

"What? No one told me!" Cassie exclaimed. The words came out shriller than she intended. She needed to take it down a notch, or her sister would retract into her shell like a hermit crab. "How is he?"

"I guess we didn't want to worry you," Sabine said.

"That's okay. I'm fine with that," Cassie lied. She mentally thanked Sabine for her tact. Her parents and two sisters kept her out of the loop deliberately. That was how they dealt with her, from small things to major family crises. She thought of what Peter had said: some things were better off swept under the rug.

"The heart surgery went well," Sabine said. "But he contracted an infection at the hospital. Now he is … we don't know. It's harder to recover at his age."

"I had no idea that he needed heart surgery."

"It was elective. He was tired all the time. He could not keep up with mom."

"Why would he need to keep up with her? She's twenty years younger than he is."

"They gave him a new valve, from a pig, or a metal valve; I forget which one."

Oh, but both would be rather fitting, Cassie thought meanly. "Is he in pain?"

"Right now, he can't seem to wake up. It's kind of why I'm calling you."

Cassie felt her knees go soft, "What do you mean?"

"He can't seem to regain consciousness," Sabine said. She sounded exhausted. And distant. "They're pumping his system with antibiotics."

"How are Maman and Odile doing?"

"Hard to tell."

"How are you?"

Sabine answered cryptically, "The same."

The front door opened. It was Jessica. Peter's Jessica. She just walked into Cassie's house, smiling warmly at her. She had this light way of walking, as though her feet were mounted on springs. She was a shade blonder than the week before and very tanned: her summer look. In her yoga pants and a bra, everything about her was enviably tight and smooth, despite her having given birth only six months ago. Jessica gave Cassie a happy wave and went to kiss Peter, who was still in the kitchen, sitting at his computer and eavesdropping on every word of the phone conversation. "How can I help?" Cassie asked Sabine.

"Maybe you should come?" her sister suggested in a small voice.

"Come to France?" The notion was a shock. Almost more shocking than the news that her father was unconscious following a surgery she did not know he was having.

"If you want to," Sabine said.

"To see Papa?" Cassie let the sentence float between them. In the kitchen, Jessica was standing behind Peter's chair and massaging his shoulders. "Is that what *they* want me to do?"

Sabine paused before answering. "You don't have to. I'm sending you an email with the name of the hospital, d'accord?"

"Oui, bien sûr," Cassie said.

Sabine hung up without goodbyes, as was her habit, and Cassie fell into her chair and glowered at Peter before he could open his mouth. "I'm telling you right now, stop looking at me that way. There is not a chance in hell I'm going."

"Oh, you're going," Peter said.

After Peter and Jessica left, Cassie sat in the kitchen, stunned. Paris? Really?

The windows were open, and the scent of jasmine swooshed through the house like a spring spirit. April, and not a cloud in the sky, only a light haze of Los Angeles smog, the sun fierce at not even mid-morning. Minutes following the phone call, Peter had booked her ticket. In a few hours, he was taking her to the airport. Was she really about to take a plane and fly to Paris to see her family for the first time in five years?

****

There had been no time to fine-tune the concept. It was good that Peter was clearheaded about the whole thing because Cassie's thinking process had turned into a foggy mess. Peter bought the ticket, while she went online looking for a hotel close to her father's hospital. Ten days seemed the right amount of time to spend there, Peter had said. Long enough for her father to recover, not so long as to mess with their writing schedule.

Why was her dad in the hospital, exactly? What had Sabine said? And why was it Sabine who called, rather than Odile, her other sister, or her mother? Could it be that they did not want her to come, or that they did not want her to know? They had not cared to consult her about the surgery. Had things gone according to plan, would she have ever found out about it?

She looked around her. Her house, her beautiful house: that was real! That was what grounded her. Or maybe not. Now that Jeanne and Alex were gone, Cassie faced the real possibility that she had been wrong about the house, and even more wrong to insist on keeping it in the divorce. It was as though she had bet the rest of her life on the concept that the house would be all she needed to be happy. This she had believed and repeated for the last eighteen years: she loved her house! She loved her house! She was a homebody, and she loved her house. It was possible that her stubbornness about the house had, if not ruined her marriage, at least not improved it. As Peter's career took off, his income increased by a hundred-fold. He wanted to move, but Cassie had dug in her heels and refused. She insisted that she was content with this quirky house, this lifestyle, and found ostentatious displays of wealth an embarrassment. "If you have money to burn, give it away to people who need it," she would say. The truth was, she did not like the way fame, money, and the trail of sycophants in his wake were changing him.

Peter wanted something very different from life. He wanted to want things and pursue things. He wanted Hollywood parties. He wanted the good life, the frisson of power, while Cassie wanted – or believed she wanted – things to be simple and remain eternally the same.

From the time the kids were five, Peter had been on a mission to find them a new house. House-hunting became his weekend pastime. He was sure that one day he would present her with a house so wonderful she would have no choice but to succumb. He often took the twins with him and tried to put them on his side. When they visited a particularly awesome house, incidentally one that cost upwards of two million dollars, the three of them would beg her to look at it. But she was pig-headed about it. "I need roots," she would say. "I left my country and my family, and I need stability. This house is my anchor." Since no one could move without Cassie's consent, Peter had been reduced to expressing his longing for exterior signs of success by buying a new luxury car each year, even a boat once, and one time a Harley and the dumb aviator glasses to go with it.

The twins were twelve years old when Cassie and Peter separated. It had been a mutual decision, albeit one precipitated by Cassie kicking him out of the house. Peter had moved into the Beverly Hills Hotel and after a few months had looked for a house to rent. Jessica was a real estate agent. They met at an open house for an ultra-modern structure made of steel, concrete, wood, and glass that he ended up buying. He was finally getting a house he liked, one that was a far better reflection of his success.

Cassie and Peter had an arrangement any divorcée would envy: amicable, equitable, fair, grown up. It was a no-brainer to invite Peter over for dinner several times a week, and then to welcome Jessica into her life as well. Jessica, too, Cassie had to admit, was a better reflection of Peter's success.

There was just that small thing she'd gladly trade the house for. This was not something she'd ever advertise, that harmless fantasy of getting Peter back. She'd never be a home wrecker. It was just a little bout of regression that kept her safe from exploring romantic options. It was just that now that Peter loved someone else, she could love him better. Unrequited love, along with microwave mug cake, was her true specialty.

****

It was a good thing that the Salvation Army truck had not materialized because all the suitcases were at college with the kids and she had to resort to using the ugly zebra one. She sniffed the suitcase's mildewed interior. The zipper looked about to give out, and she didn't like the look of one of the wheels.

In her bedroom closet were nothing but T-shirts and jeans — in other words, clothes for a world that did not include France and her chic mother and sisters. Cassie had no sense of fashion. For a French woman, it was embarrassing. Since the divorce, she felt pressured to look nice, and attractive, and well put together, all definitions she doubted applied to her. She had no idea how to dress in ways that represented who she was supposed to be. It was like trying to dress for an interview when you don't even know what the job is. What was she exactly? Single? A divorcée? A retiree from life? What were ghostwriters supposed to wear? A white shroud with holes for the eyes? In Los Angeles, among the women her age, Cassie had yet to find her niche. She was not one of those women who perfected the extremities: the nails, the hair, the makeup. She had no patience for sitting in salons, and she was afflicted with curls, tons of them, black and unruly better left au naturel. Her nails were permanently chipped, her hands scratched up from gardening. Her entire makeup routine consisted of painfully extracting lipstick remnants with the aid of Q-tips out of a dozen old tubes scattered in various bathroom drawers.

She admired the various breeds of Los Angeles female humans. For example, there were the Jessicas: women driven to physical perfection who dressed in exercise clothes during the day and like movie stars at night. Cassie bought her undies in packs of six. Her sole form of exercise consisted of taking the trash out to the street and going up and down the stairs of her house carrying laundry baskets. There were the Malibu moms, who wore flowing things: hair, dangling earrings, fringed everything, silk, lace. And then there were the women dressed to display exterior signs of a libido Cassie simply didn't possess. She admired women who dove into the dating race with great courage and grit. It's not that she was out of touch with being a woman. An apathetic side of her wished she could feel vibrant and sexy again, but not to the point of doing anything about it. She was in flux, neither able to embrace wrinkles and flab nor involved in a frantic attempt to turn back time or send sexual messages she was not willing to live up to. Her solution was to pretend the whole thing didn't exist. And if this meant that she was taking herself out of the dating game, that she was passing the baton to women of reproductive age (the age that men preferred anyway), then so be it.

Paris could feel like winter in April, but a quick peek online told her that Europe had been enjoying an unseasonable heat wave, with temperatures in the high seventies. She folded into the suitcase two pairs of jeans, a week's worth of underwear and bras, a half dozen T-shirts, three sweatshirts, all the while thinking of Odile. Her sister epitomized French uptightness in her pearls, scarves she knew how to tie just so, and mousy colored clothes to complement her mousy self. Cassie peered at the zebra suitcase with reproach, through Odile's eyes. Already, she was having an argument in her head with her sister. Sabine was ten years younger than she was, and only eight years old when Cassie had left France. In many ways, she and Sabine had never had the opportunity to get to know each other. But self-righteous Odile, just eighteen months her senior, she knew all too well. Cassie added into the suitcase a yellow and orange polka-dot T-shirt Odile would disapprove of and a pair of snazzy sandals. On the plane, she would wear her Uggs.

She pressed her foot on the suitcase for leverage to force the uncooperative zipper closed as she grappled with the notion that her father was sick, sick enough for at least one family member to ask her to come. How did she feel about her father being sick? She did not feel worried. Or upset. Or sad. She felt foggy. Foggy was good. She wasn't going to Paris for herself.

She was going because Peter thought she should. She was going because of Sabine. Sabine had been the single neutral relative and had made the most efforts, often acting as the liaison between her and the rest of the family. Sabine had never asked anything of her before, and this time, she seemed to be asking.

Cassie backed up her laptop, activated her cell's international call feature, and placed her chargers in the tote bag that would serve as her carry on. For the next week, electronics would be a lifeline to sanity. Already, she was packed with time to spare. She was more in control of things than she was giving herself credit for. It was only ten days. She had given birth to twins at twenty years old, had started over in a new country, had pushed through a divorce with her soul intact. She could survive ten days in Paris.

****

At the airport, Cassie was making no motion to enter the security line in front of the Air France counter. Peter nudged her in, handing her a plastic bag.

"What's this?"

"Just a little something from Jessica."

Cassie peered into the bag to find four small precious packages in various shapes and sizes and wrapped extravagantly in glistening paper and frilly bows. "What the hell?"

"You know how she is. It's little gifts for your family."

"She bought all this and wrapped it in one hour?"

"She skipped her massage for this. She just wanted to reach out, be nice. You know how she's always trying."

"She's always shopping, that's what she's always doing." It had never occurred to her to bring gifts for her family, and here was Jessica acing it again. "Fine. Thank her for me," she said. Over the loudspeaker, a voice in French informed them that the planes were on time. Just hearing French, Cassie experienced a bout of cold sweat. "I'm not doing this," she said, gripping Peter's sleeve. "Take me back home. Please."

"You can do this. You need to do this," Peter assured her. And with this, he opened his arms.

She sank into his hug, buried her nose in his jacket to inhale the reassuring scent of his after-shave, the one thing Jessica had not been able to change. She felt that sense of safety she could only experience in Peter's arms, even if she knew that his embrace often came with an aftertaste of longing and regrets. "What if I'm captured?" she asked.

"I'll pay the ransom, of course. I've rescued you from them once; I'll rescue you again."

"But what's your incentive now? Your children are raised, and you found someone new to warm your bed?" She meant it as a joke but saying it out loud brought her dangerously near to tears.

"I still need you for the writing," Peter said. The plain honesty of the statement befuddled her so much that she could not think of how to respond and only walked forward in the line, moving away from him. "You've got the adapter for the 220 current?" he asked.

"I packed the old one."

"That thing is antiquated. I've told you before it was crap. They have them everywhere inside the airport. Buy a new one as soon as you pass security."

Cassie rolled her eyes, "Peter, I've got this."

"It's only ten days in Paris," he said, patting her on the arm. "It's the number one item on most bucket lists."

"It's just not a safe country for me."

"Don't drink the water," he responded and with this gave her a gentle push toward the line.

She boarded the plane, anonymous among passengers, and settled into her aisle seat, far in the back near the bathrooms. Peter had remembered her preference. She tried not to read too much into this small kindness. Every time he did something nice for her she ended up, even for a brief moment, imagining they could go back to the way things were.

****

She had not been in France for five years. The last time had been weeks before her separation from Peter. The trip was intended as a family vacation but had been an epic failure. The twins, then twelve years old, had been going through stuff, no doubt acting out the discord in her marriage. They both had been monsters. Or rather they had been normal American pre-teens, but once in France, where children must be seen and not heard, they had appeared barbarous, even to her own eyes. Raymonde Lombard, her mother, then sixty, had been a quiet trap of disapproval. Gustave Lombard, her father, who was eighty-two at the time, hardly acknowledged her or the twins. Odile's children, meanwhile, had been delightful. The then two- and four-year-olds did everything right. Their prowess included the ability to speak French – the only language their grandparents spoke – their exquisite table manners, the ease with which they said bonjour and merci (which her twins, lock-jawed the way only teenagers can be, refused to do), their skill at making eye contact with grownups and at bringing smiles to Grandpapa Lombard's face.

Caught between her parents and her twins, Cassie had felt like a mediator between two countries in the grip of a cold war. She tried to sell her own children's adorableness to her parents just as she was fighting serious doubts about it, and she tried to sell her parents' wonderfulness to the twins against all evidence to the contrary.

Her children were Americans. Her children spoke English exclusively; no, she had not been able to teach them French. Her children were brooding and uncommunicative. Her children could not fit into the French mold of silence and docility. But in Cassie's view, the biggest babies were her parents. They were incapable of the most basic attempt at winning the twins over. With the hubris that characterized them, they believed that children should be the ones to make the effort. She had hated them for that. She had also hated her twins for falling short of expectation. She had hated Odile, Odile's children, and, of course, she had hated Peter.

But she had hated herself the most.

"Your kids are tuning out their grandparents," Odile had had the nerve to say.

"You have no idea what teenagers are like. You just wait and see."

"I doubt very much that I'm raising my children to turn into that kind of teenagers."

"Your kids are afraid of you, just as we were afraid of mom. Do you think their politeness is genuine? It's fear-based. I'm surprised they can sleep at night."

"So what?" Odile said, swallowing the insult with remarkable aplomb. "Life is stressful. They need to learn to handle stress. Your job as a parent is to teach your kids self-control and give them opportunities to experience failure and disappointment. They need to know that in life there are consequences when you can't get along in society."

"What consequences? Their disgruntled grandparents won't approve of them? Big deal."

"You let your kids grow like weeds, and you tiptoe around their feelings," Odile had told her. "You're giving them an unrealistic expectation when it comes to life and their abilities."

"You've only been a parent for four years, and already you're an expert."

"I might not be an expert, but I won't let my children grow up thinking they're little geniuses, and I won't let them act like mini-despots."

"I recognize Maman's rule book. Only one despot allowed. By all means, go for it. It worked for her. Too bad it didn't turn us into happy adults."

"You're not teaching your kids happiness though," Odile had said with condescension. "Everything they experience is artificial. They expect life to be smooth and people to be at their beck and call. Good luck with the rude awakening that's ahead of them."

"How about we resume the conversation when your kids are teenagers," Cassie had suggested.

"I'd be glad to."

The entire trip had been a nightmare. She had used Peter as a punching bag and a buffer. Each night, squeezed together in her too small childhood bed, they'd argued in frantic whisperings about how miserable they were making each other feel, what inept parents they were. They blamed each other for being selfish, emotionally unavailable, lousy at any form of intimacy, unwilling to deal with their respective neuroses. He blamed her for the lack of sex in the marriage while she blamed him for not giving her writing credit.

Upon their return to Los Angeles from Paris, jetlagged and at the end of her rope, she had told Peter she wanted to separate. Yes, this time, I'm sure of this, she had said.

She still hadn't been sure.

Within two years of the family trip to France, Odile's words had turned prophetic. Alex began suffering from extreme anxiety – when high school and normal life stress began to pile up; he had no idea how to cope. As for Jeanne, she chose denial, expecting life to remain one pink and pretty merry-go-round. If that meant taking drugs and booze any time the going got tough, that's what Jeanne did. Alex quieted his stress by overachieving at school, to the detriment of everything else. Jeanne got rid of hers through being promiscuous and flunking every subject. Even P.E. Odile had been right; her kids were indeed unprepared for the vicissitudes of life. In the end, maybe it was Cassie who had been the biggest baby of them all.

Cassie settled into her seat, tucked her bag under the seat in front of hers and breathed. An unmistakably French couple in their forties labored up the plane's aisle and came to sit in her row. The man wore a gray suit and a tie, and the woman stood very straight in a belted green dress, her stomach tucked in as though she was about to step on the red carpet. Neither had felt compelled to wear something comfortable for the transatlantic flight. The woman, especially, reminded her somehow of Odile. Thank goodness there was an empty seat between them.

A flight attendant walked through the cabin, handing travelers headphones, eye masks, and menus printed on small cards. The man looked at his menu and turned to Cassie. "Encore un repas dégeulasse," he said. Another awful meal.

Cassie shook her head as if to say she did not understand French.

The man turned to his wife. "Elle est Américaine," he said, referring to Cassie.

"Of course, she is," the wife responded in French. "Who else would be wearing snowshoes on a plane?"

Snowshoes? Cassie looked down at her Uggs with a sinking feeling. What exactly had she packed for the trip?

An ample woman in her sixties was ambling up the aisle. She stopped in front of Cassie and squinted at the numbers above her head. "I don't mean to bother you," the woman said, "but is it possible that you're in my seat?"

Cassie looked at her boarding pass, and sure enough, hers was not the aisle seat after all but the one in the middle. "I apologize," Cassie said as she moved one seat to her left. "Just as I was mentally thanking my ex-husband for knowing me so well and for reserving the aisle seat."

"You can't trust anyone these days," the woman said cheerfully as she settled in her seat. "Not even ex-husbands." She set a large bag on her lap. "Food," she explained. "If we're going down, at least I'm not going down hungry."

"I know what you mean," Cassie said. "Who would want to tread water for days in the middle of the Atlantic Ocean on an empty stomach?"

"The worst!" the woman laughed. Within minutes, she was digging into her bag and laying out food on her tray: a box of Milano cookies, chocolate covered macadamia nuts. "I detect an accent?" she said.

"I was born in France, but I've lived in the U.S. for the last nineteen years," Cassie said.

"What brought you to the U.S. then?"

"Love. And a burning desire to get the hell away from my family."

"Are you going to France to visit them?"

"My father's ill."

"Sorry to hear. Are you close?"

"We've hardly spoken in the last five years."

"Oh my," the woman said, removing the outer wrapping of a box of chocolate-covered Hawaiian Macadamia nuts and plopping one, two, three in her mouth, then a fourth, a fifth. "What happened?"

Cassie accepted a chocolate from the open box the woman shoved in front of her. "Where to even begin?" she said. "I left the country. I married a foreigner. I'm a pain in the derrière. My children don't speak French. And then a few years ago I had a bit of a meltdown, said the wrong things." Cassie gave a small laugh that was meant to sound joyful and came out pathetic instead. "I put those wrong things in writing, actually, in a letter they did not like very much. After that, they did not take my calls for two years. You know, the usual story."

"That doesn't sound so usual to me," the woman said.

"And since they would not let me tell them how angry I was with them, I divorced my husband instead." Cassie thought for a moment. "You know, I was saying that as a joke, but I'm pretty sure that's precisely what happened."

"Maybe this is a chance to open the lines of communication with your father, talk about your feelings."

"He doesn't do that."

"What?"

"Talk about feelings. He only talks about things."

"Things?"

"In the literal senses. Things. Objects. Architecture, furniture, rugs, cutlery even. He can ramble on about manufacturing techniques of Persian rugs, or the anatomy of a sailboat, or the leg shapes of eighteenth-century chairs. But he has no vocabulary when it comes to emotions."

"On the autism spectrum perhaps?"

"I don't think so. Once, when I was little, I had a whole cabinet fall on me – to be fair I had climbed into it – and I was bleeding from my head, and all my father was worried about was his damn crown."

"He wears a crown?"

Cassie laughed, "It's not an actual crown. The crown is what my sisters and I call it. It's an artifact. His prized possession. It's silver and gold and what not. Ancient. He calls it his finial, whatever that means. It looks exactly like a crown, only tiny. One that could fit a doll's head. Which is just what I intended to do with it when I climbed that cabinet."

"What about your mother. Could you speak to her?"

"I never can tell if she hides behind my father because she doesn't have to have an opinion, or if she is the one pulling his strings."

The woman smiled at her kindly. "Well, it looks like you have your work cut out for you on this trip."

"Me? Oh no! It won't be work at all. It will be a quick in, quick out; nobody gets hurt. I'm not going there to dig deep, believe me. I've been burned before, and I'm over it. I'm going to be on my best behavior, ruffle no feathers, gather no moss, and then come back home safe to California and resume my life."

"Well, good luck then," the woman said.

"What about you?" Cassie asked. "Why are you going to Paris?"

"I'm attending a conference on eating disorders."

Cassie tried not to stare at the candy and cookie wrappers in front of them. "You have to go as far as France for this?"

"Oh yes. It's an international symposium. I'm a professor of psychiatry at UCLA."

Cassie's jaw dropped. "I just told my life story to a psychiatrist?"

"It tends to happen," the psychiatrist said.

The psychiatrist soon fell asleep. If only Peter knew this, ha! He who had begged her to go to therapy, calling her damaged, telling her that she needed therapy more than anyone he'd ever met, and Cassie dismissing it, saying she was too private to air her dirty laundry in front of a stranger. The irony wasn't lost on her.

She fell asleep and woke up from a dream where she walked through rooms where doors fell and disintegrated like wet cardboard between her fingers. Water dripped from the ceiling onto her father's Persian rugs. She called, but no one answered, so she took her father's finial and tried to use it to collect the water falling from the ceiling. But the water ran right through the finial, and she cried and cried.

CHAPTER 4

Children of Smyrna

To gather a sense of what was happening around him, Albano learned to pay attention to what people said. Even more could be learned from what was not said the contained anger of a trembling hand, the nervousness of a sweaty forehead, the complicity in a repressed smile. Aunt Sadie was not the kind of woman who bothered to answer ten-year-old boys' questions, let alone those of a nephew who was an added burden to her, so when she sprang out of bed one morning and, kvetching the entire time, launched into a meticulous house cleaning for no religious reason, Albano knew that something was afoot. Then Uncle Joshua ordered new shoes, leather ones. A visitor was coming, an important one. Important and disliked by Aunt Sadie, which was an intriguing combination.

By the time Uncle Joshua received the letter informing them of the day of his arrival, Uncle Moshe and his merchandise were already on the boat to Smyrna, leaving the family with only a few days to prepare.

"That is just like him," Aunt Sadie said. "Not a care in the world but giving everyone else an attack of nerves."

Who was this mysterious Uncle Moshe everyone worked so hard to please? And why the undercurrent of disdain for a man special enough to precipitate the ordering of new shoes and the slaughter of a goat? Albano overheard Aunt Sadie tell Uncle Joshua that she would not allow Moshe to share a roof with her children. Yet she used her best linen in preparing his bed. She said Moshe was *hadras I baranas.* A boisterous mess. Uncle Joshua, an amicable man who knew that peace at home begins with not mingling in a woman's affairs, got more tense as the day approached and as Aunt Sadie grew more vociferous.

There was to be an expedition to fetch Uncle Moshe and his merchandise when he disembarked at the quay of Smyrna in two days. Relatives and friends were coming over to Uncle Joshua's house that night to plan the whole thing. Albano was studying at the table in the big room with Uri and Zev, who were his cousins and Uncle Joshua and Aunt Sadie's sons. Uncle Joshua nervously arranged and rearranged the chairs while Aunt Sadie busied herself at the stove. The smell of yeast and anise seeds wafted deliciously through the room, giving it a welcoming feel. Each time Aunt Sadie's back was turned, Cousin Uri and Cousin Zev took turns hitting each other hard on the head with their school books, muffling their cries of pain and laughter, which made them want to laugh even more. Aunt Sadie was not a woman you wanted to mess with, but tonight she was too preoccupied to protest. This did not mean she would turn a blind eye on Albano if he misbehaved, so he strained his eyes in the weak light of candles and tried to concentrate on his book. Uri and Zev were twelve and fifteen, older than Albano, yet allowed to be ignorant all they wanted while Albano had to study late into the night. The reason for this was that he was to become a rabbi. Aunt Sadie loved all things rabbinical yet had failed to produce an offspring who could pass the rabbinical school's entrance exam and who could, like Albano, read Hebrew, Latin, and Greek by the age of ten. Albano's father had prized education above all else. He had been a patient tutor to his children, and Albano was from a young age well versed in academic matters. Also, Albano was a Kohen, as his father had been, a priest by blood, descendent from a priest; and there was nothing he could do about that.

The cholera epidemic had also taken the life of Aunt Sadie and Uncle Joshua's only daughter, and ever since Aunt Sadie had become more pious and more afraid. She was the one who had set her mind on the idea that Albano should go to rabbinical school, and Albano had been given no choice in the matter. Uncle Joshua was respected in the community for his practicality and his good judgment, but he let that judgment be superseded by his wife's discreetly whispered admonitions at home. So the decision was made. Would his real father and mother want him to become a rabbi had they survived? Albano did not know, but Aunt Sadie seemed to think so.

As Albano squinted at his books, the men entered and were greeted by Uncle Joshua. With each arrival, the room became hotter and smaller. Rabbi Levi arrived last, his long gray beard, somber mood, black cloak, and formidable presence stealing whatever breathable air was left in the room. He sat at the end of the table, and Aunt Sadie fretted over him, bringing him tea in her best cup.

Rabbi Levi peered at Albano from above his round glasses and said, "Aren't you Yoseph's boy, the rabbinical student?"

"I am, Rabbi Levi."

"Are you a diligent student, dear boy?"

"Yes, Rabbi Levi."

Aunt Sadie brought pastries and placed them before Rabbi Levi. "I make sure he is, Rabbi. Surely Adonai must have had a design for him to make me suffer so, putting this boy in my care. Taking my daughter and sparing him."

Rabbi Levi narrowed his eyes. "Lest we forget that the boy suffered as well," he said.

"Ah, yes," Aunt Sadie hurried to say. "We have all suffered very much indeed."

Now everyone was here. Two strong men from the Jewish quarter whose names Albano didn't know, also Selig and Rafael, who were not so strong but were his father's and Uncle Joshua's and Moshe's childhood friends, and thus part of the welcoming committee. The two strong men, Selig, Rafael, Rabbi Levi, Uncle Joshua, Cousin Uri, Cousin Zev, and Albano sat around the table. Albano made himself small and hoped he would be allowed to stay and listen. Aunt Sadie placed on the table pots filled with mint tea and plates of cumin and anise breads, round, golden and warm from the oven and said, "Albano, what are you still doing here? Close your books and leave, hush." Albano gathered his book and got up.

"Albano can stay, why not?" Uncle Joshua suggested.

Albano beamed. He was about to sit back on his chair, but one look at Aunt Sadie made him freeze into place. "He's a child and a rabbinical student. He should not bother himself with men's business," she said, adding briskly, "Albano, go!" Albano, his cheeks bright red, stepped away from the table and tried to look at no one.

Perhaps it was the residue of several days and possibly nights of Aunt Sadie's constant complaining about Moshe's arrival, but Uncle Joshua reacted with uncharacteristic defiance. "This child will be a man soon enough, won't he? Albano. Sit!" Albano folded back onto the chair, hoping to disappear. He did not like to be a source of discord between his uncle and aunt, and Uncle Joshua's sudden display of authority as master of the house was almost comical.

Aunt Sadie camped herself in front of the men. "I made a solemn promise to his mother on her deathbed to raise him as my own!" she said. Her contradicting Uncle Joshua was a common thing, but to do so in front of the men was a tactical mistake. She was giving Uncle Joshua nowhere to go.

"And I," Joshua said, puffing his chest, "I too made a solemn promise to his father, Yoseph, my beloved brother now tragically dead, to raise him as my own." Then realizing that all eyes were on him, he raised his voice in a way that was unnatural to him. "And I decide when a boy can start being part of men's business and when he cannot."

"But I—" Aunt Sadie said.

"Woman, enough!"

Aunt Sadie seemed to shrink upon herself in humiliation, or perhaps anger. There would be hell to pay for Uncle Joshua later on, but for now, he had won. Albano curled back onto his chair, thrilled. Men's business!

Uncle Joshua, his voice made stronger by his own bravery said, "Moshe's merchandise is, I believe, mostly rugs. How many I don't know, the letter said nothing. Neither do I know how heavy those will be. There is a risk that we will have to make several trips, in which case some of us will need to stay behind on the quay overnight to guard what was not loaded onto the wagons."

"Wagons? How about camels?" Rafael asked.

"Camels will not do. Not with rugs. We need to borrow at least two wagons with excellent wheels and equip each with two good horses." The men nodded gravely and lit their pipes. "As I cannot be certain that proper Kosher food will be available to us in Smyrna, the women will prepare food to bring," Uncle Joshua said. "Finally," he added, the alarm in his voice betraying his concern, "we must be armed." A wave of mixed emotions reverberated around the table: anxiety, worry, excitement, but mostly excitement, Albano could tell, from the gleaming eyes and straightened postures of the men. "How do we know what we might encounter along the way?" Joshua said, looking at each face around the table. "Cholera has brought terrible loss to our community and all throughout the Empire. But now the epidemic is over, and people are back to their misdeeds. We could encounter robbers. Or worse. Each of you must decide if leaving the Jewish quarter is something that you find a risk worth taking." He added, his voice filled with oratory tremors, "Moshe is my brother. As such my sons and I must go. All of you must decide if you want to come down to the quayside."

Smyrna's quayside. The name evoked untold riches and mysteries. At home, Aunt Sadie spoke of decency and tradition and was the enforcer of both. She believed that everything in Smyrna that wasn't the Jewish quarter brimmed with vice and diseases and was a death trap for Jews. But Albano had heard other stories about Smyrna from the men. Smyrna, the City of Infidels, as Muslims called it, was said to be one of the most cosmopolitan places on earth. In Smyrna, every religion had its place of worship, and every language under the sun was spoken. From Mount Pagus and the Jewish quarter, Albano could only glimpse at the mysterious city below, the gulf, the hundreds of boats that circled the bay, moving voyagers and merchandise to and from the Ottoman Empire.

He could only imagine the wealthy Levantine families who were said to live in gilded castles surrounded with servants, and whose days were spent lounging in fragrant gardens filled with roses and fountains, and who employed people in their fields and factories by the hundreds of thousands. He could only dream of Frank Street and its myriads of shops, and of the fabled Greek department stores that sold goods from every corner of the world. He could only yearn to see with his own eyes the legendary Smyrna waterfront, where the architecture was said to resemble that of cities in Europe. But the Jews kept to the Jewish quarter for the most part, especially the children. There were people in Smyrna, and all throughout the Empire, who would kill a man just for being Jewish, or Muslim, or Christian, or for wearing the wrong clothes, or for having too short or too long a beard.

Uncle Joshua's warning seemed to ruffle no one. The danger must not have been that high, or else the men in the room were indeed very brave. In fact, for the next two hours, there was great excitement in the air as arrangements were made in the thickening smoke of pipes and the diminishing light of candles. The men discussed which road would be safest from robbers and which would be easiest for the horses and wagons. Must they bring extra wheels? How long would it take to cover the few miles down to the waterfront? Boats could be delayed, so they needed to prepare for a night or two of sleeping there. They would need to take turns mounting guard at night. How much straw should they bring for the horses? How long would the return trip take once the wagons, heavy with Uncle Moshe's mysterious merchandise, were brought back uphill to the Jewish quarter? Albano listened, transfixed. He wanted nothing more than to accompany them but he was not Uncle Joshua's son, and he wasn't yet a man, so he had neither rights nor expectations. Aunt Sadie was moving about the room with tiny steps bringing more kettles filled with tea and trays of pastries, taking back empty cups and plates, all the while not losing a crumb of what was being said.

The entire time Rabbi Levi sat glumly in his chair and did not speak, and Albano could read nothing in his half-closed eyes and crossed arms. Uncle Joshua turned to him and said with deference, "Rabbi, with all the important things that are your responsibility here in the Jewish quarter, we understand if you prefer not to partake in this arduous journey."

"I prefer not to go," Rabbi Levi said, suddenly irate. "But this crazy brother of yours is coming, so I have no choice. How else can I ensure nothing blasphemous will take place?"

"Rabbi Levi," Uncle Joshua protested. "My brother is beloved by us all."

The rabbi lifted a reproachful finger. "Beloved, yes, that is another alluring embodiment of sin. One can be beloved, as you say, for all kinds of immoral reasons. I must come to ensure that he intends to follow our rules, at least as long as he stays in the Jewish quarter."

"Of course," Uncle Joshua said, pretending to ignore Aunt Sadie's triumphant glare. She must have made her case about Moshe behind her husband's back.

"And what about Albano?" Cousin Zev suddenly asked. "Is he coming with us?" Albano's pulse quickened.

Uncle Joshua scratched his beard, shrugged. "I guess. Why not."

"In what capacity?" Aunt Sadie interjected, unable to contain herself. The men all looked at her, then at Uncle Joshua. Albano held his breath.

Uncle Joshua exploded, "In the capacity that he is Moshe's nephew! The sole surviving child of his dead brother! That's the capacity!"

And so, Albano was to go. And his life would be forever changed.

This much Albano knew about Uncle Moshe: he had left the Jewish quarter, his family, and his roots at age fifteen and only came back on rare occasions for business. Moshe was thirty years old now, a mature man, and he was frowned upon for creating a life that had little to do with the way he had been raised. He was also admired for becoming an intrepid businessman who traveled the world where he picked up precious rugs from around Persia and then went to sell them in Constantinople, Marseille, or Naples. It was said that his rugs even found homes in the high societies of Paris and London.

Uncle Moshe did not live in any particular country or any particular place. He had never married and had no children. And he was said to have reneged on God. Uncle Moshe's reputation was something amorphous. He was different and did things differently, but what did different look like? Having never left the Jewish quarter, Albano had no idea.

It was a particularly sweltering summer day when their small group made its way from the Jewish quarter to Smyrna's waterfront. By nine in the morning, they were suffocating in their black clothes. By ten o'clock, their clothes clung to their bodies and their bare feet were coated with the dirt of the road. Only Rabbi Levi and Uncle Joshua wore shoes. "They are hard as metal," Uncle Joshua said, cursing the shoemaker under his breath. At one point, he removed one of the shoes to uncover an impressive row of red-hot blisters. He stoically put the shoe back on and continued down the hill pinching his lips and sweating profusely through the pain, until he finally gave up and went barefoot like everyone else.

Notable along the way had been the conspicuous absence of danger. Walking defensively around the horses and empty wagons, they encountered none of the bandits, brigands, robbers, and fanatics the road to the city was supposed to be filled with.

On the way, they walked past groups of veiled women carrying goods on their heads, men sitting atop moving camels, the animals impassible despite their load, even small children walking alone. The Muslim people were dressed in light-colored clothes well suited for the heat and the landscape, whereas their group in black coats, black pants, and black wide-brimmed hats seemed only suited for sitting around a table and worrying about the outside world. Albano, for his part, floated rather than walked the distance, such was his excitement to be part of the caravan. He did not mind the heat. He was used to climbing up Mount Pagus in his black clothes on the way to and from his cave, and the bare soles of his feet were well callused. At one point, they had to make way for a machine coming from a distance at great speed. They stood by the side of the road and watched in dismay as a black automobile passed them in a flurry of sand and dust. In the automobile, two red-faced men in funny round hats and thick mustaches looked straight ahead.

"Who are these people?" Albano asked his cousin.

"British," Cousin Zev answered with authority.

"How do you know?"

"The round hats. They also wear funny trousers and jackets with many compartments and buttons. And they have cloth squares they take out to dab at their sweat." Cousin Zev laughed at that one. "A cloth just for sweat. And a pocket just for that cloth!"

"Why is their skin so red?"

"Because of the blood that's inside of them. It's redder than ours," Cousin Uri said.

"Redder than our blood?" But Cousin Uri and Cousin Zev exchanged a look, and Albano guessed they were not telling the truth. "What language do they speak?"

"Why, they speak British I guess."

"What does it sound like?"

"French."

"What do they eat?"

"Pig sausages, mainly. Now stop with all your questions."

Pig? Albano swallowed his disgust.

Soon, dirt roads turned to paved ones. There were people everywhere: Muslims, Christians, Europeans. People with normal skin colors, and people with red, pink, white, even black skins. People with normal noses, and people with tiny noses, or flat noses, or enormous noses. People with yellow hair. People with red hair! He saw people whose eyes were as blue as the sky. And more automobiles, and camels, and a breeze at last, but one that brought on unknown scents, strong ones: grilled meat, and spices, and strange, pleasant fragrances, and rotting fish. Leading their horse and cart, they crossed one more street, made another turn, and there they were: the Smyrna waterfront!

How could Albano have imagined the waterfront other than as a large-scale embodiment of what he already knew? He had pictured the Jewish quarter, only larger and on the water, an amalgam of gray stone houses, small alleys where barefoot children played alongside scaly dogs, and men and women dressed in black, careful never to make eye contact with one another. How wrong he had been! Before Albano's astonished eyes lay a massive esplanade surrounded by white buildings several stories tall. At the foot of those buildings were terraces of restaurants and cafés where every table was occupied by people, one stranger-looking than the next. Beyond that, the harbor, filled with hundreds of boats and the most dizzying wall of humanity Albano had ever witnessed. It was like market day in the Jewish quarter, multiplied by a hundred! A thousand! The smells of camels, horses, goats, live chickens, ducks, and rabbits by the cageful, mingled with the scent of spices, ripe and dried figs, fish, and many other things he could not name grabbed his throat, coming in wafts that took his breath away. And the noises! The cacophony of animals in close-quarter was a loud hum covered only in intervals by the strident horns of the many steamboats that crowded the harbor. Men called to one another in dozens of languages. Music mingled. Strange sounds coming from unknown instruments pierced the air without rhyme or reason. Merchant ships spilled their contents onto the dock, littering it with crate after crate of goods from across Europe. There were piles of bags, as tall as men, of dried figs, and apricots, cinnamon, cardamom, pepper, garments, precious wood, oil lamps, and tobacco all awaiting shipment. On the dock, boats were so tightly packed against one another that you could not see the water. Steamboats crisscrossed the harbor and docked noisily to unload passengers who poured onto the quayside like a human tidal wave.

Further out, a hundred or more ships crammed into the harbor, majestic three-masted barkentines, massive three-screw transatlantic passenger liners, and a flurry of vessels large and small. Further out at sea, brightly colored sails decorated the horizon like garlands on the Aegean Sea.

Uncle Joshua's shoes were back on his feet, and they all stood, confusion on their faces, their eyes searching the crowd for Uncle Moshe. They must have been an odd sight, huddled as they were around the two empty wagons, the sweat on their faces, the panting horses, the long black coats, the curled payots, the tall hats, the woolen tzitzit dangling from the sides of their bodies, so different from the rest of the crowd, and yet everyone was too busy and purposeful to pay any attention to them.

Albano had never seen so many people in one place. Out on the waterfront, there were Namibian men with skins as dark and smooth as polished stone, Muslim men wrapped in white capes, Greek Orthodox priests, pink-faced European men in funny tight pants and jackets. There were women too. The Muslim women wore headdresses, the Jewish, Armenian, and Greek women wore black, long sleeves and shawls, but the European women were so out of the ordinary, like nothing he had ever seen. They dressed in garments tight at the waist and wore brightly colored dresses and coats, wide-brimmed hats and lacy umbrellas, jewels, and beads. Albano immediately knew what his aunt had meant by "immodest." European women even had ankles, arms, and necks exposed. Some wore fur shawls despite the temperature, their pale skins reddened by the heat. It was all very puzzling, as though the European women wore clothes to make you look at them, instead of making you look away. But what amazed Albano the most was how the European women mingled with men, some even engaged in conversation in plain sight and broad daylight! The European men were just as peculiar-looking as the women in their tailored suits with wide-shouldered jackets and trousers that were tight on the leg and creased in front. And the hats, so many hats! Top hats, bowler hats, fezzes, and turbans all bobbed in harmony all over the quayside. He wondered which of these people were the rich Levantine men and women who owned the city.

Cousin Zev elbowed Cousin Uri, whispering and pointing more or less discretely. "Look! A harlot!"

Leaning against a wall was a blonde woman of extremely immodest attire. Her dress was red and black and fluffy, and some of her bosom was exposed, and she was laughing at something a man said.

"A harlot?" Albano asked, "What is that?"

"Ask my mother. She'll explain all about it," Cousin Zev said, winking at Cousin Uri.

"A harlot," Cousin Uri began, "is…." He was silenced by Rabbi Levi's striking him quite harshly on the head with a book.

"There he is!" Rafael exclaimed. Albano looked in the direction where Rafael pointed and saw a strange-looking man who stood erect and confident, as though the entire quayside belonged to him. Next to him was a formidable pile of rolled rugs at least two meters high.

If Albano had been in charge of spotting Uncle Moshe, his poor uncle would well have remained standing there until morning. The man standing on the quay bore no resemblance to Uncle Joshua or his father, or any of the bearded men of the Jewish quarter. Whereas Joshua was short and skinny, like his father Yosef had been, Moshe was tall and wide as a boulder, with a prominent belly. To Albano's amazement, Uncle Moshe did not have a beard. Instead, he wore a peculiar, thin moustache above his full, smiling lips, and instead of black, he was dressed in a light blue suit and sported a strange hat Albano had never seen before – he learned later when those began sprouting in the Jewish quarter, in shops and market stalls, no doubt in imitation of Uncle Moshe himself, that this kind of hat was called a French canotier. Uncle Moshe wore his inclined to the front of his face and slightly off center. Over his winged-collared shirt was a button-down vest – a waistcoat, as Albano later learned. A heavy gold chain went from his trouser pocket to a small pocket on his jacket.

Yet this stranger, the most bizarre-looking man Albano had ever seen, had exactly his father's smiling eyes.

Uncle Moshe and Uncle Joshua fell into each other's arms. "Now you come?" Uncle Moshe exclaimed in a thunderous voice, a voice which, Albano would soon notice, remained thunderous even when he was whispering. Tears of joy fell freely from Uncle Moshe's eyes as he admonished his brother, "I could have been robbed and mugged a hundred times!" But Uncle Joshua was too busy dabbing at his own eyes to respond.

Uncle Moshe was introduced to everyone, and he hugged them, all with equal abandon, even a very shocked Rabbi Levi who stiffened at the physical demonstration. Taking his time bantering and reminiscing with each one, Uncle Moshe did not at first notice him. This gave Albano a chance to gawk at him, open-mouthed. However strange his attire, Uncle Moshe did not seem self-conscious in the least. He wore his funny clothes in a way that was so regal that it made you wish you were dressed just as he was. And he had a way of speaking and laughing and firing questions that made even the dullest one of them with their monotonous life suddenly seem more exciting. Moshe's joy was so communicative that even Rabbi Levi had to stop himself from smiling on more than one occasion. Uncle Joshua, overcome with emotion, laughed and cried unrestrainedly. The two had not seen each other in seven years.

"And this?" Uncle Moshe finally bellowed, grabbing Albano's arm and feeling his biceps. "Is this one of the strong men you promised me as an escort?"

"This," Uncle Joshua said, "is Albano."

To this, Uncle Moshe responded by lifting him until Albano was tight against his fat belly and his feet dangled ten inches from the ground. Moshe held him there for a long while. Albano did not know how to react and just tried breathing through the squeeze. But soon he felt that Uncle Moshe's body was shaking with silent sobs, so he stayed very still for what seemed like an eternity. "Your father," Uncle Moshe roared in his ear finally, "was the best man on earth. You hear me? The very best, kindest man on earth." With this, he set Albano down, and Uncle Moshe and Uncle Joshua stood for an instant, not speaking, looking at the ground in sadness.

The men began loading up the wagons. Albano, looking for something he could do, said, "I will fetch water for the horses."

He needed to say no more. In the excitement, everyone had forgotten about the horses. "The horses!" Uncle Joshua murmured. "Yes, they must drink. At once!"

"Good boy," Uncle Moshe hollered. "He is the brain of this family, I can tell, just as his father was. And how did our family produce such a handsome child? Where did he get those gold eyes of his?"

Albano grabbed the two pails and set out to find fresh water on the quay.

Looking for a fountain or a spigot, he walked around the waterfront, his heart beating wildly in his chest through the cacophony of blaring horns, the clanging of pots falling on the stone quays, the yelling of fishmongers who sold their day's catch right out of their boats, the whistling and screeching of docking barges, and the smells of decaying fish, camel droppings, incense, vanilla, and overripe fruit.

He had heard that the architecture of the waterfront was reminiscent of Europe and built to resemble it. Now here it was, right before him on the beautiful waterfront. Who knew when he would be able to get such a close look again, if ever? Blinded by the reflection of the sun on the white façades, he walked closer to the buildings. They were two or three stories high with balconies at each window and had lace-like wrought iron banisters. On some of the balconies, people had placed potted flowers and plants cascaded down. The buildings were the most beautiful, man made things Albano had ever set eyes on.

But even more fascinating were the cafés and restaurants at ground level filled with dozens of tables at which men in their fineries sipped unknown beverages. Each terrace was shaded by colorful awnings: yellow, red, blue, orange. It was so festive, all this color. Each café and restaurant was topped by signs on which were words in languages Albano did not know. He walked closer to the terraces. The tables were set with white dishware over crisp tablecloths. Silver cutlery and etched crystal gleamed in the light. Waiters came to and fro, wearing aprons down to their feet and holding large trays filled with food and drinks in tall glasses in which ice floated. On the plates were strange, delicious smelling foods that made Albano's mouth water: stews, small roasted birds, vegetables in little mounds, grilled fish in sauces, slices of cakes, and to his relief, nothing resembling a pig.

On the quayside closer to the water, men and women strolled arm in arm, umbrellas shading them. The European children accompanying their parents wore little hats and leather shoes. Girls wore ribbons in their hair which was curled and arranged just so. If the quay was a dangerous place, it certainly did not appear to be. Quite the contrary, it was a wonderfully happy place where families could stroll or have a meal in peace, all languages and ethnicities intermingling.

"Go, move," a waiter said in Arabic as he hurried by, carrying a three-tiered dish he then set on a table with a flourish. The diners made excited sounds and spoke to each other in an unknown language. On each level of the dish was a circular tray of crushed ice, filled with mounds of nothing but treif! Shrimp, lobster, crab and shellfish all presented to be eaten as though they were delicacies. The diners, Albano figured to be mostly Levantines, Americans, Europeans, and Greek. Obviously, Christian was the religion to have if you were to eat at any of those restaurants, but if this is what they wanted to eat, they could have it all to themselves. Albano felt thankful he was not born Christian. He would likely have starved to death!

Albano moved away from the building, carrying his pails and looking for water until he saw an old woman carrying an empty bucket and decided to follow her. She led him to a large fountain where Albano stood in line awaiting his turn. The fountain was wide and squat with a single spigot that let out a powerful stream of water. A boy his age dressed in a white djellaba, a red fez camped on his head, sat atop the fountain and turned the spigot on and off, while letting out a continuous high-pitch flow of sentences in Arabic, Greek, Armenian and other languages. Albano saw that as people filled their containers, they gave the boy a coin.

Albano did not have money. He had been gone for fifteen minutes and still did not have water for the horses. He got out of the line and stood there, wondering what to do next.

"Hey, Jew!" the boy called in broken Hebrew.

"Me?" Albano asked in Arabic.

"You're the only Jew here. You speak Arabic?"

"Some."

"You want water?"

"I have no money."

The boy laughed. "So?" He hopped off the fountain and pointed at the spigot. "Then help yourself. The water is for everyone. I only open and close the spigot. What am I to do when fools think they should pay me for it? Refuse their money?"

Albano stepped toward the fountain tentatively, set his pails down, and turned on the water. The water came out so forcefully that he was splashed in the face and the pail overturned.

"Lower, turn it lower. No fool, the other way!" Albano was drenched now, and still the water was coming at him. The boy pounced forward, turned

the spigot, and let the water slowly fill the pail. "What are those things for,"
the boy said, touching Albano's tzitzit that dangled from the side of his
trousers.

Albano considered the question. "They bring me closer to God."

The boy was astonished. "How could they?"

Albano shrugged. "They just do, I guess."

The boy roared with laughter. "Those are only bits of thread! If they
brought people closer to God, everyone would have them. You Jews are fools
indeed."

"Where did you learn to speak Hebrew?"

"You're not the only Jew in Smyrna you know. I've seen others before
you."

Albano looked at the boy who smiled a bright smile and watched him
intently. "Not Jews like me you haven't," Albano assured him, a twinkle in his
eye. "I am studying to become a rabbi."

"Yes," the boy admitted. "You are my first rabbi."

Albano's pails were full. "You are Muslim?" he asked.

"I'm many things," the boy answered cryptically.

"Thank you for the water," Albano said. He lifted the pails and began to
turn around. The boy hopped on top of the fountain and was back to
jabbering to everyone in line. When Albano was a few meters away, he heard
the boy call after him.

"I'm here on the quay every day. Come back soon, Rabbi."

Albano left and turned once or twice and watched in awe as the boy
swindled more fools out of their coins.

****

The group found a quiet spot on the quay, gave the horses their water
and straw, and sat to eat their meal by the water. Sitting away from the rest of
the group on the stone parapet, Uncle Moshe and Uncle Joshua had removed
their shoes and rolled up their pant legs. Uncle Moshe had also removed his
socks, which were held together with funny little straps around his chubby
calves. They had their feet in the water and were catching up with each other,
whispering. From his shaded spot under a tree, Albano admired the Aegean
Sea and the sailboats in the distance. What would life be like on one of those
boats, covering great distances between far away countries, docking in
Marseille and Genoa, Constantinople and the great port cities in Greece or
Egypt? What did the air feel and smell like there? Did the soft wind now on
his skin come from one of those faraway places? The seagulls that danced
above had seen more of the world than he had. He had heard of cold
countries where ice and snow covered the ground, and of countries where the
trees were so dense that you could not see the sky for miles. Could one travel
to those by boat? Albano inhaled the salty air. Soon he would return to the

Jewish quarter, the rank air, the hours of studying by candlelight, Aunt Sadie's reproachful gaze.

The sea breeze carried gleams of Moshe's loud whispers, and Albano heard foreboding words that carried weight when spoken by such a jovial fellow as Moshe: words such as war, ethnic nationalism, massacres, a group called Young Turks. Uncle Joshua nodded and shook his head and combed his fingers through his beard the way he did when he was perplexed. Albano felt the chill return, the sense of doom that had been with him since the cholera epidemic had taken his family.

The time came to make the trek back to the Jewish quarter. Rabbi Levi hopped on the wagon atop the rugs because he was old and tired. Uncle Joshua posted the men around the wagons and led the caravan. Albano and Moshe walked together in back. His strange new uncle, despite his considerable girth, was bouncing up the hill more than he walked. When they were sufficiently high to see the bay from above, Moshe stopped without warning in the middle of the road. Albano stopped too. The rest of the group did not notice this and continued trudging up. Moshe faced the beautiful bay of Smyrna below and opened his arms wide, gazing at the shimmering Aegean Sea on one side, and the plains and mountains on the other. He sighed deeply, "Ha, Smyrna ... the beautiful. How I have missed you." He casually pulled a thin silver box out of a pocket and out of the box a funny little cigarette, long, thin, and perfect. He lit it with great flourish and took several large minty puffs out of it.

"You're not afraid of robbers, Uncle Moshe?" Albano asked with alarm as he saw the space between them and the rest of the group widen.

Uncle Moshe took another puff out of his cigarette and unhurriedly resumed the climb. "Have you ever seen a robber carrying loot such as one of those heavy rugs?" he asked playfully. "Three men would need to lift one, roll it, and what would they do? Scamper away stealthily up Mount Pagus?" The thought made Uncle Moshe howl with laughter, and it was such an infectious laughter that Albano laughed along with him. "Say, chap," Uncle Moshe said, "your Uncle Joshua says that you want to become a rabbi, huh? That is a great honor for our family indeed. I'm sure your father would be proud."

Albano looked at the dirt on the road. "Yes, Uncle Moshe."

"Is it yes, your father would be proud? Or is it yes, you want to become a rabbi?"

"Both," Albano answered. He thought about it and added, "But mostly the part you said about my father." Uncle Moshe laughed, so Albano laughed too, not knowing why. He had now laughed twice in a minute. It was a strange thing, to laugh. He had forgotten how good it felt.

"It's your aunt, isn't it?" Uncle Moshe said. "Why not have one of her sons become a rabbi and leave you to do as you wish?"

Albano shrugged, "It is because I have an aptitude for studying."

Uncle Moshe shook his head. "That woman ... A wonderful, pious woman don't get me wrong, but why would she have the final say?"

Albano hesitated and timidly asked, "What else is there to do for a boy like me?"

Uncle Moshe raised his eyebrows, "A boy like you? What kind of boy are you?"

Albano looked away, afraid that Uncle Moshe's piercing gaze might bring on tears of self-pity in him. "A boy with no mother and no father," he said.

To this, Moshe opened his arms wide again, as though he were embracing the entire world. "My boy, this could be the freest you will ever be! Think of it: no parents to disappoint, no wife to tell you what to do, no children to worry about. Why, you could do anything! You could become a sailor, a teacher, a merchant. Once your muscles come in, you could even become one of those dangerous carpet robbers that haunt the flanks of Mount Pagus." Uncle Moshe laughed at his joke and Albano laughed too until tears sprang from his eyes.

"But what about God, Uncle Moshe? Am I not supposed to serve Him. I'm studying the Torah, and then to stop ... Wouldn't I disappoint God?"

"So, God takes your entire family, and you're worried about disappointing Him? You should be the one who's disappointed." Albano balked at the sacrilegious words. "Listen," Uncle Moshe continued. "God and I, true, we've had our differences, but for the time being He is leaving me to live life as I wish. In exchange for this, I try to be the man He intends for me to be. God created all kinds of creatures, you see. The giraffe and the starfish, the gazelle and the flea; they each have a purpose on this earth. It is the same thing with men. Some men are supposed to be rabbis, and some are supposed to be robbers. You can be a rabbi if this is what you truly believe it is the purpose for which you were brought forth on this earth, nephew. If not, then find your purpose and do that. Don't you think God would be more disappointed in a rabbi who loathes being a rabbi than in a robber who truly accomplishes his God-given destiny as robber?"

****

That night, dinner at Uncle Joshua and Aunt Sadie's was an unusually joyous affair. Friends and relatives came from all over the Jewish quarter to visit Uncle Moshe, admire his famous rugs, or any other excuse they could conjure up to see the man who was fast becoming a legend.

To everyone who visited, each bringing a delicious dish, Uncle Moshe gave the greeting of a long-lost brother, even to those he didn't know. He had such an infectious, warm air about him that it was impossible for anyone not to be charmed, especially the little children who were fascinated by this man who spoke their language but was loud and colorful as a jester and so different. And he ate and ate, and he drank bottle after bottle of sweet wine. Soon, neighbors were bringing their violins and accordions, the family dinner transformed into a massive celebration of nothing in particular.

Later, Uncle Moshe let his little nephews climb on his lap and crawl all over him. Nothing about him was stern, nothing about him was proper, and everything about him felt generous and open-hearted. Albano camped himself near him and would not budge, hanging on to Uncle Moshe's lips for the extraordinary stories he strung together.

Cousin Toby, who was just five years old, said, "Uncle Moshe, is it true you own a motorcar?"

"Do I own a motorcar? Of course, I don't own a motorcar! I own *nothing*, my boy. I am a free man, owning nothing, and owned by no one."

"You own rugs."

"I merely move them from one place in the world to another."

"But you are rich. You could buy a motorcar if you wanted to."

"Bah!" Uncle Moshe said. "I usually travel by whale."

"On top of a whale?"

"Inside, there is a special cavity for voyagers."

"Like Jonah?"

"He made it popular. I personally find it quite rank and dark," he added mysteriously. "I much rather travel by air."

"How do you travel by air, Uncle Moshe?" Albano asked.

"Why, I travel by magic carpet!" The little children opened their mouths, transfixed. "Although magic carpets are temperamental, much like donkeys. One day they're in the mood, the next day they are not. You could be sitting on one for hours and nothing, and then suddenly, for no reason at all, they will soar through the sky and take you wherever they wish."

"You fly through the sky?"

"All the time."

"But isn't it windy up there? How do you hang on?" one little girl asked.

"As long as you fly at the precise speed of the wind, which carpets know to do instinctively, you will not feel the wind at all."

"And what about rain?"

"You must make sure there will be no rain. Any little drop of water and the rug plummets to the ground, and you with it."

"And what about clouds? Do you travel through clouds?"

"Ha, clouds are a tricky business. Clouds are the reason I will never again ride a magic carpet to Paris." He scrunched up his eyebrows. "I had an incident once … but I do not want to bore you."

"Tell us!" the kids cried out in unison.

"Have you heard of the Eiffel Tower?"

"No."

"The Eiffel Tower is an immense tower in the center of Paris, which is the most beautiful city in France, and it might well be the most beautiful city in the world outside of Smyrna. This tower is made entirely out of tremendous beams of metal. Yet from a distance it appears to be made of very fine lace." Uncle Moshe drew the shape of the tower in the air with his finger. "It is also the tallest building ever created by man."

"Is it as tall as Mount Pagus?"

"Far taller."

"Can one climb it?"

"You can climb it but it may take many days, and you must do it by foot. I attempted once to climb it by camel, but they refused. And I don't mean the authorities refused; the camel refused to go up those steep metal steps. So, as I was telling you, the tower is so very tall that it reaches all the way up to the clouds, and the stairs get thinner and thinner as it goes up, so much so that the base is as wide as a village, and the very tip is sharp as a needle and twice as long as a sword. This sharp tip I discovered the hard way. I was riding one of my favorite carpets through the clouds of Paris. It is my fault. I blame myself entirely for this, as I had an important business meeting to attend in Vienna, many countries away, and was in a hurry. (Now you must know that it is important to hide in the clouds, and ride at night if possible, especially when you're flying in a foreign country; you do not want to draw attention to yourself.) When suddenly, was it the clouds, was it the moonless night, or a combination of both, I felt a sudden sharp tug and heard a great sound of tearing; my carpet had caught on to the spear at the top of the Eiffel Tower! And just like that, in one instant, the carpet was sliced in half. I barely had time to hang on to the tip of the tower. I dangled there for a while, wondering what I should do next. Then I had no choice but to climb down the side of the tower, meter by meter. And believe me when I tell you that is a lot of meters, and as you can see, I am a man of considerable size. Adonai be thanked, it was dark, so no one saw me. When I finally reached the ground, the clouds had subsided, and it was daybreak. My clothes now hung loosely on my body, as I had sweated off half my weight. When I lifted my eyes, I saw my poor carpet, still caught at the tip and dangling miserably."

"How did they get the carpet down?"

"They dispatched a team of specially trained monkeys. The French are quite organized. They always use monkeys to go up and down the Eiffel Tower and take care of those details."

In bed that night, Albano wondered if Uncle Moshe was the way he was because he had been away when cholera struck. The fact was, the entire Jewish quarter had stopped being happy then. And here was Uncle Moshe, reminding them how it was done.

****

The day Uncle Moshe left, a month later, everyone was crying. Albano felt a deep sense of loss. Who else was there in the entire Jewish quarter who could make the impossible feel possible, who could use tragedy to laugh at himself, and make the threat of war appear like a golden opportunity for much-needed change? Albano had hoped he would be allowed to be part of the escort that brought Uncle Moshe back to the harbor, but this time Aunt Sadie made sure he was busy. Aunt Sadie had never warmed up to Uncle Moshe. "This man, he eats like ten men. You can be sure I am relieved he is gone," she told anyone who would listen.

"Why don't you like him, Ma? Cousin Zev asked. Everyone else does."

"He makes a joke of our traditions. That's why."

"Because he did not marry?"

Aunt Sadie had a small laugh. "Your Uncle Moshe has ... other interests," she said mysteriously.

The day of his departure, friends and family congregated at the door of the Jewish quarter, and Uncle Moshe embraced everyone with the same gusto, pinching children's cheeks, flattering the women with compliments on the handsomeness of their children and deliciousness of their food, shaking hands and hugging everyone in sight.

"Where is my rabbi?" Uncle Moshe called out. People made way for Rabbi Levi.

"My boy, I hope that you will soon rethink your sinful ways," Rabbi Levi said, but although he tried to sound stern, it was obvious Rabbi Levi was as much under Uncle Moshe's spell as everyone else.

"Sin, what is sin?" Uncle Moshe laughed. "Everything that is beautiful you call sin, Rabbi. Food is sin, love is sin, traveling the world is sin, dressing this way and that is sin. But tell me then, Rabbi, why did God bother Himself to invent so many sins?" The men laughed. Offended, Rabbi Levi mumbled in his beard.

When it was Albano's turn to be hugged, Uncle Moshe spoke in his ear. "Son, don't let people tell you what sin is or isn't. Fearful people call sin everything they do not understand."

The weeks after Uncle Moshe left, Albano did not feel like himself. He was both more excitable and sadder. Although his days mirrored the days before Uncle Moshe had come to Smyrna, now nothing felt or tasted the same. He was sad in a new way. It was not the old sadness of crying quietly at night for his family. It was a new sadness about the very nature of his days. Now the endless rising before daybreak, studying, and reading did not feel like something he was meant to do, but something he was made to do. Energy brewed inside him. Staying in one place felt painful to the point of screaming. He wanted to escape and run to his cave, but there was never time. His cousins were outside, running, fighting, screaming while he pored over ancient texts. Watching the Hebrew letters blend into each other, he thought the inside of him, his brain, his heart, his muscles, could no longer be contained by the outside of him: his skin, his clothes, even his shoes. At night, he dreamt wildly of monkeys, of flying carpets, of boats, of whales that swallowed him whole. During the day, he longed to return to the harbor and talk to that curious boy who spoke so many languages. In the short hours he had spent on the quayside, Albano had smelled odors he did not know existed, felt the ocean breeze right on his skin. He had seen the European buildings, and the clothes, and the hats, and the boats, and the people. What other sensations and sights were there to experience?

The harbor became his obsession. In those short hours he had been there, he had not felt lonely. How could it be then that here in the Jewish quarter, among his cousins, his blood, placed among his people, he felt forlorn, like an outcast. His trip to the harbor had permanently erased the notion that the city was dangerous. Now it was the thought of never leaving the Jewish quarter that terrified him. He constantly thought about Uncle Moshe's words on life's purpose? How was Albano to discover his if he stayed put?

He began to devise a plan. It was not a smart or well-thought-out plan at all. Aunt Sadie would never let him go back; this much was clear. If he wanted to visit the harbor again he would have to do it without her permission or knowledge. And whatever he did, he simply would have to face the consequences. His plan was just to go. Early one morning he would take the road down to the city instead of the road to shul. His plan was that once he came back, he would be punished. There was no escaping the punishment. A beating he could take, he reasoned. He had been beaten before. He knew what to expect. And whatever punishment and chores were given to him, he could simply do. And that was the whole plan.

He searched in his books, in the Torah, and didn't find any signs that to walk down to a city filled with Muslims and Christians constituted a sin. He would be doing something forbidden, yes, but not by God. There was racial tension everywhere in the Empire, but judging from the mingling of races and religions on the quayside, Smyrna appeared immune to it. He did not fear the Muslims, but he had been taught to mistrust Christians who had persecuted Jews from time immemorial. His own ancestors had been driven away from their Spanish homeland by King Ferdinand and Queen Isabella's edict in 1492. The Christians had given them a few months to take a boat to any country that would have them. This was how his family had ended up in the Ottoman Empire. Sultan Bayezid had welcomed Jews with open arms. According to the story, he had declared the king and queen of Spain fools for chasing away their brightest and most prosperous subjects and letting him have them. The Torah finials were all that remained of that time for his family, who had smuggled them, buried them, hidden them under clothes, and passed them down from one Kohanim to the next for nearly five hundred years, and now they were hidden in Albano's cave.

So, if Albano was not committing a crime against God, and he wasn't endangering his life, then this was simply an act of family disobedience.

Even with all the thinking Albano had done on the subject, when the day to go came at last, he had not planned it. Not exactly. He rose at three in the morning, as usual, went to the kitchen alone to have the bread that Aunt Sadie left out for him for his breakfast, and dressed in his rabbinical school uniform, in black from top to bottom except for the stiff, white buttoned-down shirt. Only, instead of walking south toward shul, he found himself wandering toward the boundaries of the Jewish quarter and, in the dark still, down the hill instead of up.

He walked by the light of the setting moon and under the fading stars and continued downhill in the slowly lightening sky. The silence and aloneness, rather than intimidating him, filled him with a sense of awe and possibilities. Dawn broke just as he arrived at the deserted pier. Having only experienced the waterfront at the busy hour, Albano had eagerly anticipated the same activity and had not imagined it any other way, but to be part of Smyrna's awakening was uniquely mesmerizing. The waterfront seemed longer and wider in its emptiness. Muslim men swept and washed the pavement sleepily. As the sky filled with streaks of pinkish hues and the sea went from black to cobalt blue, the waterfront revealed itself, stretching unhurriedly like a cat. Boats on the docks rocked gently to the low clanking of buoys.

Albano inhaled the delicious moment, the sea air, the merry clinking of bells, the clapping of sails. On the waterfront, cafés were just beginning to open: awnings unfolded, busboys lifted piles of wicker chairs and set them on terraces, white cloths were spread squarely on tables.

Soon, a handful of early-rising, impeccably dressed European and Levantine businessmen were sitting at scattered tables. The businessmen took spectacles out of their coat pockets, pinched them on their noses, and unfolded newspapers as waiters brought them coffee in tiny cups and plates filled with pastries. Albano did not doubt that those men were the kinds of men who, with their money, their work, their importance, their newspapers, shaped the world. He stood transfixed. This is what he wanted to do with his life! He wanted to be one of those men who, in early morning hours, sat in peace and luxury at the terraces of cafés!

Standing alone on the pier, intoxicated by the clean scent of the sea and the aroma of fresh coffee and pastries, Albano felt inexplicably alive.

He sat right on the pier, let his bare feet dangle toward the water, unfolded the cloth in which he had placed his bread and a chunk of goat cheese, and as he watched the sea, began to eat. Surely God would want him to know about His creation. God could not possibly have meant for him to be ignorant of anything that was not the Torah and Jewish affairs. He watched the sailboats and the ever-brightening blue sky and began to imagine with great pleasure what it would be like to ride in one of those boats, what it would be like to explore the strange cities those boats came from, what it would be like to be a sailor moving about the world.

He vaguely heard a high-pitch call, "Rabbi!" but in his reverie, he didn't react. A few seconds later, someone was sitting right beside him. "I thought it was you, Rabbi!" Albano looked in amazement: it was the boy from the fountain! "Did you come here to see me?" the boy was asking in Arabic.

Taken aback, Albano muttered, "I did not." Although in a way it was true.

The boy camped himself in front of him. He wore the traditional dress of Muslim men, a white djellaba, a red fez. Next to him was an extraordinarily large leather satchel filled with newspapers. "I knew you would come back," the boy said. He spoke animatedly, but his eyes remained fixed on the horizon, as though he was looking at something. "In fact, I thought to myself, when will my friend the rabbi pay me another visit?"

Friend? Albano thought. "How did you learn to speak Hebrew?" he asked.

"And how can you speak Arabic? I thought Jews only spoke Hebrew."

"Everyone in the Jewish quarter speaks Arabic. And my family speaks Ladino because we're Jews from Spain."

"There are not too many rabbis your age walking around the pier," the boy noted.

"I'm not yet a rabbi. Only learning."

"What is your name, Rabbi? Mine is Hagop."

"I'm Albano."

"Where is your group from last time? And your horses?"

Albano was surprised that the boy knew so much about his last visit to the pier. "I came alone."

"They let you go?"

"They do not know I'm here," Albano admitted.

Looking at the horizon, Hagop whistled between his teeth appreciatively. "A disobedient rabbi," he said.

"I'm only curious about Smyrna," Albano said defensively.

Hagop nodded in understanding and pointed to the place on the horizon where his gaze had been fixed. "See that Ferry over there? That is the first ferry of the day, and with it comes mayhem. Then it's one after the other. I will not lie to you: this is not easy work. But these people coming on those boats, they are starving for them; they haven't gotten any since they have been at sea. They will pay anything for them."

Albano looked at the boy, dumfounded. "Starving for what?"

Hagop turned to his enormous bag and laid it between them. "News!" he said. "Newspapers: Greek, French, British, even American." He pointed to the horizon again. "See the steamboats arriving? Those are passenger liners that come in each day from all over the world, not just the Empire. People sail here from Genoa, Marseille, Trieste, London. They arrive every hour, and in those boats are men from all those countries. Most of them only speak their own language. They're from America and Africa and Europe and Russia and everywhere. Do you know the single thing they all have in common?"

"They are seasick?" Albano suggested.

"They want news. They want newspapers!" Hagop exclaimed. He continued excitedly, speaking a mile a minute. "They are ravenous for them! They are desperate for them! They want newspapers more than they want food to eat or air to breathe. And now that war is on everyone's lips and in every headline, they need news more than ever. They want to know how the world's affairs will affect their travel, their business, everything. They are so desperate for newspapers that I can set my price; they will pay double, triple! And whatever they pay over cost is my benefit."

"Can they not purchase newspapers at the kiosks over there?" Albano jutted his chin in the direction of the small tent that had sprouted on the quay and where a merchant was busying himself arranging newspapers and periodicals.

Hagop shook his head impatiently. "The key is to present them newspapers right as they disembark. Smyrniots aren't the ones who buy from me. They know that in only a few steps they will purchase it at the regular price. But all the others, especially those who have never set foot in Smyrna, those people are ripe for the picking."

"Isn't this dishonest?" Albano inquired.

"It is called supply and demand."

"What does this mean?"

"They don't know if there will be a supply," the boy said assuredly, "so, they demand. I'll tell you what, Rabbi. Do you want me to show you Smyrna?"

Albano looked at Hagop dubiously, but the boy's wide smile and enthusiasm were contagious. "Maybe."

"I'll make a deal with you. You help me sell the newspapers this morning, and in exchange, I will show you Smyrna."

Albano pointed to the way he was dressed. "Will people buy from someone like me?"

Hagop ignored him. "Here in this satchel, I have newspapers in Greek, Armenian, English, French, and Italian. The minute people dock we can see what nationality they are, and we present that language to them. The two of us can go twice as fast, and then we have the rest of the day to explore."

"I'm not supposed to be here," Albano admitted.

"What, you think I'm supposed to be here?"

"I would not know how to sell. What do I tell people?"

"You tell them nothing, you shove the newspaper right under their noses, they read the headline, and they're hooked. Like a big juicy tuna fish." Hagop considered Albano, tilted his head, assessing him. He reached for Albano's chin with dubiously clean fingers and moved Albano's face this way and that to see it from several angles and nodded knowingly. "You will present the newspapers to the ladies."

Albano widened his eyes in horror. "Why the ladies?"

Hagop laughed. "Have they no mirrors in the Jewish quarter? Just go to well-dressed ladies, the ones with the laces and jewels. They might even give you a tip. But I get to keep all the money, is it clear? You earn a tour of the most cosmopolitan, the most exciting city on earth, by one of the city's top guides."

"You?"

"Me!" The next moment, Hagop was on his feet. He took half the newspapers out of the satchel and thrust them into Albano's arms. "Follow me," he said, and before Albano had any time to think, they both started running toward the docking steamboat, Hagop holding on to the red fez on his head and Albano to his wide-brimmed black hat.

What followed was indeed a whirlwind. The incoming steamboat was filled with French citizens coming from Marseille. Hagop moved French newspapers to the top of his and Albano's piles and, while advancing against the disembarking crowd, began screaming, "Le Figaro! Le Monde! Dernières nouvelles! Achetez Le Figaro, Achetez Le Monde!" Albano was astounded that Hagop, a Turkish boy his age, could know Hebrew and the French language. Mute, his stomach in a knot, the newspapers moistened from the sweat of his gripped fingers, Albano rigidly stood where Hagop had told him to stand. Fancily dressed men and women made their way down the ramp, holding on to handrails and a flurry of Turkish men fretted around them, offering to carry their luggage. The French ladies clutched their bags and held dogs the size of rats. The French gentlemen took out their wallets. Albano went stiffer still. Hagop summoned him in Hebrew, "Closer, Rabbi! Come close to the women!" and then he resumed calling out the names of the newspapers in various languages. "Tribute, Figaro, Corriere de la Serra!" Newspapers were flying out of Hagop's hand while Albano still had not made a single sale. And how could he have? He did not look like a salesman at all. He looked like a child in rabbi clothing, dumb, stiff, and mute, who happened to be standing there gripping a pile of French newspapers.

A beautiful woman, surely the most beautiful woman Albano had ever seen, came down the ramp, all cream lace, silk clothes and pink cheeks. She held on to the arm of a mustachioed man who wore the same funny straw hat Uncle Moshe had worn that first day he arrived. "Là, le journal," the woman said, pointing in the direction of Albano. "Vous avez Le Monde?" the man asked. Albano could not understand them. He looked at his papers as though this was the first time he was laying eyes on them, which is exactly what it was. Unable to read the names of the newspapers written in languages he did not know, he just presented them in a pile and let the man find the one he wanted. "Combien?" the beautiful French lady asked. Albano, unaccustomed to being addressed by a beautiful woman, European or otherwise, blushed violently. "Il est si beau," the woman laughed. "Donne-lui de l'argent, Eugène." The man handed him a coin. Albano looked at the coin dumfounded. "C'est suffisant?" the man asked. Albano only stared, so the man gave him another coin, and a third. Albano must have looked terribly confused because the lady smiled warmly at him and the man just shrugged, exasperated. Albano, frozen, the coins still sitting on his upright palm, watched his first ever customers walk toward the restaurants. He was still watching them when the lady turned back toward him and flashed him a smile so alluring that Albano dropped half the papers onto the pavement.

Hagop gave him a light tap on the cheek, plucked the coins from Albano's hand and announced, "I was right about the ladies."

Albano picked up the newspapers scattered at his feet. "I only sold one."

"You'll get better at it."

The rest of the morning, as the cafés became a sea of hats and open newspapers, Hagop and Albano sold newspapers. This was the most exciting thing Albano had ever done. Once Hagop recognized a docking steamboat and figured out what the nationality of the travelers might be, he showed Albano how to pronounce the title of the papers the travelers would most likely purchase. He also taught him how to pronounce the prices in a number of languages and gave him huge slaps on the back when Albano pronounced correctly.

Hagop was fearless in his approach, but Albano rapidly figured out how to repeat the feat of his first sale. Yes, Hagop was right. For some reason, all Albano had to do was stand there and one lady or another would notice him and nudge her husband in his direction. She would smile at him. Some ladies would speak to him, ask him questions in languages he could not understand, so all he did was repeat the name of the newspaper in their language and tell them the price. Effortlessly, the papers sold themselves. Exclamations of "Muy caro" and "bel ragazzo" and "gentil garçon juif" and an outraged "das ist die Zeitung von gestern," followed them, but he did not know what those meant.

"These European people," Albano asked Hagop once the sun was high in the sky and most of the newspapers were sold, "why do they not haggle?"

Hagop shrugged, "They don't know how."

"Everyone knows how to haggle."

"It is considered rude in Europe."

Albano decided he had much to learn. Either the rest of the world was upside down, or else it was right side up, and it was the Ottoman Empire that did things wrong. It was all so confusing. The one thing Albano tried not to think about was the beating that awaited him when he came home. He also tried not to think too much about sin. Was spending time with a Muslim boy a sin? Was smiling at European ladies a sin? There were no rules against commerce that he knew of, and he hoped this was commerce, not robbery.

When the last steamboat had docked, Hagop held up his hand. "Give me my money, Rabbi. Are you hungry?"

"I have no food. And now," Albano added, dropping his earnings into Hagop's hand, "I have no money either."

Hagop laughed. "You are funny, Rabbi. Come with me. I will feed you and show you Smyrna."

"What do you do with the money you earn selling newspapers?"

"I spend it."

"What do you buy?"

"More newspapers!" Hagop said.

They walked across the quay and away from the sea. "See the road to the Jewish and Turkish quarters are up to the right, south of the quayside. The Armenian quarter begins straight across from the ocean to the east, just past Frank Street. Have you seen Frank Street?"

"Everyone speaks of it."

"Northeast is the Greek quarter. To the north there is the American Consulate and Sporting Club, and after that the European quarter where most of the Levantines live. Now, if you've never seen wealth, you will be amazed. I'll take you to Frank Street, and then to the Turkish Bazaar, and then the Armenian quarter."

As they walked toward Frank Street, Hagop pointed to white marbled façades, minarets, intricate mosaics, stained glass, and stone stairs that lead to massive buildings, naming everything faster than Albano could make sense of it. "This is the French Bank! And this is the Greek Bank!" Each time he seemed as proud as if the establishment belonged to him alone. "And this to the left is the entrance to the Hamman! And this is...? I don't know what this is.... And this is the brothel! And this is the English Consulate! This is the Imperial Ottoman Bank! Over there is the Opera house. This is the Crédit Lyonnais, the French Bank. This is the headquarters of an international insurance company. This is the Catholic Church of Saint Mary, the Greek Orthodox Cathedral. And this is the entrance to Frank Street...."

The narrow street, encased on each side by buildings made of stone and wood tall enough to shade it completely, was long, sinuous, and narrower than Albano had pictured. Frank Street was barely wide enough for the dense crowd, yet all manner of vehicles and people squeezed themselves into it: men atop camels, horse-drawn buggies, barefoot peddlers pushing carts filled with goods who stopped in the middle of the road to sell merchandize to passersby. Every centimeter of the cobblestone pavement was dense with people in all sorts of strange shapes, sizes, and appearance, animals, dead and living, and mounds of merchandise, some of which he could recognize, most of it entirely mysterious to him. In the center of the pavement, you quickly learned to avoid the gutter that carried off soiled water and animal excrements. There were men in kaftans next to men in three-piece suits and top hats, women veiled from head to toe next to women dressed in the latest

European fashion. Greek, Jewish, Armenian, Levantine, and European women and children, each wearing the attires of their respective people, pressed themselves into the crowd. At the stores' thresholds, merchants shouted the merits of their goods and switched to honeyed voices to coax shoppers into entering their stores. Everyone was buying or selling. Everyone was yelling and calling. Everyone was eating, cooking, singing, walking, arguing, bartering, or haggling. The street was loud with ethnic music and voices in every language. Periodically, the traffic would come to a standstill, and Albano and Hagop compressed themselves into this sea of humanity.

Above, the buildings on each side had balconies spilling bougainvillea and pink laurel, and clotheslines with drying laundry went from one side of the street to the other like playful banderoles. Painted signs in wood and metal attached to the façades stuck out into the street, and colorful awnings jutted from walls naming the various shops and eating establishments. Albano's head spun to the right and the left as Hagop breathlessly explained things: "This is Xenopoulos, the famous Greek flagship store." Albano knew enough written Greek to recognize some of the words painted on the fancy walls of the shop: silk and wool, dresses, ribbons, lace, umbrellas, blankets. "This is the French store Au Bon Marché." Hagop continued excitedly, "They carry goods from Europe and the whole world, and that's where the Levantines, the Europeans, and all the rich people shop."

But next to this luxurious establishment, out of which fancy women in corseted dresses walked, followed by servants with arms filled with bags and boxes, there were stores for regular people too. Stores for Muslims, stores for Christians, stores for Jews, more stores than he could imagine existed: hat makers, shoemakers, jewelers, watchmakers and goldsmiths, apothecary shops, shops that sold olives and raisins, oils and dried fruit, tobacco leaves, tea, and coffee. There were grocers, gambling parlors, butchers, fish sellers, coffee shops, horse and wagons for hire, each store with its own stench, or perfume, each with colorful signs written in a dozen languages. In shop fronts were displays of meat — cooked and raw — live goats and poultry, piles of vegetables and fruit, dried goods, spices and grains in open baskets. Everyone had something to sell, and there was something to buy for every budget. The many cafés spilled their customers onto the streets by setting chairs and tables out on the pavement. American sailors, drunk into a stupor, coexisted there with pipe-smoking men donning fezzes, turbaned Bedouins who sat around small tables and drank Turkish coffee in silence, Greek men with long beards who drank ouzo out of metal goblets, and still more red-faced British men and their funny rounded hats. As he spoke nonstop, Hagop carved their way through the dense crowd. Albano kept bumping into people because he was looking up and down, to the left and to the right, trying to keep up with Hagop's tour and at the same time being overwhelmed by the sights, sounds, and scents all around. The smells reminded Albano that he was hungry, but his stomach could wait. He would, in all likelihood, never lay eyes on a more amazing spectacle than Frank Street, never again witness a sight more capable of taking his breath away, and never again feel more excited and alive than he did at this very moment.

Albano followed Hagop who continued to speak in a high-pitched voice. They made their way up a small alley that sprouted off Frank Street and arrived in the heart of the Turkish bazaar. The street was narrower and barely wide enough for three men to stand side by side. Merchandise dangled from walls and spilled onto the street. Everything one could want to purchase was in the bazaar: fabric, mosaics and tiles, metal lamps, crystals, pipes and hookahs, raw meat, fur and cloth, rugs, pottery, hats, tobacco, tea, spices. But this was not a place where Europeans shopped. Gone were the rich people, the banks, the temples and churches. In the bazaar everything was more rugged, the dress and language coarser, and many of the men more dangerous looking.

Hagop did not seem intimidated in the least, and no one was paying attention to them, so Albano began to relax about his surroundings, even though he looked conspicuously Jewish in this predominantly Muslim area. Suddenly the nagging thought he had tried to ignore awakened in him. By now, the people at shul must have noticed he was missing. It should not be too much of an issue as long as he got back to his house on time, which was still a possibility if he left right now. The problem was, he was not about to leave. Not so soon. Not now that he had a friend in Smyrna, a friend who knew the city. The thought of never returning home just to avoid the inescapable beating flickered through his mind.

Hagop, who had ignored every other store they walked past, came to a halt in front of a table piled high with angora blankets, silk garments, cotton clothing, and hats. He began fingering the merchandise, unfolding fabric, trying on this hat and that one. The merchant, a turbaned old man with bushy eyebrows, crossed his arms menacingly the instant he saw Hagop. "Salamalekum, may God be with you," Hagop clamored happily to the man.

"I don't know what you're up to," the man shouted angrily. "But I will call the police on you unless you stop coming here."

"Noble merchant, I don't know what you mean. I have done nothing wrong but admire your merchandise."

The old man raged, "I know you are stealing from me!"

Hagop looked contrite and, holding out his palms said, "Honored merchant, may Allah be with you. But before you accuse me and my Jewish friend of a crime, perhaps you need to see that our hands are empty." Hagop twirled, then made a show of opening his satchel, which was empty now. He bowed deeply. The man showed him his fist and screamed at him some more in Arabic as they walked away.

Albano waited for them to be out of earshot and asked, "Why is this merchant so angry with you? Is it true that you stole from him?" Then he noticed something. "You lost your hat!"

"Quite the contrary," Hagop said. "My hat is not lost; it has found its way home."

"What do you mean?"

"It's simple," Hagop beamed. "Each morning I walk past this foolish man's shop, I borrow a fez and put it on my head. When I come back home, I return it. The man knows that something is happening yet he doesn't know what!"

"But why do you do this?"

"If anyone in my quarter sees me with a fez on my head and tells my parents, I will not live to see another blessed day."

Albano did not understand. "So you steal, then you return?"

"I borrow. It is a business arrangement."

"One where only one person benefits," Albano pointed out.

"Oh, quite the opposite. I am the one who gets the least. I only get a stupid hat, while this man gets a puzzle to exercise his brain."

"Soon he will figure it out."

"Why worry? There are more fez merchants in Smyrna than there are boats in the Smyrna harbor."

"Why would your parents not want you to wear a fez?"

Hagop did not respond. Albano followed him up a narrow, sinuous street, admiring his new friend's self-confidence, his fearlessness. This was how he wanted to be: he wanted to be more like Uncle Moshe or like Hagop. Except that for every action he took, Albano could imagine hundreds of possible outcomes. The possibility of danger, of hurting someone, of being caught did not usually measure up against his curiosity and the thrill of adventure. And yet, here he was, following a reckless boy full of laughter.

"Now I will take you to the finest bakery in the Armenian quarter," Hagop said.

"But Armenians are Christians. Can a Jew and a Muslim be safe there?"

Hagop burst into roaring laughter. "I'm not Muslim! I'm a Christian. Apostolic Armenian, to be exact."

"This is why you can't wear a fez?"

"This is why I can't wear a fez."

"But why pretend to be Muslim?"

"When you dress like a Muslim boy in Smyrna, no one pays attention to you. I can walk around the city however I please."

"Do you not have school?"

Hagop shrugged in a way that expressed his utter disinterest in the matter. "I am a baker's apprentice. By the time the sun rises, I have already done my day's work. So I just head here before others awake, and I'm the first one on the quay."

"When do you sleep?"

"In the afternoon. Such is a baker's life, which is why I hate it so. We are lucky if we see the sun at all."

On Frank Street and in the bazaar, there were many Jews dressed much like him. But as they entered the Armenian quarter, Albano felt aware of his dark coat and tall black hat, the fringes that came down from his pockets, the long hair that spilled from his hat on both sides of his face. Now he knew what Hagop meant. If Hagop could transform into a Muslim simply by donning a fez, then it was possible that the difference between a Muslim, a Christian, or a Jew was even shallower than skin deep. Could he himself remove his clothes, cut his hair, and pass as a Muslim or a Christian boy? Would he want to? His skin was fair, his hair was a light shade of brown, and his eyes were that pale color that everyone noticed and was so unusual in the Jewish quarter. Were he to don short pants and long socks, and wear a European sort of hat, would he ever be mistaken for a French child? The funny thought distressed him. It made him anxious that his deepest sense of identity could be stripped from him simply by taking away his clothes. "Is a boy dressed like me safe in the Armenian quarter?" he asked.

Hagop considered this. "We don't like Jews much." He scratched his now fez-free skull. "But we don't like Greeks and Muslims either. And we don't like the Levantines. Or the Europeans. We just like to sell them things and work in their factories. Do Jews like Armenians?"

"I don't think so," Albano said.

The Armenian quarter was not unlike the Jewish quarter, Albano noticed. The same women's voices clamoring, muted sounds of donkey hoofs on dirt paths, laundry drying at windows, girls carrying jugs of water on their heads, grimy, barefoot boys chasing each other, men getting shaved on chairs set out by barbers in the street, old women gossiping on benches. The greatest difference was the smells. The quayside had smelled of fish and perfume, the bazaar had smelled of tobacco and raz el hanout, the Jewish quarter smelled of yeast and cinnamon, and now, in the Armenian quarter, it smelled of fried oil and honey. Hagop walked proudly through the streets, calling people by their names and laughing. Albano soon became acutely conscious of the many sets of eyes on him. Hagop read his thoughts. "Maybe take off that hat," he said helpfully. "But don't worry, my new Jewish friend, no one will harass you when you are with the son of Yori."

"Is your father a powerful man?"

"Better than that. He is the best baker in the Armenian quarter. No one here would take a chance of being refused his famous dolmas." Hagop rubbed his belly and licked his lips to illustrate. Soon he pointed at a bakery up the street and exclaimed, "This is it!" Inside the bakery it smelled heavenly, of warm bread and honey. The place bustled with activity and animated conversations. There were a dozen wooden tables and chairs where customers sat, drinking coffee and eating pastries. The length of one of the walls was covered in a beautiful fresco depicting men and women working together in a field of golden wheat. Hagop signaled for Albano to follow him toward a small table in back of the store. "That painting you're looking at, it's over one hundred years old. That's how old this bakery is. It belonged to my grandfather, and his father before that." Hagop noticed that many were staring at Albano. "What?" He told a gawking boy and his mother. "Is this the only Jew you have ever seen? This one is extremely holy, as you can judge from his extremely holy clothes. I found him down on the quay." Hagop plopped down heavily on a chair. "Sit," he said with much emphasis and pride. "And wait to feast on the best pastries in the whole Ottoman Empire." He added royally, "You can have anything here you desire." Albano sat, and Hagop began extricating coins out of his many pockets, spreading them on the table and gathering them into little stacks by currency: lira, pounds, French and Swiss francs, American pennies. He began counting, cursing, counting again.

There were perhaps twenty people inside the bakery. Some sat at the tables lined against the whitewashed walls, some stood in line, waiting to be served, pointing at merchandise, while two women who looked like mother and daughter hurried about the room. The two women wore their jet-black hair the Armenian women's way: severely parted in the middle and into one long, thick braid that reached way down their backs. They wore white blouses, long black skirts and a heavy crimson apron that came down to the floor. The mother, a heavyset woman with a kind face, did all the talking and interactions with the customers, taking orders, receiving money, and giving change with authority. The girl, who was about Albano's age, came in and out the back of the store carrying large trays filled with steaming pastries. Long sleeves covered her arms, and the collar of her dress was buttoned up to the nape of her slender neck. She carried her head high, and her eyes were unflinching. Her skin was very pale, her face a perfect oval, her nose small and straight, but it was her grave black eyes that made Albano lose his breath. Her eyes were immense and luminous, her eyebrows finely delineated, her lips crimson and full. Albano opened his mouth and forgot to close it. He was jerked away from his admiration by Hagop's reaching across the table and putting a hand on his collar. "When I tell you that you can have anything you want here, I am only speaking of pastries."

Albano decided Hagop had to be a magician to be able to read all his thoughts. "Wha, What do you mean?" he stuttered.

"If you look at her like this I will have to gouge your eyes out."

"She is your wife?" Albano said, astonished at Hagop's good fortune.

Hagop laughed. "What wife? I'm ten years old! She is my sister." Hagop and his sister looked very much alike: similar eyes with heavy lids, similar mouths, and bright, straight teeth. But Hagop's features were more pronounced and asymmetrical, which gave him the crazy air of a jester. His eyes bulged almost. His mouth was rapacious, whereas Xandra's features were so perfect they seemed painted on the lovely oval of her face. "Xandra!" Hagop called. "Meet my new friend."

"Nooo," came the strangled sound out of Albano's mouth. But already the girl was standing before him, holding a tray of pastries, her gaze amused and inquisitive.

"I found a rabbi on the quay, and now he is my friend," Hagop told her in Arabic so that Albano could understand what he was saying. "He and I are going into business together."

She looked at Albano and spoke in Arabic. "Are you certain? My brother may not be the most reliable of partners. He's never on time." Albano's stomach made 360-degree flips inside his belly. Xandra spoke to him, and the effect this had on him was something new and incredible. He could barely look at her and was unable to utter a word.

"Time, time, time!" Hagop clamored. "All you bakers think of is time. And rising in the dead of night. And shelling nuts by the boatful. And breaking your backs carrying bags of flour. Not me. I am meant for sunshine and adventure! I am meant to be a businessman." Hagop frowned at the narrowness of his dream and revised it. "I am meant to be a banker!"

"My brother the adventurous banker." Xandra laughed, looking at Albano. Albano laughed too, not even knowing why.

Hagop was furious. "One day you will see I will have my own seat on the train with my name on it, just like a rich Levantine."

"You always said you didn't want a partner," Xandra pointed out.

"I'm an ugly fellow, so I need a good-looking partner. You have to see Albano with the ladies. The key to success is who you associate with."

"Are you good with ladies?" Xandra inquired.

Albano could only come up with a strangled, "I ... don't—"

"Isn't he handsome?" Hagop said with pride. "I will change his clothes, and he will look just fine."

"What is this for?" Xandra asked, pointing to Albano's sidelocks.

Albano felt his face redden. "Ahem ... tradition, I think."

"Can you cut them?"

Albano widened his eyes, "Oh no!"

"Can you tuck them behind your ears?" Hagop asked pragmatically.

"I think so."

"What is your name?" Xandra asked.

"A, Albano."

"Can I give you something to eat, Albano?" she said, nodding to the tray she was still holding which was filled with pastries, some in the shape of crescents topped with powdered sugar and others like well-leavened rounds that glistened with honey.

To hear this beautiful girl pronounce his name, Albano nearly jumped out of his skin. He didn't know what the pastries on her tray were called. "I would like ... a pastry?" he said stupidly, his voice barely above a murmur.

Xandra turned her coal-black eyes to her brother. "He isn't *that* good with the ladies," she said. "But it is true, Hagop, you have found yourself a handsome-looking rabbi."

CHAPTER 5

La Parisienne

Cassie stood by the conveyor belt waiting for her luggage when a chuckle emanated from the crowd. Then another. Then everyone was giggling. She looked for what was so amusing and found it; right there, moving on the conveyor belt, a single white, high-waist cotton panty was traveling alone. She laughed. It was all so incongruous and well, hilarious. It wasn't until a yellow and orange polka-dot shirt was ejected from the bowels of the terminal and began its own rotation of shame that Cassie understood that those were, in fact, *her* panties and *her* polka-dot shirt! They were followed by another T-shirt, this one purple, and a bra, an electric toothbrush rolled down, and, finally, the pièce de résistance: her zigzag suitcase, gutted, its innards of clothes and undies disgorging out of it like a cartoon zebra road kill.

She sprang forward waving her arms calling. "C'est à moi!" and began a humiliating scavenger hunt along the conveyor belt, apologizing and fishing out clothes and shoving them, red-faced, into her tote bag. "Merci," she mumbled to the psychiatrist who bent down and retrieved the polka-dotted T-shirt and held it between two fingers. "Merci," she told a beaming five-year-old girl who handed her the toiletry bag. "Merci," she whispered to a large man who waved a pair of socks in her direction. "Pardon. Je suis désolée," she blurted out to two pairs of feet next to which she scooped another T-shirt. "Merc" – recognizing the feet belonged to the French couple, Cassie switched to English – "I mean, sorry!" and she fished a lime green viscose bra from atop a still rotating suitcase.

After a few grunts, head shakes, and clicking of tongues, the Charles de Gaulle Airport baggage authorities washed themselves of any responsibility, pronouncing the gutted suitcase, "très vieille avec une fermeture à glissière en mauvais état." Antiquated, with a broken zipper. Cassie was given the options of a large trash bag or duct tape and agreed to the duct tape.

She exhaled as she exited the terminal and stepped out into the morning air. Then she inhaled and stopped in her tracks. It was freezing! Or perhaps a degree or two above freezing, judging from the pouring rain. There was supposed to be a heat wave! With her two layered, long-sleeved shirts made of ultrathin cotton, a lavender one over a light pink one, she might as well have been wearing tissue paper.

She considered the Frankenstein-looking suitcase sausaged in duct tape at her feet and renounced trying to retrieve her jacket. She eyed the taxi line and decided to make a run for it. Her suitcase, grinding against the wet asphalt, twisted and turned on itself with each step. In the line, a little man with a receding chin camped himself right behind her much too closely and lit a cigarette. Adjust, adjust, she thought. Ahead of her in line was the French couple from the plane. The wife wore a warm coat and seemed quite smug about it. She observed Cassie's unruly hair, the too thin clothes, the mangled suitcase, and the Uggs acting as fast-absorbing sponges on the soaked pavement. When a taxi Parisien whisked the two away, Cassie breathed better. If she could not handle the disapproval of complete strangers, it didn't bode well for the rest of the trip. She could not have been in Paris more than ten minutes, and already she was cold to the core and felt defeated. When it was her turn to enter a cab, her suitcase came off-balance. She turned her head in time to see one of the wheels fall off like a ripe fruit off a tree and go rolling off into the distance.

It was already three in the afternoon in Paris and six in the morning in her brain. She was filled with a strange, hollow, out-of-body energy but decided she better get to the hospital before the hotel. "Hôpital Saint-François. Dans le dixième arrondissement, s'il vous plaît," she told the driver over the blaring radio. The cab driver wore a white prayer hat and drove too fast for comfort, honking rather than slowing down when people or cars got in his way. Outside, it was as though she had never left. The city was familiarly gray, hazy, and wet. People in rain suits and umbrellas jumped over puddles. There were bakeries and cafés, shops with brands she recognized and some new ones. The windshield wipers moved with the rhythm of the music. In the city, the top edges of buildings melted into the thick sky. And then she saw them, the first giant billboard, then a second one, and a third, with smaller versions of them on the bus stops and métro entrances: posters of *Women in Black, Part Two*, the words in green lettering against black. "Oh God," she moaned. "It's everywhere."

"Comment?" the driver said.

"Where is the heat wave?" she asked in French.

"C'est fini," he responded in his thick North African accent. "L'hiver est revenu," he added. Winter is back. And with this, he laughed.

She leaned against the headrest. "When they throw a hook, don't bite," Peter had said. It was interesting, the use of the pronoun. They. A monolithic block, or so it seemed. "They're horrible people," she had told Peter on her way to the airport. "Even parents of serial killers don't refuse to take their own child's phone calls for two years over *one* stupid letter."

"They're thick-headed," Peter had said. "Like someone I know."

"What makes it worse is how many heads the beast has – my mother, my father, Odile, and perhaps even Sabine, all united against me."

"Look, you can fix this," Peter said. "You need to fix this. Especially with your dad; the guy is old."

"Not that old."

"Honey, you're in denial."

"Oh, stop it. I forget my dad's age: I'm in denial. I say I don't want to look for a boyfriend: I'm in denial. I say that I'm comfortable being an empty nester: I'm in denial. I'm always in denial with you, and you're always wrong."

"Except when you're in denial."

"It's my prerogative not to dwell on some things."

"That's the definition of denial," Peter had said. "The thing about your dad is, you can't go on for the rest of your life weeping every time you talk about him."

"I'm weepy just thinking about him. I can't help it."

"He's capable of a heart," Peter said. "Look how he adores Odile and her kids."

In the cab, Cassie tried to think of an answer she could have given to Peter. Because that was precisely the thing: when they were little girls, and to this day, her dad had always adored Odile.

****

Cassie stood in front of the austere entrance of Hôpital Saint-François. She was drenched. Her hair, her too thin clothes, her boots, were soaked. Past the gate, the architecture reminded her of the Place des Vosges; there was a rectangular courtyard with a fountain in the center, arcaded walkways, colonnades. She entered the building. As she walked through the corridors, her duct-taped suitcase dragged on the side where the wheel was gone and made a terribly high-pitch screech against the marble floor. People stared at her with a mix of amusement and disapproval as the screech echoed through the vast hallways and bounced off the cathedral ceiling. At least those hideous pterodactyl noises covered the embarrassing squish-squish of her wet footsteps.

She followed the brightly colored signs. Could they really practice cutting-edge medicine in a castle-like building that, according to a sign, had been built in the 1840s?

At the reception desk of the intensive care unit, a thin, morose-looking woman in a greenish smock read Télérama and chewed gum. She had frizzy hair and colorless skin. "Excuse me," Cassie said, "I'm here to visit my –"

The woman pointed a finger toward a sign that said "Vestiaire." Cloakroom. "Change over there," she said without lifting her eyes.

"Into what?" Cassie said, expecting in return the kind of bonhomie that took place between people when one attempted humor.

When the woman looked at her glacially, Cassie said, "I was joking."

"It's all in there," the woman said, not amused in the least.

Adjust … adjust, Cassie thought.

Inside the changing room, she found written instructions. "For reasons of hygiene, all visitors to the intensive care unit must wear a paper gown over their clothes, a paper bonnet over their hair and paper slippers over their shoes, and a surgical mask." She wasn't convinced that those would provide much protection against all the germs she carried from her exposure to the plane, the taxi, or life in general. Nevertheless, she put on the gown, tied the paper belt, and slipped the paper over her boots. Instantly, the paper soaked up the humidity in her hair and boots. She poked her head out of the room. "May I bring my suitcase in the room?" she called.

Rather than say yes, which is what she meant, the frizzy woman said, "Non! C'est complètement interdit! It's strictly forbidden to leave personal belonging in the cloakroom." Complètement and interdit. How French people loved to use those two words together. The woman's tone implied that this was a question of rare idiocy. "The mask too, Madame," she told Cassie as she exited out of the room. Cassie slipped on the mask and looked at herself in a mirror. She looked moronic. This was how her family would see her the first time they laid eyes on her in five years: eyes blood-shot from a night spent on a plane, wrapped in paper from head to toe, and at her side, a suitcase mummified in duct tape. She reminded herself to breathe and pushed open the door that led to the patients' rooms. The bright lobby was strangely quiet. Two dozen people, doctors, nurses, staff, and visitors dressed in paper, moved about in morgue-like silence. The effect sobered her up. This was no joke; her father's condition, foggy and theoretical until now, became real.

She looked for the room number. The door was closed. She turned the knob and opened the door ever so quietly.

In contrast to the lobby, the room was very dark, and she saw nothing at first. There was the smell of bleach and the ominous beeps of machines. Her vision adapted to the low light, and she saw a hospital bed perched up high and, on the bed, an old man whose face was half-hidden by a plastic mask. Briefly, she hesitated, refusing to believe that this was her dad. There was an enormous bandage on his chest. Dark purple bruises covered his bare legs. All manner of clunky apparatus connected to his arms via wires. Tubes went from his body to hanging IV bags and pouches down below. There was a thick tube coming out of his mask, and it made him look like some insect, a fly, a mosquito. His eyes were closed. Overwhelmed with what she was seeing, she did not immediately notice the two motionless human shapes sitting by the bed, dressed in paper outfits and surgical masks identical to hers. They were staring at her soundlessly, the weight of their gazes piercing through her, judging her already.

"Maman? Odile?" Cassie whispered.

One of the human shapes got up and gestured to follow her out of the room.

In the hallway, Odile removed her mask. "With these ridiculous things they make us wear, I wasn't sure it was you. It's all theatrics if you ask me." Odile had aged in the last five years, Cassie noted, and not a little. It wasn't just the wrinkles; Odile now looked a lot like their mother.

"How's Papa? Was that Maman in there?" Cassie asked, but her words came out all muffled.

"You know, you can remove the mask now," Odile said with irritation.

Cassie slipped the mask down to her neck. "Sorry," she said.

"Well, you didn't change one bit," Odile exclaimed, maybe with a hint of envy.

"Neither did you," Cassie lied. "Is Papa feeling any better?"

Odile stiffened. "Doesn't look like it, does it? He's stable, whatever that means. You know they're the ones who put him in this state in the first place."

"They?"

"The hospital. The heart surgery went fine. They had to put him to sleep to intubate him, at some point, I don't know why," Odile said. "Then they removed the endotracheal tube and weaned him off the ventilator, and that's when they realized he had developed an infection in his lungs."

"I've heard that those tubes are tricky. People get pneumonia from them."

Odile shrugged defensively. "We don't know what's at the root of the infection."

"I thought his heart was the problem?"

"Changing the heart valve went fine. I just told you what the problem was."

"Yes, but –" Cassie decided against trying to explain herself. She did not want to slip into the family dynamic that fast. Already she was walking on eggshells. "Is he sleeping now? I mean, can he wake up? Sabine said that—"

"He can wake up when they take down the sedation. But each time they try to he gets agitated and jerks around, and pulls at his IV, which he needs for the antibiotics. And so, they sedate him again."

"How is Maman?"

"A real bitch about the whole thing, as usual. You'd think all this is happening to her."

But it *is* happening to her, Cassie thought. "I should say hello to Maman," she said. The two of them put their masks back on and reentered the room. Raymonde was still sitting in her chair, looking straight at the door, just as she had been doing minutes ago. Cassie walked toward her, afraid to look in the direction of the bed. "Bonjour Maman." She kissed her mother on both cheeks, over the mask. It was funny how Americans felt that kissing on both cheeks was too intimate, and instead put their entire bodies into a hug.

The last thing she could have done at the moment was to hug any of them. Far too much vulnerability and love went into hugs. With their surgical masks, though, the exchange of kisses felt idiotic. "How are you holding up, Maman?" Cassie asked.

"When did you arrive?" Raymonde asked, her voice muffled by the mask. If she was glad to see Cassie, the two inches of face above the mask did not show it. If she was unhappy about it, there was no sign of that either. The same could be said of Odile. They both seemed intent on showing no emotion. Cassie felt that she had no choice but to mirror their lack of expression. On the bed, her father stirred. They looked in his direction, held their breath. He stopped moving. They turned back to each other.

"I landed two hours ago," Cassie said. "I haven't checked into my hotel yet," she added in case her mother offered for her to stay at the apartment. But Raymonde didn't say anything, and Cassie tried not to read into it. "The instant you're around them you get sucked into the family dynamic," Peter had said, then added, "well that's a misnomer actually – the family apathy is more like it."

Cassie turned toward the bed and dared to take a good look at her father. He was breathing with difficulty through the plastic mask. A pump was rhythmically sending air into the mask. His slack jaw that seemed to gasp for air at intervals was heartbreaking to watch. Cassie stood next to him, not sure what to do next. Should she bend down to kiss his cheek and risk waking him up? But if she did not, would Odile and her mom see her as uncaring? The short gown her father wore did not cover his legs and was wide open at the chest. She had the urge to pull all the tubes and wires out of him, and an even stronger urge to put a warm blanket over his body.

She realized she was shivering from her wet clothes. Was the room warm enough? He only wore a thin hospital gown. If he was chilled, he could not express it. She wanted her dad to be covered but realized it was not only because he might be cold. All his life, he had taken such pride and care in the way he presented himself. He had worn a suit and a tie even on the weekends. In the evenings after dinner, he'd methodically remove tie, trousers, and jacket and put on a long bathrobe over ironed pajamas. She had never seen him any other way than meticulously dressed. She was certain that had her dad been conscious, he would have been sickened to know himself unshaven and in this state of undress. The bruises on his legs were hard to look at. Why so many bruises? Old people bruised easily. Was that the reason? Had she ever seen her father's bare feet before? Probably in her childhood when they went on vacation, but even then, he wore seersucker suits, summer loafers, and a starched, buttoned-down shirt. She brushed the tip of her finger on her father's hand. "Do you think he can hear us?" she asked.

"You were just on an airplane; maybe you should not get too close," Odile suggested.

"I washed my hands," she said apologetically. Odile's comment had the immediate effect of making her feel soiled. "Is Sabine here?" she asked.

Odile shrugged, "Who knows?"

Raymonde's silence was already sending Cassie into mental overdrive. Was this meant as an icy reception or a manifestation of grief? If she suggested the three of them go outside in the hallway to talk, would it be interpreted as bossy? She went to fetch the empty chair in the corner of the room, and recognized, folded over it, one of her father's coats. The presence of this particular coat struck her as incongruous. It was what her mother had always called "the relic," a gray coat made of heavy wool. The cut was oddly outdated, and it hung in the closet. Her dad never wore it but kept it for unknown reasons. Cassie moved the chair next to her mom and sister and, finding no other place to put it, folded the coat over her lap. She instantly felt warmer. There was a yellowing label at the neck, not printed but embroidered. P. Germain, Tailleur. The coat smelled of her father's lavender aftershave, a smell so particular to him, the smell of a childhood where her father was invincible and the most wonderful human being in the world.

They stared at beeping machines in strained silence. Cassie's brain was on overdrive, but her body lagged in dull fatigue down to her bones. Now that she had gained weight, Odile looked so peculiarly like Raymonde. Her mother and her sister had similar small, straight and narrow noses, straight blondish hair, and blue eyes, very Nordic, whereas Cassie and Sabine had black hair, more aquiline noses, and this unusual eye color, a light amber hue that was hard to define. Sabine, who had gotten away with the best of both gene pools, was, unlike her, blessed with straight hair.

Ten interminable minutes passed during which Cassie didn't dare budge. At last, Odile got up from her chair and approached Gustave's bed. She felt his forehead with the back of her hand and sighed. She turned to Cassie and whispered, "Let's go outside."

In the hallway, Cassie was relieved to return to the world of ringing telephones and hurried footsteps. "Maman hasn't said a word to me," she told Odile.

Her sister rolled her eyes. "That one, she's driving me crazy."

Cassie pondered the meaning of this. "It's a weird time in my head. I need to get to my hotel to sleep, at some point."

"You're not staying at Maman's place?"

"Last time I heard I was not on speaking terms with her ... or Papa." She omitted to state the obvious, which was that she did not know if she was on speaking terms with Odile either.

"It's time you bury the hatchet, don't you think?" Odile said coldly.

"I have no hatchet," Cassie said, although she knew this to be a lie.

Odile made a small grimace, a familiar, slight, downturn of the lips to mean whatever. The dismissal was not verbalized, but it might as well have been. Cassie fought the urge to confront her. Instead, she managed to say, "How are your kids?"

"I had to leave them with their dad and come here. I can't tell you the nightmare that it is to get here all the way from Poitier. But they're in school. What could I do? Uproot them for an indefinite amount of time until Papa recovers?" The reproach was clear: Odile was sacrificing herself to be here, while Cassie, whose children were grown, was of no help. Forgotten perhaps was the fact that they had not bothered to tell her about the surgery. Although if she was honest with herself, would she have come had she known?

"Are you staying at Maman's?" she asked.

Odile shrugged at the apparent idiocy of Cassie's question. "Where else would I stay?"

"Where is Sabine?"

"That's the million-euro question," she said.

"What do you mean?"

"She was here earlier. Yesterday too. But she won't come into the room. She stays outside in the hallway. Does that make any sense? She works nearby and comes during her lunch hour. But what's the point of showing up if it's to stay in the hallway?" Odile thought, hesitated, and then added, "Oh, and I'm telling you right now since you'll discover it soon enough, she ended the pregnancy."

"Who was pregnant? Sabine was *pregnant*?"

"You didn't know? Well, it happened, the abortion I mean, after Paul left her."

"Paul *left* her?"

"She didn't want to be a single mother, understandably."

"When did this all happen?" Cassie said, trying to hide the distress in her voice. But perhaps she didn't do such a good job because Odile clammed up.

"I guess it's her business if she opted not to tell you."

"But still –" Cassie stopped herself; it was when she cared and showed it that she most rubbed the family the wrong way, but she said it anyway, "– it's a pretty momentous decision."

"She's an adult. It's not like she needed our permission."

Was that it? Did the family hide this from her for fear that she would try to talk Sabine out of it? "Did Maman encourage her?"

Odile looked at her with a brewing storm in her eyes. "You really think this is the time and place to criticize Maman?" Odile's act of virtuous daughter was crumbling already, the composure of her face making way for something else.

"I'm not criticizing anyone."

Odile pointed in the direction of the garden, behind the glass door a hundred feet away. "It's still lunchtime for Sabine. She's probably smoking somewhere." Odile put her hand on the door to their father's room. "Oh," Odile added, "actually, I wouldn't mention it to her."

"It?"

"No one talks about it. It makes her upset."

The hospital's garden lay behind a wall of glass. In the center of the garden was a large fountain and stone benches where paths edged with neat rows of boxwood converged. The rain seemed to have stopped. A few convalescents walked on the path or sat in wheelchairs pushed by nurses. Cassie stood by the glass door looking for Sabine and spotted her. Her younger sister was leaning against a wall, her thin frame wrapped in a black coat elegantly tied at the waist, looking as she always did, inscrutable. Odile and Cassie had grown up together. They knew each other the way only sisters close in age could. They knew what made the other one tick; they knew which buttons to push. Sabine, being younger by ten years, was nearly a stranger. Her sister's enviably straight hair was shorter now, cut just above the shoulder. Sabine was the elegant one in the family. Odile and Raymonde looked provincial in comparison. Not that Cassie, who dressed like a Californian slob, was a good judge in the matter.

The glass door opened, and a handsome young doctor came out of the garden and into the hallway. He held the door for her. She did not move. "Dedans ou dehors?" he said. In or out?

"Out," she said in French. "I mean in. This garden should be out but the hospital is built all around it and –" The cute doctor smiled politely and walked away. The moment she stepped outside, the cold air slapped her with big angry hands. She walked toward Sabine. "Well hello!" she said.

Sabine had a faint smile and moved to kiss Cassie on both cheeks. "You'll freeze without a coat," she said.

For no good reason, Cassie exclaimed, "I'm fine! I've missed the cold in fact. I'm sick of perfect weather, you know."

Sabine took out a pack of chewing gum from her purse, "There's no smoking in hospitals any more. Some law they passed, apparently" she said, offering her a piece of gum.

"No thanks, I don't smoke," Cassie said idiotically. Then she laughed just as idiotically. She was nervous as hell. Everything she was not supposed to say wanted to jump out of her mouth. "How are you? Maman and Odile seem shell-shocked."

"You think so?" Sabine let her sentence trail off. She moved her hair away from her face. Sabine was the beautiful sister, but at the moment, her beauty was dulled by sadness.

"Thank you for calling me. About Papa, I mean. I can't think of why Maman and Odile didn't tell me."

"They would have, eventually."

Why had Paul left Sabine, Cassie wondered? They had been together for years. When was this? A week ago? A month? A year? She and Sabine must have spoken on the phone during that time, which meant that Cassie had been left out of the loop deliberately. Peter's assessment would be the same as it had always been. "Don't get emotionally tossed around," he would tell her. "These people are emotionally crippled."

"Where are you staying?" Sabine asked. "You can stay on my couch if you want."

"Oh no, thank you, I made a reservation at a hotel. Oh, hmm, Sabine?"

"Yes?"

"I'm thinking I'm going to die if I don't get next to a heater in the next five seconds."

"That's what I thought," Sabine said.

Inside the hospital, they walked but not in the direction of their father's room. Sabine was silent, which was disconcerting and gave Cassie the urge to talk for two. "Odile says you don't want to go into Papa's room? You don't like to? Is it too depressing?"

Sabine sighed, "I'll go in with you."

In the dressing room, Sabine removed her coat. She looked brittle. It would have been the right moment to say something, but Cassie could not find the words. Sabine was neutral in the conflict, or was she? Maybe it was not the moment to ask questions. Already, Cassie had this reputation of unnecessarily stirring things up.

As they put on their paper gowns, their differences lifted. Now they were two daughters terrified to enter a room.

They entered and were assailed by the smell of bleach, detergent, and lavender aftershave. As though time inside obeyed different laws, Odile and Raymonde still sat in their chairs, wrapped in paper gowns, surgical masks over their lower faces, motionless, expressionless. There was still the ominous beeping of machines in the background. When you live in a paper dress, don't throw stones, Cassie thought absurdly. "Can he wake up?" she whispered.

"Only when they stop the sedation," Raymonde said.

"But when they do, he gets erratic," Odile added.

Cassie looked at her father's bare legs. "When Alex needed surgery for his broken arm a few years ago, they put compression devices on his legs, to prevent blood clots."

"Well, here they must not," Odile said sharply.

"He might like a blanket don't you think?"

"It feels like an oven in here," Odile said.

"Maybe it would be comforting for him to feel tucked in." Cassie began pacing the room, opening cabinets. "Hmm ... nope, none here. I'll ask a nurse."

Odile's eyes filled with tears. "Papa's on so many drugs: morphine, antibiotics, sedatives."

"Why morphine? Is he in pain?"

"They can't tell. Papa doesn't talk, as you may have noticed. He's *unconscious*." She emphasized that last word, as though Cassie was in some way to blame.

"Are we sure he needs all that?"

"If they give it to him there is a reason!" Odile said sharply through her tears.

"Maybe if they cut the sedation, he'll be able to tell us if he is in pain. Or if he is warm, or cold."

"Maman and I have been here for days, and you just show up here and tell us what to do!"

"I would have been here earlier had anyone bothered to tell me that he was about to have heart surgery," Cassie said under her breath.

"I've stopped my life to be here and take care of Papa," Odile cried, "and you just waltz in here knowing nothing about the situation and start telling us we're not giving him the right treatment."

"I'm not telling anyone anything. I'm asking questions." But now both Odile and Raymonde were looking away with pointed purpose. "I'm going outside," Cassie said, "I'll ask for a blanket."

"He does NOT need a blanket!" Odile said with a savagery that made Cassie freeze into place.

"What the hell, Odile?"

"It's always like that with you," Odile said with fury. "You have to create problems. You have to be difficult!"

Sabine made a motion toward the door with her chin, got to her feet, and left the room. After a beat, Cassie ran out behind her.

They walked down the hallway in silence, removing their masks, and sat on a bench a good distance away from the room.

"Oh. My. God," Cassie said, deflating with each syllable.

"She was going to say that no matter what," Sabine said with a shrug.

"Who? Say what?"

"Odile. She was going to call you difficult."

Cassie stared at Sabine. "You can't possibly know how grateful I am that you're acknowledging this."

Sabine pushed her hair away from her face. "That was decided long before your plane landed."

At that moment, the cute doctor walked right past them and surprised Cassie by giving her a nod of recognition and a smile. Cassie beamed, waited for him to be out of earshot, and said, "Did you see how adorable that doctor is?"

"I noticed," Sabine said. "But you can't have him."

"I can't?"

"Oh no, you're much too difficult."

Cassie burst out laughing and Sabine, after a moment, laughed softly.

****

Aside from the modern cars and the cell phones inches away from everyone's nose, the city was nearly identical to when Cassie was eighteen and dreamed of escape. Cigarette smell. Exhaust. Narrow streets. The roar of mopeds. Trashcans rolled into the street by apartment buildings concierges. Old ladies with transparent plastic bonnets over their heads and straw baskets in the crook of their arms. School children in colorful raincoats. Men smelling of wine coming in and out of a Bar-Tabac. People in line outside a charcuterie. The hotel was a few blocks away from the hospital, but in this weather, it might as well have been on the other side of the earth.

She felt smashed from a toxic cocktail of jet lag, hunger, chill, and the rising anger she was trying to suppress. In the rain, Cassie pulled and dragged her suitcase, avoiding cars as she crossed streets. On the narrow sidewalk, she bumped into people. Had she lived in Los Angeles so long that she had forgotten how to walk on crowded streets? She got poked in the head by someone's umbrella – twice. Her hair dripped with rain; her cheeks felt both feverishly hot and cold enough to fall off her face. Were it not for the threat of hypothermia, she would be tempted to curl into a ball at the foot of the first building and wait for Peter to rescue her. Already, she no longer felt like herself. Already, discouragement loomed.

She passed the fantastic aroma coming out of a boulangerie. All she needed was a meal and a bed. She dug deep for the last of her strength and pushed forward. To be here was surreal. It felt as though she had never left, and at the same time, everything felt alien, as though she could have imagined the last twenty years in the United States and awakened suddenly to the life she would have had in Paris, had she stayed.

The day was ending. Streetlights lit up one by one, and the wet cobblestone pavement glistened. The green neon sign above pharmacies crackled and brightened. Plants set outside in the rain in front of a flower shop were taken back indoors. Nothing had changed, and everything had, because she had.

She arrived at her hotel at last. The lobby was ultramodern and impeccably designed, all metal and polished wood. Peter would approve. She liked things to look a bit more organic, but the sleek minimalism of the place reassured her. She had booked it online, had chosen it for the pictures. It was an expensive hotel, an expensive room. But there was a restaurant inside and a spa, and since something resembling mental illness overtook her when she was around her family, this was no time to skimp on material comfort.

Behind the desk, a young French beauty with yellow hair held in a tight ponytail said, "Bienvenue à l'Hôtel de la Seine." Her smile faded when she took in Cassie's soggy Uggs and duct-taped suitcase. In a clipped tone she added, "Puis-je vous aider, Madame?" May I help you? Cassie out of exhaustion gave her name in English. The woman peered at her computer screen, nervously fingered the orange silk scarf tied around her neck and said in a thick accent, "I see not the reservation under that name."

"I booked online," Cassie said.

The woman shook her head, looking at the screen, "I'm apologize, I don't see it."

"I have this!" Cassie produced a printout of her reservation and handed it to her.

The woman frowned at it. "Ah, oui. It happens since many time, Madame," she said, modulating her intonation to one of patient annoyance. "You made a reservation with a different hotel."

"What? Absolutely not!"

The woman hovered a reluctant index finger above the piece of paper, as though touching it might contaminate her. "It say Hôtel *Petite* Seine, vous voyez? This here is Hôtel *de la* Seine."

Cassie looked at the paper. "I don't understand."

"Yes, Madame, and the two hotels, they are on the same street. People make a lot that mistake. It's often confused, the both." Cassie opened her mouth, realizing what had happened. Stupidly, she must have clicked on the wrong link when making the reservation! Nearly the same name, and in the same street, how could she have not? It had happened so fast, and she had been in a state. "Never mind," she said, "I would like a room then."

"Impossible, Madame! There is a doctor's symposium at Hôpital Saint-François. We are fully booked."

"Not even a tiny room for one?" Cassie pleaded, "I'm exhausted. I just need one night if that's all you have. Just a pillow and a shower, honestly."

"Non. Impossible. Vraiment." The woman brightened and added in a tone that Cassie did not like, "And besides, this is a four-star establishment. You might find that Hôtel Petite Seine —" she paused, looked at Cassie's soggy boots and gutted suitcase, searching for the right word — "for all budgets."

Cassie was astounded. What had the woman implied? That she was downtrodden? A homeless woman? In all fairness, if she did not get a room immediately, she would be homeless indeed. Heat rose in her. In the most imperious tone she had in her she demanded, in French this time, "What's your name, please?"

The woman gave her a patient smile. "We do not give out our names, évidemment."

"Then give me the name of your supervisor."

The young woman shook her head energetically. "We do not give out names of supervisors."

"Like hell you don't," Cassie said between her teeth. And then she remembered. She was in France. The American way to do business, the concept of customer service, of servility of any kind, did not jive here. In the United States, customers had tantrums and got their way. That's how it worked. But the customer wasn't always right in France, and in this particular case, Cassie wasn't even a customer.

The telephone rang. The woman picked it up and, with the most expert of dismissive looks, proceeded to ignore her. Cassie examined her options: throw herself at the yellow-haired monster and strangle her with her dumb scarf or turn around on her soggy fur heels, tuck her tail under, and find Hôtel Petite Seine.

She walked out into the street followed by the screech of her suitcase. Anger had worked its magic, and she no longer felt cold or tired. A few blocks down the street, she found the street number indicated on the reservation printout. But this could not be right; all she saw was a bakery and – uh-oh! On the door to the right of the bakery was a black plastic plaque no larger than a postcard with an engraved inscription in washed-out gold paint: Hôtel Petite Seine. She lifted her head. A smallish neon sign affixed to the façade of the building blinked on and off weakly. The many small windows sported an assortment of curtains without unity of style. Petite all right. At this point, it would have to do. She'd crash here for the night and look online for a better hotel in the morning. Defeated, Cassie pushed open the unadorned door.

She found herself inside a dark, minuscule reception area. No one was behind the desk. French television commercials blared in the background, and the smell of cabbage soup filled the air. She found a bell and pressed it. Nothing happened. She pushed twice more.

"Ça va! Ça va!" A man well in his eighties with a thick white mane emerged from the back room and looked at her with puzzlement. "Oui Madame?" he said in the baffled tone of someone who finds a stranger has materialized in his living room.

"Good afternoon, sir," she said in French. "This is Hôtel Petite Seine isn't it?"

"I sure hope so," he said jovially, "or else I've just spent the last six hours working here in error." His shirt was open at the neck, as though he had been in the process of putting on his pajamas. He buttoned it all the way up, hiding the abundant white hair that escaped from it like straw out of a scarecrow.

"I have a reservation," she said. She gave her name, but the old man only stared at her. She pointed to the large black book set on the counter. "Maybe it's in here?" she said helpfully.

"Ah, bien sûr!" He felt in his pocket and having found his glasses adjusted them over his nose in slow motion. He traced down the page with a shaky finger.

She read the book upside down and pointed to her name. "Here I am!"

"Ha, oui! Room twenty-three, the fifth floor. My niece will do the paperwork later. She does all those things."

"And the elevator is…?"

The man raised a bushy white eyebrow. "The elevator?"

"You know, to go up."

"Oh no, we most definitely don't have one."

"Do you have a room on a lower floor?"

"Je ne sais pas. My niece, she does all these things. But people seem to like room 23."

"When will your niece be back?"

"Soon."

"How soon?"

"Next week."

"Can anyone help me bring my luggage up to the room?" She rattled the suitcase for further effect. "It's broken, you see."

The man removed his glasses with extreme slowness. "There is only me."

She sighed. "I'll manage." She took the medieval-looking key he handed her. "I assume you don't have internet access?"

The old man took offense. "Mais bien sûr que si, Madame," adding with sarcasm, "as well as running water."

Cassie grabbed the suitcase, lifting it up against her chest, and proceeded up the stairs. The dark stairwell had the scent of old Parisian buildings, slightly rank but not in an unpleasant way, the smell of things ancient but well cared for. Despite her exhaustion, she went up the five sets of steep, uneven, narrow stairs without breaking a sweat. Years of schlepping baskets full of laundry up and down stairs in her house were paying off.

Numéro vingt-trois. She turned the archaic key into a matching wrought iron keyhole.

The room was small but adorable. The bed was perched up high and covered with a cozy-looking comforter and lacy pillows. The wood floor creaked pleasantly underfoot. The high ceiling was ornate with stucco moldings, disproportionate to the size of the room. A crystal chandelier dangled from the center. The wallpaper, a pinkish Toile de Jouy motif, peeled in several places, and the bedside table was a flimsy thing barely sturdy enough to support the heavy lamp where carved cupids supported an ambitious lampshade. But everything was very clean. There was a pretty mantle over a fireplace. Overall, the effect was cozy and shabby, charming in an old-world sort of way.

She turned on the bathroom light and was astonished to find, rather than the standard cheap remodel she expected, a black-and-white-checkered marble floor, an age-blotched mirror, framed and gilded above the ceramic sink, copper pipes running up and down the walls, well-polished faucets, an anachronistic bidet, and underneath the large window, an honest to goodness claw-foot tub.

Back in the bedroom, she opened the glass door and stepped out on the balcony as the last of the sun's rays pierced through the rain clouds. A tiny table and folding chairs filled the entire space. She leaned over the railing. The sky at dusk had taken on a golden pink hue that was reflected on a forest of rooftops and chimneys slick with rain. Beyond that, Paris, its edges softened by haze, with thousands of glass panes reflecting the last of the day's light, glimmered and seemed to float in time and space. Minuscule in the distance, like a beacon, the ghost of the Eiffel Tower sparkled.

Beautiful Paris!

In the same breath, she thought of Peter. This was the most romantic little hotel room, and she had no one to share it with.

She stayed on the balcony and looked at the city for a few more minutes, assailed by images of her father on his hospital bed, the machines, his unshaven jaw. First and foremost, she had to keep in mind that her dad's apparent helplessness did not mean she should put down her guard. He knew how to hurt her even when he did nothing. Especially because he did nothing. Like that time when she had come to Paris with Alex and Jeanne when they were five years old. They were at the perfect darling age. She had convinced herself that her father would fall in love with them. How could he not? But he had hardly given them – or her – a shred of interest. She had come to Paris with lofty hopes and had left with the sense that she and her kids were barely tolerated strangers. At the end of that trip, she had returned to Los Angeles not just sad, as she had in the past, but furiously angry. Suddenly the little things in her childhood that she had fought to ignore became proof of his neglect. What were the clues? What did they mean? How far back could she go to best torture herself? There was the time at the public pool when she had felt awkward and awful in her bathing suit, and her dad had made fun of her lack of breasts. And that time when he had shrugged and walked away after she had shown him a piece of art she had made in school. When Odile said something, he fawned over her. When Cassie did, he seemed annoyed, unresponsive. And there were the excellent report cards he took for granted while he made a fuss about Odile's lower grades.

It could be argued that none of this ever happened. Her sense of not getting the love could have been a projection. If her dad was mean to her, it could be argued that he had not been *intentionally* mean. If he ignored her, it could be argued that he had other things on his mind. If he did not praise her, it could be argued that she was overly sensitive. It could be argued that she imagined all of this, the sense that she was not getting the love, that she became less visible to him every day, because he had not always been that way with her.

When she was little, he was fabulous. He adored her. They were peas in a pod. And then he seemed to change. As a teenager, she was overwhelmed with powerlessness and incomprehension at her dad's change in attitude towards her. So she tried harder. But the more she fought to be visible, the more she excelled, the funnier and livelier she tried to be, the more deliberate his indifference, the rarer the eye contact. But it was also possible that she was a bitter, paranoid person. She had to stop measuring everything. She had to stop being jealous of Odile. But she was in Paris again, and it was as though the rooftops, the sidewalks, the sky, the smell, made her swing back in time. Her entire life had been spent fighting the profound sense that the problem wasn't her father, but herself, that she should have been somehow different, that there was an entry code to her father's heart that she time after time failed to break. An entry code only Odile could access.

She stepped away from the balcony and returned inside the room, shaking off her resentment, her childish feeling of injustice. She was a grown-up now, and her father was a sick old man in the hospital.

She peeled the duct tape off the suitcase, opened it on the floor, and went through its contents in disbelief. Each item of clothing she had brought was more weather inappropriate than the next. But she was only here for ten days, and it did not make sense to buy a winter wardrobe that she would never use back in Los Angeles Maybe she could email Sabine and ask to borrow a warm jacket or a coat. She looked at her Uggs, pitiful by the room heater. She would have to buy shoes, toot sweet.

She decided to send Peter a quick email to let him know she had arrived. She emptied the contents of her tote bag onto the bed, lined up the sleek, thin laptop, the smartphone, their respective cords and chargers, and the old converter. No matter how hairy things got from here, no matter how out-of-body the experience, she would be connected to the real world: electronics as a lifeline to sanity.

She searched beneath the bedside table, found the electrical outlet and plugged in her converter, which had two prongs so that she could charge both her laptop and her cell phone at the same time. She plugged in her cell phone charger. She plugged in her laptop charger. She then brought her charger cord to her laptop and plugged in that.

She smelled it and heard it before she could see it and instinctively leaped away from the bed. "NO!" she screamed. But already it was over. In one instant, the charge of 220 current buzzed and hissed, and a tremendous heat charged through the electrical outlet, through the chargers and all the way to the depth of her laptop and cell phone. WHOOSH!

Then silence.

Cassie blinked at her laptop. The screen was black. The space between the keys was black too; a faint smoke seemed to emanate from both the laptop and the cell phone. After another long moment, she tentatively brought her finger to the on switch on her laptop and pressed. Nothing. She tried to turn on her cell phone. Nothing. She sniffed them. Both had an ominous smell of burnt plastic.

She looked around the room, her heart in a vise. She now understood with perfect clarity the nagging emotion she had felt all afternoon but failed to pinpoint. Disappointment. Her father was unconscious. She had known he would be; Sabine had warned her. And yet ever since she had bought her ticket, she had let herself dream up something very silly. She had imagined arriving at her father's bedside and him being, at long last, happy to see her.

****

There was a phone booth in the hotel lobby. Cassie entered it, slid the door shut, sat on the single stool, and looked around. It was bizarrely upholstered wall to ceiling in a burgundy-red velvety fabric. Above, a single fixture cast a dim light. It was like sitting inside an upright coffin – one that smelled of cabbage soup. She called Peter collect. "Were you sleeping?" she asked.

"Darling, I have a newborn," Peter said, "I'm never sleeping." He added, "Also, it's ten in the morning here."

Hearing his voice, Cassie felt better. "I haven't slept yet," she said.

"You're going to be cranky. You always get testy when you don't sleep enough."

"I went to the hospital straight from the airport. I only got to the hotel an hour ago."

"How's the old goat? And the rest of that gloomy cast of characters? I swear to you, I could put each member of your family in a screenplay and terrify the world."

"Don't. I'm the one who's earned the right to fictionalize my family's dysfunction. Listen. This is bad. My laptop. Well it, hmm, broke down."

"Did you back up the files?" Peter cried out.

"Relax, your precious screenplays are backed up in half a dozen places."

"But your laptop is brand new!"

"Well, it was. And, hmm – about my cell phone: it kinda stopped working too."

Peter burst into laughter. "You fried them!"

"Of course, I did not fry them!" She waited for Peter to stop guffawing. "You know what I miss the most about you?" she asked. "It's your gift for empathy."

"How in the world did you manage? Phone *and* laptop? You're a genius at this! It was that lousy converter, wasn't it? Am I right? I bet I'm right. The charger short-circuited, didn't it? You knew this was a piece of obsolete shit. Now, that should have gone to the Salvation Army instead of the kids' baseball trophies."

Cassie realized she could lean and rest against the velvety wall and it felt nice and mushy against her back. "The point is, I can't be reached for the time being. I'll give you the number at the hotel, and you can leave a message, but I'm warning you, they don't speak English."

"In what hotel in the Known Universe do they not speak English?"

She closed her eyes. "I can't get into this right now."

"No way!" Peter exclaimed, gleeful. "You botched the reservation too?"

She did not bother to respond. "I can't be called, or call," she said. "I can't send or receive emails. I'm not sure what the solution is because I can't even go online to search for a repair shop until morning. I'm only here for ten days, so I'm tempted to wait it out. I have warranties."

"Honey, warranties work when the merchandise malfunctions, not when its user does!" Peter laughed at his bon mot. "You won't last in Paris without a phone or laptop. How about you buy new ones and return them before coming back home?"

"You can't buy things and return them for a full refund on a whim here."

"Why not?"

"That's not how businesses work in France."

"Even at Target?"

"There is no Target here."

"No Target?" Peter repeated, dismayed.

"Whatever I buy, I'll be stuck with it. And it would be set on the French system, and then I'd have to use a converter for it at home."

"And repeat this fiasco in reverse," Peter laughed.

"Look, tell Alex and Jeanne that I'm here and I'm okay," Cassie said, although she felt very much not okay. She gave Peter Sabine's cell number and the hotel number and hung up. Now all she could hear was the silence buzzing in her head. She gently poked the soft red velvet of the wall with her index finger. It sank into the fabric, leaving a small dent. Slowly, the wall reverted to shape, and the mark was gone. Mushy walls? This phone booth wasn't a coffin after all, but a giant, cabbage-smelling womb. A 1980s womb, from before the invention of the internet, the worst kind of womb there was. She searched for the doorknob, but there wasn't one. She pushed the door, shook it, immediately feeling trapped, until she remembered that it slid open.

It was almost seven p.m. Her eyelids felt coated with sand, but she was thirsty and hungry. If she did not take care of herself in some basic way, she'd lose her mind very quickly. She decided to brave the cold and find something to eat. At the reception desk, she asked the old man for a place to eat.

"The closest is La Jument Bleue," he said. "It's not fancy, but the food's good." He paused, looked at her and said, "You might need a coat."

"Ha!" she told him, "I'm made of strong stuff."

La Jument Bleue was right around the corner, so she did not have to freeze for too long. As soon as she pushed the glass door of the bistro, she was welcomed by the heat and the smell of coffee and greasy food that every cell of her body craved. This was the kind of place where they sold cigarettes and lottery tickets and served cafés and plat du jour to neighborhood residents. She walked past the zinc counter and found a table in the back, set against the glass window. From there, she could observe the people who stood at the counter and sat at the few occupied tables. The door to the kitchen swung open and closed as a waiter and a woman in her sixties with red cheeks and abundant bosom, who appeared to be La Jument Bleue's owner, came in and out carrying plates of food. From her position by the window, Cassie also had a good view of the street, which was getting dark.

La patronne, the owner, came to her table. "Bonjour Madame, what will it be for you tonight?" she asked.

"Do you have a menu?" Cassie said.

The woman's smile froze. "The kitchen has closed," she answered tersely.

"I was told you served dinner."

"You were told wrong," she said icily.

Cassie briefly wondered what she had done wrong for the woman to go from jovial to antagonistic in two seconds flat and then realized that she had trampled over the most basic rule of French engagement by omitting to say bonjour! When it came to being served anything, by anyone in France, you better remember your manners, and she had blown it. Was that what had happened with that blonde at the hotel? "Je suis désolée," she apologized. "I am jetlagged and exhausted. I'll have … a glass of milk, I guess."

The woman softened, "What would you like to eat?"

"I would not want to be an inconvenience to the chef."

"The chef is my husband, and I decide whether he should be inconvenienced or not."

"In that case, do you have ketchup?"

"Ketchup? That's all?"

"Whatever you want to serve, I will be happy with."

The patronne considered this and seemed to approve of her subservience. "A steak au poivre et frites then? To go with your ketchup."

Unlike Cassie, the average French person did not dip her string beans in ketchup or use it as a pasta sauce. Ketchup was for fries only. Cassie preferred her food well coated with a layer of Americanness. That particular condiment reassured her taste buds. "That would be perfect," Cassie said. "Thank you."

"And one assiette de crudités to start?" the patronne declared more than asked. Cassie dared not decline.

As businesses and offices closed for the day, people who worked in the neighborhood began pouring into La Jument Bleue, filling the tables one by one. Soon, the zinc counter was lined with customers. In the space of fifteen minutes, La Jument Bleue went from sleepy to bustling. The patronne's step quickened; waiters zoomed to and fro, holding large circular trays filled with drinks high in the air as customers continued coming in.

Her crudités arrived: grated carrots and celery roots, delicate pink radishes, sliced hearts of palm and a small vinaigrette dish. At first, Cassie felt a little self-conscious to be eating alone, but no one paid her any attention. She was a fly on the wall. Une mouche sur le mur. She tossed the translation around in her mind. In French, it had no meaning whatsoever.

At the next table, a teenage boy and girl sat holding hands across the table. The waiter walked up and set two tall, foamy beers in front of the young couple, whom Cassie, and any American, would have considered children.

She devoured her crudités and sponged vinaigrette with the best bread she'd ever eaten, watching as three young women entered La Jument Bleue, removed their coats, and placed them on the communal coat hanger. One of them was the mean blonde from the hotel. The three women were dressed in the hotel's uniform: a sky-blue blouse, a tight navy cardigan and matching skirt, and that square of orange silk tied at the neck. They stood at the counter, laughing and talking with animation. And was this not the old man from her hotel, in the funny Cossack fur hat? He saw her and tipped his head. This was what he had meant by "everyone goes there." La Jument Bleue appeared to be the quartier's preferred watering hole. Cassie noted the contrast with her local Starbucks, where patrons were careful not to infringe on others' space. People here knew each other. Those who arrived were greeted with handshakes or a flurry of kisses on cheeks. The noise level rose. There was laughter, and opinions were loudly thrown around. People two tables removed got into a heated political discussion. She overheard a sexual joke. The three women from the hotel sat at a table and were soon joined by two men. There were more kisses on cheeks.

When her dish arrived, Cassie scraped the pepper cream sauce off her steak with the back of her knife, poured ketchup on top and dug in. Best French fries ever, she thought. Best ketchup ever.

Her table had a perfect vantage point to observe without being too obvious about it those who entered, those at the counter, and the passersby on the sidewalk. The blatant flirting that went on around La Jument Bleue fascinated her. The men sweet-talked the women, who responded in kind. Women, even women her age and older, smiled and chatted away, whispering and giggling. The flirtatious energy in the room intensified with the arrival of four men in their early thirties dressed in sweater vests, scarves, and loafers. As they came through the door, cigarettes in mouth, the patronne pushed them back out. They finished their smoking outside in great inhalations, tossed and crushed under heels butts of cigarettes, and returned inside.

Cassie leaned back in her chair. Nothing felt quite real, as though she were watching the scene on TV. She dug a pen out of a purse, removed the paper mat from under the plate, and wrote:

1- Find electronic repair shop
2- Buy cheap cell phone?
3- Ask Sabine for coat tomorrow
4- Think of questions for Papa's doctor

She lifted her pen. Would her father be alarmed by her presence? The fact that she had flown in from the United States to see him might worry him about his own condition. He looked so helpless in that hospital gown. It angered her. It didn't matter, considering the situation, that his bare legs and feet were exposed. But what about his dignity? He was proud of his appearance. He always dressed to the nines, even when he took her and Odile to the Zoo de Vincennes, the Jardin d'Acclimatation, or the Musée Grévin when they were little. Back then, she and Odile were dressed identically by their mother, as was the style, in matching plaid dresses, coats, and high socks. She remembered clinging to their dad, fighting with Odile to be the one nearer to him, the one holding his hand. Memories came in, jumbled: the bus and métro rides through Paris, competing to be the one to sit on his lap. Always a competition with Odile. And the endless strolls through Paris's quartiers. Her dad knew Paris comme son mouchoir, like his handkerchief, which in English translated to the back of his hand. He was a Parisian, born and raised. That's about all he ever said of his childhood. Those outings with her dad stopped at some point. Why was her father so intent on taking his daughters out of the house? Was it to escape Raymonde's noxious moods? But if she thought about it, it was not that the outings stopped, it was that she no longer came along. If there were reasons for this, she couldn't remember them. But on second thought, she had begun to feel unwelcome, as though she and her sister had been competing for their father's love all along, and Odile had won.

And where had Sabine been this whole time?

She wrote on the placemat.

5- Ask Papa about his childhood, when he wakes up.

6- Be strong!

Night had settled over the street. Now, the light came from the old lampposts and the neon signs across the street from the pharmacy and the flower shop. She leaned against the glass pane to look outside when the huge roar of a motorcycle startled her. She watched the motorcyclist maneuver his heavy machine expertly onto the curb and park on the sidewalk on the other side of the window, inches from where she sat. The man wore a bomber jacket reminiscent of Indiana Jones. He turned off the engine and, still straddling his motorcycle, removed his thick gloves, and then his helmet. He was in his late forties, with wide shoulders, a thick mane, and piercing blue eyes, and was not a bad-looking guy if you liked them rugged.

His helmet tucked under his elbow, he disappeared as he crouched next to his motorcycle to wrap a chain around a pole. Cassie brought her face closer to the window to watch how he was going about it. The man lifted his face, and all of a sudden, they were eye to eye on opposite sides of the window pane. She continued staring, perhaps because she had accepted the idea of being invisible. But invisible she was not. He knitted his eyebrows into an interrogative frown, and Cassie jumped back in embarrassment. When the man entered the café a minute later, he seemed to look in her direction with reproach, but a moment later she was invisible again, and he was surrounded by the preppy men. Cassie asked for the bill and, bracing herself, asked la patronne. "I'm wondering if it would be possible for me to receive a call here, in the case of an emergency?"

"What kind of emergency?" la patronne asked.

"My cell phone broke. I don't imagine I should need it, but just in case?"

"Alright," la patronne grumbled. "But don't make a habit of it."

Cassie paid, stepped into the night, and, shivering through and through, walked back to her hotel. In her room, she removed her clothes and let herself fall, face first, onto the bed. She was asleep in seconds.

CHAPTER 6

The Baker's Daughter

His payots tucked behind his ears and held in place by an embroidered cap, Albano left his cave and climbed down the flank of Mount Pagus in the direction of Smyrna's quay. Only a year ago he had been frightened to skip shul and leave the Jewish quarter alone for the first time. Now the whirlwinds of Smyrna's streets, the busy quayside, selling newspapers with Hagop, earning money, and disguising himself as a Muslim boy were natural things. He had left the Jewish quarter long before sunrise, had briefly gone up to his cave by the moonlight and changed clothes, and was now walking down the deserted hillside with only the buzz of crickets as companions. It was cold; his ears were cold, and so were his cheeks, but he felt warm inside. The moon was thin, but once his eyes were accustomed to the obscurity, he felt he could see very well. On occasion, he thought he felt near him the breath of mountain lions or coyotes, but he did not feel scared. Under the stars and inside his cave, Albano felt protected by a force he could not name. More than a force, it was a sense of joy, a sense that God was near. It was a peculiar thing that he never felt the divine in his books and prayers, but always when he was alone and in nature.

As he walked down the mountain, he thought of that day when he had returned home after selling his first newspapers with Hagop and meeting Xandra. He had been resigned to the anticipated beating but was astonished to discover that no one had noticed his absence. Even his deep sunburn from being in the sun all day raised no suspicion. At shul, it had been assumed that Albano was sick. At home, it had been assumed he was at shul. Either no one had paid attention, or else no one had cared.

The next week, emboldened, Albano had returned and found Hagop on the quay. "I have something for you," Hagop had said, and out of a burlap bag he had pulled new clothes for Albano and insisted he put them on. "Here. Now you're a good Muslim boy." Hagop had placed a 'borrowed' fez on Albano's head. Then he had adjusted his own and grinned that Hagop grin, full of mischief and bravado with something ferocious under it.

Uncle Moshe had been correct. Having no parents of your own when the adults around you are busy with children, businesses matters, bouts of gout, funerals, tooth abscesses, weddings, and leaky roofs could be a blessing. Especially if what you wanted to do was lead a double life. Now, his teachers frowned at his absences, but Albano was not the only boy to skip shul, others skipped to earn money for their family. This was the excuse he gave his teachers, and that was only a half-truth, since Uncle Jacob and Aunt Sadie knew nothing about his work, and since Albano and Hagop kept the money for themselves, or rather for the enlarging leather satchel hidden inside the cave. His grades remained excellent no matter how much of shul he missed, and when one of his teachers took it upon himself to tell Uncle Joshua about his absence, Uncle Joshua only limply admonished him. Often, though, Albano wished there was a grown-up to rely on for guidance. Someone like Uncle Moshe, whom he hadn't seen in a year. Uncle Moshe had a different way of looking at the world. Perhaps he could help Albano decipher the meanderings of his heart.

****

To Hagop, Albano soon learned, nothing was serious, and nothing was sacred. He laughed at the droll and the tragic with the same affected insouciance. Hagop was the eldest and only boy with four sisters, the oldest of which was Xandra. Their parents, Yori and Ina, relied heavily on them. Xandra helped her mother at the bakery and for deliveries, and Hagop worked nights at the mixes and the baking. Yori presided over the baking, and it was on Hagop that fell the thankless task of shelling nuts by the thousands, a tedious work he abhorred. Hagop's other responsibility was to watch over the family's secret yeast blends. And so Hagop always smelled like uncooked dough and Xandra like a sweet bun fresh out of the oven. Hagop laughed at his father but only when his back was turned, for his dad could turn spiteful, especially when he drank. When Hagop did not work to his liking, Yori would grab a walnut or a hazelnut and throw it hard at Hagop from across the room, so Hagop's body was covered in mean little bruises.

"One day, when he is drunk, I will shove my father into his oven and let him cook like one of his bread loaves."

"But if he is dead, then you inherit the bakery," Albano pointed out. "And you end up becoming what you don't want to become: a baker." This was the kind of verbal jousting he and Hagop enjoyed. It was a game, an exercise, although one that often ended in Hagop sulking if Albano did not let him have the last word.

"My brother will run the bakery," Hagop said.

"You have no brother."

"I will eventually. Why do you think I have so many sisters? My parents keep trying to make a replacement for me." Hagop went on to loudly imitate the sounds his parents made in bed so that Albano, who was according to Hagop a prude rabbi at heart, would have to cover his ears.

****

Rather than meet Hagop at the quay, Albano usually headed out early to the Armenian quarter to eat a fresh pastry from Yori's bakery before they set out for the quay. Pastries weren't the reason Albano awakened at three in the morning, rather than four, and walked all the way from the Jewish to the Armenian quarter in the night, but it was the reason he gave Hagop. After breakfast, Albano and Hagop would then walk down to Frank Street, purchase their stock of international newspapers, and assume their respective spots on the quayside where they sold to arriving travelers for a couple of hours. By late morning, the papers were gone. Albano would hurry back to the Jewish quarter and arrive at shul having missed the morning classes. Learning from rabbis, who hardly ventured past the Jewish quarter or their conservative viewpoint, or from stale texts with no basis in the modern world paled in comparison to what Albano learned on the quay. From reading newspapers and listening to the people, he learned about politics and the world. He learned languages the same way; French and other Latin languages were easy for him. He had also become excellent at counting their earnings. He now was the one who decided which papers to buy and in which quantity, based on past sales and profits.

That day, as he entered the Armenian quarter, and although the seeds of secrecy between Hagop and him had already long sprouted, Albano had no idea he was about to start a triple life.

That morning there was a peculiar, uneasy atmosphere throughout the Armenian quarter. Men talked animatedly. Women cried. The unease grew as he approached the street where Hagop's family lived. There were men on horseback from the Turkish police stopping people and asking questions. Albano had picked up sufficient Armenian to converse, but he wasn't able to understand what people were upset about.

Before entering the bakery, he stopped on the other side of the street and discretely watched Xandra as she laid trays of freshly baked baklava, birds nest and fig cookies in the window. The scent of yeast and honey wafted through the open door. His heart thumped at the sight of her small, precise hands and the pale skin of her neck. She lifted her face, and their eyes met for just an instant. Usually, that instant was enough to weaken Albano's knees for a good ten minutes. But today, he saw with alarm that she had been crying.

When he entered the bakery, Hagop jumped at him. "Did you hear? Silla, the butcher, was arrested."

"Is that why everyone is crying? For the butcher?"

"He beheaded his eldest daughter, Szophia."

"Beheaded!" Albano had to sit down at this news. "Szophia? The one who served at his shop?"

"Last year she left her husband because he was beating her," Xandra said, her voice breaking. "She had come back to live with her parents above the butcher shop, but then her father thought that she –"

"–There was proof!" Hagop interrupted.

"Proof of what?" Albano asked.

"That she was seeing a man," Hagop said. "She brought dishonor upon her father. Her whole family, shamed."

It was too much for Xandra who burst into tears. "He carried her head by the hair up and down the street."

Albano wished he could comfort her, hold her, but that was impossible. "Will he be put to death?" he asked.

"There will be a judgment," Xandra said, but her expression showed she doubted any harm would come to the butcher.

"She was a whore." Hagop spat.

Xandra's eyes turned to fire, and she yelled, "And what is her father? A hero?"

Hagop shrugged at Xandra's outburst. "Women cannot understand," he explained to Albano. "They think with their heart. A man must protect his honor and the honor of his family, whatever the law says."

Xandra ran to the back of the store and buried her face in her hands. Albano thought of what he could say to soothe her but found nothing. And what could he do? Come near Xandra and speak to her, alone, as he dreamed? No, that was impossible. There were rules for girls and boys. They were twelve years old, and in the last few months, Xandra looked more like a woman, even if he still only looked like a child. If there were people around them, they could speak up, but they could not speak to each other.

Later, as Hagop described the scene vividly with many more details than he cared to hear, Albano thought of what he could tell Xandra if he was able to speak to her in private. As Hagop excitedly described the scene, the butcher's arrest, the blood marks on the pavement, the butcher's wife's wailing with grief, Albano had an idea.

****

Albano and Hagop did their usual route, bought their stacks of newspapers, and waited for the boats to arrive. By noon, their stock was sold. Hagop ran back to the bakery to shell a fresh arrival of almonds, and they parted for the day.

But rather than head back to the Jewish quarter, Albano headed toward the Levantine quarter. Albano loved the Levantine area. He would go there often just to admire it and to dream up an alternate, unlikely future for himself. Despite his poverty, in stark contrast to the Levantine families' wealth, it never occurred to Albano to feel resentment toward them. He admired them, in fact, for having prospered to such extent despite being of mixed blood. Here in Smyrna especially, the Levantines had triumphed. They were crucial to Smyrna's abundance of work. The Levantine families' factories employed hundreds of thousands of Smyrniots, and they did not care which religion the workers were, or which nationality. The Levantine bourgeoisie of Smyrna were like benevolent parents to the population. Had they not existed, hundreds of thousands would have starved. Many believed that as long as the Levantine families maintained their monopoly over commerce and continued to control shipping, textile and rugs, and the exports of all the goods produced, Smyrna would continue to thrive.

Of all the breathtakingly beautiful parts of Smyrna, the Levantine areas were the most breathtaking. Most Levantine families lived a few miles outside of town in communities with names such as Paradise or Boudja, which connected to Smyrna via a steam train with designated seats for its more prominent members. The first time Hagop took him to the European quarter where many Levantines had primary residences, Albano had not wanted to believe that those were mansions for single families. The Levantines homes were palaces with architecture inspired by Italy; sprawling villas with loggias, and fountains, and rooms upon rooms, and dozens of servants hurrying about to make everything perfect. In the gardens and front yards, there were rows of cypress trees, magnolias, and citrus trees, pergolas and glass houses, climbing jasmine, tall hibiscus borders, bougainvillea draped over rooftops and rose gardens tended by meticulous gardeners.

Next week was Christmas, a festive time in the Christian quarters. Everyone in Smyrna loved to live outdoors, and the Levantines were no exception, and so anyone could watch them having meals and enjoying their manicured paths and gardens. The children, girls in summer dresses, boys in shorts and long socks, played croquet on the lawns and chased after pet goats. Men in leisure clothes, canotiers on their heads, light vests and open shirts, smoked on balconies. Women in straw hats and lacy dresses sat on chairs and couches set under pergolas as servants brought refreshments. Albano passed a group of carol singers. The people listening were clapping and having a lovely time.

Albano, his heart racing, found a central spot from which he could survey the street. He waited.

He spotted Xandra as she exited the back door of a Levantine house. She was walking to her next delivery now. She had a large woven basket on her back and one on each arm. She walked fast despite the load and had on her face that determined expression that both intimidated him and made him want to take her in his arms. Because of the horrors of today, she looked sad too, and her eyes were red. This was not Albano's first time observing her as she made her delivery, and yet this was the first time it occurred to him to speak to her. Today, he had an excuse to. He felt nauseous, and his legs were almost paralyzed at the sight of her. But the idea of speaking to her had come to him, and he felt the urgency of carrying it through. Today, at last, he had a reason. The thing had happened with the Butcher, and it would be a natural thing to discuss.

Xandra walked right past him, and then he stepped out of the corner so that she saw him. She stopped in her tracks, either in surprise or fright. Her face was very pale and her hair and eyes so black that they seemed to absorb the light and every bit of Albano's courage. "Why are you here?" she murmured, her eyes cast down, not looking at him.

Albano's heart was beating too fast. He too was afraid to look at her. His plan had gone as far as deciding to come and speak to her, but he had not prepared what he would say. "I sometimes wonder if it is safe for a girl alone in the streets," he said, improvising.

Her eyes shone with angry tears. "Fathers will behead their daughters in the name of honor, but they are not so worried that they won't let them walk alone in the street. As long as it brings money."

"I am here so you will not be bothered by anyone," he said. He was conscious of how preposterous this was: a scrawny boy without a hair on his chest could not do much to protect himself, let alone a girl, but Albano said this with assurance, and as he did, he straightened to make himself look taller.

"You can carry my baskets then if you want to help," she said. She removed the straw basket that weighed heavily on her slender back and helped Albano put it on his own back. Then she put her hand baskets over each of his arms and said, "Come donkey! Come."

Albano pretended to be a donkey for a few steps, and she laughed at that. Then they walked, making sure to remain ten feet from each other, as was the unspoken proper distance between a boy and a girl. As they walked, they did not look at each other; they looked straight ahead. They spoke, but it was as though they spoke to the street in front of them.

"Tell me why you are really here," Xandra said to the street.

"I wanted to tell you something."

"How did you know where I would be?"

Albano could not tell Xandra that he often followed her from afar since she had taken over the task of delivery from her mother who was expecting another child. He had always felt uneasy about her being alone, even in Levantine streets filled with gilded houses and pleasure gardens. He would follow her until he saw her reenter the Armenian quarter and he felt she was safe again because the community watched over its own. Now he was no longer so sure about the community. "I was only hoping you would be here," he lied.

"What is it you wanted to tell me?"

"The man, the butcher," Albano said. "He should be imprisoned. Or put to death for killing his own daughter."

"Why not say this earlier?"

"Hagop is like a brother, but he and I have different minds."

"So?" she asked, defiantly. "Do you not think a man has a right of life and death over his daughters?"

"No one has the right of life and death over another human being. That's what I think."

Xandra did not respond. She continued to walk somberly. But despite the event that had just occurred, Albano could not feel somber. He walked alongside her feeling the soft air on his skin every time they stepped in the shade, and the heat of the sun every time they came back into the light. He felt that this moment was full of grace and perfection, and he was happy. "Do you not think those are heavier than your newspapers?" she asked. "Hagop says the newspapers are much heavier." The baskets were full of bread and pastries, and they were heavy, but Albano could not feel the baskets at all. Walking with Xandra he was weightless.

"I could help you with your deliveries," he heard himself say. He did not even think this ahead of time, and it just came out of him, and there was nothing he could do to stop himself from speaking. "I would carry the baskets for you, and you can bring the merchandise to each house."

"Albano!" She laughed, her laughter like a bird's song, "you're already doing this!"

"I mean, on other days," he said while looking at the street so their eyes would not meet. He hesitated. "Every day. If you want."

Xandra looked down at her feet as she walked. The silver threads of her embroidered slippers and skirt gleamed in the sun. "And what will Hagop think?" she finally said.

"I'll help him with the newspaper in the morning, and I'll help you with the pastries in the afternoon."

"Will you tell him?"

"I don't need to."

"But I can't pay you. The money I earn is not mine."

Albano smiled. "It's all right," he said.

The next day he met her at the entrance of the Levantine quarter, and he authoritatively took the baskets from her hands. He followed her from house to house and waited in front of each house as she pushed through the gates and went in the back of each house into the servants' quarters to deliver her goods. That week, it was a miracle Albano could manage to sleep at all, such was his happiness.

By the end of the first week, Xandra insisted that Albano come to each door with her and not wait for her in the street. This was how Albano discovered the courtyards of the rambling villas, like personal oases inside the city. There were elaborate water fountains, play areas for the children, gravel paths, bird baths, tiled barns where gleaming motorcars were tended by drivers, mosaic pools. Some of the houses were right on the Aegean Sea with private beaches and floating docks onto which pleasure boats were tied.

There were children in white clothes playing badminton or hide and seek between the boxwood hedges of French gardens. As Albano marveled at their surroundings, Xandra entered the kitchens or the servant quarters through back doors and made her deliveries. Then they both walked out of the house and toward the next one.

"Sometimes," Xandra said one day, "I imagine that I live in a beautiful house, with a fountain and a garden. And in the gardens, there are roses and jasmine, and it always smells wonderful."

"How many rooms does your house have?" Albano asked.

Xandra smiled with pleasure that Albano was playing along. "It has seven rooms, and there is one room just for bathing. And water arrives inside the room through a pipe; you do not even need a well."

"Does electricity come to your house?" The Ottoman Electric Company's first coal-fire electricity-generating station was now powering the Sultan's house in Constantinople, and the word electricity was on everyone's lips.

"Of course," she smiled.

"Tell me more about your house."

"It is painted white, with columns. There is a large deck all around overlooking the sea, and there are palm trees and climbing roses everywhere."

"It sounds beautiful."

"Also...."

"What?"

"I have a little dog all to myself."

"Do you have children?"

"Yes," she laughed. "But no more than three."

"And...." Albano paused, then asked tentatively, "Who is your husband?"

She blushed. "I don't know yet."

"Is he Christian?" The question, which came to his lips before he had a chance to think it, changed everything.

Xandra became grave. "My family will want that."

"Will he be Armenian?" Albano dared to ask.

Xandra lifted her eyes toward him. "It is the tradition. I have to." They continued in silence until she entered the last house on her route and took the baked goods out of the basket Albano was carrying. This was his favorite part when she got things out of the basket and for a moment stood centimeters from him. She walked into the house and out of it, and suddenly it was time to say goodbye. This, was Albano's least favorite part.

"There are places in the world where traditions are different," Albano told her as they headed back toward the Armenian quarter. "In France, in Italy."

"What are the traditions there?"

"To Americans and Europeans, we are all the same. Greek, Armenians, Muslims, and Jews. They cannot tell the difference."

She shook her head, "How is that possible?"

"They see us all as inferior. Or else they see themselves as superior. You might not believe this, but they can't tell us apart. Our eyes aren't blue; our hair is not red or yellow. They can't even tell our religion from our clothes. We're just poor people to them."

"How do you know all this?"

"I read the newspapers."

They continued walking for a hundred yards, and Xandra said, "What about you? Will you marry a girl from the Jewish quarter?"

"I only care about what my heart says," he murmured.

"What does your heart say?"

"My heart says...." Albano was bursting with love, and he did not know how to express it, and part of him felt he should not. Xandra had given no indication of how she felt. "My heart says that I want to live in one of those beautiful houses with a garden, with my wife. And give her just the life she wants."

"I think your wife will be very happy with you then," Xandra said.

Day after day they met at the same place. Now she waited for him. He'd hoist the baskets on his back and over his shoulders, and they'd set out on the delivery route. The conversation between them lost its awkwardness; now it was as though they had always been able to speak and laugh together. They'd speak of Hagop and giggle at the crazy things he did and said. She told him about her life at the bakery, and he told her about life in the Jewish quarter. They discussed their religion, injustices, family. But there was a subject they avoided since that first talk they had about marriage. They did not speak about love.

One day, nearly a month later, as delivery ended, rather than go their separate ways, they followed the road past the last house of the European quarter and walked along the beach. The sun was low in the sky on this January afternoon. There was no wind at all, and the sea was as smooth as mercury. They walked on the sand in silence and sat on a large flat rock under the low branches of a dense tree with waxy leaves that had found a way to take root right into the sand.

"Tell me again about the places in the world where traditions are different," Xandra said. They were both acutely aware that the two of them should not be here: a boy and a girl sitting under a tree in the setting sun. And yet they had headed there as though it was the natural thing to do.

"Their traditions are different, but not always better."

"Then tell me about places where people do not kill each other over religion or race."

"In Europe, there are zoos with humans in them," he said.

"I don't believe it."

"At the Jardin d'Acclimatation in Paris, they have enslaved an entire family from the continent of India so that people can buy tickets to look at them. The Indians wear feathered headdresses, and they paint their faces. There also have other kinds of people, from other parts of the world. They have short people from Africa. They are called pigmy, and they are very small. The children are even smaller."

"Like birds?"

"Larger than that. They are in cages. There are signs that say, 'do not feed the indigenous.'"

"Like animals?"

"Exactly, like animals. They call these ethnographic exhibitions."

They were quiet for a few minutes, pondering the meaning of this.

Xandra broke the silence. "Things are changing in the Empire, Albano. I do not like the way men are talking about politics. Everyone is thinking about war. The men want war."

"I do not want war."

"It is as though all the men are turning mad."

"I promise you I will not turn mad."

"But what if everyone else does?"

Albano held his breath and finally said, "Then I will take you away."

She looked at him and beamed. "You will?"

"I will take you to France. I will save the money from newspapers. After a few years, I will have enough. I will take you on a boat to France or Italy where no one is mad."

"But what if they put us in a zoo?" she laughed.

"As long as you and I are … in the same enclosure … I wouldn't mind." Realizing what he had just dared to say, he added quickly, "The sun is setting; you better get back."

"Not yet," Xandra murmured. She raised her face to him, and her face reflected the pink of the sky.

"Your family will worry about you if you do not hurry back," he insisted.

Xandra's eyes filled with tears. "Take me to France, Albano. Take me to a place where an Armenian girl can marry whomever she likes."

"Don't cry," he said, and he took her hand, which rested on her lap. Her face was next to his, and her body was next to his, and the next thing he knew he was taking her in his arms and they were kissing.

CHAPTER 7

Paris in the Rain

Cassie was wide awake, ready to start the day, but when she looked at her watch, she realized it was not daytime at all, but two in the morning. She groaned and pulled the blanket to her chin. There would be at least three more hours before daybreak, three hours without the internet, and she had finished her book on the plane. She got up and peeked out the window at the darkened Parisian skyline, like a Japanese painting, charcoal on charcoal. Even the Eiffel Tower was asleep. It was surreal, being alone in this Parisian hotel room at two in the morning. Surreal, but not unpleasant. She turned on the light. This room, new to her just a few hours ago, now was as familiar as if she'd always lived in it. How strange this was, the hotel room after a single night, the street below, La Jument Bleue bistro filled with patrons, all felt so much more tangible than her life in Los Angeles. Everything that had been so crucial less than twenty-four hours ago, her garden, her habits, her house even, now receding into vagueness. Even the faces of her children were more opaque to her now that they were in college. It was almost as though she had just awakened from a dream where she was an ex-wife, a mother, a writer, an American, only to realize that none of it was real.

What would her life be had she not decided to marry Peter? But was anything that happened in life a decision? It felt more like a series of happenstances, of forks in the road that led to this life. Had she not, for example, met Peter years ago in a Parisian café much like La Jument Bleue, her life would resemble nothing it was today. She would not have the twins. She might not even know how to speak English. Would she even be writing? Despite all evidence to the contrary, she knew herself to be unadventurous by nature. She did not seek this life. Things had happened to her as she had just floated along the river of life.

Now the river was at a standstill, it seemed. Left to her own devices, without Peter to nudge her forward, she was stuck. The thing was, with Peter it had been easier to go along with most things. He was all willpower and certainty. Raising twins, her life with Peter, their working together had made her happy for the most part, but with an undertone of rushed bewilderment.

Refusing to move from their house on the hill was an arbitrary line in the sand that gave her the illusion of continuity when in fact life was nothing but grasping at straws.

Without warning, loneliness gripped her, and she spent the next few moments fending off dread. She went to the bathroom and splashed cold water on her face and thought of how awful it was to wake up alone in a strange place. If another fork in the road appeared today, she would steer clear of it this time. She needed predictability in life. She needed the exterior to be predictable because lately her emotions were all over the map. Suddenly, she needed to be out of the room.

Of course, that was what she would do! She would go to the hospital, right now, and be by her father's side. It would be horrible for him to wake up alone in a hospital bed, tangled in a mess of wires and machines.

She layered clothes, and minutes later, she was outside. She gasped at the frigid night air. The sky was like ink. The neon signs in the shop windows had been turned off, and the only light was the yellowing hue of the street lamps. Without the car noises, the humid air muffled all other sounds, and she walked in the direction of the hospital in cottony silence.

At the ICU desk, a bleary-eyed receptionist worked on her Sudoku in the harsh light of incandescent bulbs. "But Madame," she told Cassie. "It is the middle of the night."

"I know," Cassie said, cheerful. "I've just flown here from the US where I live. I'm jet-lagged, and I could not sleep." To the receptionist's look of incomprehension, she said, "No problem. I'll wait here until it opens. At least I see you have medical brochures to read, that's better than in my hotel room."

"But, Madam...." There was a pregnant pause. "Visiting hours are between one and eight in the afternoon."

"What? How about morning visits?"

The receptionist pronounced carefully, as though she were speaking to a simpleton, "Visitors are allowed between the hours of one and eight in the afternoon."

"But, why?"

"That's how it is."

"That's ridiculous; what kind of hospital is this?"

"It's the same in all Parisian hospitals, Madame."

She considered the clerk's glacial tone. The words were beyond reproach, but the intonation and absence of eye contact told a different story. "Ah, I see," Cassie said. Remembering that to demand things would bring her nowhere, she said sweetly, "I apologize. You see, as I mentioned, I live in the United States, and we do things very differently there. I flew in yesterday. And I was hoping to be in the room with my dad. How about just for a few minutes, just to say hello? If he is asleep, I'll come right out."

The woman crossed her arm, not the slightest bit charmed. "C'est absolument impossible."

Cassie's blood turned hot. "In that case, may I please speak to whoever is running the ICU unit?"

The receptionist looked at her. "I don't understand." Her puzzlement was genuine. "What is it you want, and whom do you wish to speak to?"

"I don't know. You tell me. A doctor? An administrator? Whoever has the authority to let me visit my father outside of visiting hours."

The woman looked at her with suspicion. "What's the patient's name?" Cassie gave her dad's name, briefly holding the notion that the woman was changing her mind. It turned out she only wanted to confirm the existence of a real patient to rule out the probability that Cassie was a lunatic who ambled into hospitals at night making ludicrous demands. The woman then dialed an extension. "There is a woman here at the desk," she added mezza voce. "She says she is here to visit a patient." She stopped there, needing to add nothing to convey the strangeness of the request.

A minute later, a lanky doctor in a white coat and balding cranium approached. "Madame, may I help you?"

"I'm American," she said, words rushing out of her mouth all at once. "Although I might not understand how things work vis-à-vis visiting hours, well, I'm here now, and I'm told that I can't see my father."

"That would be correct," the doctor said, scratching his forehead.

"This is the middle of the night, I get that, but they say I won't be able to visit him until one in the afternoon."

The doctor pondered, looked at her not unkindly, and said, "Between one p.m. until eight p.m."

"But that's nonsensical! What could be the reason for this?"

"In order for the staff to do their work without interruption, and so that the patient can rest."

"Rest? They've been resting all night! Listen, I took the first plane from the United States, and you're telling me I won't be able to see my sick, elderly father, whom I haven't seen in five years, for another eleven hours?"

The doctor looked at his watch and said helpfully, "Ten and a half hours."

"They would never treat someone like this in the United States!"

He sighed, as though drained. "Madame, forgive me, but this is not the United States."

"I think that what my father needs right now is his family."

"What he needs right now is rest and capable medical care. And this is what he is receiving."

"Well, let's talk about his medical care, shall we? Why are you pumping so much morphine into his bloodstream that he can't even wake up?"

"I am not at liberty to discuss patients' files."

"I am his daughter."

"Even if you were the president of the United States, Madame, there is such a thing as patient privacy here." He added, "In France."

****

Cassie slumped all the way back to the hotel, the steps up to her room steeper and in greater number than they had seemed before. What was she going to do for the next ten and a half hours? Sabine, her only semi-ally here – and that was not a given – would be working all day. As for old friends in Paris, she had none. She had managed to let that go in her manic effort to put space between her and her childhood. She could not call anyone; she could not email anyone; she could not get any work done.

She undressed, got back into bed, tossed and turned, counted sheep without luck, and resigned herself to an interminable night.

At five in the morning at long last, after checking all night long for signs of street life outside her window, there seemed to be some activity down at La Jument Bleue. She figured this was a reasonable hour to activate the howling of water pipes. She took a shower standing in the tub, got dressed, layered clothes, came down the stairs, and walked a block under the night sky. She entered the café at the very moment it opened and felt swept up by a feeling of everlasting gratitude for the smell of fresh coffee and the sight of another human being. She sat at the same table and ordered a café au lait and a croissant. The coffee arrived, piping hot and smelling like hope itself. The croissants were crumbly, buttery, and all around gorgeous. As dawn lifted, the street became visible from her table. She wasn't the sole early riser in Paris. Soon a dozen people were ordering breakfast: sanitation men on their break, delivery men, two women in fishnet stockings and high heels. The old hotel manager entered and went to stand at the counter. When he saw Cassie, he gave her a friendly wave.

There was a roar outside the window. It was the motorcyclist from the night before as he made his thundering arrival. He parked his motorcycle in the same spot as the evening before. He entered the café and walked in her direction. When he saw her sitting there, he frowned, turned around, and went to sit a few tables away. She heard him order a café crème et baguette on which he slathered butter and confiture. He ate while reading Le Monde, as if this were his private dining room, and paid her no more attention.

In a caffeine-induced rush, Cassie dusted croissant flakes off her placemat and began scribbling. Lists, thoughts, resolutions, recriminations, bits of dialogue, runs at the perfect sentences she might use with her dad the moment he woke up. She wrote on both sides of the placemat and only lifted her face when she ran out of writing space.

When she lifted her head, the people who had been in the café earlier were gone and replaced by new patrons. Indiana Jones – that's what she called him in her mind – had left as well, and she had not even heard his motorcycle. It was seven in the morning. She paid, returned to her hotel, and was overwhelmed by a wave of fatigue. Just a tiny nap, she thought, but immediately fell into a deep, dreamless sleep.

She woke up to bright daylight aiming straight at her face. She looked at her watch for a long time to make sense of what it said. One in the afternoon? How could this be? She had slept for six hours straight, and now she was late for visiting hours.

****

Odile, Sabine, and her mother were already sitting in the waiting room. No matter that Cassie had beaten them to the hospital by ten and a half hours, she now looked like the one who didn't care. Odile's eyes were puffy, her nose red. Raymonde looked exhausted, and Sabine just gave her a look resembling reproach, although she wasn't sure. "Is everything all right?" Cassie asked. Odile shook her head no and disappeared into her tissue. Cassie's heart quickened.

"We tried to reach you on your cell," Sabine said.

"My phone broke, I'm sorry."

"They cut the sedative this morning, and he is waking up. We were worried that you would miss that."

They were ushered into the changing room and hustled into their paper gowns, paper masks, and paper slippers, and took turns tying the flimsy cords behind each other's backs. Cassie was so nervous that her fingers turned rubbery, and she was having trouble making simple knots.

When they were done, they looked at each other. Paper everywhere, above which were four sets of confused eyes. It was unclear who had the first giggle. Cassie noticed that Odile's shoulder shook and that she was trying to stop herself. When she understood that her sister was laughing, she was instantly affected. It was bad and irrepressible, coming from the belly and wanting to burst out. Before she knew it, Sabine was looking away to control the urge, and Raymonde was emitting mousy little chortles from under her mask. It was infectious, but apparently only to her family because the other people in the dressing room did not see the humor in this and looked at them with displeasure. And the guiltier the four of them felt for laughing, the more hilarious and wrong it was.

They managed to calm down at last by refusing to look at each other. They were about to enter Gustave's room when a doctor with gray hair and a plump physique stood between them and the door. The embroidered badge on his coat indicated that his name was Docteur Dumant. Pompously, and with such slowness that Cassie was tempted to push him and enter the room in a stampede, the doctor enunciated:

"We now have the result of the sensitivity … test. We are starting him on a new course of antibiotics more specific to his … particular infection."

"He is better then?" Odile asked.

"There are many factors. The age of the patient adds to … the complexity of the case."

"But is he *better*?" Cassie asked again.

"We have a long road ahead. But the side … effects of morphine on the elderly vary. As you know from previous … attempts, he was somewhat cognitively impaired to some … extent. He may exhibit signs that resemble delirium and be more excitable … than usual."

"I'm surprised that you are not using compression devices on his legs," she said.

The doctor looked at her askance. "Are you a physician?" he inquired.

"No," Cassie said.

"In that case, I don't see how this would be … hmm … relevant."

Cassie started to say, "But in the United States—" when Odile's hand on her forearm interrupted her.

"Thank you Doctor Dumant," Odile said. The doctor nodded curtly and left. Odile turned to Cassie, her voice muffled by the surgical mask she still wore. "What are you doing questioning Papa's treatment? And yes, we know, Americans do everything better."

"I'm not hurting anything by asking a couple of questions."

"You're antagonizing the doctor, and who knows how it will affect Papa. And us."

"What are you talking about? We have every right to advocate for him. It won't affect him negatively. Quite the opposite!"

"Not in France!" Odile snapped under her surgical mask.

"France or not, he's an ICU doctor, not a disgruntled waiter you're worried might spit in your soup."

"Don't be a child, Cassandra," Odile said.

Cassie clenched her jaw. As they filed into the room, they looked idiotic, like a procession of paper-cloaked clones. Gustave turned his face toward them and stared at them with wide open eyes, showing no other emotion than confusion. They had removed his oxygen mask, but the machine by his side still made rhythmic swooshing Darth Vader sounds. He's so weak, Cassie thought. Can he even recognize us? Dressed like this they might as well be surgeons about to operate on him or candy factory workers straight out of an *I Love Lucy* episode. They gathered around him in silence and Raymonde said, "Ça va Gustave? We all came here to visit."

He did not respond for a long time, and then he whispered, "I'm making do." Odile bent over him, took his hand, and asked him if he needed anything. "A prettier nurse," he said with great effort. "They all look like horses." Cassie smiled with relief under her mask. Humor! A terrific sign.

"We'll work on it, Papa," Odile said. "Is there anything you want to drink or eat?"

"Chocolate pudding," he said, and closed his eyes from the effort.

In his weakness and confusion, Gustave had not yet registered Cassie's presence, so she stepped forward and said, "I'm here too, Papa, I'm so glad you're feeling better." Gustave opened his eyes and stared at her. He raised his eyebrows perplexedly and said nothing. He was disoriented, clearly. She lived thousands of miles away and had not seen him in such a long time. She pushed her mask away from her face so that he could recognize her. "It's me!" she said. "I came all the way here to see you."

But right then, her father did something peculiar. He closed his eyes shut and shook his head vigorously back and forth on the pillow.

"What is it, Papa?" Odile said.

"No!" Gustave barked. Then he opened his eyes again, looked around the room, flummoxed and angry. He raised a trembling finger in Cassie's direction. "Why is she here?" he said, his voice quivering with something that sounded like rage.

"Papa! I'm here to visit you," Cassie whispered, blinking away tears. "I took a plane. I came yesterday, but you were sleeping." Gustave had shut his eyes tight again, as though looking at her was beyond his strength. He was shaking his head forcefully, his mouth a tight line, like a baby refusing to be spoon-fed.

"Come on." Odile pulled on her sleeve a little. "Step back maybe," she whispered. "I think you're tiring him out."

Cassie wanted to step back. She wanted to run away right this minute, but she planted her feet on the floor while her stomach flopped around in her abdomen. "Jeanne and Alexandre couldn't come. They're in college," she said, knowing full well that her dad had never shown interest in her children. Did he even remember their names? She added, "Peter had to stay in Los Angeles."

The rhythm of her father's heart monitors accelerated. Without warning, Gustave bolted upright, opening his eyes wide and dragging with him all manner of tubes and wires, and pointing at Cassie, roared, "I don't want to see her! Make her go away!"

Dread, bafflement, and shame swept through Cassie like a wave. Suddenly, she could not move had she wanted to. Sabine came between her and Gustave and put a protective arm around Cassie's shoulder.

Cassie turned to her mother, helpless. "He doesn't want to see me?" she asked. Raymonde and Odile looked as confused as she was.

Raymonde shook her head with genuine dismay. "I don't know."

Gustave was shaking now, the heart rate monitor beeping faster still. Cassie had the vague sense that Sabine was tugging at her to make her step away, but she could not move. "It's me!" she told her dad.

"That whore!" Gustave bellowed. "That bitch!" The heart monitor triggered an alarm, and in seconds, the room was filled with a strident beeping. Nurses appeared. Cassie, Sabine, Raymonde, and Odile were kicked out of the room, but Cassie could not make her legs work. She felt Sabine's firm grip on her hand, pulling her. At last, they were all in the hallway, tearing at their masks.

"Merde" was all Cassie could say.

"Are you all right?" Sabine asked.

"What the hell just happened?"

"Don't take it personally," Odile told her.

Raymonde said nothing.

They waited outside the room without speaking. Cassie was too numb with incomprehension to utter a word. After ten minutes, a young doctor came out of Gustave's room. "He got over stimulated, but he is fine now," he said.

"Can we go back in?" Raymonde asked.

"He's asking for chocolate pudding," the physician said.

"I don't know about you," Sabine told Cassie, "but I could use a cigarette first."

"Maybe it's better if Maman and I go first," Odile agreed. "Just in case he is still agitated, you know."

"No! I don't know," Cassie barked. But she did not reenter the room, and Sabine stayed with her.

While Raymonde and Odile returned to Gustave's room, Cassie and Sabine removed their paper clothes and walked in silence out of the hospital and into the street where smokers had taken refuge. In the cold, nicotine-saturated air, and amid the pandemonium of car honks and ambulance sirens, Sabine lit a cigarette and took a long drag. "Are you okay?" she asked Cassie.

"I don't even know my own frigging name right now," Cassie murmured.

"The morphine is making him mean; the doctor told us this might happen."

"Papa could be mean to me before the morphine."

Sabine considered this. "This probably has nothing to do with you."

"I don't know how I'm going to be able to go back in there."

"I don't want to spend another minute in there either," Sabine said. "It reeks of crazy."

They did return, eventually, back into their paper gowns and into the room. Odile was bringing a spoonful of pudding to Gustave's mouth. He lapped it up, his eyes half-closed, like a cat. The moment belonged to Odile. She oversaw it all, capable, efficient, necessary. Raymonde was standing back, useless, and Cassie felt sorry for her.

Gustave was peaceful now, so Cassie stepped closer to the bed. Odile was bringing to his lips another spoonful, which Gustave ate. He watched Cassie as he chewed, his eyes rolling in a bizarre way that did not seem like him. Odile brought another spoonful close to his mouth, but Gustave shut his mouth and turned away. He rolled his head on the pillow toward Cassie, pointed his finger at her again, slowly and measuredly this time. His voice clear and unwavering, he said, "Get that bitch out of here!"

They all froze. Cassie shriveled back and away from him, from the emotional impact. "But Papa," she murmured. "It's just me."

But Gustave growled, "Get Marceline out of here!"

Marceline? "Who's Marceline?" Cassie asked the whole room.

"Get her OUT!" her father shouted, and the heart monitor went beep beep at an ever-accelerating pace. "I DON'T want her here!"

Stunned, Cassie removed her hat and mask, threw them on the floor and left the room.

In the hallway, she placed her forehead against the wall and tried to breathe. What had just happened to her?

Twenty minutes later, Gustave was sleeping again. Sabine, Odile, Cassie, and Raymonde gathered around a hospital cafeteria table. Odile seemed invigorated by the visit. Raymonde was practically catatonic, and Sabine kept looking around, as though scanning the place for an emergency exit.

They ordered espressos, and Cassie stared at the cafeteria menu without understanding what she read. She got up and piled her tray high with everything that looked good, and everything did: salade composée, lapin confit aux pruneaux, camenbert, tarte Tatin. Only in a French hospital, Cassie thought. She was denied ketchup – apparently, they only served it on days that had French fries on the menu. She paid and returned to the table. They all stared at her tray.

"You're going to eat at this hour?" Raymonde asked.

"Why not?" But she knew why not: because her French mother could not conceive of eating a meal outside of the appropriate time range.

"It's almost two in the afternoon," Raymonde said.

"I'm jet-lagged," she reminded her. "It's early morning in L.A."

Between tearful bouts, and with irritating self-importance, Odile detailed Gustave's treatment, the infection in his lungs that refused to be tamed, how it had started somewhere in his throat as he recovered from his heart valve replacement. How the heart surgery had been a success, and how the inexplicable infection, now in his lungs, had nothing to do with the reason he had first entered the hospital. As Cassie wolfed down her food, and as Raymonde and Sabine sat in silence, Odile proceeded with a detailed description of Gustave's medicine. The name and dosage of his antibiotics. The name and dosage of the antibiotics before that. She described his pudding intake, even the state of his bowel movements.

Why did Sabine look so miserable? Her jaw was tense, her eyes absent. Was she also annoyed by Odile, or by her? Raymonde's expression was of dull resentment, but towards whom? Raymonde should have been the one giving updates, listening to doctors. She should have been the one feeding Papa pudding. Maybe she resented that Odile was robbing her of those functions. Cassie asked, "Maman, do you think it's the morphine that made Papa angry?"

Odile was going to answer, but Raymonde said, "The last time he woke up, he shouted racial slurs. He called the nurse a dirty Jew."

Cassie gasped. "What? That's awful."

"We know that Papa isn't like that," Sabine said.

"Drugs can make you feel and say crazy things," Odile said.

"How did the nurse respond?"

Odile laughed. "She was Asian. She said that she had been called many things in her life, but this, never."

"Could Papa be a closeted anti-Semite?" Cassie asked.

"He doesn't think about ... anything Israelite," Raymonde said forcefully.

"You mean Jewish?"

"Oh, by God, Cassie. Always stirring the pot."

"I'm only asking."

"It was the morphine," Sabine said, addressing the elephant in the room. "He was not speaking to you. He didn't recognize you."

Cassie sighed. "A man able to make a specific request for chocolate pudding should be able to recognize his own daughter."

"Maybe it was a hallucination," Raymonde offered.

Cassie shrugged, "There's also the possibility that the morphine allowed him to express how much he hates me."

"Oh please," Odile said, rolling her eyes. "Not this again."

"Again?"

"With you, it's always one conspiracy or another."

They all knew what conspiracy theory Odile was referring to: the Letter. Cassie inhaled, braced herself, and said, "Maybe without the drugs, he is better able to disguise his dislike of me as indifference."

"It's not because you repeat something over and over that it makes it true," Odile snapped.

"Well, if you needed proof, what about this latest outburst?"

"It wasn't about you, you, you!" Odile exploded. "The more we tell you that it's not about you, the more you insist. Every time it's the same thing: you disappear, then you barge in, tell lies, and leave me behind to clean up the mess you left."

"What are you referring to? If I disappeared, it's because I was written off. Cast away by all of you!"

Sabine and Raymonde looked down at their food, but Odile was galvanized. "You wrote a letter of insults; Papa and Maman had to defend themselves!"

"Defend from what? From my feelings?"

"From your inventions and your lies."

Cassie had the urge to reach across the table and slap Odile. She tucked her hand between her knees and looked at her mother who showed no expression. She said, "In this family, the minute you share an unpleasant truth you're called a liar."

They all looked down at their empty espresso cups for a long moment, no one knowing what to say next. Sabine broke the thick silence. "Maman, why do you think Papa mentioned this name? *Marceline?*" She said this with deliberation. It was unlike Sabine to cross-examine anyone. It was as though she was encouraging their mother to speak up about something only she knew about. All three sisters held their breath and looked at Raymonde.

"Me? I— how would I know," Raymonde said, staring at the table.

"Does he know someone with that name, maybe?" Sabine insisted. "Someone from his *past?*" Sabine was looking at Raymonde fiercely, impelling her to answer.

Raymonde's eyes darted from one daughter to another angrily and finally blurted out, "I can't remember!"

Despite the fight just a moment ago, an invisible current passed between Odile and Cassie. Their mother was lying, it was obvious. The lie floated between them. Something unusual had just happened, but neither of them was ready to cross-examine Raymonde.

"I'm getting a smoke," Sabine said. She got up. "You want one?" she asked, giving Cassie an excuse to leave. Cassie stood up.

Odile and Raymonde returned to Gustave's room, and Cassie and Sabine walked into the street. They leaned against a stone wall to protect themselves from the falling rain. Cassie observed her sister as she took a cigarette out of a pack and brought it to her lips, lighting it, inhaling, and exhaling deeply. She was tense, and her eyes were sad.

"Okay, you're going to say I have too much imagination," Cassie said, "but didn't Maman look embarrassed when we asked about that Marceline person?"

Sabine inhaled and said, "That's clear."

"First, she says Papa hallucinated. Like instead of seeing me he was seeing someone else? And then why would Maman pretend not to know that person unless...."

"Unless Maman is manipulative."

"Well, I was thinking, is it possible that Papa had some kind of affair?"

"No," Sabine said. "It's something else."

"You do know something!"

"I heard things," she said, exhaling smoke through her nose into the cold air.

"What?"

"The expression 'that bitch Marceline.' Papa used it when we were growing up," Sabine said. "I heard it when he and Maman were talking."

"I never heard any of that."

"If some woman named Marceline was his mistress, he would not commiserate with his wife against her."

"You didn't ask who she was?"

Sabine had a small smile. "You know how it goes in this family. We're not supposed to ask questions, and anyway, no one will answer them."

Cassie looked at Sabine wide-eyed. "That's right! That's exactly how it goes! I thought I was crazy to think that. Everyone in this family thinks I'm crazy."

"No one believes that you're crazy," Sabine said, laughing a little. "We just want you to *think* that you are."

"I'm about to fall to my knees to thank you for this," Cassie said.

Sabine lifted her chin and blew a cloud of smoke up at the sky. "You're welcome," she said.

After Sabine had returned to her work, Cassie paced in the waiting room. She had heard of ICU psychosis. Hallucinations and paranoia were known side effects of heavy sedative use and ventilation. She needed to ask the doctor if that was what he had meant when he had warned them of possible delirium. It would explain everything. Also: she would be innocent.

Behind the front desk, the frizzy desk clerk was looking as glum as ever. "I'd like to speak with my father's doctor," Cassie said.

"He's busy," the woman responded without looking up.

Cassie inhaled, exhaled an already much hotter air. "I'd like to make an appointment, then."

"Doctor Dumant doesn't take appointments." The woman made everything sound as though the person in front of her was stupid, in the wrong, or both. It was oh so subtle, nothing you could pinpoint, but the contempt was there.

"I've never heard of a doctor who doesn't take appointments," Cassie said. "That would be like a teacher who doesn't see students," she explained. "Or a butcher who doesn't handle meat."

The woman stared at her with a vacant expression. "You might be able to see him when he is making his rounds," she said.

"When is that?"

"I don't manage his schedule."

"I've been walking up and down this hospital, and I don't see him. I'm starting to wonder if he is playing frisbee in some deserted hallway instead of treating sick people. Shouldn't the doctor be doctoring?"

The clerk shrugged, uninterested. "He sees the patients who need to be seen when they need to be seen."

At that moment, Cassie spotted him. Doctor Dumant was charging through the hallway, half a dozen interns trotting after him. She thought she recognized one of the young men she had seen at La Jument Bleue that first night. She began to trot along with the group. "Excusez moi, Docteur Dumant! I'm wondering if you would have a minute."

The doctor stopped in front of a patient's door, picked up a file, and put his hand on the doorknob, ignoring her.

"Excuse me!" she said loudly. "I know you aren't deaf, and I'm pretty certain that I'm not invisible, so please speak to me." The interns were stunned into immobility, a collective horrified expression on their faces.

"What is … this?" Doctor Dumant said.

"I need to talk to you about my father's treatment," Cassie said.

The doctor looked at her with impatience. "I am extremely … busy, Madame."

Flustered, Cassie forgot why she wanted to talk to him, so she improvised. "I heard that there is such a thing as taking too strong a course of antibiotics."

The physician was perplexed by this. "And?"

"I heard it could lead to kidney or liver failure."

"Are you suggesting we stop the antibiotics, and let … him fend for himself?" Doctor Dumant asked, inspiring a collective mirth among his entourage.

"No, of course not," Cassie said. "Also, I'm wondering about the degree of inclination of his bed."

"What about it?"

"I heard that feeding tubes can leak into a patient's lungs with the wrong degree of inclination. Are we sure that it won't happen?"

The interns looked at her with bemusement, waiting for Doctor Dumant to react. "Quite certain," the doctor said.

Suddenly Cassie remembered her original question. "My dad shouted at me out of nowhere yesterday. Is it possible that he has ICU psychosis?"

"Possible," the doctor said meanly, "but in your … specific case, unlikely."

What an a-hole! Cassie, anger swelling in her chest, went on the offensive despite herself. "You'll understand my concerns; my father entered here for a heart valve replacement and contracted a nosocomial infection, you know, a *hospital-acquired* infection?"

"I'm well acquainted with the term," Dumant said icily.

"I bet you are," she said.

"Has the patient authorized you to … speak on his behalf?" Doctor Dumant asked sharply. The interns, attuned to the doctor's emotional temperature, shifted on their heels.

Cassie shrugged. "I imagine my mother, my sisters are. I'm probably as well."

"Either you are, or you are not. Why don't you … find out." With this, he opened the door.

Cassie raised her voice. "If you're unwilling to answer basic questions, I'll speak to your boss." But the doctor and his interns had disappeared into the room.

Cassie scanned the now deserted hallway for something to break. Feeling like ramming her fist into the wall, she headed for the front desk. There were four people in line ahead of her. The frizzy clerk was busy dispensing her non-help to everyone. Cassie waited, furious. When it was her turn, she said in a voice she tried to keep even, "I want to make an appointment with the director of this department."

The frizzy clerk made her repeat, as though the request was beyond the grasp of her understanding. "You want a what?"

"An appointment."

"With the head of the intensive care unit?"

"That's right."

"Madame, c'est impossible! He doesn't deal with patients, let alone the family of patients. He's an administrator."

"Well, I have an administrative issue. What's his name?" Behind her, a half a dozen people stood in line. Sensing they would be made to wait now, the line emitted a collective sigh of annoyance.

"Madame," the clerk responded in a tone of personal outrage, "we obviously don't give out names of the faculty, or administration."

"Why not?"

"But Madame, if people came here and got the names of people on staff, it would violate their privacy. This is a hospital. We have rules."

Behind her, sighs made way for groans of impatience, which Cassie tried to ignore. "This is nothing but obstruction," she said. "Once the director finds out what is going on here, I am quite sure he will find it interesting to learn that this department makes people sick, not better, and that the patients are treated like cattle."

Far from being intimidated, the clerk had an exhausted smile. "Next!" she called.

****

The heavy rain had turned into a mean and windy sort of drizzle. Cassie walked fast, trying to put as much distance between her and the hospital as her soggy boots would allow. She walked down Boulevard de Magenta and crossed Boulevard de Rochechouart toward rue de Clignancourt. She passed graffiti-covered walls, African beauty shops, kosher butchers, porn shop signs, fake leather purses hanging like grapes on the outside walls of discount stores. The sidewalks were as crowded as the street and smelled of exhaust pipes, cannabis, and cooked lamb. The crackling sounds of mopeds faded by the time she reached rue Pierre Picard. Suddenly, there were trees. Pedestrians disappeared, and she found herself alone in the street. A minute later she was at the foot of Montmartre.

The stairs leading up to the Sacré-Coeur were empty save for a few intrepid tourists battling the weather with overturned umbrellas. She climbed, and the street noises became muffled and then disappeared. Montmartre, wet and glistening, was all hers. Below her, stone stairs and trees. Above her, more stairs and trees, many of them starting to show signs of spring. The texture of the air changed. An icy draft bit her hard.

There were no more street noises, only the chirping of a few brave birds, as though she had climbed out of the city and into the countryside. She emerged on the Sacré-Coeur's esplanade. The basilica was massive, so much bigger than it appeared from the bottom of the butte. Above her were the gray sky and the stillness of bare trees and branches. Below, Paris was grey, muted.

She stood by the balustrade. The cold wind slapped her without mercy as immense pangs of sadness and guilt beat down on her. No wonder she usually took a shortcut to anger. It was a readily available emotion, simple, immediately accessible, energizing, an emotion far less painful than the alternatives: sadness, grief, envy, self-loathing. Anger felt good.

Until, of course, it destroyed everything. The Letter to her parents, that irreparable fracture, written in a single day when she had needed to blame someone for her unhappiness, had been the product of anger.

She had penned the Letter the day that followed her return to Los Angeles with Peter, after that disastrous trip to Paris. On that day, they had fought. He had accused her of blaming him for things beyond his control. She had called him a narcissist, he had called her a professional victim, and she had accused him of having an affair, had called him a man-whore and a douchebag. She had shouted that she wanted a divorce, that she wanted him gone. Out of the house right this instant. He took all the writing credit. He was ignoring her. They did not even talk anymore. She had not meant this, at least not the part about wanting him gone.

None of this had been a new argument. Only, to her dismay, Peter had packed a bag this time and spent the night at the Sunset Marquis. A week later, he still had not returned. A month later, he was filing for divorce.

The day Peter had left, she had decided that she was done with lies and compromises, that she wanted to tell the Truth. In the Letter, she told her parents how horrible visiting them had been. She accused her father of playing favorites, her mother of being complacent, and Odile of reveling in the whole mess.

Just like her threat to Peter, she had only meant to vent. The Letter should have been no problem at all – had she not mailed it. A week later, she received a terse response from Odile notifying Cassie that, in return for the calumnious web of lies, her parents no longer wished to speak to her.

She had not expected this. She hadn't expected that her anger could make all of them angry.

Her parents' reaction to her letter had floored her. They had written her off so easily, validating all her suspicions. The heartbreak she experienced was so violent that she knew what the term meant now. She felt it, her heart. She felt the physical shattering of it.

She had scrambled to fix things with Peter. But it was as though she had hit an off-switch with him. He said that he had failed at making her happy for years and that he no longer had it in him to try.

The years that followed the separation were abysmal. The children, as predicted by Odile, began to act out. Jeanne fell in with the wrong crowd. It's always about other children having a bad influence on yours, but what happens when it is your child who is caught selling pot to other middle schoolers? Jeanne was expelled and put on juvenile probation. For the next few years, Cassie had to chase after her daughter to get her to pee in a cup to prove her sobriety to juvenile court. Alex, meanwhile, disappeared into AP classes and Robotics Club until – she was the last one to find out, through Peter – it was revealed that he had been suffering from debilitating bouts of anxiety and was under the care of a psychiatrist who had prescribed heavy-duty psychotropic meds.

When Peter was picked like a ripe plum by Jessica, it was the last straw. A giant sinkhole of pain and guilt swallowed Cassie whole. Peter was her best friend, possibly her soul mate, and she had pushed him away. She had kicked him out, as Peter reminded her, sending him straight into Jessica's arms.

Watching Peter and Jessica together, witnessing their happiness, was torture – Jessica's youth, the pregnancies, the fact that their life together was only picking up steam whereas hers had collapsed, all of it brought her to her knees. She would have agreed to anything in the divorce, as long as she could continue to have Peter in her life. She did not know how to live without him. They agreed to work together, and those were the crumbs on which she fed. And thus, she saw Peter every day, and she starved.

After a year without speaking to her parents, and at Sabine's suggestion, Cassie found the courage to call. She had told her parents about the divorce and apologized to them. Or more to the point, she had grovelled. Cassie had blamed her behavior on the stress of her marriage falling apart and recanted all she had said. The apology hadn't been sincere, but she was at a low point and in desperate need of their love.

But the love didn't come. For the next four years, she made every effort, struggled through perfunctory, strained conversations (as if in a permanent act of contrition, she was the one expected to call; they never did). The relationship with her father stalled to nothing. Her calls seemed an annoyance he avoided. The more Cassie did the talking, with an increasingly manic intensity, the more aloof he seemed. He did not ask questions and went from vague and disinterested to not coming to the phone at all. And on the rare occasions when he picked up the phone, he handed it to Raymonde. When Cassie asked to speak to him, he was always out or napping.

She confronted her mother and Odile about it, but they assured her that nothing was the matter. Once again, she was making things up. Over time, she called less. Every other week, and then once a month. And then only for Christmas and on birthdays. It was no surprise that they did not feel the need to tell her about his heart operation; she was barely part of the family.

Leaning against the parapet, Cassie shivered. It had started to rain again. Her fingers were numb. She walked across the esplanade and stopped in front of an engraved plaque stating that the construction of the Sacré-Coeur was completed in 1914. She looked up at the basilica, so intricate, so ancient, immutable-looking, when in fact it was only about a hundred years old! She could have grandparents that age. She did not. Her mother's parents had passed away, and come to think of it, she had never met her paternal grandparents and did not even know their names. Her dad never spoke of them.

He was so hard to know, her father, so hard to read. He had always been a silent, secret man. She had tried to read him, tried to connect, but he had not let her. Sacré-Coeur, sacred heart. Peter. Her father. This longing for the love of two men who could not give it to her in return was akin to masochism. And yet she continued to want it.

Shouldn't her heart be sacred too? Did it not need protecting?

****

It began to rain hard. Cassie hurried back down the stairs. Her first order of business was not to get hurt. By anyone. What could they do to her that they had not already done? Her dad had clearly lost interest in her a long time ago. This outburst was more of the same. Who cared who Marceline was, or why he had confused her with Cassie? He was out of his mind because of the drugs. It meant nothing. If the rest of the family gave her the cold shoulder, so be it. At least she had showed up in Paris, done the right thing. There was a family narrative, "Cassie est dure," they would say, which might be translated as tough, or harsh, depending on the intention. Cassie was thought to land on her feet. Cassie was not *sensitive* the way Odile was. She could have perceived this as a compliment but took it as a reproach. It made her feel self-serving, unfeeling. But she could not defend herself from this reproach without appearing *dure* indeed, so she embraced it. She was tough. She was strong. She had grit. She did not need anyone. Not Peter, not the kids now that they had left for college.

But strength, toughness, and grit implied self-sufficiency. No one thought that people like her needed tender loving care. The needs of tough, strong, gritty people tend to be overlooked, first of all by themselves.

****

Just as she arrived at the hospital, a voice over the loudspeaker informed her that visitation hours had come to an end. Dozens of family members began to file docilely out of patients' rooms, removing their hats, masks, and paper gowns and tossing them into nearby wastebaskets. Cassie ran back into her father's room as Odile and Raymonde were leaving. She peeked inside the room; her dad seemed to be sleeping peacefully. Sabine wasn't there.

"Do you want to have dinner together?" Cassie asked.

Raymonde looked at Odile, signifying that the two had agreed on this. "We're exhausted. Maybe another time if you don't mind," Odile said. She nudged Cassie out of the room before she could get closer to her father's bed. "He's sleeping now; better let him be."

They walked out of the hospital. Rain poured. Odile and her mother, in their warm coats, opened their umbrellas. Cassie stood under her mother's umbrella. The three formed a little tent, steam billowing out of their mouths as they spoke. "Maman?" Cassie said, "I'm wondering about something."

"What?"

"How come we never got to meet Papa's parents?"

Raymonde looked at Odile as if she needed her authorization to respond, but Odile gave her a blank stare. "You ask this now?" she protested. "It's your dad's business."

Odile surprised her by coming to Cassie's aid. "They are our grandparents," she said.

Raymonde shrugged. "Your grandfather died during the war, and your grandmother died when you were little. After that, there was a … falling-out."

Cassie avoided looking at Odile, but she was sure her sister had registered it too. Odile said, "A falling out with whom, if they were both dead?"

Raymonde eyed her with panic, or perhaps anger. "Oh, I don't know!"

"Where were they from?" Odile asked. "Our grandparents, what were their names?"

Raymonde's jaw clenched. "I can't remember! It's too long ago!"

Cassie narrowed her eyes. "You can't remember your mother-in-law's name?"

"I only met her a couple of times!" Raymonde protested. It was one thing to brush Cassie off, and another one to deflect questions when her daughters were united. Tapping her boots on the pavement and gripping her umbrella, Raymonde raised her voice. "I did not meet with her approval! She was all hoity-toity. I was too working-class. I don't know what she imagined for her son, some duchess or something? That's what she was into — status. But I was penniless. A shop girl." She added defensively, "I wasn't after Gustave's money. And his family never gave him a franc. Not that he would have taken it were it offered!"

Cassie and Odile exchanged a furtive look. A current of excitement passed between them. This was a long-taboo subject. The topic of their father's past would not have been allowed had he been present. But now that Raymonde was entangled in her explanations, a little push could result in something interesting. From whom was Gustave estranged? As far as the story went, he had no living relatives.

"Papa was what? Forty years old when he met you?" Cassie said, craftily. "Maybe his mother did not approve of Papa's choice of a twenty-year-old bride?"

Raymonde, reeling from what appeared to be a reopened wound, said, "So what? I was young and pretty, I'll have you know. You saw the pictures of me back then, thin and all. Who wouldn't want this for their son? But not her. Oh, no. Her Majesty never wanted to know me. I could not bear the way she was treating me, in that house of theirs, their castle," she said, pronouncing that last word with a mix of resentment and admiration.

"A castle?" Cassie said.

"Well, not exactly. But the way they had their décor, they would have you think it was Versailles."

"How *did* she treat you?" Odile asked.

"Like I was dirt," Raymonde spat.

"What did you say Papa's mom's name was again?" Cassie said, knowing full well her mother had claimed not to know.

"Lucienne." Raymonde realized her mistake. "I guess I remember now," she grumbled.

"And then what happened?"

"Then your father wrote a letter and said he wanted to have nothing to do with them." She pinched her lips. "That's all I know."

"How familiar," Cassie said. "I disagreed with Dad, and he wrote me off too."

"We were tired of being insulted!" Raymonde barked, all too happy to bring the conversation back to something she and Odile agreed on. "Your letter was nothing but lies."

Cassie expected Odile to come to her mother's rescue, but she didn't. Instead, she pressed on. "Them?" Odile asked. "His father was dead, so who is 'them?' There was Lucienne, Papa's mother. Who else?"

"Well," Raymonde said evasively, "there was his sister."

In unison, Cassie and Odile exclaimed, "What sister?"

"Papa had a sister?"

"Has. She's still alive as far as I know."

"Did you meet her?"

"Is she younger or older?"

"I met her," Raymonde said, defeated. "You were little. This wasn't her first marriage. She was marrying a count. Not her first count, at that! I imagine that's why we were invited: so that they could rub our noses in it."

"Do we have cousins?" Odile asked, excited.

"Perhaps. I don't know. No. I don't think so. Maybe."

"What was the name of the count?" Cassie asked. She needed to gather as much info as possible before her mother closed up like a clam.

"Some ridiculous aristocratic name."

"Can't you remember?"

"Not really."

Odile and Cassie pondered this. A sister. A living relative. An aunt! "What's her name?" Odile asked with authority.

Raymonde shrugged, as though the answer was obvious, "Well, Marceline."

Cassie and Odile exchanged an excited glance. The name hovered between them, ripe with mystery and speculation. *Marceline, the bitch.*

"That's who he was ranting about?" Odile said.

Raymonde wasn't listening. The discussion had brought her back to a loop in her thinking, whatever had happened, still undigested. "By marrying me, your father went from the bourgeoisie to working class. A step down. They didn't approve, oh no. He was never good enough for them, and neither was I."

"Why did Papa never tell us about Marceline?" Cassie asked.

"Your father hates his sister. That's why you never met her. He despises her like you have no idea."

"After today, I'd say that we got a pretty good idea actually," Odile said. She turned to Cassie. "As I suspected, this was not about you. He was confused, that's all."

"Why would Papa agree to go to his sister's wedding if he hated her so much?" Cassie asked.

"I guess they wanted us to witness their grand airs. I don't know why he went." Raymonde paused and looked around as if searching for a quick exit route. Outside, the rain was relentless. The umbrella wasn't broad enough, and Cassie felt the cold, wet fabric of her thin jacket against her back. She was cold to the core, but not about to move. She could tell that Odile wasn't budging either, physically or mentally. She was just as curious as Cassie was.

"Why would Papa not tell us any of this?" Odile said. "Why the big secret?"

"That's all I know," Raymonde said, pinching her lips.

"What's Marceline's last name?" Cassie asked.

"Oh, I don't know. A complicated name." Raymonde was getting flustered. "You can ask your father when he wakes up!" She turned to walk away and suddenly said, "Ah, yes! I remember," perhaps because the name had just popped into her mind or because she had burned to pronounce it all along. "Marceline Bécasel D'Alompe! No, *Comtesse* de Bécasel D'Alompe, believe it or not." With this, she turned away and walked down rue Ambroise Paré. "I'm cold," she told Odile. "Let's go."

Odile looked at Cassie, shrugged, and hurried after her mother.

"I'll see you tomorrow," Cassie called after them.

Now that the umbrella was gone, Cassie was left standing in the rain. She watched them walk toward the metro station. Neither had asked a single question about her life, her children, her divorce, how she fared, or even where she would be staying.

Cassie rushed back inside the hospital and into the intensive care area. At the desk, she asked for a piece of paper, and she jotted down the words Comtesse Marceline de Bécasel D'Alompe before she forgot. The woman at the desk was a new nurse that Cassie had yet to alienate. She decided to take her chance. "Excuse me," she said, trying to appear sweet and obedient, "I realize visitation hours are over, but I forgot my wallet in my father's room."

The woman hesitated. "Hurry then. And don't get near the patient, you know, because of germs."

"He won't even know I was there," Cassie assured as she rushed toward the room.

****

Her father lay on his back, asleep. On his face was the mask to help him breathe, connected to a tube and a machine. The only signs of life were the beeping of the heart monitor and the laborious up and down motion of his chest as he labored to breathe. "Poor Papa," she whispered. "What have they done to you?" She brought the thin blanket up to his chin. She found two other covers and spread those across his body, but when she looked up at him again, his eyes here wide open, unblinking. "Papa?" she said.

Gustave gripped her arm. His eyes rolled around, taking in the room, his expression close to panic. He began to moan, or perhaps to speak. "Are you trying to say something?" Cassie asked urgently. She looked at the door, then down at her hands. Were they clean enough? She lifted his mask off his face. "What is it?"

Her father murmured, "I saw his ghost."

"What?"

"Baba."

"Baba?"

"It wasn't my fault."

"Of course, relax now, just rest."

"You have to find Baba," he muttered. "You'll see. He'll tell you."

An instant later, his eyes were closed. Cassie waited a moment and placed the mask back on his face. She tiptoed to the other side of the room, snatched her father's coat and ran out of the hospital.

****

Wrapped in her dad's coat, and for the first time since she had gotten off the plane Cassie felt warm. The coat was too wide, too long, but she liked how it weighed on her shoulders, how rough it was to the touch, like a coat of armor, one that smelled of her father's lavender aftershave. The coat, or "relic" as her mother had labeled it for some reason, had been a presence in her childhood. It existed in her parent's closet without ever being worn. In fact, the coat did not fit her dad either. It was too wide for his build, and the cut was from another era. Why keep this old thing, she wondered? And why, of all the coats he owned, had her father chosen this one to bring to his heart surgery?

Cassie, looking increasingly less chic and Parisian in the strange coat, walked toward the hotel and clambered into La Jument Bleue.

At the door, she came shoulder to shoulder with Indiana Jones, who appeared intent on beating her to it. He let her in first, with a reluctant, "Après vous."

"Merci," she said. But as soon as she passed the threshold, he walked past her and then did something so rude that she nearly gasped in indignation: Had he actually rushed ahead to steal her table? Yes, he had! He was stealing her table, just like that. Robbery in broad daylight!

The only empty table left was the one across from where he was sitting. Seething, Cassie headed for it, removed her coat and folded it over her chair. She sat down and crossed her arms, intent on not looking in his direction. The waiter arrived to take her order. Unprepared, and feeling Indiana's eyes on her, she fumbled with words and ordered the same steak au poivre she had eaten the day before. "Avec du ketchup," she added. She waited, impatient, pen in hand, for the waiter to set the table. She removed the white paper placemats from the table and began writing, feverishly laying on paper the thoughts that lay in a jumble inside her head.

Something extraordinary had taken place today. Her father had mistaken her for his sister. A living sister! One he kept secret from his daughters. Why? How? And who was this Baba?

She wrote:

1- Look online for relatives, family tree, <u>something</u>
2- Find internet café
3- Tell Sabine the story
4- Find out more about Marceline. Who is she?
6- Do I <u>look</u> like her?

She gazed up to find that Indiana Jones was watching her with keen interest. She put her arms over her placemat, hiding her writing like a school girl, and looked pointedly away. A moment later he opened a book, and it was her turn to observe him. No ring on any of the fingers. Could be gay. Or not. In Paris, it was hard to tell. She cared about none of this, of course. However, a handsome man at the next table was proving himself difficult to ignore.

Her steak-frites arrived and with it a laughably minuscule ramekin filled with about a tablespoon of ketchup. "Pardonnez-moi," she told the waiter, "I'm going to need a whole lot more ketchup." The waiter returned with a bottle. She used the back of her knife to scrape the sauce off her steak and poured ketchup on her plate. She ate, setting her fork down every so often to write on her placemat, and made every effort to ignore Indiana Jones for the rest of the meal.

It was dark when she left La Jument Bleue. As she crossed the street, she stepped down from the curb and into a deep puddle. Instantly and effortlessly, the Uggs absorbed the dirty gutter water like high-efficiency sponges. She stood in shock. Icy water was up to her ankles inside her boots! She dragged her now much heavier feet all the way to the hotel, cursing the rain in French.

****

Inside the hotel's phone booth, she sat on the bench, removed her boots and socks, and called Sabine. The call went straight to voicemail, twice. No point in leaving a message since she could not be called back. The day had been so hard, and she was so tired, and her toes had turned to shriveled little blue things. What she did next was just plain stupid. She dialed Odile's cell phone. "I'm thinking I'd like to get in touch with that Marceline woman," she told her older sister.

"Why?" Odile asked coldly. "What would that accomplish?"

"I'm curious about her, that's all."

"I think you should drop the idea."

"Okay. But I would just need a tiny favor from you though. Could you help me out?"

"Depends."

"Could you go online and look for her address?"

There was a long silence as Odile considered this. "Why can't you do it yourself?" she asked.

"I don't have any access to the internet at the moment. It's just a quick look on google. I wrote down the name."

"Sorry, I can't," Odile said.

"How difficult would it be for you to spend the five seconds it takes to look up a single address?"

"I can't—"

"How hard would it be to give me the time of day for once in your life? How about that?"

"And how about I'm at Maman's, and she doesn't have a computer."

Cassie leaned her forehead on the glass door and bumped it gently a couple of times. "Okay," she said. "You don't want to look on your phone?"

"No, Cassie, I do *not* want to look on my phone right now."

"Okay."

"Are you going to do it anyway?"

Cassie hesitated. "Probably," she admitted.

Odile's voice changed pitch, something either near tears or explosion. "Do you think that's appropriate?"

"What?"

"Going behind Papa's back?"

How did she do it? Odile had a gift. Between the withholding of emotions, and the reproachful, judgmental undertone of everything she said, Odile could give a master class on how to be passive-aggressive. "I am not going behind his back!" Cassie snapped. And realizing that in fact, she was, she said, "Fine! Don't help me."

She then dialed Peter's cell phone collect. She needed to speak to him. Needed to! Peter was, she was now convinced, her last friend in the world. She was never going to be able to cope without him. In a few sentences, he would calm her down, put things in perspective, make fun of her.

She dialed and dialed again, but each time her call went to voicemail. She had no luck reaching Peter at home either. She tried again, feeling more rejected and alone with each try.

The reason she could not cope with life without Peter is that she had never developed a life of her own. In the marriage, she had remained in a safe, little world. She had never quite learned to function outside of her house and outside of her role as wife and mother. As an expatriate, those roles had felt safer than to attempt to integrate into a new country or a new culture. But really, it was not Peter's fault, even if it had been convenient for him to keep her available to him and ignorant of everything else. Now, for the first time, she accepted the blame for making one man her Everything, and then for pushing him away the way she had. Now she was confused, forgetting digits and fumbling with the phone like in a bad dream. She had lost Peter. He was no longer hers. That was the absolute truth.

What am I doing?

She stopped dialing and hung up. She had spent half her life counting on Peter to solve her problems, but now she needed to fend for herself. I need to move on, she thought, the words resounding in her head like a terrible fatality. She could no longer afford to need Peter or his friendship. It wasn't fair to him, it wasn't fair to Jessica Rabbit, and, ultimately, it wasn't fair to herself. She wasn't giving herself a proper chance at life.

She had been a daughter, and then a wife, and then a mother, and now she was nothing. She burst into tears, alone in her red velvet padded phone booth. She cried for a good long time. And when she was bored with crying and with feeling sorry for herself, she walked up the stairs.

In her room, she brushed her teeth and took off her clothes. She lay on top of the covers, brought her dad's coat to bed, wrapped herself in its coarse wool, and fell asleep protected by the scent of lavender aftershave.

CHAPTER 8

The Armenian Visitor

On a warm October day, Albano watched incoming ferries, his back propped against burlap bags filled with grains awaiting shipment. The 1914 harvest had been spectacular and the succession of hot days and dry nights had made the conditions ideal for the drying process, thus ensuring another year of prosperity for Smyrna.

The Ottoman Empire had bombed Russia's Black Seaport and officially entered the war, and the mood on the quay had turned festive almost overnight. Among the citizens of the Empire, there was a sense of great anticipation and the giddiness of men preparing for heroism. Men who had always worn simple peasant clothes, some who had never worn shoes in their life, looked grand in their fresh uniforms.

Albano did not like the air of authority the uniform gave them. Humble men now turned soldiers seemed drunk on patriotism and pride. In the cafés and restaurants, on the pier and throughout Smyrna, rumors flew, and temperaments ran wild. On the quay, the flurry of activity had doubled in intensity. Few foreigners remained. Those from countries that had allied with the Ottoman Empire and were now part of the Central Powers, Germany, the Austro-Hungarian Empire, and Bulgaria, stayed in Smyrna unless they had been mobilized to fight by their respective governments. Foreigners from the Allied Powers, Great Britain, France, Russia, and Italy, had been repatriated with their families. Other foreign families who had lived in Smyrna longer and had deeper roots here had required more time to liquidate assets and were now hurrying to leave. The loading docks were filled with mounds of luggage and anxious foreigners wringing their hands.

Albano opened the last of his French newspapers and read its content avidly. Of all the languages Albano had learned over the two years since he had first met Hagop, he loved French the best. Learning new languages was easy for him. He would read newspaper articles in Turkish, Arabic, Greek, or Armenian, then look for corresponding subjects in the contents of a French, Italian, or British newspaper and over time would start to make sense of it. When pronunciation eluded him, he listened in on conversations between men from London, Milan, Paris, or Prague and sponged up the accents. Then he practiced to himself out loud as he walked between the Jewish quarter, Mount Pagus, and the quayside. He studied how Europeans dressed, how they greeted one another, trying to decode the subtlety between classes. Sometimes, when Albano was alone in his cave, he practiced standing and walking the way French people did. France held the most charm in his mind ever since Uncle Moshe had made it so vivid with his tales of monkeys and Eiffel Towers.

With the Europeans being repatriated, a gaping hole was opening in the very fabric of Smyrna. Gone were Danish bankers and Italian insurance men in their silk suits. Gone were English women in large skirts and lace, French women wearing the new fashions from Paris. From the quay's restaurants, the smell of tagine and Greek stew no longer mingled with the aroma of boeuf bourguignon and sauerkraut. The top hats, canotiers, and feathered hats were mostly gone. All that was left were turbans, fezzes, and felt embroidered caps. With the political agitation, he and Hagop had sold out of European newspapers within the hour. Hagop had gone to the store to fetch more, but already he was heading back to Albano empty-handed. "Starting tomorrow it will be illegal to sell anything printed by any country of the Triple Entente," Hagop morosely said as he plopped down next to Albano and leaned against one of the burlap bags.

"This is the end of our prosperity," Albano said.

"We need to think of something else we can sell now," Hagop said bitterly. "Ammunition? Coffins?"

"We could sell your father's pastries just like Xandra does in the Levantine quarter. Sell them here, on the quay."

"Think about it, Albano," Hagop said. "Those baskets are heavy." Albano bit his lip to keep from responding. If Xandra was strong enough to do it, maybe the two of them could do it as well. But Hagop did not find much value in hard work. What he found value in were shortcuts – the least amount of effort for the highest return. Cleverness, to Hagop's way of thinking, not sweat, was what made men rich. "We could take them in a wheelbarrow," Albano suggested.

"We could," Hagop shrugged. Then he thought about it. "It's below us. Men don't go around selling pastries."

They watched in silence as the hundreds of boats covering the marina moved about. Attracted by the fishing boats, seagulls dove madly into the waters, zooming through the sky and dive-bombing. The late October sky now had the soft haze that preceded the arrival of cooler days. A group of soldiers walked by proudly, but judging from suppressed winces of pain and the way they hopped from foot to foot, they were still unused to stiff leather boots. Albano was about to point out how comical they looked when Hagop said, "Why can't we be wearing uniforms too?"

Albano shrugged, "Because we're too young."

Hagop pointed to the French newspaper Albano was holding. "You said you were out of newspapers."

"I want to keep this last one for myself."

"Hide it then. You don't want to be seen reading it, starting today. Besides, you ought to be less in love with France. Everyone in Smyrna seems to want to be French, but there is more pride in being what and who we are."

"What and who are we?"

"Obviously, you and I are not the same," Hagop mused. "You're a Jew. I'm a true Armenian."

"What is a true Armenian?"

"One who only aspires to be Armenian, speak Armenian, eat Armenian, marry Armenian. A true Christian." Saying this, he took out his knife and made a small incision in the burlap bag against which he was leaning. A tickle of sunflower seeds fell into his hands, and he popped a handful in his mouth.

Albano did not like when Hagop did these kinds of things, but he was tired of fighting him about it. Still he pointed out, "Aren't Greeks also Christian?"

Hagop spat out sunflowers shells at a pigeon. "Armenians are the only true Christians," he said.

Albano had heard it all before. Lately, that undertone of nationalistic and religious pride seeped into everything. He shook his head. "Greeks say the same thing. It's nonsense. These days each ethnic group is pulling the blanket toward itself and away from its brothers."

Hagop ignored him. "My father thinks we need to return to our roots, go back to the stricter rules of the Armenian millets. We must remain pure of race. Father says we need to start by forbidding people to intermarry. Then both races lose. The children are forever bastards and communities are weakened."

"Your father says all this?" Albano asked feebly.

"Each ethnic group should separate," Hagop announced. "Those who already have intermarried must not be allowed to have children, and the new cases must be made a punishable offense, with tribunals."

"But … why?"

"So that we can achieve a pure race."

Albano's heart sank. "What is so desirable about a pure race?"

Hagop thought for a moment, "I don't know. I will have to ask Father." He spat sunflower seeds shells on the ground. "I have to go. I'm sick of doing what he wants. I'm a man of action, not destined to live in the basement of a bakery. As soon as I'm old enough to enlist, I will. I'm wasting time here. I want to help my people."

"Soldiers need bread. You can help your people by making it."

Hagop snorted at this preposterous notion, spat out the last of the sunflower seed shells, and left. Albano waited for half an hour before walking across the width of the quayside toward the Levantine quarter.

There, among the white-washed stone walls of beautiful villas, climbing jasmine, fountains, and statues, it was almost possible to forget the war. There were no soldiers in sight, only privilege, and beauty, luxury, peace, and comfort. Between the houses, he glimpsed the private docks where pristine boats bobbed gently. He thought of what it would be like to have a boat that could take him away from shore on a whim. He thought of what it would be like to have enough money to buy safety. With money, he thought, a lot of it, you could even buy invincibility from the war.

He spotted Xandra, who had already started her deliveries. She was dressed entirely in black, with petticoat and layer upon layer of black clothes, an apron, and long sleeves, and she had tied her hair back. When she saw him, she beamed and set down the heavy straw backpack that contained the pastries. Albano approached the bag, which was enormous. "This is far too heavy for you. You will hurt yourself," he said, trying to make it seem effortless for him as he hoisted it up and onto his back.

"Business is good," she said. "We have more orders. Mother says the war makes people crave sweet things."

They set out the way they had now done for over a year: Albano reading the addresses and the items ordered, Xandra retrieving them from the basket, tapping at doors, and handing out the baked goods to servants. If things went smoothly and no one tried to make conversation with her, Xandra and Albano would be able to spend some free time together. Thirty minutes at most. Thirty minutes stolen from a life that conspired to keep them apart. It wasn't enough, but this is what they could have, and they were thankful for it.

Albano was in love with Xandra. And Xandra was in love with Albano. This time was all they had, but it was theirs and theirs alone. Neither mentioned their fear that one day she might be called to another task, that one of her little sisters might be told to take over the route. Neither mentioned Hagop anymore, fiery Hagop, whom they sensed could never be told about their daily meeting in the Levantine quarter, let alone about their love.

When the basket was empty and the deliveries made, they headed toward the beach. As they stepped in the sand, Albano removed his sandals, but Xandra had to remain clothed from head to toe, for modesty. They arrived under their tree, that gnarled thing with wiry black trunk and spotty leaves that had decided to grow in the sand, against nature. The tree provided them with shade and enough privacy so that they could be together mostly unseen and undisturbed. Before them, the Aegean Sea shimmered, and sailboats glided in the distance. They spoke in Armenian, with Xandra gently correcting his diction. They never ran out of things to say because everything either of them said was interesting to the other. In the early days, they had spoken about their families, the war, their apprehensions. But now they were speaking of more dangerous things. The future. A future where a Jewish boy and an Armenian girl could have a life together.

As they spoke, Albano feasted on the sight of her: her large, marvelous eyes and the way she covered her mouth with one hand when she laughed.

"I overheard servants talking," Xandra said. "The Levantines are feeling anxious. Levantine families with French or British ancestry worry they might soon be considered the enemy."

"Most of them have never set foot in Europe."

"It is hard to imagine anyone could be fearful possessing all that wealth."

"I want to be rich one day," Albano said.

"I don't need you to be rich, Albano."

"The rich can marry whoever they want, even in Smyrna."

They watched the sea in silence, dreaming their shared dream. Xandra smiled mysteriously and looked at her hands. "A rich man such as yourself might prefer those fair-haired European ladies with their nice manners."

"I will never marry anyone else but you."

She looked at him eagerly. "If I didn't exist, if you had never met me, would you not rather marry one of those beautiful European ladies, rather than a Jewish peasant girl from a village, even a pretty one?"

Albano smiled and shook his head, sensing the trap. On occasion Xandra needed to hear that she was the only one, the most beautiful one, and that there would never be anyone else in his heart, so he told her so. But later, after they parted and headed back to their respective quarters, Albano had to admit to himself that he was smitten by Europeans. Not by the ladies, but by the entire lifestyle. It was not just about the blissfulness of wealth; it was the idea of being somebody. To be recognized and respected within an upper layer of society was something he would have liked very much. It was clear to him now that the money he and Hagop made, which had seemed like a fortune before, was laughable in comparison to the way the Levantine families lived. As impossible as it may be, these riches, these clothes, these beach houses, and cars, and servants, those were things he wanted now, for himself and for Xandra.

As he made the trek toward the Jewish quarter, remnants of a conversation with Hagop a few days earlier polluted his thoughts. They had been sitting on the dock, facing the water, waiting for the next steamer and Hagop had said, "When the time comes to enlist, we will need to know which side to fight for."

War was on everyone's mind, but he had been making a conscious effort not to think about how it would affect him. "Perhaps war will come and go before we are of age to enlist," Albano had answered. "But I guess we'll have to fight for whatever side the Empire is on."

"The Turks do not speak for the entire Ottoman Empire!" Hagop had snapped, raising his voice. "Why should I enlist into an army that wants to annihilate my people?"

Albano kept his voice low and spoke in Armenian should there be a spy here on the quay. Lately, even he, the foolish optimist, had begun to function in a state of mistrust and suspicion. From the onset of war, everyone could now be a spy. There were so many mingling cultures in Smyrna that it was impossible to be sure where to place your allegiance. "It's hard to tell what is true. The Armenian papers speak of mistreatments by the Turkish nationals, but the Turkish newspapers don't."

"And it is those you choose to believe? They are spreading false rumors that Armenians are on the side of the Russians. Why would we be? We have nothing to gain by that!" Hagop had spoken loudly and in Arabic. He wanted to be heard, to set the record straight. But he switched to speaking Armenian to add, "This is just an excuse to persecute us. The Turks have always hated us."

It would have been easier to agree with his friend, but Albano thought it his duty to reason with him. "Why would they hate you?"

"They hate us because we are Christian."

"The Greeks are Christian. Do the Turks hate them too?"

"The Greeks are powerful and can defend themselves. The Armenians are not."

"You and your family have not suffered," Albano said, his heart in a vise. Hagop, so full of street sense, so able to make light of situations, now held the same incendiary discourse as everyone else. War seemed to galvanize spirits in ways that peace never did. People found reasons to hate when what was needed was calm and reason. Racial and ethnic tensions had always existed. But now it was bubbling up to the surface, and those most strident and hateful awaited, like a pack of wolves concealed in the darkness of the woods, for the moment to pounce.

"Sometimes you want to see nothing and understand nothing, Albano! You want to convince yourself that everyone is good. If you don't believe me, then come to my house. Tonight. There is a meeting. You will hear for yourself."

Albano looked at the many soldiers on the quay and the anxious Europeans who lined up at the dock with their families. He thought of Xandra. A new chill overtook him. "The war cannot come between us, Hagop? It won't, will it?"

Hagop put his arm around Albano's neck. "You and I are brothers. Our bond cannot be broken."

****

The room was filled with men from the Armenian quarter. The grey-skinned Yori, who lived at night by his bakery's furnace, his brother Petrak, close-shaven and fiery-eyed, Emmanuel, the shoemaker and community elder who was permanently hunchbacked from a lifetime bending over his work.

There was also Silla, the butcher, who had once killed his own daughter and severed her head. He had spent three months in prison for it and now walked around the quarter like a shining example of fatherly morality. There were ten other men Albano did not know. The men spoke in a low, grave tone, furrowed their brows, and pulled on their pipes. Dinner was served. Albano and Hagop, knowing their place, sat at a corner of the table and did not speak. Ina hurried around, putting down trays of bread, and in the center of the table a large dish of fragrant goat stew with olives. Xandra served wine in every goblet. The men ate as they discussed business, farming, the war, and the price of goods. Albano was careful never to look at Xandra for even a moment.

When the food was eaten, the women served bowls of dates and figs and poured Artsakh into small glasses. It wasn't until they left the room that Yori finally addressed the old man who sat among them and had not said a word thus far. The old man had a terrible time eating. His hands trembled so violently that he could hardly bring his spoon to his lips, which were nearly gray. His entire face was burnt and peeling. His left eye was clouded and opaque. He was emaciated as only the very old, and the very sick, could look. His clothes were too large for him, and his thin neck and wrists protruded from his shirt. It wasn't until he started to speak that Albano realized that the man wasn't old at all. He was so frail and sick that he looked twice his age.

"He came two days ago," Hagop whispered to Albano. "He has done nothing but sleep and eat. At first, when he ate he got terribly sick. He arrived with just shreds of clothing on his body. The community has been taking care of him."

"Tell us what you saw, Toros," Yori told the man with gentle insistence.

Toros gazed up from his plate as if surprised. When he understood what was expected of him, he set down his spoon and with great effort began to speak.

"I saw. I saw everything," he said in a hollowed voice, looking at no one. "Then I escaped. And then I walked. And then I was found." Toros paused as if worn out from the effort of speaking. But perhaps he was hesitating to continue. In the room, there was silence. "It was morning when they came. Men on horses, with guns, screaming and going through the village. There was no warning. It all happened in a few hours.... The Turks come in with their horses and their bayonets, and they tell us we're being relocated. Every Armenian in the village must go. They say we must leave at once or be shot. And then it goes very fast. Everyone is sent into a panic and a frenzy of preparation. We are given less than an hour. All the Armenian families are rounded up. Few can bribe their ways out because we have nothing left, no commerce, no farming, from all the men being gone into the military service."

"But you were still in the village?"

Toros looked up and said fiercely, "When they say that men must report to military service, don't go. We think now that this is how they weakened the village. They tell the men they have to report to military service, and they wait for all the men to be gone to go after the women and old people." He pointed to his face. "I am blind in one eye, so I stayed back in the village when all the men left."

Yori asked, "They said that the Armenian presence creates unrest with Turkish villagers. Was it true in your village?"

Toros shrugged, disgusted. "There was no unrest. We have been living side by side with the Turks, and there was no more unrest now than before." He lifted his glass of wine with a trembling hand and drank avidly, red liquid coming down his chin. And then he began again, as if in a trance. "Fear is in our heart as we leave the village in silence. There is only the cries of children and the shouting of soldiers. Fear is in our heart but also hope. We hope that they are telling the truth. The women hope that they are taking us somewhere where they will be reunited with the men. I feel hopeful because we're all together in a group of one hundred people, and it is reassuring. The Turks order us to bring nothing but what we can carry. So the women pack up only what we can lift. Many have babies in their arms. The children old enough to walk must walk. The old people too old to walk must walk. Some are taken from their beds, and they must walk too, and those who can't walk, we have to carry. As we leave the village, we feel terrible sadness and disbelief that we are being uprooted from our ancestral homeland. The other villagers, the Jews, the Greeks, the Muslims, watch us leave. Some spit and throw stones at us. Others weep for us. We weep too. But deep down, we think we will come back.

"As we walk inland, we pass through many other villages. Here too the Armenian families are made to leave their homes. Our group grows. We wonder where they will take us. Sometimes we see a familiar face from a nearby village, and this brings us some warmth and courage, to be reunited. We act brave, and we try not to upset the children who already are tired and hungry. So, the group is quite large now, perhaps five hundred of us. And the men on horseback are all around us like we are a herd of cattle. We've been walking for hours. Those who slow down or try to rest are threatened by the Turks on horses. And so, adults carry the young ones, the healthy carry the sick, and we go on.

"Later there are many thousands of us walking in silence but for the cries of children. When night comes, we sleep on the dirt without making any fire; anyway, there is no food to cook. Children are asking for food and water, but there is none.

"In the morning, we wake up to the smell of excrement. Everyone asks where the camp is. The Turks now take to whipping us when we ask questions. Now some of us notice that the Turks, unlike us, have food in carts pulled by horses. They have food and water for days, but only for themselves. We are afraid of what this means. There are rumors that we are being taken to Mesopotamia or Syria, but that is much too far away to be believable.

"By mid-day, no encampment has appeared. It is hot, and we are very thirsty. We pass a river. We all rush to collect water into our gourds. A few men throw themselves into the river and begin to swim away. That's when the Turks start shooting. People stop jumping in the water. We watch the bodies of the men float down the river, but now we also see other bodies, coming from upstream. Now we know that more of this is happening upstream to others, and we are terrified.

"That night is bad. We hear the wails of women who are being raped, but we can't do anything without risking being shot, and so we hold the children closer. In the morning, we wake up to see that several have found a way to run away from the group. But those who have children or old people in their care have stayed. Their absence enrages the guards, and now they watch us even more. We realize that the chance to escape is gone. Now there is only desert ahead of us and desert behind us, and those who are seen trying to escape are gunned down. I know that I missed my chance to run, and I hope for another river.

"On the third day, no one has any food and the water collected at the river is gone from our gourds.

"We keep going. When we've been walking for four days, people start to collapse from dehydration. We witness with terrible sadness when one of us falls. Some people are simply too old, too sick, or too young to survive several days of walking in the hot sun with hardly any water or food. We are not allowed to bury the dead. We are threatened with guns and bayonets if we stop. So we leave the bodies behind, and people weep. As we walk past them, we grab rocks, and everyone puts one rock upon the dead bodies, to try to show respect for them as much as we can.

"We are heading deeper into the desert. There are no more rivers. We see a long black line on the horizon. People. At first, we're excited. We think it is the camp. We are about to rest. We will have food and water. But we get closer, and soon we suspect the terrible truth: these are hundreds of thousands of villagers from across Anatolia. This is not a camp: these people are walking just like we are, and we're about to join their ranks. When we meet them, we finally understand everything.

"They are covered in sand and dirt. Sand inside their mouths. Flies all over, and filth. These people are walking skeletons without any light left in their sunken eyes. They don't speak. Many in their group have also died; all the old people are gone. What is left are the few men, the older children, and the mothers. The mothers refuse to give up. They continue going until the last one of her children dies, which is usually the babies because they are fed until their mothers' last drop of milk or their last breath. There is a mother who carries two children in her arms. They are both dead and covered in flies, but she will not let go of them. When the woman falls to her knees, the guards do nothing. I see that the mother has set her babies on the dirt and has covered them with her body. They don't shoot her. They are saving their bullets. There is no need to shoot her because she will die anyway here in the desert as soon as the group has moved on.

"That is the purpose of the walk. There is no relocation. There is no camp. They are just walking and starving us until we all die. And so, we continue walking. The guards aren't as vigilant, only patient. They know that even if we escape, we cannot go back on our tracks, it is too far, and we are all so weak.

"One morning, I don't know how long we have walked, I awaken, and the children aren't crying anymore. All of them have died. And I tell myself it is better to be killed than this. I decide that I will not continue. Before that, I felt a responsibility to stay with the group, but not now that the children are dead. Now I decide I will run away. And if they shoot me, they shoot me. I know that they want my death anyway, and I decide to choose how I will die.

"The guards need water for themselves, and so they steer the group along a river. When we get to the river, thousands of us plunge. They are shooting, and many are killed. But I am not shot. I float with whatever strength I have left. I don't know how long I float, maybe a day. As I float down the river, I think of the mothers with their babies. Then I open my eyes, and it is days later. I am inside a house, in a bed. I'm in a village. People have found me and rescued me."

"So there were still Armenians in some of the villages?" Emmanuel the shoemaker asked the man.

Toros shook his head in disbelief. "I woke up in a Muslim house. They found me and rescued me. And they knew I was Armenian. They helped me at great risk to themselves." The men in the room let this information sink in, drawing on their pipes. "When I could walk again I set out and found my way to Smyrna," Toros concluded.

"Do you think anyone made it to Mesopotamia?" Petrak asked.

"I want to believe that some did," Toros said. "I want to believe that there is a camp in Mesopotamia or elsewhere. But everything I wanted to believe didn't come true. Until their last breath, the people from our village hoped that God would take care of us. Even as we were made to step over the bodies of our family members, we continued praying to God not to forget us."

"Could you have rebelled earlier on?" Silla asked, embarrassed by the insinuation that they were in any way responsible for their fate. But he was right to ask. It was important to know.

"Without weapons?" Toros said, visibly exhausted by the effort of reliving the events. "How can unarmed women and children and the elderly rebel? Most of the men were away at military service."

"What about all the men in military service?" Petrak asked. "Where are they?"

Toros only shook his head to signify that he didn't know.

Petrak exclaimed, "There is no military service for us! It is a ploy to round up Armenian men without raising suspicion. Once we report to service and arrive in camps, they kill us."

"How can you be sure?" Yori asked.

"They walk the helpless women and children to their death," Emmanuel the Shoemaker said, "and you think they are keeping the men alive?"

Silla said, "The villagers were caught by surprise. If they had known the truth like we do, they would have fought. They believed they had a better chance of surviving if they went along. But they did not know of the plan until they were too weak to revolt. Once they understood the plan, it was too late; there was little they could do."

"Still, the Turks had horses and weapons," Petrak said.

"But the villagers had the greater number," Silla insisted. "They could have attacked them with rocks. They could have overtaken them."

"What can we do to prepare?" Emmanuel mumbled as though to himself.

"Believe nothing they say," Petrak said. "When they tell us to turn in our weapons, give them some, and hide the rest. When they say to report to military service, hide in the mountains. When they come to take our women and children, attack."

"Governor Rami Bey won't let any of this happen to the citizens of Smyrna. We're not like those hidden from sight in remote villages—"

"Rami Bey could easily be overthrown, and then we have no defender," Petrak interrupted.

Yori shook his head. "This is a big city. All of Europe has political or business interests here. There is the Red Cross. There are ships of every European country moored in the bay, and the eyes and ears of every government's representatives are on us. They would not let any of this happen here because...." But no one was listening to him.

Silla turned to Petrak and said, "We should take the offensive."

Emmanuel spoke. "What we must do is watch for the signs when they start to imprison or kill our leaders, draft the young men, tell us to hand in our weapons because we're allegedly a threat ... those are all the signs we should watch for. So far, nothing of the sort has taken place here."

"What do you think your family will do?" Albano asked Hagop later on when they had walked to the edge of the Armenian quarter. "Will you hide as Toros said to do? Will you wait? Will you fight?"

"You Jews have it good," Hagop said. "You make alliances; you see where the wind is blowing. Armenians aren't like that. It's not so easy for us. We have pride. We won't just hide. We want revenge for our people."

"The Jews are worried too," Albano said.

Hagop scoffed at the thought. "What is it the Jews ever have to worry about?"

"We are all the same, Hagop. We all have to decide the best course of action to survive."

"All the same, you say? How about the Turks? When they kill our children and rape our women? Are they like us?"

"There are monsters among them, it's true. But also, righteous people, like the Muslims who rescued Toros."

Hagop laughed an angry laugh. "One good Muslim out of a thousand and you think that Muslims and Armenians are the same?"

Albano wanted to mention the butcher and what he had done to his daughter. "Men have a bestial nature. Jews, Muslims, Christians, it does not matter. It is within some of us more than others. As is goodness."

In the months that followed, calm and reason did not prevail. War, which unified in patriotism countries such as Germany, Italy, and France, seemed to tear apart the Empire. The sense of nationalism within the various groups turned from pride to zeal. Religious and ethnic strife between people who had coexisted for centuries reawakened inexplicably over one rumor, one newspaper headline, or one comment from a neighbor of a different ethnicity. It was as though sleepy little sparks of hatred spontaneously ignited everywhere. How long before those sparks turned into uncontrollable blazes?

Albano needed to know what to think of the Armenian man's account. Had he told the truth or was he a crazy man? He wanted to ask Uncle Joshua what he thought, but he did not have the kind of relationship with his uncle in which he felt safe to ask questions.

One morning when he came back from the quay and entered his uncle and aunt's house, a great surprise greeted him. Uncle Moshe was sitting at the kitchen table.

"Uncle Moshe! You are here? No one said you were coming."

"Your Uncle Moshe surprised us all," Uncle Joshua said. He tried to keep his tone light, but his face was tense.

Aunt Sadie was pacing the room, resentful. "I had no time to prepare the house."

Uncle Moshe's mustache was shaved off, and his ample girth ampler than it had been two years before. "I refuse to believe this young man is my child nephew. Impossible!" he said in his booming voice as he squeezed Albano in his arms.

"It is truly me, Uncle Moshe!" Albano laughed. "Are you here to sell rugs? How long will you stay?"

Uncle Moshe looked him up and down and, away from Uncle Joshua's and Aunt Sadie's earshot, said, "I have seen rabbinical students before, and they do not usually look this healthy. The ones I have seen have glabrous, ashen faces and the delicate physiques of those whose sole physical effort is to squint at the Torah." Because of his daily treks from the Jewish quarter to the quay and the heavy lifting of newspapers and pastry baskets, Albano looked healthy indeed. Uncle Moshe raised a suspicious eyebrow. "And you obviously carry the Torah up and down Mount Pagus as well, what with those muscles?" Albano could not suppress a smile.

All, including Cousins Zev and Cousin Uri, sat down for dinner. They learned that Uncle Moshe was only here for a few days to settle some business. He was on his way to Chile and Argentina where he would, as he put it, wait out the war.

"When the war is over, I will return to France and try to obtain citizenship," he said.

"Why would you want to become French, Uncle Moshe?" Cousin Zev asked.

"My nephew, the Ottoman Empire is dying. The millets are deteriorating. The Empire is at risk of becoming a patchwork of disparate countries, and who knows how favorable the area will become to Jews." He turned to Uncle Joshua. "Perhaps you should consider a change of life sometime soon, Brother."

Uncle Joshua sighed. "My business is here. My life is here. At my age, to start over—"

"And find ourselves surrounded with people of your sort?" Aunt Sadie interrupted shrilly. "The problem with you, Moshe, is that you have no attachments. We have a community here; people respect us."

"Well, you can stay here if you wish, and your husband can move to France," Uncle Moshe mused. Aunt Sadie gave Uncle Moshe a murderous look.

"But why France?" Uncle Joshua asked.

"France values artists, intellectuals. There is an openness of minds," he remarked and paused. "People with my ... predisposition are left alone for the most part."

"What predisposition is that, Uncle Moshe?" Albano asked.

Uncle Moshe opened his mouth to answer, but an uneasy exchange of glances between Uncle Joshua and Aunt Sadie silenced him. "You must visit someday, Albano. I have many friends in Paris I'd love you to meet." Aunt Sadie scoffed at this and stomped out of the room.

Later, during dinner, the men all agreed that no matter the unrest throughout the Empire, for now, the city was as racially eclectic, energetic, and prosperous as ever. "To imagine Smyrna any other way is impossible," Uncle Joshua said.

Albano, who had been sitting nearby and missed not a beat of the conversation, found the courage to ask his uncles the question that had been torturing him. "Is it true?" he asked, "what is said about the Armenians who are outside Smyrna? That terrible things are happening to them?"

"Why does it matter to you, dear boy?" Uncle Moshe asked.

"I have an Armenian friend now."

Uncle Joshua nodded, unconcerned. "It is probably true." To which he added, "But not in Smyrna,"

"Why not, Uncle?"

"Because our city holds a privileged place in the heart of everyone, including the Turks. Smyrna is a city destined for the enjoyment of life, for trade, a city where people take pleasure in the diversity of cultures."

"I'm afraid that you are naïve about Smyrna, my dear brother," Uncle Moshe said. "There are persecutions against Armenians, it is true, and they are widespread. It is only a matter of time before it reaches this city." He turned to Albano. "You should tell your friend to leave."

Albano felt a terrible chill. "But where should he go?"

"Anywhere outside the Empire."

"But Uncle Moshe, war is everywhere."

"Then your friend is out of luck," Uncle Joshua said.

Uncle Moshe patted Albano on the head. "At the first hint of racial persecutions, there are three things a man can do: fight, run, or hide. It seems that when outnumbered, one would be mad to attempt the first. So I say, run."

"Hide! Hide is better," Uncle Joshua said.

"You don't think it cowardly to run or hide, Uncle Moshe?" Cousin Zev asked.

"For your enemy to win, he must eliminate you. For you to win, you must refuse to be eliminated by any means at your disposal. If fighting decreases your chance of survival and running and hiding increases them, it is mathematical."

"But what of honor?" Cousin Zev pressed.

Uncle Moshe dismissed this with a raised hand. "Warmongers invented the notion of honor and cowardice so that they can put weapons in men's hands and have them do their bidding. It is quite a clever scheme, truly."

"We are Jewish, so we are safe," Uncle Joshua said peremptorily, as though this had been the sole thought on his mind. "When we Jews have a country to call our own, then we'll worry about it."

"I disagree, Uncle Joshua," Uncle Moshe said. "Jews should always worry." To Albano, he said, "Keep your ears and eyes on alert. When people start nationalistic rhetoric, all a Jew needs to hear is the drumbeat of anti-Semitism. It was always the world's favorite form of xenophobia. Anti-Semitism has been developed and perfected over thousands of years."

"What would happen to the millets if there was a dissolution of the Empire?" Albano asked. "Would the Jews be forced to go into exile the way it was after the Spanish Queen chased us away?"

"That is the bad thing about having no land to claim as our own," Uncle Joshua noted somberly.

"If the Ottoman Empire were to decide to turn against its Jews, then we would go elsewhere. As Jews have done for centuries before." Uncle Moshe said gravely. "It has not been pleasant, but it has made us who we are."

"But you said it yourself, Jews have enemies everywhere," Uncle Joshua pointed out.

"We also have settled everywhere, and so we count many friends at every far corner of the earth. In some countries, Jews have even shaped policies. That is why I choose France. It's a country where, since the Dreyfus affair, anti-Semitism is clearly unfashionable."

"Ha! Imagine that," Uncle Joshua said. "All the Jews of the Ottoman Empire taking refuge in France. Anti-Semitism wouldn't be out of fashion for long."

****

Four years later, in 1918, the Great War ended, and as Uncle Moshe predicted, the Ottoman Empire, which had been on the losing side, was partitioned, cut into chunks like a cake. And while Europe got busy rebuilding itself, a new war started in the region, this time between Greece and the Turkish National Movement. Smyrna, placed under Greek control, was for the moment protected.

Albano and Hagop were sixteen years old. As if by magic, their bodies now manifested hair and muscles, and they had grown to the size of men. Hagop was taller than Albano by a head, and he had bulk. Albano was still rail thin, no matter how many Armenian pastries he clandestinely ingested. Yet it was Albano who provoked the admiration of women, whether this was something he wished for or not. Hagop used to find that endlessly funny, but now there was resentment in his voice when he said that Albano was too handsome a friend and that he was hurting his own chances with women.

Hagop didn't know that Albano had no interest in stealing women away from him or anyone. His heart, mind, and blood were so thoroughly occupied by thoughts of Xandra it excluded thoughts of anyone else.

Now that they looked like men and had the steady income from the sale of newspapers, they no longer sat on a rock near the dock, but at the terraces of cafés. That morning, Albano and Hagop were sipping the bitter Italian espressos they had acquired a taste for as they read the headlines of newspapers. The more sensational the headlines, the better the sales for the day. Albano loved that moment in the early morning, reading the paper, sitting at a café terrace. It made him feel cosmopolitan and sophisticated, like the European men around them, or so he hoped. He looked across the pier. Smyrna was back to looking very much the same as it had before the war, with Europeans promptly returning to their commerce and interests in Asia Minor. But something in the mood had changed. The men in uniforms no longer displayed any gaiety unless they were drunk. Those who had returned from the war in one piece had come back humiliated. Their faces were hard, their eyes those of killers. The mistrust between ethnic groups was at a high, each suspecting his neighbor of being a spy, a turncoat, a coward, a fomenter, or a crook.

Hagop, who had been reading quietly across the table from Albano, let out a roar of frustration and crumpled the Turkish newspaper he was reading. "Armenians are not betraying the Empire!" he cried out. Across the terrace, men peered at him from above their opened newspapers.

"Who is betraying who?" Albano said softly, hoping that Hagop would mirror his tone.

"It says it, right here," Hagop said, tapping the printed words violently with his finger. "It says that the Armenians plan to join the Russian forces. Lies! All lies! Just another scheme to unleash the fury of the Turks."

Albano shifted uneasily in his chair. He looked around. Hagop needed to be careful. Why did he refuse to be careful? "None of that has reached Smyrna," he said.

"Smyrna? Who thinks of Smyrna? It is happening all over," Hagop exclaimed. "They arrive in Armenian stores demanding to collect war contributions, and when the merchants refuse, they loot and set the shop on fire!" Hagop was angrier these days. His fiery temperament could barely be contained. He was angry with this father, angry with his community, which he accused of being too passive, angry with the Turks, the Greeks, and the Jews. "And what about the mass deportations of Armenians away from the coast?" Hagop continued. "How can you speak of Smyrna alone when we know that the entire populations of villages are being displaced, or worse." He was referring to the persistent rumors of Armenians being marched to their certain death under the guise of relocation. The story that Toros had told them years ago had been echoed by many more witnesses and was impossible to ignore. Yet such inhuman cruelty toward civilian population was not something Albano wanted to imagine possible.

That afternoon, Albano, as he had continued to do in secret from Hagop for years now, walked to the Levantine quarter to help Xandra with her baskets. The risks of doing this were something he and Xandra never discussed. Perhaps they both had managed to convince themselves that they were doing nothing wrong. But Albano knew better. He knew the contents of his thoughts, which were not innocent thoughts, far from it. Now the way he looked at Xandra was hungrier, more desperate, and nothing felt simple anymore. It was no longer enough to see her or speak to her. He urgently wanted to touch her, and kiss her, and hold her in his arms, but there was no place where this could happen. Eyes were everywhere and a boy and a girl, even from the same ethnicity, especially these days, could get into great trouble being seen as much as holding hands in public. Already this morning, he had twice been stopped for identity checks. Once, Greek soldiers had asked to see his papers. Another time, he was asked to provide proof of residence by Turkish policemen. The racial tension was tremendous, and uniformed men needed no excuse to stop those they wanted to harass. The uniforms themselves appeared to give them license to misbehave as they wished, abusing their power, taking bribes, or threatening populations the instant their superiors had their backs turned. There was so much of this going on that to take on cases of such misdeeds one by one was impossible. No tribunal, civilian or military, had that kind of manpower. Each time he saw Xandra, Albano tried to make her feel safe and at peace. But in truth, time felt as though it was closing in on them. Travel routes out of the country were cut. There was nowhere to go unless by boat, and even that was not safe. In the last few months, to make matters worse, Xandra's parents had begun to discuss whom she should marry. She was, after all, sixteen. With all this on their minds, Albano was surprised to find Xandra happy. He had to wait until the end of their delivery route to find out why. As soon as the two were alone on the beach, she said, "I know what I will do so that they don't marry me!"

"What is it?"

"Someone needs to take care of my parents in old age. I will volunteer to remain unmarried. Mother loves me best. If she agrees, then we could convince my father."

Albano considered this. "They will want to marry you first, not only because you're the oldest, but because you're the most beautiful one."

She grew pale. "So, this is what gets in the way of my happiness?" she asked. "Beauty? If it didn't mean that you would stop loving me, then I would make it so that I am no longer beautiful."

"That is impossible. That cannot be changed."

"There are ways," she said, her teeth clenched. "I could scar myself, cut off my hair. I could break my front teeth."

Her intensity upset him so that he decided to laugh it off. "Oh, that would never work. Even with no teeth, no hair, and missing a leg, you would still be the most beautiful girl in all of Smyrna."

"You would not want me either if I would be ugly and disfigured." She added sadly, "But I can't bear being married to anyone if I can't be with you."

"Men are being drafted every day. People might not think of marrying their daughters to men who might not return. That is what you should tell your family to gain time."

"If men are being drafted, then you could be as well, as soon as next year when you turn of age." She tore at the skin around her fingernails with her teeth. Lately, her hands had become the battle zone of her anxiety. "There is nothing Hagop wants more than to fight."

"Hagop has not been the same," Albano said. "You think he suspects something about us?"

Her back straightened and, looking out at the sea, she said, "If Hagop suspected something about us, he would have long ago killed me with his bare hands."

Albano felt the hair on his skin rise on end. "You cannot mean that."

She shook her head. "My brother is furious at everything and everyone. All he talks about is enlisting, and he would if my father didn't threaten him with bodily harm. Hagop feels powerless about what is happening to our people. We all do. He is angry. And he'll never show if he is afraid or sad. That is his way."

"I had a dream about you," Albano said soothingly. "In my dream, you walked in through a front door with marble columns on each side, and everywhere there was the smell of jasmine and roses. A servant took your shoes and washed your hands. All around, there were beautiful blooming trees, and fountains, and rugs. You were dressed in lace, and silver, and pearls. Servants stood, waiting for your command, one in every room. You sat, and they brought you mint tea and rose-flower flavored pastries." Albano did not mention that it was a daydream more than a dream, that he was in it, and that he had imagined much more afterward.

Xandra, forgetting for a moment about being seen, placed her palm on his cheek and sighed, "Albano, my dreamer. To live this kind of life you would have to be born into it."

Albano shook his head adamantly. "That is not true. There are men who started without a name and family fortune who now live in abundance."

She laughed, "Crooks you mean?"

"My Uncle Moshe was born right here in Smyrna. But he took his chances, traveled the world, and became a rug merchant."

"Your uncle is an exception."

"Xandra, I will do this. I too can be an exception! And you will be my exceptional bride."

Xandra smiled her beautiful smile. "I do not want a castle, or lace and pearls. But I do want to be your bride." Then she added somberly, "But people here will never let us marry. Not for the next hundred years. Things have been the way they are for centuries, and they cannot change."

"After the war, when the sea roads reopen, we could sail to Europe. I think that if I were to ask my uncle, he would let me work for him in France. We would tell no one that I am Jewish and you are not. In fact, my uncle says that no one would ask."

She looked at him. This was not a vision or a dream: this was a plan. This was a possibility. "The two of us, in Paris?" she murmured.

"I can speak Armenian nearly without an accent. We can both say that we're Armenians."

"Let's be Jewish then! It is much safer than being Armenian." She set her hand between them so that her baby finger touched his. Together they watched the sea and the sails of the boats heading, they imagined, toward the beautiful architecture of Paris, the wide boulevards, the many cars, the shops and restaurants, which they imagined as a larger, more magnificent version of Smyrna.

Later that evening Albano walked up to the Armenian quarter, nervous as he was every time he was invited into Hagop and Xandra's house. Their mother, Ina, was a kind woman who did not mind a Jew sharing their food and had taken a liking to him. The three little sisters, Clara, Agda, and Octavia, worshiped him, and the new baby, Tessa, loved pulling on his tassels. Yori wasn't quite as welcoming. He had not shown Albano antipathy, but neither had he quite acknowledged his existence. Albano hoped that if he maintained model behavior and made sure not to look conspicuously Jewish, perhaps one day Yori would, if not warm up to him, at least not act as though he did not exist. One day, Albano would be rich. That day, he would come to Yori and offer him a gold watch like the ones he had seen in the window of the French department store Au Bon Marché over on Frank Street. He would wear a suit and ask him for Xandra's hand in marriage, and Yori would remember that this was the same boy his son trusted, and his wife liked, and he would say yes.

The Armenian community in Smyrna scrambled to secure political allies, but its fate was the last thing on everyone's mind. The Turkish-Greco war raged, rapidly transforming Asia Minor into a battlefield. Tales of horrifying acts perpetrated against Armenians continued to come from every corner of the Empire. But there were also accounts of atrocities against Muslim civilian communities, against Greeks, against Jews. All these terrible things appeared to stop at Smyrna's door, and so they did not see it happen. Was any of this true? The accounts of decimated villages, of mass killings, of beheadings, of rape and torture often conflicted. You would hear the same story from every corner of the city, only depending on who spoke, it had happened to a Muslim community, or a Greek one, or an Armenian one. This inflamed people's spirits and cemented the bitter chasm between the millets.

For the moment, Smyrna remained under Greek control, and in the city reigned a semblance of peace, or rather the sense that everyone was holding their breath. On Smyrna's quay, commerce went on. The sky was still piercingly blue. Restaurants and cafés were once again full of Europeans. On the sea, the same sailboats, pushed by clement winds, glided on the horizon by the hundreds. But what would happen to the non-Muslims if the Turks won the war and the Greeks lost control of the city? No one felt secure. Nothing seemed permanent. Everyone was afraid.

Over the course of the following months, there was an increase of questionings and searches by the Turkish police in the Armenian quarter. And then, in the last weeks, there had been arrests. A few men were accused of plotting a conspiracy. What could Albano possibly say to Xandra now? How could he assure her that her father and Hagop would be safe?

He could not. So he began to prepare.

He did not tell Hagop of his plan. If he did, Hagop might refuse, and if he refused, the way Hagop was these days, thickheaded and angry, he would never go back on his decision. Albano did not tell Xandra either, in part because he thought this would alarm her, and in part because there was no guarantee any of it would work.

Each day, Albano gathered supplies, dried fruit, blankets, firewood, candles, mats, dried meat, and everything he could think of, and he brought everything to his cave. This became the focus of his days, and he no longer even had the pretense of continuing his rabbinical studies, Kohanim or not. It did not matter that Aunt Sadie threatened him, screamed at him, and even beat him at times. In the morning, he would leave. If she didn't want to feed him, he had enough money to feed himself.

Most days he spent in Smyrna. Most nights he spent in the cave, preparing it for Hagop, Xandra, and their family. By now, Uncle Joshua and Aunt Sadie had renounced trying to influence how their sons occupied their time, let alone what Albano did. Cousin Zev was married now and lived with his wife just a few streets away. Cousin Uri had become a shoemaker apprentice and was engaged to the butcher's daughter. As for Albano, they understood that notions of rabbinical studies had long been abandoned and that he preferred to live alone in some cave up on Mount Pagus. People in the Jewish quarter had even taken to calling him the troglodyte.

Through 1919, Xandra's face betrayed her exhaustion and the pressure her family was under. She was pale and too thin in a way that broke Albano's heart. Even so, and even as he prepared in secret, Albano did not seriously believe a day would come when he would have to put his plan into action. And then, in May 1920, that day came.

The instant he saw Xandra arrive at their usual spot in the Levantine quarter, he knew that something bad had happened. "They arrested Emmanuel and his son," she said, her face pale with anguish but her voice steady. "The police came in, and there was nothing they could do."

Albano was stunned by this news. "How is an old shoemaker a risk to them?" he said.

Xandra shook her head. "He has done nothing. Nothing at all!"

"They must see him as a leader of the community," Albano said. "That is what my uncles spoke about. They silence those at risk of speaking their mind first."

"Albano! If that is the case, my father is next on their list."

"You must talk to him. Tell him that perhaps now is the time to hide."

"He doesn't take advice from women, especially not a daughter. And besides, all my father ever wants to do is wake up, and make his bread. You could never tell him to leave his bakery. He is as stubborn as my brother."

Absorbed in their conversation, Albano and Xandra did not see a shadow approaching behind them. When they, at last, noticed him, Hagop was standing a few feet from them, arms crossed over his chest, jaw clenched. "Albano, what are you doing here?" he said icily. His eyes were bloodshot, his skin greenish like a man about to get sick. Albano and Xandra had just been caught speaking to each other, standing inches from each other. The air turned thick. Redness came to Albano's cheeks, and Xandra's face drained of life. They looked at Hagop, finding nothing to say. "Explain to me why you are holding my sister's basket," Hagop said, each of his words pronounced like a threat.

Albano inhaled and said, "I was just in the neighborhood, and I saw Xandra … and I thought I should help her with her heavy load … and—"

Xandra interrupted in a tiny voice. "Hagop, why are you here?"

Hagop's eyes filled with furious tears. "They arrested Father!" he shouted. Albano heard Xandra's quick intake of breath and felt his body drain of strength. "They had a gun to his chest!" Hagop raged. "And not just Father. They arrested about thirty men, Petrak, and Tadeos, and Silla, and Emanuel! They arrested them all!" He lowered his face, his mouth distorted into something that resembled crying, but he stopped himself. "I was just getting home, and I saw them in the distance, so I ran away. They might have taken me too." He lifted his face and looked at Xandra. "This is why I came to get you!" Then with a rage that seemed directed at them, as though they, somehow, were the cause of all this he asked, "What am I supposed to do now?"

Xandra was crying softly, but her voice was steady when she said, "You can't return there."

"I am not a coward!"

"Mother needs you not to be imprisoned. If Father is in jail, it makes you the man of the house. You cannot get arrested. I will go home to Mother while you go into hiding."

"Nowhere is safe, idiot woman," Hagop spat. "They are searching the houses."

"Here is what we need to do, please, Albano," Xandra said. She did not seem like a scared young girl suddenly but like a woman able to think with a cool head. "Beg your aunt and uncle to hide Hagop in the Jewish quarter. The Turks won't be looking for Armenians there."

"I don't belong with Jews!" Hagop roared.

"I will help you," Albano said.

Hagop looked at him with distrust and growled. "Help me? Like you are helping my sister?"

****

This was how Hagop came to live in Albano's cave.

In Smyrna, Armenian men continued to be arrested under pretexts ranging from unpaid taxes to suspicion of treason. Many of the younger men, those most at risk of being sent to labor camps, found their way into hiding. Only the older men were left in the Armenian quarter to haul, make, or sell merchandise. Without supplies and deprived of the men's skills, stores closed one by one. In short succession, Armenian commerce froze, services became paralyzed, finances sank into limbo, and the unprotected women and children became vulnerable to assaults, and soon to hunger. Without Yori to bake goods, and because he had never revealed his techniques to his wife and daughters, there were no bread, cakes, or pastries to sell. Hagop, Xandra, their mother, and four little sisters would soon depend on the money Albano and Hagop had saved up, which was kept safely inside the cave in two leather satchels.

Through winter and spring, Xandra made the long trek up Mount Pagus to bring Hagop the clothes she had washed for him the day before and whatever food she had managed to buy with the money they gave her. She brought with her news of the family and the community. Each day, she would return with a few coins, hidden in the hem of her skirt, which Hagop dispensed parsimoniously, telling her how their mother was to spend it. Yori remained in prison. However, unlike so many of the men, he had not been sent to work camp. They speculated that it was because they needed his baking skills at the prison. Albano continued to sell newspapers in the morning and then rushed back to the cave, in part to distract Hagop, but mostly to keep an eye on him. Confinement did not suit Hagop. He was mad with boredom and frustration. His body was weakened by inactivity, his thoughts circular. During the day, he remained hidden in the cave, pacing and throwing rocks into the stream. At night, when the moon was high, he walked outside, never venturing far from the cave, and threw more rocks. Much of the time he slept, and when he did not sleep, he lamented and raged. One day, after many months of this, Albano was horrified to find Hagop sitting outside the cave in broad daylight. "I need to do something!" Hagop said, seething. "Anything is better than this. Death is better than this!"

They went inside the cave, and Albano rekindled the fire that Hagop had let die. The sun was high, and it was the time of the day when a bit of the sun radiated through the crack between the boulders above, brightening the cave in a way that made the rocks shimmer. This was the most beautiful time of the day inside the cave, but Hagop was immune to the beauty of the cave. The fire grew, basking their skin in a warm orange hue and turning the rough walls to gold. "If you go out during the day, you might reveal yourself and our cave," Albano reminded him softly.

"It will be summer soon. How long can I stay here without losing my mind?"

"If you are seen, someone might report you. Your mother told the police that you had left the country. They would know that she lied. You would put her and yourself at risk."

Hagop crouched and poked at the fire with a stick. Sparks flew. "This mountain is more barren than the moon," he said angrily. "Who will report me? Coyotes? Owls? And why do you come every day? Am I a sick man on his deathbed?"

"I'm only trying to see how you are doing."

"I am a man in jail. I'm every bit as jailed as my father is. This is not freedom you have given me. It is captivity! And you are my jailor."

"But it is better than risking labor camp."

"But I want labor! I need labor. I'm made for action, not for cowering under a rock."

Albano shook his head. This was the same conversation they had every day, with Hagop arguing with him until Albano managed to coax him into staying. Until the next day, when it all started again. "People are not coming back from those camps," he said.

"You and Xandra are making me mad with your help and your kindness. You want to help me? Find me a weapon. Then I would go at night to the jail and I would free the men."

Albano knew better than to tell him that this was madness. With Hagop these days, it was better to say nothing. On the other hand, Albano could see that Hagop never turned his threats to action. He could have left the cave a hundred times, he could have snuck out to the Armenian quarter or anywhere he wished at night, but he had not. Albano took a folded newspaper out of his satchel. "Look, I have a French newspaper left. If you want, I can translate it for you."

Hagop peered at the newspaper with distrust. "Lies. Every written word is a lie, and you are the greatest fool of them all for reading them. And a French newspaper, of course. You and my sister, enamored with France. A couple of fools." Hagop's face hardened. "We need to speak about Xandra," he said, looking at him with suspicious eyes. Albano, disconcerted, poked at the fire. "I've been observing her when she comes here," Hagop continued, "and I have come to a decision." He paused, scrutinizing Albano's face. He got up and began pacing as Albano sat on the mat. "She has too much freedom now that there is no man to watch out for her."

"I will watch out for your whole family," Albano said tentatively.

Hagop was standing behind him, and he felt his stare on the back of his neck. "Tell me, what are my worthless sisters doing these days?"

"They go to school, still. The baby stays with your mother. She and Xandra go to the jail every day with the other women and beg for news of your father. Xandra works very hard, wakes before dawn. She and your mother bake, the best they can to try to make a few sales. You must reconsider how much money you give them. It is not quite enough to make do."

Hagop was not listening. "Men must be looking at Xandra. She needs to marry."

Albano swallowed. Why did he have the impression that Hagop was looking for his reaction? "She is young still," he said, trying to sound unconcerned. He needed to look Hagop in the eyes now. He inhaled, stood up, and faced him.

Hagop had a crooked smile. "But she is not too young for you, heh?"

Albano's mouth went dry. "For me?"

Hagop laughed. "I know you too well. I've seen the way you look at her," he said. "Yes, I know, she is beautiful. And this is why she needs a husband and not a moment too soon. I will choose to whom she should be married. Now that Father is imprisoned, the duty falls to me." He watched Albano's face and added, "And you shall help me look for a suitable husband for her."

Albano felt a sense of dread. Why was Hagop saying all those things now? "Most of the men are gone," he said.

"Not the old ones," Hagop said with a smirk.

"You want Xandra to marry an old man?"

Hagop shrugged, "If that's all that's left. Better an old Armenian than a young Greek." Hagop thought about this and mumbled to himself, "A Greek would be a terrible thing."

Albano decided to try his chance. "You are not worried that a Muslim might court her?" He swallowed and added, "Or a Jew?"

"Even my daft sister wouldn't consider a marriage so far below her," Hagop said with savagery, a bit of spit coming from his mouth. "The point is, I need to safeguard her honor, and the longer we wait, the more we take risks. What if she loses her honor? What use would she be to us then, when no man will marry her? I want you to speak to my mother and ask her to make a list of the men. Bring me the list tomorrow and I will make my choice."

Albano went to the entrance of the cave. He crawled outside to catch his breath and hide his emotion from Hagop. Outside, he leaned against a rock, peering at the horizon. All his thoughts were in a jumble. He felt a sense of mounting panic. Hagop was his friend, and oftentimes he made sense. He was in fact a very smart person. Perhaps he did mean this, in which case Albano could try to talk him out of it. But then why did this feel like a test? Or was it another empty threat, like his threat of leaving the cave, something Albano had to humor for a day or two but was expected to do nothing about?

The day was hot. Judging from the sun, it was about ten in the morning. Xandra would be here soon to bring food. Albano contemplated the arid beauty of the landscape. Long after men were done slaughtering each other, the earth would still stand, and lizards and bushes and seas and clouds would remain, in peace and harmony until the end of time. Animals did not know war. They were not self-aware. Why was it that the only creature God created that could name Him and know Him was the most ferocious, the most mercenary one?

When Xandra appeared at the foot of the hill, his dark thoughts vanished. "Here she is," he murmured to himself. He walked down toward her and around the boulder. From that angle, Hagop could not see them by looking through the crawling space, unless he stepped out of the cave as well. He had to warn her now, about the marriage nonsense, before Hagop saw them.

She should have seen how upset he was, but instead, she jumped at him, nearly taking him off balance. "Albano, I have wonderful news. My father was released! He is back at home!" She laughed a laugh of pure joy.

Albano forgot all about his worries. "How is this possible? This is indeed a great blessing!"

"Some of our Levantine customers you went to see intervened on his behalf. The police had nothing against him. He was no political instigator, just a simple baker. Finally, they let him go. It is thanks to you, Albano! You were the one who spoke to the Levantines. You did this!"

"How is he?"

"He is skin and bones. Mother is delousing him now," she said, laughing. "But you know my father; he said he would start looking for flour and sugar right away and start baking. Oh, Albano, I am so thankful!"

"I am so happy for your family," Albano said, overjoyed. "There is hope now." This would distract Hagop of his notions of marrying Xandra. And it was true that he may have been instrumental in Yori's release. He had written letters and brought them to the Levantine quarter, and had asked the servants to forward them, letters pleading for Yori's most loyal customers to intervene. Even if they had not been reached through their hearts, he made sure to appeal to their stomachs by adding a list of the wonderful pastries which were part of Yori's repertoire, French éclairs, baba au rum, mille-feuilles. And they would have these again when he was released.

"I can't wait to tell Hagop!" she said as they made the turn around the boulder.

"Tell me what?"

Hagop was leaning against the rock at the entrance of the cavern, his arms crossed over his chest. "What news is making both of you smile so much?"

"Father is back, Hagop! He was released."

Instead of his expression changing to a happy one, Hagop looked sourer still. He dangled something white in front of them. "What is this, can you tell me?"

Albano and Xandra looked at what Hagop was holding. It was an embroidered handkerchief. They knew precisely what this was. Xandra had embroidered it herself and given it to Albano on his birthday.

"It is mine. I made it," Xandra mumbled.

Hagop ignored her and only addressed Albano. "Why do you have my sister's handkerchief folded with your things?"

"I ... I found it." Albano lied.

"Where? Where did you find it? And why did you keep it, instead of returning it to her?"

"I found it ... on the ground."

"You are lying to me," Hagop roared. "Did you take it from her or did she give it to you?"

"I took it," Albano lied again.

"Because she cannot give you something," Hagop said, his voice lowered to a threatening hiss. "This would mean she has feelings for you. She cannot have feelings for you. Don't lie to me."

Albano looked at Xandra apologetically. How could he lie about this? "I have ... feelings for her," he admitted.

Hagop threw the piece of cloth to the ground and crushed it with his foot. The beautiful handkerchief became the color of the dirt. "Well, you cannot. She is not for you. She will never be for you."

Albano nodded and looked at his feet. Things made sense now. Hagop's rant about marrying Xandra had indeed been a test. He was planning to confront them all along. "I know this."

Hagop turned to Xandra. "Did you know that our Jewish friend here has this that belongs to you?"

Xandra did not answer. She and Albano looked at each other. Their silence alone was an admission of guilt. Albano felt a terrible uneasiness in the pit of his belly. Hagop advanced toward Xandra and pushed her, making her stumble back. "You have feelings for him too?" he asked menacingly.

Albano took a step toward them, partly to protect Xandra, but mostly to stop her from speaking. If Xandra told her brother the truth, there would be no turning back.

But it was too late, tears sprang from her eyes as she said, shouting almost, "Albano and I are in love!"

The words were not yet out of her mouth when Hagop released like a spring and threw himself at her, pushing her to the ground. It happened so fast that Albano did not have time to stop it. He rushed to Xandra, helped her up, and then stood between her and Hagop.

"Take your hands off her," Hagop screamed, red-faced. "You cannot be in love. You must stop immediately!"

"We did not plan on this," Albano said.

"You have destroyed her honor!" Hagop howled. "How can you betray me, your own brother?"

"Xandra's honor is safe. We have done nothing that...."

"We want to marry one day," Xandra said, defiant now. "It is not for you to stop me. Papa is back. You are not the man of the house now."

Hagop looked at her with disgust. "You can't. You will never. You can't marry a Jew. No one will let you. I won't let you. How long have you two conspired behind my back?" He peered at Albano, his eyes like slits. "I trusted you with my life, and instead you took what was even more precious: my sister's honor."

Albano stood in front of him. "Xandra's honor is intact. We have done nothing. I swear this to you!"

"You think our father will accept this? He will lock her up and never let her out. And he will beat her. He should beat her. In fact, I should beat her myself."

"You will not beat her," Albano said firmly. "Hagop, you must calm down."

"If we can't marry here, then we will go to Europe," Xandra said. "In a place where Armenians and Jews can marry, and where there is nothing you or Papa can do about that!"

Hagop scoffed. "You are a disgrace. You have dishonored yourself and us. You will never find a husband now." He looked at Albano. "Were you going to take my money too?"

"Our money," Albano corrected, "and no, I was not."

To this, Hagop answered nothing and rushed inside the cavern. A minute later he was out again, wearing his sandals. Both money satchels hang over his shoulder.

"Where are you going, Hagop?" Albano cried out. "You know this is the only place where you will be safe."

"I'm taking all the money. This money was never yours, Albano!" Hagop raged. "You were only my tool in amassing it and hiding it."

"The Turkish police are everywhere; you don't have proper papers!" Xandra said.

"Now I know why you wanted me in this cave," Hagop spat. "It was so that you could hide your disgusting secret. You never wanted to protect me! You wanted to keep me in the dark."

"Don't do anything stupid," Albano said.

Hagop turned to Xandra. "You, come," he ordered. But Xandra did not budge. "Come, I say!" he yelled, and seeing she was looking at Albano and not moving, he hurled himself at her. In an instant, he had seized her by her hair. She screamed and he pulled her hair, shook her head hard.

"Hagop, stop!" Albano yelled, but Hagop pulled harder and began to drag Xandra who pinched her lips and remained silent through the pain. "Let go of her; you're hurting her." But Hagop did not let go. Albano lunged at Hagop, all his body forward, his fists forward and put all his weight into a terrible punch to Hagop's stomach. Hagop let go of Xandra's hair and dropped to the ground, doubled over with the pain of the punch as he struggled to breathe.

Xandra rushed to her brother screaming his name, but he lifted himself to his knees and slapped her so hard that she fell to the ground. Before he could make another move, Albano charged Hagop and wrestled him to the ground as Xandra got to her feet. Albano punched Hagop, and Hagop punched him back again and again. "Don't hurt each other, I beg of you!" Xandra cried out.

Albano let go and stepped away from Hagop. He stood, breathing hard, his fists ready for another round. "I'm in love with your sister; it is true. And as long as I am alive, I intend to care for her."

Hagop slowly got up. There was blood coming down his nose, staining his shirt. Instead of charging again, Hagop rushed to the money satchels and grabbed them. "Then you must both die," he said. "And I am the one who will kill you." Hagop's face was distorted into something hideous. There could be no doubt that he meant what he said.

Albano called to Xandra. "Please go in the cave. Now." Xandra stepped back, but she seemed torn between her desire to obey and her fear of leaving him alone to fight her brother. To Hagop, he said, "It is between you and me. One of us will kill the other." Albano's eyes were full of tears, but he was resolute to do whatever it took to protect Xandra.

Hagop looked at Albano in disgust and astonishment. "You called yourself my brother? What brother would betray our whole family like this?"

"I have committed no betrayal. Neither has she. Our love is pure. I will convert to your religion. I will speak only your language. I will learn your customs. Your family might never accept me as one of them, but I will become Armenian. Our children will never know that I once was Jewish."

"You can no more become Armenian than a scorpion can become a hawk," Hagop said, his voice strangled.

Albano knew that behind his friend's murderous rage was sadness and the accumulated losses of an entire people. He shook his head and only said, "I love Xandra with all my heart."

It was as though the words pierced through Hagop, who seemed to deflate. He slumped until he was sitting on the rocky earth with his head in his hands. His shoulders shook violently. "I cannot kill you," Hagop admitted as if to himself.

"I'm sorry," Albano said. "I'm so sorry."

Hagop drew his knees to his chest and, with his face buried in his arms like a child, he sobbed softly, periodically wiping his nose with his sleeve. Albano did not know if he should sit next to his friend and put his arm around him or stand guard and be ready to fight him. But after a few minutes, Hagop stood up. "I cannot stay here," he said. "Not when my brother and sister fornicate before my eyes."

"But we have not! I told you this. You must believe us!"

"I'll go into town," Hagop continued in a hollowed voice. "I will give Father the money so that he can rebuild his bakery. Then I will enlist."

"Take the money," Albano said, thinking that letting go of his share of the money was a small price to pay. "But you cannot return to the Armenian quarter, and you must not enlist. It's a slaughterhouse, throughout the country."

"You give me no choice," Hagop said as he hoisted up the satchels. He began to step down the rocky path. "Tell my whore of a sister that she better not show her face in the Armenian quarter ever again."

Panic and sorrow gripped Albano's heart. "Will you come back for us?" he asked. "Will you tell people about this place?" Hagop pulled the satchels straps tight and walked away without answering.

They watched him walk down the mountain and returned to the cave. Albano shivered despite the heat. Xandra watched him gravely. In the light of the fire, her face was golden and still. Albano slumped on his mat and tried to breathe, but he was overcome with grief. Xandra took both of his hands in hers. They had never been able to face each other, be so close, look at each other in the eyes, and hold hands before. "It's over," she simply said.

"I will speak to your family," he said, mouthing the words but not believing them. "They'll understand."

"I am dead to them now," she said.

"I will go to your house and—"

"They will lynch you, Albano. I know what happens to girls suspected of losing their virginity before marriage. And with you who are not Armenian? Even if my father wanted to forgive me, the community would shun him. He *has* to reject me. He has no other choice."

"Xandra, it's all my fault."

"It is better this way," she said, adding resolutely, "It is what I wanted. It only came early."

"I will think of a solution," he muttered. "There has to be a solution." Xandra did not respond. Instead, she proceeded to undo Hagop's bed. She lifted the blankets and brought then outside. Albano heard her shake the blankets with vigor. Then she did the same thing with the straw mattress, dragging it outside and tapping it violently with a broom. The entire time, Albano sat on his own mat and watched her come and go out of the cave. The harder he thought about the situation, the fewer ideas came to him and the more despondent he felt. He was heartbroken about Hagop's reaction, and he felt so stupid. Blinded by both his love for Xandra and his friendship for Hagop, he had rehearsed for years the way he would tell Hagop, and how Hagop would understand and accept the notion of Albano and Xandra as husband and wife. Each time he imagined this, it went better in his mind. He had been terribly foolish. Now, any moment, Hagop could come back to the cave and give them away. Or, just as upsetting, he could be intercepted by the Turkish police on his way to the Armenian quarter and be sent to forced labor or to jail. As unimaginable as this was, because of Albano's stupidity, Xandra could risk her life at the hands of her own father and brother, simply for loving him.

When Xandra reentered the cave, her face was grave and resolute. Instead of setting the bedding where Hagop's bed had been, she laid it right next to Albano to form a larger bed.

A bed large enough for two.

Albano watched her in incomprehension. And then he understood. "Xandra!"

"This is our home now," she said, and she gave him a weak smile. She approached him and he stood up. She brought her body close to his, "I am your fiancée now," she said. She took his face in her hands and kissed his mouth.

They kissed, and Albano felt a fire rise in him. He jumped away from her. "I ... I cannot," he muttered. "I must continue to respect you ... I won't...."

"Hold me," she said.

And for the first time, Albano got to hold Xandra in his arms. He held her for a long time, overwhelmed with sadness and with joy, with fear for Hagop, and love for her.

That night, they lay side by side. He could not sleep at all. His mind was a battleground of sadness, and excitement, and fear, and hope. He was mesmerized by the soft movement of her sleep, up and down with each breath. He tried not to get too close to the warmth her body emanated. Was he, with his love, destroying Xandra's life, and that of Hagop? If anything happened to either of them, it would be entirely because of him. Tomorrow, he decided, he would try to find Hagop on the quayside and he would speak to him. If he let Hagop fight him, perhaps then Hagop would be able to be reasoned with. At that thought, Albano felt guilt and anguish grab him tighter still, and yet, when he finally fell asleep, he was touching Xandra's hair with the tips of his fingers, happy like he had no right to be.

For the next few days, Albano was too worried about Hagop returning, or Xandra being alone in the cave, so he did not look for Hagop in Smyrna. After five days, there was still no sign of Hagop or Yori. If Hagop did not tell Yori about the location of the cave, then they would be safe. After a week, Albano took his chance and went down to the quayside. He looked for Hagop in all their usual spots. Not only was he not there, but no one he asked had seen him. He could not take the risk of looking for him in the Armenian quarter. If anything happened to him there, Xandra would be powerless and alone.

He returned to the cave, and they stayed there for days, wondering what had come of Hagop, and if he had told their family the situation. But after a few days, they ran out of food and walked up to the Jewish quarter to get supplies, food, and candles. When he arrived, Uncle Joshua was waiting for him. "I don't like not knowing where your cave is. What if I must reach you? One day you will break your leg and be stranded, and no one will be able to rescue you. And people will say, 'Where is your foolish nephew, the one who is supposed to be a great rabbi' And I will say, 'Oh, he is a troglodyte now, or perhaps a corpse somewhere on Mount Pagus. He has renounced God for a couple of boulders.' By the way," Uncle Joshua added, "an Armenian woman came yesterday asking for you."

"An Armenian woman?"

"She gave me this note for you." Uncle Joshua handed him a piece of paper, which Albano unfolded. He tried to read, but although he could read some Armenian when it was printed on paper, the letter was handwritten and incomprehensible. "She was walking around the Jewish quarter asking people where you were, and they sent her to me. Why is an Armenian woman looking for you, Albano?" Uncle Joshua asked. But Albano was already running back to the cave.

Xandra was cooking bean soup on the fire. He presented her the note. Xandra stared at it. "It is from my mother," she marveled. "My mother went all the way to the Jewish quarter to give me this note!"

She read in silence, her eyes scanning the letter in disbelief. Then she read it again, and again. "My mother," she said, breathless. "She is imploring me to not come back. She says Father is wounded by my betrayal. No Armenian man, young or old, will have me now, he says. She tells me that I must stay away in hiding and not come back." Xandra should have burst into tears at that point, but to Albano's amazement, she went on. "Mother says that if I come, my life is in danger. They will beat me and might kill me." Xandra read the rest of the note to herself, and her face whitened. "Oh my God," she mumbled.

"What?"

"Hagop! Mother says he was taken! And they stole all the money!"

Albano sat on his mat, his legs suddenly limp. "Taken where?"

"Mother doesn't say." Xandra's chin trembled when she added, "Mother says she loves me and wishes me great happiness."

"I am to blame," Albano muttered. "Everything that has happened is because of me."

Xandra crouched, facing him, and looked into his eyes in the dim light of the cave. "Hagop threw himself into the lion's mouth. You know that."

"He did that because my action left him no other choice."

"His actions were wrong; yours were not."

They sat in silence for a long time, thinking of Hagop and of what the future might bring. Finally, Albano said, "I will ask my uncle for help."

Albano went to the Jewish quarter and told Uncle Joshua everything. "Does Moshe know about this whole fiasco?" Uncle Joshua asked. "It all seems like his kind of meshuggah ideas."

"It was all my own doing. Uncle Moshe knows nothing about it."

Uncle Joshua paced the room. "If you are thinking of asking me to take that girl in, don't. Your Aunt Sadie would never stand for it. But also, my nephew, you must understand. There is a war. Everyone's situation is precarious. The tension between the ethnic groups is too strong. I cannot put my family in the middle of it. If I were to welcome her into our house, I could be accused of all kinds of evil."

"I understand," Albano said.

"Food, clothes, you can have anything you like."

Albano returned to the cave with a heavy load of supplies and food, and thus Xandra and Albano began their life together.

There is something I want to show you, Albano told Xandra one evening as they sat by the light of the fire. He lifted one of the mats and dug up from the ground a wooden box he had hidden there. When he opened the box to reveal the golden finials, the light of the fire shone on them, and Xandra gasped. "What are those?"

For the first time in his life, Albano could show them and reveal how happy and proud he was to possess objects of such beauty. "They are the kele kodesh," he said. "It means sacred vessels. It is all that is left of a very ancient Sefer Torah that once belonged to my family. Here," he said, handing them to her. "You can touch them."

She took one between her fingers and inspected the graceful lace-like engraving, the tiny bells, the polished edges. "What is a Sefer Torah?"

"The Torah is the Jewish people's holy book. It contains the first five Books of Moses."

"Like a bible?"

"Yes, but not in the shape of a book. The Torah is a scroll. It is made of parchment and handwritten by scribes, and then rolled over wooden rolls. We call the rolls the Tree of Life, but I don't know why. After the Torah is read, the rabbis roll it and place it in its case, and then they place the sacred vessels at the top. There is a sort of larger crown in the middle. That was lost too. And then these two smaller ones are set atop the tree of life."

"They are so beautiful."

"I will pass them down to my first-born son. That is the tradition. He will be Kohen too."

"Kohen?"

"A special role. The role of priest."

"Are you a priest?"

"I guess I'm supposed to be."

"Hagop doesn't know about them?"

Albano admitted to Xandra at the same time he admitted to himself, "I feared showing them to him."

For a long time, they admired the finials in the light of the fire.

"They look like little crowns," Xandra noted.

Albano placed one above her head playfully. "And you are my queen."

Xandra placed the other above his head and said, "And you are my king." They looked at each other and laughed.

Albano was reluctant to leave the cave. Every moment he spent away from Xandra seemed fraught with peril. Hagop could return, leading others to them. A woman living alone on the mountain was an aberration. And yet, the very cave that had felt like a jail cell to Hagop was to them as warm, inviting, and full of love as any home he could imagine. He should have been sad and worried, and he was, but not merely that. He was with Xandra, and this filled him with joy. His heart was so light in his chest it was as though a giant balloon lifted him up as he walked. She was his fiancée now. When he would come back to the cave after having picked up supplies for them, there she was, waiting for him, her beautiful smile like a million suns radiating straight to his heart. "You're an excellent troglodyte," he would tell her, mimicking Uncle Joshua.

Xandra had none of her brother's impatience, and she was incapable of the brooding that consumed him. She never ran out of things to occupy herself with, and she was indefatigable, always at work. She sewed and she weaved, she melted bits of candles to make whole ones, she found ways to create a small oven with stones that she hand-picked and that Albano lifted and placed how she instructed him to, and now she even baked. She collected scented plants and hung them around the cave; she managed to make traps to catch prairie dogs that she skinned and rubbed with herbs before roasting them. By her mere presence, Xandra brightened and lightened everything. Her sadness was there, under the surface, but she never complained, never uttered a word of pity for herself. Albano would arrive, and she would rush to see what he had brought, finding a use for everything and marveling at the bit of candle wax, the strip of leather, the chunk of goat cheese, the few marinated olives. She was utterly accepting of her predicament and boundless in her expressions of love. Albano in return did everything for her. One of the things he did for her was one of the hardest to give. They endlessly kissed, but those kisses were chaste. Albano kept the promise he had made to Hagop and to himself to respect her.

For a full month, this was their life. Xandra was tormented with questions about her family. Was her father able to bake and earn a living? How did her mother and sisters fare? What if Yori was arrested again? Didn't her mother need her now more than ever? Because of the folly of men, she and Albano were forbidden to help. Having not heard from Hagop, they feared the worst for him. Hagop had only been in the Armenian quarter long enough to tell his parents about them, but not long enough to make it back to the cave. Had he changed his mind about getting his sister back, or was he arrested before he did?

For two months, Xandra and Albano slept side by side in the cave. At night they were anxious, and sleep was difficult. But during the day, Albano was happy. He had Xandra all to himself, and each minute with her was a gift. Happy, as well as consumed with desire, around Xandra, Albano was a timorous boy. His dreams and thoughts were filled with visions of her. He tried not to look at her lustily and was failing at this. Each time he chased an impure thought away with splashes of water on his face, or a strenuous walk up the mountain, another thought would come, bringing with it a wave of ardor. It was as though his brain had turned to soup and he could think of nothing else. Their near-constant physical proximity, the solitude of the mountain, his youth and energy, and the way they were physical with each other, kissing the way they kissed, did nothing to help. Albano had no idea how long he could go on in such a manner.

One evening, like many others, they were sitting together in the cave, on the mat, their backs propped against pillows set against the coolness of the stone. Albano was reading out loud from an old French newspaper they had kept, translating as he went and helping her with her pronunciation. The fire, still warm, flickered and lit up the walls of the cave. "You see," Xandra suddenly said, "the ground has not opened up from beneath our feet. We are happy. The war will never reach us here. We can stay together here, safe, forever."

"But very soon, we need to be married," he answered urgently. "But how? No priest, no rabbi, will accept to marry us," he added, sounding pathetic.

"When the time is correct, we will be husband and wife," she answered enigmatically.

That same week, she gave him a long list of herbs and minerals to bring back from the city. "What is it for?" he asked.

"A remedy," she answered.

"For what ailment?" She smiled and did not answer. It took him a while to gather the proper herbs from various shops on Frank Street. When she had them all, she made a brew. "Are you sick?" he asked. Again, she did not answer.

That night, instead of simply going to bed, she asked him to add logs to the fire. Then she knelt by the spring and removed her petticoat in front of him. Usually, she washed in private when he was out, but now she was before him only wearing a shirt, her arms and legs bare. She poured water in a bowl and using a cloth washed her face and arms. From his mat he watched, mesmerized, her arms so white, the skin so marvelously smooth. Feeling his gaze on him, she turned and beamed. "Outside, in the night, your face is smooth and white and bright enough to rival the moon," he told her. "But here, with the fire, it is orange and it glows like the sun."

Xandra stood up to face him, and said, "Tonight, we will be married."

"We … will?" Albano stuttered. And then he watched Xandra do something incredible: she let her shirt fall to the floor.

Albano stopped breathing. He remained on the mat as she stood facing him, the dappled light of the fire flickering on her bare body. "You are so beautiful," Albano whispered. He needed to look away. He needed to run out of the cave. He jumped to his feet, "I ... I cannot be here. I have to go," he muttered, and yet he did not look away, and he did not run.

"Stay," she said, extending her hand to take his.

Albano knew with every cell in his brain that he mustn't take her hand, just as every cell in his body moved his hand forward toward hers. "I cannot be here next to you like this and still respect—"

"I know," she said, gently, slowly, placing his hand on her bare breast.

"No, no," he murmured, but an instant later he fell to his knees and embraced her bare body in his arms, letting his head rest on her stomach. "I mustn't do this."

She caressed his hair and whispered, "Please, my love, I am ready for you."

Albano took her in his arms and kissed her, but this time, he let himself kiss her the way he had always wanted to kiss her. Overtaken, she began to melt, so Albano gently laid her on the mat. And just like that, they were married.

****

That night, after they had made love for the first time, Xandra consumed her brew. "It is against babies," she explained.

"How do you know how to make it?"

"Women pass down this knowledge."

"Isn't it against your religion?"

"Women have to be practical. If we are taken by force and we are not married, the alternative is death. My mother made me memorize it. It does not always work, so I will have to be careful about cycles of the moon."

"How so?"

Xandra's answer filled him with awe. "The moon decides when a woman is fertile and when she is not," she said.

The next morning felt like the first day of their lives. They made love, again and again, amazed at the big secret that was now theirs. They ate cheese and bread, fresh figs, and dried fruit. When it was night, and no one could see them, they went to a nearby stream and removed all their clothes. They bathed in the cold water and further discovered each other's body and their own. Albano held Xandra in the water as she floated, her body glistening in the light of the moon. "You are my moon lady, weightless in the night."

"When I am in your arms, I feel safe."

"I will hold you forever, and forever keep you safe," he swore.

CHAPTER 9

Cité des Fleurs

Cassie awakened from her second night in her Parisian hotel room to the revelation that she had slept ten hours straight. Outside her window was nothing but gray skies and rooftops sleek with rain. She took a bath and washed her hair. The humidity in the air did not bode well regarding follicle cooperation, but she had not thought of bringing a blow-dryer, of course. She put on her jeans, layered three T-shirts, forced her last two pairs of dry socks on top of each other, brushed on mascara, and applied lipstick. She could almost picture herself acing this day. But when she slid her feet into Uggs that had the feel and consistency of a wet sponge, dampening her last pairs of dry socks all the way through, and when each strand of her hair began curling malevolently upon itself, suddenly she was not so sure. How could she expect cooperation from anyone in her family when her own hair was giving her the finger?

She went down to the deserted lobby. The sound of French cartoons played on a nearby television, and the lobby smelled of freshly brewed coffee and burnt toast. She entered the phone booth and dialed Sabine. In one breathless sentence, she explained to how she had managed to book the wrong hotel, how she had obliterated both her cell phone and her laptop, how she had borrowed their father's coat, and how the only shoes she had brought were turning into festering swamps. "I have moss growing between my toes," she joked.

On the line, there was no laugh, not even a polite one. "What's your shoe size?" Sabine asked. "I'll lend you a pair. I'm a thirty-eight."

"Forty," Cassie said. "That won't work but thanks for the offer. But that's not why I called you. Okay, so here is the scoop: You were right. That Marceline character, she was not Papa's mistress."

"Who was she?"

"Are you sitting down? She is Papa's sister!"

"His what?"

"He has a sister! Isn't it incredible?"

"Has or had?" Sabine asked.

"Apparently, she is still alive. She's two years older than Papa."

"We have an aunt?" Sabine sounded incredulous, but also excited.

"And we knew nothing. Absolutely nothing!"

Sabine was quiet for a beat. Then she said, "When Papa had his weird blow up, he thought you were her?"

"Better than the alternative," Cassie said. "I'm pretty relieved that it wasn't actually me he called all those names."

"That's what Maman meant when she said he was hallucinating," Sabine said. "She knew perfectly well who Marceline was the whole time."

"You'd think she would have volunteered the information to make me feel better."

"She likes it better when she holds all the cards," Sabine said, pragmatic.

"Wouldn't it be incredible to meet relatives we didn't know existed?"

"Considering how well we fare with the ones we already have, I'm not so sure," Sabine said.

"Do you think you could look up her name and see if you find anything? I wrote it down. A name straight out of a Flaubert novel." Cassie unfolded her paper. "Here it is: Marceline de Bécasel D'Alompe."

Cassie heard the swift sound of fingertips on a keyboard. "Comtesse Marceline de Bécasel D'Alompe. 4682 Cité des Fleurs in the seventeenth arrondissement," Sabine said. "Papa's sister is a countess?"

"She's listed?" Cassie marveled. "What kind of miracle is this?"

"It's called the internet."

"She's not even hiding a little bit? Incredible. What do you think I should do?"

"Buy shoes," Sabine said.

"Any telephone number?"

"I don't see one listed."

"Maybe I should go to the address, see what I find. Anyway, I have nothing better to do before visiting hours."

"You're going back to the hospital?" Sabine sounded surprised.

"Well ... yes, why?"

"I guess that makes sense. That's why you came here but...."

Cassie waited for the rest of the sentence, which didn't come. "Are you all right?" she asked.

There was a long silence. "I'm alive, I guess," Sabine said.

Alarm bells rang in Cassie's ears. "We should get together just the two of us," she hurried to say. "Talk. Catch up."

"I better go," Sabine said. "My boss is getting fidgety."

After they had hung up, Cassie wondered about Sabine, the way she said things. Cynical. Or maybe sad. If she knew Sabine the way she ought to, she would be able to tell. Here she was getting all excited about a new relative, and she was incapable of getting an accurate reading on her own younger sister.

Cassie shuffled into the street in her frizzy hair, her father's shapeless coat, and squishy boots. Give her a couple of trash bags and people would start handing her money. Although she kept repeating to herself that she felt fine and didn't care about her looks, it turns out that she wasn't fine. She did care. Could she present herself at the door of Madame la Comtesse sporting a road kill on each foot? Because now it was decided: she was, without giving it any thought, finding herself heading in the direction of the seventeenth arrondissement. Cité des Fleurs, wherever that was, and whatever it was she might find there, or not find there. She had nothing better to do she had told Sabine. But mostly, she was curious. And angry. At what? At whom? She wasn't quite sure.

But first, she needed shoes. Paris did not offer many shopping options at eight in the morning. Cassie walked down rue des Martyrs, her Uggs growing wetter and heavier by the minute, searching the shop windows for a solution. Cafés, bakeries, and grocery stores were open, but everything else was closed. She stopped in front of a small vintage shop. Someone with an abundance of black curls was inside, folding T-shirts. She looked through the window. The shopkeeper was a thin woman in her fifties in a long black skirt with fingers covered in silver rings. Cassie stepped back and considered the merchandise on display in the window. It was a hot mess, part resale store, part gift and novelty, part porn video rentals. But amidst the dusty radios and food mixers, feathered whips, and old books was a single pair of red cowboy boots. The boots embodied the closest definition of shoes Cassie would not wear. For one, "secondhand shoes" struck her as a horrifying combination of words. Secondly, the boots were bright red, pointy enough to stab someone, and just so visible, so … exuberant.

Cassie continued down rue des Martyrs. As she walked, she pondered the kind of woman who would wear cowboy boots such as these. It would have to be someone with opinions. Someone who liked being seen and heard. Someone obnoxious, to be sure.

Cassie, not even clear as to why, walked back up the street and returned to stare at the boots in the window.

Yep, she thought. Here they were. On the plus side, they were not much of a risk at twenty-five euros. Odile would despise the sight of them, which added to their appeal.

She pushed open the door and entered. "Bonjour, Madame," she made sure to say. The shopkeeper jumped, startled. Her eyes were heavy with black eye makeup. Her hair was as black and wavy as Cassie's, but on her it was a fashion statement. "I must have forgotten to lock the door," the woman said. "We are not open. I'm only doing the inventory."

"Oh well, thank you then." Cassie turned around to leave.

"But since you are here, is there something you wanted to look at?"

"I need to buy a map of Paris."

The woman stepped toward a display of postcards and maps. "Here they are."

"Also, I was wondering about the...." Cassie hesitated, embarrassed. "Those red boots you have in the window."

"Les bottes de cowboy?"

"What size are they?"

The woman went to the window to retrieve the boots and handed them to Cassie. On close inspection, they looked even more rugged than they had seemed behind the window, but in a well-loved sort of way, not raggedy. Holding them, Cassie felt guilty for no good reason. "Size Forty," the shopkeeper announced. "Elles sont manifiques."

"That's my size," Cassie said, surprised. "I guess there is no harm in trying them on. They're not my style at all." When she removed her boots, her drenched socks stayed inside the Uggs. "You don't happen to sell socks, by chance?"

"We do have some, but they are spéciales," the woman said. Spéciale, in French, did not signify special at all, but plain weird.

"How spéciale?"

The woman walked to the glass counter behind which was an assortment of leather, lingerie, Eiffel Tower-shaped vibrators, and furry handcuffs. She handed her a pair of high socks in a vibrant pink covered in a small penis print. "C'est tout ce que j'ai." That's all I have.

"Penis socks?"

"Oui, Madame."

Cassie sat down and contemplated her toes which increasingly looked like miniature drowned corpses. She sighed in surrender and put on the penis socks. The penis prints stretched obscenely.

And then she slid her feet inside the boots.

Words could hardly describe the perfection with which they fit. The arch was perfect. The height was perfect. The way her feet felt, safe, warm, dry, and protected after all the abuse, was perfect. She took two steps back and looked at herself in the mirror. Not so bad. Pretty great in fact. Not at all like her, but awesome in their own genre. "I can't believe they're only twenty-five euros!" she exclaimed.

"Ha, non," the woman said. "You missed a zero. Look at the tag: They're two hundred and fifty euros."

Cassie looked at the tag, looked at the woman, then looked at her boots.

"I'll take them," she said.

She walked to the soundtrack of her cowboy boots pounding the sidewalk. Comtesse-Marceline-de-Bécasel-D'Alompe, Comtesse-Marceline-de-Bécasel-D'Alompe. What a mouthful, that name. In truth, aristocratic names triggered mixed emotions in her, something ingrained in her subconscious to which she had never given a second thought until now. Those people. They clung to their bloodline like an amulet against the evils of all things progressive. Out of principle, she resented the thought of power, or money, passed down across generations. Or did she? Could it be that she was unconsciously parroting her mother's prejudice? Growing up under her mother's dominance, Cassie had adopted much of her mother's tastes and opinions as her own, so much so that it was at times difficult to sort things out, even now. It wasn't until she was in her thirties, when she began to catch herself wondering how her mother would react to things in order to know how she should feel, that she had realized this. She had cured herself of this compulsion during her marriage by an exhausting daily practice of rebelling against Peter's authority. A calm, confident husband was the perfect person against whom to practice having a mind of one's own. With Peter, she had rebelled, and fought, and stood her ground. Not for what she wanted (that remained kind of murky) but against what he wanted, which was nearly as good.

The air was cold on her cheeks as she walked up rue des Abbesses toward the métro station. She unfolded her Paris map. Cité des Fleurs. The City of Flowers. What a lovely street name. For the first time since she arrived in Paris, Cassie felt equipped for the weather, and since she could think better when her body was in motion, she decided to continue on foot rather than take the métro. It was strange to feel so at home in Paris. It was not only how things looked and smelled and sounded, but it was also the people. In the United States, even after nearly twenty years, people felt opaque to her. Friendly, easy to categorize, yet amorphous. But here in Paris, it was as though she had an immediate, gut-level knowledge of the collective thinking, the yearning of souls, the take-no-prisoner sense of humor, the contrarian thinking, the deep and so very French appetite for anarchy, a uniquely rebellious spirit that inhabited even the most conventional individuals. She could feel the zeitgeist of the place in her bones. From rue des Abbesses, she walked down rue Joseph de Maistre along the Montmartre cemetery's wall. Maybe for a few days she could cope with her mom, her sisters, her father, and forget about her children in college, the void in between their calls, Peter, the loss of it all, starting from scratch, not wanting to start anything, not knowing where to start. The rhythmic, clipped sound of her heels on the sidewalk had a way of saying, "You exist." That was better than what Sabine had said. Sabine had said, "I'm alive." It sounded horrible, the way she said it. To be alive was to occupy space. To exist was to claim significance, to demand it. Something was wrong with Sabine, but Cassie had no idea how to bring it up without everyone in her family telling her to go to hell.

As she walked through the unknown neighborhood, she felt a sense of déjà vu. She was pretty certain that she had never been on this street, so why did the sidewalks, the sycamores, and in particular the buildings feel so familiar? What did it mean to be a countess these days, she wondered? Picturesque names – what her mother called noms à charnières, names with hinges – and useless titles, were all that was left of the French nobility. Aristocracy's power was long gone. Their great wealth had shrunk to nothing for most. Families that had passed down land, properties, and estates for five or six generations, these days often had to sell everything just to pay the inheritance tax. Fabulous properties that had been in families for several hundred years were being sold and turned into museums or hotels.

"They think they're better than us," Raymonde would say about anyone she perceived as richer, happier, or better-educated, though the underlying fear may not be how much better they were but how insignificant she felt. The neighborhood was lively, busy like a village. Boucheries, pâtisseries, cordonneries, flower shops, and cafés all teemed with activity. In front of the school, mothers held the hands of children with colorful backpacks and raincoats. Ladies with shopping baskets greeted each other and chatted in the doorways of buildings. Men in green overalls swept the sidewalks. Cassie's cowboy boots clip-clopped on the pavement, and the rhythm was beginning to sound a lot like I think I can-I think I can.

****

Cassie arrived at rue de la Jonquière and had to stop to collect herself. She stood on the sidewalk, the drizzle of rain in her face. What was going on? She had never been here before, she was certain of this, yet she still could not shake off the growing feeling of déjà vu. It was as though she knew what the next block looked like instants before seeing it. This porte cochère. The shape of this window. That gate, the sign over the butcher shop – she knew them, but how could this be? Also, something struck her suddenly. How was it that she knew all those architectural terms? She was finding herself able to recognize an arc-boutan and a travée. Why? How? She did not know any of those words in English, which means she had learned them in French as a child. And then it came to her like a poke in her heart: she had been here before! With her father.

It was years ago when she was a little girl. It was not a linear memory. It came in bits. Her hand in his. Odile was there. Him pointing at rooftops and windows. An arc-boutan, a travée. This was one of the things he did: name objects. It was not too fascinating at the time. He tended to ramble on about subjects of no interest to little girls. But as they walked, he pointed to churches, to windows, and to rooftops and told her and Odile the names of things: une rothonde, un pillastre. He was going to show them a house, she remembered. A special house. Sabine would have been an infant. She was not there. Where was their mother?

Cassie arrived in front of a metal gate with a sign that read: "Cité des Fleurs. Rue privée. Closed to the public from seven in the morning to seven at night. Chiens interdits." She walked through the main gate just as the sun managed to pierce through and the sky was revealed, blue in patches between dark, billowy clouds.

She could not believe her eyes as she advanced through the private alley. Not only had she absolutely been here before, but it was unfathomable that she would have forgotten it until now. That such a place existed in the middle of Paris was amazing enough. This was not a place you forgot. Cité des Fleurs was a long cobblestone alley about four hundred feet long and wide enough for a car, although there were no cars, not even parked ones. On each side of the alley were walls, fences topped with pointed finials painted black, blue, or green, and gates. Each gate was framed on each side by a rectangular stone pillar about ten feet high. Atop each pillar sat a large urn shaped like an inverted bell out of which tulips, narcissus, and daffodils burst like fireworks. Budding trees, cascading wisteria in purple hues, and white clematis running wild spilled from behind gates. Ivy climbed on walls, birds chirped and dashed around, and cats lay in the sun or walked around like they owned the place. The rest of Paris had felt frozen in winter, but Cité des Fleurs, perhaps because of the ray of sun, or perhaps because of the vegetation, was a pocket of spring. Behind the gates were three- and four-story houses built most likely in the late 1800s, each pretty as a jewel box, each with a small garden in front. They were what the French called hôtel particuliers, townhouses, technically, but with flair. From her vantage point in the alley, she could only see what was above the gates, the higher levels of each house. The houses all looked different, but the matching urns, out of which vegetation escaped and framed the gates, gave the street its architectural unity.

She recognized the house instantly. It was the most beautiful one on the street, painted in a pink-tinged white. She counted four stories with three large windows on each floor. The fourth story had two smaller windows nestled within the slate roof. The house had handsome proportions; the symmetry of windows gave it gravitas, but the façade had whimsical details: dainty stone carvings above the windows, a stone cornice that ran the width of the façade, intricate wrought-iron balconies. The center windows had small balconies on two of the levels. A lush, massive pine tree framed the house on one side, and the general effect was straight out of a children's fairy-tale book.

Money, Cassie thought. And lots of it by the look of things. If Marceline lived here, perhaps not all aristocrats had lost their properties to inheritance taxes.

Her castle. Was this what her mother had meant?

Buried under a thick layer of ivy she detected an aging intercom with a single button and beneath it the name Bécasel D'Alompe. She hesitated, her finger hovering above the buzzer. Her clothes gave her pause. The jeans, her father's terrible coat, and now the red cowboy boots. To press or not to press, that was the question.

She pressed.

The buzzer emitted a tiny pterodactyl noise, and Cassie's heart bounced in her chest. For a while, there was nothing. Then came a sputtering sound and a woman's voice, drowned in crackles from another world, said, "Allô, oui?"

Cassie took a deep breath. "Is this Madame de Bécasel D'Alompe?"

"What is this regarding?"

"My name is Cassandra Lombard," Cassie said in French. "I'm visiting from California. I think it's ... ahem ... possible that we might be ... related?" She cringed. Why had she ended her sentence with a pathetic question mark? There was a long silence, but she could still hear the static. "Allô?" she said.

"Un moment, s'il vous plaît," the woman's commanded.

Cassie looked up at the house. There was no reason to feel nervous really. Except for the nagging sense that her life was about to swing wide open. It was like standing at the edge of a cliff. There was still the possibility of taking a step back. Scamper away. Hide. At one of the windows of the lower floor, a curtain parted briefly. And then another curtain moved at the window above, followed by more creaking from the intercom.

"You will now be received," the voice said. With this came a buzzing sound and a small door within the black metal gate clicked open. Sésame ouvre-toi, Cassie thought.

She flattened the frizz of her hair with the palms of her hands, readjusted her coat, and pushed open the door.

She found herself inside a large, airy, gardenlike courtyard where clipped boxwood framed a central path that led to the porch and the entrance door. To her left, a stone maiden extended her hands in a graceful beckoning. To her right, a gazebo made of six small marble columns covered with blooming clematis shaded a wrought iron patio table and chairs. She heard clipping sounds above her and lifted her head. Up on a towering thin ladder, a North African gardener, pipe in mouth, handsome and spry despite being most likely in his late eighties, was trimming a hedge, one hand holding the clipper, the other hanging on to the ladder for dear life. He nodded his head at Cassie and resumed his task.

She advanced on the narrow path and this time again saw the distinct motion of curtains in at least two of the windows. She was being observed. The thought that her curiosity was reciprocated gave her courage. The front door was flanked on each side by gas lanterns and protected by a lacy awning of glass and iron curlicues. This particular architectural element was called une Marquise, she knew, thinking how fitting it was that she had to go past a Marquise to get to the countess.

At the door, she wiped her palms on her jeans in preparation for a blue-blooded handshake. Before she could knock, a squat woman in her late forties in a buttoned-up black dress and a strict hairdo had come out of the house and onto the porch, looking at Cassie interrogatively. "How may I help you?"

Cassie propelled her hand forward and gave her a vigorous handshake. "Bonjour, Madame," she said, thinking that the woman was way too young to be her aunt. "Are you Madame…?" But in her nervousness, the name had vanished from her brain. "Madame de, de … Bbb … De, de … Aloup? Aloppe?"

"Alompe. But … which one, Madame?"

"There are several?" Cassie felt heat come to her face. "I believe she may be your … mother? Ha, yes! Marceline! I'm looking for Marceline!"

"May I tell her what this is regarding?" the woman asked. She showed no intention of letting her in.

"I'm looking for relatives of my father."

"Yes?"

"My father is hospitalized, and well, I've just heard that he might be related to Marceline – I mean, to the duchess. I mean, the countess."

"Would you please follow me dans le vestibule," the woman said.

Vestibule? The words Vulva Vestibula intruded into her mind: the entrance to the vagina. And here she was, entering the vestibule while wearing penis socks.

The vestibule was a circular entrance hall at the foot of a sweeping staircase. In the center of the room was a round mahogany table and on the table was a profuse flower arrangement overflowing with lilacs, roses, and lilies. The ceiling had been painted with elaborate and delightful trompe l'oeil of sky, clouds, cupids, and birds bashfully carrying flowing ribbons to mask the cupid's private parts. The woman pointed to a seat against a wall. "If you would please wait for a moment?"

If Cassie thought she had regressed to the eighties by losing her laptop and cell, this environment felt like going back in time a whole century. She raked the drawers of her brain for the vernacular of this world, the etiquette. Downton Abbey meets Marie Antoinette, and every other cliché bounced around in her head. She was nervous as hell. Out of place. The cupids on the ceiling, the ornate stucco molding, the beautiful wood floor, the smell of lilac; everything here was perfect. She had no clue how to sit, stand, or even hold her head in this room. She looked like a vagrant, had gotten her nobilities mixed up, had botched Marceline's name, and now had the sneaking suspicion that the woman who had opened the door was not her relative, but the maid. What now?

The woman was back in the room. "If you would please follow me," she said.

They walked on the inlaid parquet floor, Cassie trying to put as little weight as she could on the floor as her boots clip-clopped obscenely and entered a salon with ceilings that were at least twelve feet high. In the room, beautiful light poured in through the windows. Sunlight reflected on a monumental crystal chandelier in the center of the ceiling. The walls were painted a light shade of yellow with gold trimmings and covered with art, heavily framed oil paintings of bucolic settings, still lifes piled high with dead pheasants, apples, and grapes. On the floor lay dozens of immense Persian rugs. Her father too had a prized collection of Persian rugs. The more you walked on them, the more beautiful they become, he would tell visitors.

"Would you please have a seat on the bergère," the woman said pointing in the direction of a group of three chairs. Two of the chairs were matching golden fauteuils with ornate woodwork and high backs that resembled thrones, and one was a low chair upholstered in blue fabric. Cassie sat in the chair, expecting to sink in the upholstery, but finding herself perched on a hard surface with no give whatsoever. "Monsieur et Madame D'Alompe will arrive in just a minute," the woman announced before leaving.

Cassie looked around feeling dwarfed by the room. The salon was filled with Louis XVI furniture and a few Regency pieces. The desk was Regency, if not the real thing, at least a beautiful imitation. And she knew this how? From her dad. And why did her dad know those things? Wasn't this unusual knowledge in a working-class man whose schooling was cut short by the war? Above the limestone fireplace, a painting caught her eye, surprising in its modernity in such a room. It was a portrait of a woman, half figurative, half abstract, like a Modigliani that would have been reworked by Basquiat. Half of the woman's face was figurative: black mane, piercing gold eyes like those of a cat, and an ironic smile. The other side of the face looked as though it had been reworked and blurred, the mouth redrawn as if by a three-year-old. A person who would put such a painting on a mantelpiece could not be all that stuck up.

The sound of hurried footsteps preceded the arrival of a small man and small woman in their sixties. They scurried into the room and Cassie got to her feet. "Don't get up!" the woman ordered. Cassie stayed up. They advanced toward her with extended hands and took turns shaking hers as they smiled the same precise smile, with the same thin mouth, perhaps the smile they reserved for the kind of strangers in the habit of showing up unannounced at their doorstep. They introduced themselves, as Jean-Bernard de Bécasel D'Alompe and Armelle de Bécasel D'Alompe. It was immediately obvious to Cassie that the two were twins. They seemed the male and the female version of the same human being. They had taut, almost wrinkle-free skin, high cheekbones, funny little pointy noses, and arched eyebrows that gave them a permanently surprised look. They both had blondish hair, hers in a well-crafted bun at the nape of her neck, and his full on top and mounted like a toupee. They were dressed elegantly, Armelle in a pale gray cardigan, a matchstick black skirt, and a strand of pearls, Antoine in a light blue shirt and a navy sports coat with some sort of embroidered armor on the left pocket. They had the worried expressions of people propelled into a situation of emergency.

Armelle and Jean-Bernard sat on the large, golden, throne-like chairs. Down on her seat, Cassie had to look up at them. "Thank you so much for seeing me," she said. "I hope it wasn't rude to just knock at your door. Your number was unlisted."

They nodded in noncommittal unison. Jean-Bernard crossed one leg over the other, clasped his hands over one knee, and opened his mouth, but it was Armelle who spoke. "Laure said you are looking for relatives? How interesting."

"Laure?"

"Our executive assistant who opened the door."

Cassie took mental note: not the maid, but the executive assistant. She hoped she had not embarrassed herself. "My father is very ill in the hospital," she said. "I guess I am looking into his genealogy for the first time. I'm wondering if it is possible that we might be … perhaps … cousins?"

Jean-Bernard crossed his leg to the other side, clasped his hands again, opened his mouth again, and again no sound came out. "How fascinating," Armelle said, and they both exhibited the same pinched smile of polite disinterest, which seemed to indicate that the visit would be over before it had a chance to begin. Something about them was obnoxious. It was as though they were playing a game of poker and Cassie had not even been given cards.

But maybe she did have one card. "I learned only yesterday that my father has a sister," she said.

"How interesting," Armelle said again. She did not seem interested at all.

"My father told us this name we had never heard before, and then my sister found your address online."

A light of recognition came to Jean-Bernard's face but soon faded. He crossed and uncrossed his legs affectedly. Clasped and unclasped his hands.

"But of course," Armelle said.

Now Cassie was annoyed. Who were those two dinguses? And what game were they playing? "Is Marceline your mother?" she insisted. "May I meet her?"

Armelle's and Jean-Bernard's eyes darted to the portrait above the fireplace. "Our mother?" Armelle said. These people did not want to help her. And now she doubted she was related to them at all. If these two shared DNA with anything, it would be with small furry animals, perhaps hamsters or, from the way they stared at her with wide eyes and panicked expressions, prairie dogs.

Jean-Bernard crossed and uncrossed his legs again, and then clasped his hands, put them on his lap, clasped them again, then looked around the room again like in a time loop. "Mother indeed had a brother," he suddenly said in a bleaty, much too loud voice. "But he disappeared in the course of World War II!"

Armelle looked at Jean-Bernard with displeasure. "Très cher Jean-Bernard, forgive me, but you are confused. It was Mother's *father* who perished, in World War II." Jean-Bernard became enthralled with the tip of his shoelace, poking it through each hole of this black patent-leather shoe, one after the other, and then back from the top.

"My father is eighty-seven years old," Cassie said. "His name is Gustave Lombard. He went in for surgery, but a lung infection has developed. They're trying different intravenous antibiotics."

"And which hospital is this?" Armelle asked casually.

"Hôpital Saint-François," Cassie answered, realizing that the question revealed more interest than Armelle was willing to let on. "He was born in 1925. I wish I knew his parents' names, but I don't." Armelle and Jean-Bernard stared at her, riveted by what Cassie might say next. "He's been going in and out of consciousness."

Armelle cocked her head. "How awful," she said.

"He's been calling me Marceline." As she said the name, both Armelle and Jean-Bernard glanced at the portrait above the fireplace, and then away. It happened in fractions of seconds, but now the portrait seemed like the fourth person in the room, and it was beckoning Cassie to be more audacious. "So, tell me, does Marceline live here?" she asked. "Does she have a brother named –"

"Operation Storm!" Jean-Bernard blurted out, so loud that both Armelle and Cassie jumped. "Algiers!" he nearly shouted. "November 1942!" Jean-Bernard stopped speaking as abruptly as he had started. His eyes darted to everywhere in the room at once, and he went through a frantic cycle of leg crossings, hand clasping, and eye darting. Armelle now appeared deeply annoyed, but before she could say anything, Laure, the executive assistant, materialized and stood there, wanting to speak. Jean-Bernard turned to her, irritated. "Merci, Laure, we are fine," he said.

But Laure did not leave and was about to speak when Armelle got to her feet. "I wish we could help you," she said. "This is most unfortunate, but I'm afraid we know nothing." Mirroring his sister, Jean-Bernard too sprung up from his seat.

Cassie understood that she was expected to leave. She unfolded from her terrible chair and got up as well. She tried one more time. "Your mother, could I meet her? Maybe she knows something about my father. He was born in the eight arrondissement. On January 3rd, 1925."

Armelle put a nervous hand to the pearls around her neck. "I'm afraid that won't be possible. Her health, you see...."

Jean-Bernard echoed Armelle in tone and pained expression. "Her advancing age...."

"Let us accompany you to the door."

Cassie followed them out of the room. If they were related to her dad, this was more of the same crap. The same secrecy, the same silence, but why? What for?

They were back in the vestibule. Laure, who had followed them, coughed to get their attention and said, "I wanted to let you know that tea is served."

Armelle seemed taken aback; she pivoted on her heels and faced Laure. "That won't be necessary. Our visitor was just leaving." She took Cassie's elbow lightly but with urgency as she guided her toward the front door. "I very much hope the rest of your search will be more fruitful."

"Pardon me," Laure insisted. "But tea is served," she paused and put more emphasis on the rest of the sentence "... in Madame la Comtesse's library."

Armelle tugged at her pearls and moved her mouth into a forced smile. "The library? But of course," she said and promptly took Cassie's elbow again but this time guided her away from the door. "Would you join us for tea?"

Cassie felt something odd and exhilarating in the air. *Something* had just happened. What, she wasn't sure. She looked at Laure interrogatively, but the woman's face revealed nothing. "I would love to," she said.

Armelle and Jean-Bernard went in the direction of the stairwell, but as Armelle put a foot on the first step, Laure said, "I believe Madame la Comtesse intends to meet with Madame ... alone."

Armelle blanched. Jean-Bernard said not a word of goodbye and stomped out of the room. There had been an upset; that much was clear. But whatever it was, Armelle's good education was well ingrained, and she regrouped quickly. "Very well then." She took Cassie's hand, shook it rather limply, and gave her a practiced smile. "It's been a pleasure, au revoir then." They were standing at the bottom of the stairs. Armelle walked off after a last sharp, military nod. Cassie now stood in the vestibule, lightheaded with giddiness. A mysterious master puppeteer was inviting her to tea, and Armelle and Jean-Bernard had been given the boot! Feeling as though she had just aced the most important interview of her life, Cassie followed Laure up the stairwell, and then through a high-ceilinged hallway lined with small oil paintings of landscapes and hunting scenes, and finally to a large door with gilded woodwork. She opened the door and let Cassie in.

The room was so unlike the rest of the house that Cassie might as well have entered an alternate universe. It was so impolite. So bohemian. The air was heavy with the smell of women's perfume and the licorice hints of pipe tobacco. It was part library, part cabinet of curiosities. On every wall were shelves upon shelves, and those were filled with books, newspapers, magazines, and bizarre, exotic artifacts: clay moldings of human parts, postcards, ostrich eggshells, Venetian masks, animal skulls, crystals sprouting out of rocks, feathers in vases. Everywhere, scattered and piled high, were cardboard boxes and trunks. Every surface and even the floor were strewn with magazines and newspaper clippings. Shelves and tabletops alike were covered with chinoiseries, porcelain vases, ashtrays, primitive sculptures, African masks, and a rather macabre assortment of taxidermy animals, from birds to bats to a large cat that could well be a lynx or a bobcat.

Next to the window, on a low, ornate Napoleon III table flanked by two Chesterfield chairs, was an Edwardian teapot, small silver forks and spoons, two delicate Limoges plates and teacups, and a three-tiered serving tray filled with an assortment of petits fours, small éclairs, and raspberry tarts no larger than small matchboxes.

Cassie was standing in the center of the library, taking it in, when a door on the opposite side from the entrance opened. A very old woman, perhaps ninety years old, marched into the room, her chin high. Her hair was perfectly white and tied in a bun, her skin thin and rosy. She was dressed to be noticed, in an extravagant, floor-length dress of red and yellow madras fabric. Around her neck was a heavy layering of two dozen strands of beads, pendants, keys, and amulets. There were bracelets on her wrists, ethnic rings on every one of her narrow, knobby fingers. Her handshake surprised Cassie: it was young and full of vigor. "Marceline de Bécasel D'Alompe," the old woman said, her golden eyes evaluating Cassie with interest. "I'm told you wanted to meet me."

Cassie recognized her immediately as the woman in the painting. Marceline was the most handsome and confident elderly women she had ever seen. Although something in her face felt familiar, one thing was for certain: she bore no physical resemblance to her father. Cassie could not help beaming as she introduced herself. Could this woman really be her father's sister? It was as though she had been invented the day before and now appeared, fully realized, a mythical creature turned to flesh and blood.

"What is your name again? Forgive me, I am tragically old and must have people repeat things to me," Marceline said.

"Cassandra Lombard."

"And what do you want from me, Mademoiselle?"

"Well, I ... I'm looking for my father's sister."

Marceline studied Cassie's face with an expression of innocence layered with mirth or puzzlement. Or disapproval. Finally, cryptically she said, "But why only *now*?"

Cassie was not about to tell this stranger, especially if this was her aunt, that she had learned about her in a bout of morphine-induced rage filled with an expletive associated to her name. "I live in the United States," she said instead. "This is my first visit to France in five years." She added lightly, "So I thought, why not."

Marceline repeated in the same tone. "Why not?" adding, "You've met Laure haven't you? She's my everything. My brain, my eyes," she added with a wink, "and sometimes my ears."

Cassie turned to Laure. "Glad to meet you," Laure said.

Marceline nodded towards the table, and they sat down by the window. From where she sat, Cassie could see the garden through the window. The old man on the ladder was clipping a hedge in slow motion, a cold pipe between his teeth. "I hope you like Earl Grey," Marceline said. "Or perhaps you'd prefer coffee. Americans like their coffee watered down and tasting burnt. This was the kind of coffee they drank during the war. They were nostalgic for it, the taste of terrible army coffee. Quite telling, don't you think?"

"Earl Grey will be perfect."

Laure poured tea in their cups and left the room. "So you hate France I take it?" Marceline asked.

Cassie widened her eyes. "Not at all; what makes you think that?"

Marceline peered at her. "You left. You haven't been back in five years."

"I came here because my father has fallen ill. I came from California." She improvised, "And while I'm here I thought I would look for people he lost touch with."

"Lost touch, eh?" Marceline said in an acerbic tone that did not feel all that kindly. With a steady hand, she took a few petit fours and set them on her plate. Cassie drank her tea avidly. She was thirsty and badly needed to pee. In the weirdness of the moment, she had not felt it appropriate to ask the countess for a pot de chambre. "I wonder what about me makes everyone so eager to get to know me of late," Marceline mused. "Everyone wants to get back in touch, it seems. It must be an irresistible scent people my age start emitting."

"A scent?"

"A whiff of approaching death combined with money. It is quite the seductive scent."

Cassie looked at her, horrified. "I hope you don't think that's why I'm here!"

Marceline gazed at her with her yellow, cat-like eyes. "Dear, that's why *everyone* is here."

Cassie gasped, insulted to her core. Maybe it was the stress of the last few days, but all her restraint and good manners went out the window in a flash. "I'm not here as a strategy to claim anyone's money. I won't try to convince you of the opposite. Think what you like."

"The ploy of the long lost relative, you mean?" Marceline said sweetly as she poured more tea into Cassie's cup. "Why now, then?"

"I'll tell you why now," Cassie said, more abruptly than she wished. "Because up until yesterday I did not know that my father had a sister." Marceline who had been looking straight at her blinked a few times and looked out the window. Cassie continued, "And a week ago, I was in the United States, living my life, minding my own business while my family was planning my father's heart operation without any desire of keeping me informed. Not that this has anything to do with you, but so that you get a sense of how my family functions. Or doesn't. Neither my dad nor my mother and sisters made the smallest attempt to connect with me before taking him to the hospital for a life-threatening surgery. And no, come to think of it, I don't like France all that much."

"Oh, I see," the old woman said with a cryptic smile. "So I might not be the *only* long-lost relative you have in France."

The comment struck Cassie as accurate. She chose from the tray of petit fours a tiny chocolate éclair. "I'm pretty sure I suck at being part of any family," she said, popping the éclair into her mouth. "Let me ask you something. If you think I'm after your money, why even let me in?"

"Boredom?" Marceline suggested.

Cassie leaned forward, reached for her tea and looked straight into Marceline's eyes. "Don't tell me you're not just a little bit curious about me."

Marceline laughed. She seemed entertained. "Admittedly. In that case, what is it you want from me?"

"I would like to talk to you about the past."

"That is indeed all I have going for me," Marceline said with a sigh. "There's a point when things cease to happen. All that looms on the horizon is one's mortality. At that point, it becomes all about the past. Rehashing it, wanting it to have mattered. Could haves, should haves. You hope you made a difference. You hope it wasn't all for nothing."

"Your children will attest that your life wasn't for nothing."

Marceline raised an eyebrow. "My children?"

"They're twins, aren't they? I have twins too."

"Ah, them," Marceline said with an eyeroll.

"They weren't too keen on my meeting you."

Marceline pointed to the stuffed wild cat on a shelf above them. "This lynx has more life in him still than those two ever had." Cassie looked at Marceline in stupefaction, and Marceline laughed. "Could you think a little more quietly? I can read every one of your thoughts!" She waved an impatient hand. "They never made a life for themselves. I was told it isn't their fault. They weren't mothered properly."

"That's quite a pronouncement to make about yourself," Cassie said.

"Oh no, not me … I'm not the mother," Marceline quickly explained. "Theirs died when they were teenagers."

"They called you Mother."

"When it suits them. They certainly never called me that growing up. I did not want children, let alone hormone-laden, brutish adolescents. We've never exactly warmed up to each other. This was my second marriage. Bécasel D'Alompe was a widower." She said with no small amount of satisfaction, "I was a beauty in my youth, you know. There is little left of my looks now, of course," she added coquettishly, perhaps waiting for Cassie to compliment her. And although Cassie could very well imagine how beautiful Marceline might once have been, she did not want to pander to her, so she said nothing.

Marceline registered this and seemed pleased. "A count, a widower, and wealthy to boot. You can imagine his appeal to women. But he wanted me, a fifty-year-old divorcée and older than he was by seven years." She shrugged, "I did warn him, told him that I would make a most unsuitable mother. My career demanded that I travel the world; I was never there. Armelle and Jean-Bernard had nannies – au pairs they call them these days, young women in over their heads. My becoming their stepmother did not improve things. Still, I cannot bear grown people who whine about their childhood. Once an adult, one must suck it up and start taking responsibility for oneself, wouldn't you agree?"

Cassie took that one square in the jaw. "Armelle and Jean-Bernard say that you aren't well."

Marceline cackled. "They *hope* I am not well. I get the use of the house until my death, and then they inherit. Meanwhile, we live under the same roof. Granted there is space, but I have been enduring their gloomy presence for close to forty years. Meanwhile, they've been so busy waiting for my death they forgot how to live their lives. Armelle is married to her last name. Some women are. She was never willing to give that up through marrying into a lesser milieu, and prospects of comparable ranks did not present themselves. As for Jean-Bernard, he's not right in the head as you may have noticed."

"What's wrong with him?"

Marceline shrugged. "A loose screw. Who knows? He never married either, and we should be glad of that." Cassie recoiled at the insensitive remark, and Marceline seemed to notice. "I say things as I see them," she said.

That would be the understatement of the century, Cassie thought. The more Marceline spoke, the less it seemed possible that she and her dad shared DNA at all. Marceline was too vivacious, too sharp, too willing to speak her mind. "Listen, I am just looking for answers to questions about my family."

"Families are more trouble than they're worth. A tremendous source of disappointment and heartache, the lot of them."

"That's what my father seems to think."

"But he suddenly remembered he has a sister?"

Cassie decided that perhaps Marceline would appreciate bluntness. "It was under strange circumstances. When he saw me yesterday, the first time in five years, he got very angry. He cursed at me. He called me names. One name in particular: yours."

Marceline had a little laugh at this and said, "Would you care for another cup of tea?"

"With pleasure."

"And you found me just like that? The next day."

"My sister and I twisted my mom's arm. She told us your last name."

"How did you find me?"

"Your address is listed. You should change that, by the way."

Marceline looked out the window, apparently pondering what Cassie had told her. Outside, the rain had begun falling again, and the strands of wisteria that framed the window swayed in the wind. The old gardener was no longer on the ladder. "Very well then," Marceline said with regret in her voice. "Why don't you ask me what you want to ask me and let this amusing game of charades end."

Cassie wasn't sure she wanted the game to end. She was afraid of Marceline's answers. This woman was far too interesting to learn that they were in no way related. "All right," she said. "Do you have a brother named Gustave Lombard?"

Marceline's expression remained unchanged. Her piercing look revealed a playful intelligence and perfectly sharp mental capacity. And something more: keen interest. Marceline was more engaged in conversing with her than her father would ever have cared to be. "I don't have a brother by that name," she said.

Cassie felt struck by disappointment. And embarrassment. She had congratulated herself for the ease with which she had found his father's sister, but she had found nothing. Instead, she had made a fool of herself with strangers. She leaned back in her chair, her bladder now threatening to burst. "I was wondering if...."

"Yes?"

"I was wondering if I could hmm ... be excused."

"I beg your pardon?"

Cassie burst out laughing at her own ridiculousness and Marceline's dumbfounded expression. "I'm sorry. I can't come up with the polite way to speak of bodily functions while in an aristocratic company. I need to go to the bathroom. It's all this tea."

"Oh," Marceline said, "we aristocrats have no shortage of bathrooms or bodily functions. There is one right outside. Actually," she said, changing her mind, "why don't you go to the bathroom right that way instead?" She pointed to the far side of the room, the back door she had come from. "Over through this door. Down the corridor, and then four doors to your left."

Cassie hurried across the room and found herself in a narrow hallway and counted the doors. One. Two. Three. What a letdown. Marceline would not lie to her face, would she? And yet, the portrait: something in Marceline's countenance, the shape of her chin, her eye color.... But no, Cassie should not read everything that was missing from her life into this.

She arrived at the fourth door and turned the porcelain doorknob. She was in a sort of boudoir, a delightful room basking in warm light filtered through pink silk curtains. The light caressed the bookshelf, the daybed, the comfortable chair and ottoman. This was no bathroom; Marceline had made a mistake. Cassie turned around to leave when something incredible caught her eye on the vanity table, among the perfume bottles, the powder boxes, the ivory combs and tortoise hairbrushes. She gasped. Her pulse skyrocketed before she even knew what to make of what lay before her eyes.

Marceline, Marceline, she muttered to herself. You, naughty girl.

A few minutes later, after finding a bathroom behind the second door, Cassie was back in front of Marceline, but this time she had a triumphant smile on her lips. "You have a lovely home," she said.

"What I'd like to know is," Marceline said, "why you should be so preoccupied with your father's personal affairs. Clearly, he wishes to turn the page. Does he want you snooping into his past? Besides, for all you know he might only be attempting to shield you from it."

"I think I can handle his past."

"But what about his wishes?"

"So, you did not answer my question. Why did you accept to meet me?"

"I told you. I don't get to meet new people too often. And the people who already know me tend to find me insufferable. The sentiment is, by the way, quite mutual." She waved her hand, chasing away an objection Cassie did not express. "People find aging in others odious. I know I certainly do. It's nice to meet someone young occasionally. Someone new. So, tell me, if your father did not decide to talk about that sister of his, why get involved?"

"The truth?" Cassie asked.

Marceline smiled thinly. "Preferably."

"I don't care what my dad wants or doesn't want. I'm looking into this for me."

"And yet, some secrets are best left alone."

Cassie narrowed her eyes, "And you *know* the secret, don't you?"

Marceline chuckled. "Do I?"

"And you *do* know my father. You didn't send me to the wrong door by accident. You wanted me to find *it*."

Cassie and Marceline came to a standstill on either side of the tea tray, watching and measuring one another. Marceline broke the silence. "So? Am I the long-lost sister? Is he the long-lost brother?"

"You know you are."

Marceline smiled. "But can you prove it?"

"Other than the fact that you and I look alike? Same curls. Our eye color is similar. Not a common color, is it? Even the way our hairline is the same, the narrow forehead. With all due respect, since you're far prettier than I am."

Marceline nodded with renewed interest. "We do indeed seem to bear a certain resemblance with one another. My hair used to be black and fluff up much like yours."

"But that's not what gave it away."

"What gave it away, good grief?" Marceline laughed, "Are you Hercule Poirot? Is this like in those detective stories?"

"That object I saw in that pink room, on the vanity. *The finial.* My father owns the very same one. He said there were only two in the world, that they were a pair. One was stolen from him. You have it, right there in that room!"

Marceline sat back. She seemed to be enjoying herself tremendously. "The long-lost sister and the long-lost finial!" she said, beaming.

Cassie frowned, "Why would you not tell me the truth?"

"Point to a single lie that came out of my mouth."

"You denied knowing my father."

"You asked if I had a brother named Gustave … how did you say it? Lombard? The answer to this question is still no."

"But it is him, isn't it?"

"A woman of my rank … not that rank means anything these days, but someone of my wealth must always proceed with caution. Scams are perpetrated on the elderly. And even then, why come here after all these years if you're not here for a piece of the pie."

"The pie?"

"My fortune."

"I have no interest in your fortune," Cassie said, rolling her eyes. "That's not what I'm after. I'm interested in everything that happened before you got any of this."

"So what you're after is my memory."

"Precisely."

"I haven't lost any of my intellectual capacities you know."

"It does look that way."

"But what if my memory conflicts with what you want to hear?"

"I have no preconceived notions of what I want to hear."

"Everyone does. Aren't you worried I might tarnish the way you see your father?"

"Listen," Cassie said. "I need this."

"Why?"

"To figure things out."

"Such as?"

Cassie hesitated. "He and I don't have the closest relationship. As a child, he was wonderful to me. But as I grew up, I don't know … everything changed."

"How so?"

"When I was about twelve years old he became distant and…." She stopped, partly because she was getting choked up, partly because she felt obligated to add a disclaimer. "So that you know, as far as my family sees it, I'm inventing this." Now she felt mildly disgusted with herself. "I hate to rehash old recriminations."

"And why not?" Marceline croaked. "That's all your father ever did."

Cassie was stunned. "I … beg your pardon?"

"Twelve years old, you said?" Marceline asked pensively. "Yes. It would make perfect sense." She grabbed a silver bell and shook it. "I'm calling Laure. We're going to need a whole lot more tea."

****

They remained silent as Laure brought in a new pot of tea. Cassie could tell that the old lady had gone inward. Her haughty defensiveness was changing into a mood Cassie could not decipher. Laure poured tea for them and retreated from the room. Marceline broke her silence. "Perhaps the past is best as you remember it. The way it was told to you has shaped you in ways you might not even realize."

"I want to know the truth about my father."

"The truth? How vague."

"Vague? There only is one truth."

"Nonsense!" the old lady cackled. "There are as many truths as there are human beings experiencing them."

Cassie thought of how her family perceived her vision of the truth as lies. "My dad never spoke of his childhood, of his family, of any of his experiences. He met my mother when he was already forty years old, and it's as though he was born then. There are no pictures. No stories. You'd think he was an amnesiac."

"Trust me on this; he *remembers*," Marceline said. "That's precisely the problem. What does your mother know about your father's youth?"

"If she knows anything, she's tight-lipped about it."

"What if I told you that your father did not just try to make a break with the past, but that he actively proceeded to erase it?"

"What do you mean?"

"Gustave Lombardi," Marceline said, looking straight at her. "That's my brother's name."

Cassie marked a pause. "It sounds a whole lot like Gustave Lombard, doesn't it?"

"They are one and the same."

Cassie was astonished. "My father would have changed his name?"

"It would appear so."

"And you are my aunt?"

Marceline nodded gravely. "I believe I am."

Cassie beamed. "Well, hello. Lovely to meet you!"

Marceline did not waste time in pleasantries. "Do you know much about your grandparents, Cassandra?"

"Please call me Cassie."

"I will call you Cassandra. Cassie feels common. Too American. And don't you even consider calling me Marcie or anything horrid of that sort."

Cassie sensed there was no point in insisting. "Cassandra it is then," she said. "I've never met my grandparents. I saw a picture of my grandfather once, I think."

Cassie had only seen the picture once, but the man in the photograph, and the context of finding it, were perfectly preserved memories. It was summer. She had lost her first tooth. Her mother was wearing an ultra-short dress with large orange and yellow flowers that were the fashion in the seventies. Her mother looked pretty with her well-applied coral lipstick, her tanned legs and arms, her hoop earrings, and her ash-blonde hair, smooth along her back. But as always, her mother was threatening, somehow, behind the veneer. Raymonde's moods turned quickly, without warning, and she was a slapper. You'd find yourself with a burning cheek, left to ponder what you had done wrong. That morning, her mother had seemed amenable, chatty. She had brought along a Polaroid camera and taken a picture of Cassie's new gap-toothed smile. Once the Polaroid was dry, they had opened the family album where photos were few and far between, entire years left unrecorded. A picture had fallen out of it.

It was a black and white photograph of a man in his forties. He wore a straw hat, pants rolled up at the bottom. He was holding a fishing rod in one hand, and in the other hand a medium-sized fish. He was very handsome. He looked like one of those silent movie stars. But most of all he had her father's smile. He was standing on a balcony. In the background, Cassie remembered the ocean, boats in the distance, palm trees.

"Who's this man?" she had asked her mother.

"That's your father's dad, your grandfather," Raymonde had answered.

This was the first time Cassie had ever heard of a grandfather on her dad's side of the family. "Where is he now?" she had asked.

"He's long dead," Raymonde had said.

The album was closed, and so was the conversation. But Cassie thought about the man in the picture a whole lot for the next few days. However, when she opened the album to look for the picture again, it was gone. At dinner one night she said, "I can't find the photo of your dad, Papa. It's not in the album anymore."

Her father had blanched and looked at his wife.

"What?" Raymonde had said innocently.

"The picture of the man with the fish. My grandfather," Cassie had insisted. "It's not there anymore."

"I have no idea what you're talking about," her mother had said with an air of perfect honesty, so much so that after a while Cassie wondered if she had imagined the whole thing.

"He was handsome, I remember," Cassie told Marceline. "He was smiling. On a terrace. There were stone pillars. He held a fishing rod and a fish."

Marceline turned wistful. "Ah yes," she said. "I know the photograph. World War II. The photograph was taken shortly before he died."

"He wasn't wearing a uniform in the picture."

Marceline looked out the window; her face was drawn. "There are many ways to die in a war. Our father's death was the kind that will tear a family apart."

"I was under the impression that *all* my father's family had died in the war. His mother too."

"We lived, obviously. Although with great sadness after losing Father. I imagine it was the same for Gustave. My father's name was Albano. Albano Cohen Lombardi." Marceline's eyes moistened. She dabbed at them with a pressed monogrammed handkerchief. "In the picture you saw, was the balcony overlooking a bay?"

"Yes!" Cassie exclaimed. "A bay with boats in the background." The picture existed! Cassie's fists tightened. She should have felt vindicated. Instead, she felt angry. Why had her mother denied it all? These were the kinds of things she did. She'd do or say one thing, and then deny that she had, and in one fell swoop imply that Cassie was the one who was lying, or worse, that she was crazy. "It looked like the South of France."

"Not the South of France," Marceline said, shaking her head. She was looking tired now, and her words came out more slowly. "Algeria. Algiers to be precise. The picture was taken around October 1942, shortly before Operation Torch. I was on a mission for the OSS, part of setting up that operation."

Operation Torch. This was what Jean-Bernard had blurted out. "The OSS?" she asked. "You were a spy?"

"I guess one could call me that."

"What about my dad? Was he a spy as well?"

"That's a matter up for debate. We were children. I was nineteen years old. He was just seventeen. This was war, and we did things. I was given a mission and…. You see, there are many reasons a family's story might get erased. Sometimes, the people are no longer there to talk. Sometimes it is erased on purpose because the collective family suffering is too great. To go on, some people decide to forget."

"And in the case of your family?"

"I'm afraid both were true. You see, Gustave and I were very different. We looked different physically, and our temperaments are opposites indeed. I was the kind of person who took action, whereas he was kind of a dreamer. Also, we had different upbringings."

"Weren't you raised together?"

Marceline closed her eyes. She, who had looked indomitable ten minutes earlier, now looked her age. For an instant, she seemed to forget that Cassie was there, and silence floated between them. "Raised together?" Marceline finally echoed, opening her eyes. "Well, we were. But in all fairness to

Gustave, we were not raised in the quite same way." Marceline, lost in her memories, seemed to speak to herself. "To understand Gustave, you must understand Albano," she muttered. "To understand the story of the son, you must know the story of the father. And you must understand the time and place in which each one was born. Albano, your grandfather, was the only one in his immediate family to survive one of the last great cholera pandemics of the nineteenth century. He was born in the Ottoman Empire, you see, in 1900, in Smyrna. He left Smyrna when he was twenty-two after it burned to the ground and the Ottoman Empire collapsed. Smyrna as such doesn't exist anymore. It was renamed Izmir. It's in Turkey. Albano was raised by his uncle. He was the orphan son of a prominent rabbi. He was destined from birth to become a rabbi himself."

"How interesting. So my father must have had some Jewish blood?"

"Some?" Marceline had a dry little laugh that turned into a long cough.

Laure, who must have had a sixth sense about Marceline's physical state, arrived in the room. "Madame," she said. "You don't want to exert yourself. The doctor said...."

Marceline ignored Laure, took a sip of tea, and stopped coughing. "Both our parents were Jewish," she told Cassie. "As were their parents, and their grandparents before that. Your father was as Jewish as they come."

"I don't see how that would work," Cassie said. "We are Catholic. Kind of. I mean, my father was, and my mother too. I think. But we weren't religious. My sisters and I weren't baptized. We didn't go to church or anything."

Marceline looked appalled. "Are you telling me that Gustave hid his entire Jewish heritage from his daughters?"

Cassie frowned at this. "He wasn't hiding it ... I don't think. Religion was not a topic of conversation in our family. I never gave it any thought and—"

"Are you an anti-Semite?" the old lady interrupted, peering at her intently above her cup.

Cassie nearly squirted tea through her nose. "Of course not! But I know very little about Judaism one way or another."

"Clearly."

"I'm not familiar with the religion, or the tradition. It doesn't mean that I have negative feelings," Cassie said. "I studied the history of Europe like every other French student. I know about the Holocaust. Although I never understood why anyone would have issues with Judaism or the Jews. That has never made sense to me."

"Even those who take issue with Judaism have to fabricate reasons why they do. The idea that your father would not tell you about his roots surprises me, but I guess it shouldn't. I had no idea how far removed he was trying to get from us. Perhaps it is to be understood in context; I can try to explain if you have the patience."

"Go as far back in time as you need to."

Marceline set her cup down, and tapped her bony fingertips on the table, gathering her thoughts. "All right then. You should know that both your grandfather and grandmother were Sephardic Jews. They were descendants of Jews exiled from Spain in the thirteenth century."

Cassie moaned inwardly. What had she gotten herself into? Marceline continued, "To refresh your memory, this was when King Ferdinand of Aragon and Queen Isabella of Castile issued the edict that expelled all Jews from Spain in 1492. Jews were given a few months to convert to Christianity, leave, or die. You did learn that in school, didn't you?"

No, Cassie did not remember a thing about it. "It rings a bell," she answered.

"I should hope so," Marceline said. "The Ottoman Empire seemed like a reasonable destination for exile. It wasn't a shabby place either. The Ottoman Empire, at its apogee, spanned no less than three continents from Europe to Asia to parts of Africa. A single man, Sultan Bayezid II, had the fate of our family, and perhaps that of an entire segment of Jewish culture, in his hands. He was incredulous that Spain would willingly weaken its economy by evicting its wealthiest and most educated citizens, and he issued a decree extending to the Jews of Spain immediate citizenship. For good measure, he declared it punishable by death to disagree with his edict and went so far as to ridicule Ferdinand and Isabella for impoverishing their kingdom and enriching his – which the Jews most certainly did, for centuries after that. The idea of different races and religions cohabitating in good harmony is a pipe dream nowadays. So you can only imagine how things were throughout the world in the 1400s.

"Well, the Ottoman Empire of the time may have been such a dream. This was perhaps the single place in the world that would find Christians, Jews, and Muslims living and able to worship side by side, protected by a decree of the government. All religions and ethnicities were allowed to coexist in relative peace. Armenians, Turks, Kurds, Greeks, Christians, and Jews did just that, for centuries. And each group was established in free, autonomous societies called millets. Millets followed their respective religion in the places of worship they built – the Jews, the Christians, the Orthodox Greeks, the Muslims, and so forth. Millets functioned according to their own religious and civil laws, spoke their own languages. Their children were educated in their own customs, in their own schools, all with the legal supervision and protection of the Empire in exchange for loyalty to it. Not to mention stiff taxation." Marceline stopped and said, "I don't mean to bore you, but your family's roots can be traced back to the fifteenth century."

Cassie realized that she was sitting on the edge of her armchair, her body forward. "There is nothing I want to hear about more," she assured her. But it wasn't just the story she found fascinating; it was Marceline herself. The way she spoke with conviction, her sentences unclouded by hesitation, like a person who never doubted for a moment that what she had to say deserved attention. The sort of woman Cassie had never known she wanted to be. And with this realization, Cassie felt immensely guilty of liking Marceline too much, of liking her and wanting to be liked by her, which was even worse.

"Thus arrived your grandfather's ancestors," Marceline continued. "After being evicted from Spain with their riches, talents, and education, they promptly went to work building, learning, trading, and innovating. Many Jews grew to prominent roles in finance, politics, medicine, manufacturing, and commerce all over the Ottoman Empire. This went on for centuries with everyone living in relative harmony, give or take a fair share of massacres and wars. And then it all came to a halt by the end of the 1920s."

"World War I?" Cassie asked.

"Even in 1902," Marceline continued without bothering to respond, "when my father, Albano, was born, the Ottoman Empire, after centuries of unparalleled greatness, was ailing. Well, it had had a good run. In the early 1900s, the mood of the world was tipping toward nationalism. It happens every so often; you will discover that for yourself should you live as long as I have. The budding nationalistic hysteria that would soon bring nations to wage war against one another saw itself played out within the Ottoman Empire. What had made the Empire so remarkable, its capacity to embrace immigrants regardless of their religion or nationality, was now at the very core of its demise. It was, shall we say, too mixed. Whatever aggrieved them, people found ways to blame those who weren't like them. Greeks fought Turks, Turks massacred Armenians, Arabs revolted, and everyone hated the Jews."

Smyrna was different, at least for a time. The Ottoman Empire was losing its power and girth, but Smyrna, where my father resided, remained the Pearl of the Orient. Its location on the Aegean Sea put it at the intersection of many nautical roads between Europe and the Orient. Sure, there must have been the same racial hatred there as everywhere, but the world's commercial interests kept Smyrna out of the fray, and there were fewer manifestations. When the Turks, who were on the side of the Axis, lost the Great War, World War I as it is known, the Treaty of Sèvres gave Smyrna and other chunks of the Empire to the Greeks. Another war between the Turks and the Greeks started over land control that lasted for years until Greece was defeated in Anatolia. As the Greek army retreated, Christian and Muslim populations suffered reprisals at the hands of both the Turkish army and the defeated Greek army. Villages were destroyed, crops set on fire, women and children killed, daughters raped. This news, reported by the influx of refugees, brought the ethnic communities that had previously respected one another to a paroxysm of racial hatred. This culminated for Smyrna in September 1922 when the city was burned to the ground.

"How?" Cassie asked. "By whom?"

"No one can agree. The Turks accuse the Greeks of burning it down when they saw that they had lost control of it, and the Greeks believe the Turks did it, in reprisal against the Greek and Armenian populations. The Smyrna fire raged for days. It is said that hundreds of thousands who had taken refuge on the quayside were killed. My father left Smyrna at that point."

Corine Gantz

CHAPTER 10

Flames

Albano walked across the Smyrna pier with joy in his heart. Throughout the Empire, the war between the Greeks and the Turks still raged. Endlessly conflicting rumors as to which country was winning and which was losing never amounted to anything concrete. One could no more trust the printed news than the alarming gossips that rippled through Smyrna. But today, Albano did not feel concerned. Men could go on slaughtering each other to their heart's desire for all he cared. In only a few weeks he would become a father, and shortly after that, he, Xandra, and their child would board the boat that would take them away from the Ottoman Empire and toward their new life in Paris.

Xandra's medicinal brew had worked; until it had not. When they first understood that she was expecting, Albano and Xandra were overwhelmed with equal measures of joy and dread. They now lived a life of outcasts, and the guilt and pain of Hagop's disappearance clung to them like a shroud. For over a year, he and Xandra had been deeply happy in the cave. But with the discovery of the pregnancy came a new set of worries. It would be months before the birth, but they had to think ahead. Taking care of a newborn by themselves was daunting. At first, they had fantasized that Xandra might be accepted back into her family now that she was with child. But Yori, they had learned, had openly sworn to give her a beating or worse if she ever reappeared, and he had even boasted about killing Albano. Would Yori do it? They did not think so. They hoped that the bragging was his attempt at keeping his standing, but the more they discussed it, the less they were willing to take the chance. They resigned themselves to Xandra giving birth without the support of her mother or her community. They had then decided on the next best thing: a hospital birth at the American hospital. It would be expensive, but they could save for it if Albano added more hours of hard physical labor on the quayside and around the city.

After much discussion with Xandra, Albano decided that there was nothing to lose and everything to gain by daring to write a letter, the most important letter he would ever write, the response to which could change everything.

Dear Uncle Moshe, Albano's letter said.

I have a wife now. Her name is Xandra. Well, we are not properly married, but we have just found out that we are expecting a child. Xandra is Armenian, and because of our illicit union, her family has repudiated her. She risks her life if she as much as sets foot in the Armenian quarter, but she isn't welcome in the Jewish quarter either. We have been living on our own on Mount Pagus for the last year, with much help and generosity from Uncle Joshua, but we fear it isn't much of a future to offer our child. We have thoughts of leaving Smyrna to make a life elsewhere. What do you think of France? Do you believe it is a good place for Xandra and me? Might there be possibilities to work there for someone coming from the Ottoman Empire? Xandra and I have been learning French just in case.
Yours truly,
Albano

"How long before the letter reaches him?" Xandra asked.

"A month at most. And another one to receive his reply."

They waited patiently, barely daring to make plans out loud. Each day, Albano stopped by the post office hoping for a letter. When it came at last, Albano resisted opening it until he was back in the cave with Xandra.

It was evening, and the fire was ready, with soup cooking in the kettle. Xandra, who was rounder and more beautiful by the day, opened the letter ceremoniously and gave it to Albano to read out loud.

"*My dear Albano*," began Uncle Moshe's response.

In the aftermath of the bloodbath that was the Great War, France is eager for able bodies to work on their farms and factories, and desperate enough to seek out the help of foreigners. Visas are easy to obtain, especially if you are in possession of a promise of employment, which I am enclosing. Come work with me, Albano! My rug commerce has blossomed, and I have recently sought to expand into the diamond trade. I could use someone I can trust, and I trust no one as much as I trust my own blood. Come to Paris, Albano! Bring your Xandra. I will find a place for you to live. Xandra will need to do nothing further than raise your precious child. Let me know what else you might need, and I will help you.
Warmly,
Your Uncle Moshe

Incredulous, Albano lifted his eyes from the letter. Xandra looked stunned. "Does he mean this?" she asked, her expression full of wonder.

"Uncle Moshe can be a joker, but he is a man of his word."

"France," she murmured. "We can go to France and start a new life."

"Not just a new life, my love. A better life. You read what he said. He wants me to work for him!"

Xandra laughed. "My Albano, the French businessman!"

They discussed this for hours, but every conclusion they came to was the same. They had a chance of starting over in Paris, and they should grab that chance. That meant leaving Smyrna and their families behind and becoming strangers in a foreign land. But in this foreign land, they would be together without hiding, without risk to their lives. Albano wrote a second letter:

Dear Uncle Moshe,
Xandra and I will remain forever in your debt. What you are offering goes beyond our wildest hopes and dreams. We thank you from the bottom of our hearts and accept your generous invitation and offer of work. I hope I can be of help to you, although I know little about rugs, and even less about diamonds, having never even seen one.
I hear that there is anti-Semitism in Europe. Is this something I should be concerned about?
Albano

My Dear Nephew,
Paris has a thriving Jewish community that has prospered here for generations. I'm afraid the brand of Judaism practiced here might not meet with your admirably devout pursuits. Yes, people go to synagogues and light candles for the Shabbat, but I have not seen strong signs of devotion. I am afraid most of this will offend you terribly.
Uncle Moshe

Dear Uncle Moshe,
I hope it is not I who will offend you, dear Uncle. I have renounced becoming a rabbi, and both Xandra and I have vowed to renounce any religion that conspires to keep us apart.
Albano

Dearest Albano and Xandra,
Your choice does not offend me in the least. I am of the mind that it is love, not war, or religion, or power that should be humanity's chief pursuit, and thus, I trust that my personal life choices will not be of a nature to vex you either.
Uncle Moshe

Albano lifted his eyes from the letter. "What does he mean?" Xandra asked.

Albano shrugged. "I don't know."

Albano set out to write another letter in which he told Uncle Moshe he would be working hard to save up money for the boat ride. For the time being, he explained, their savings went to pay for the hospital birth, but as soon as the child was born, he would save for the trip. If all went well, he had calculated that it would take about two years before they could pay for the boat trip to Europe.

Albano set out to work even harder. There was plenty of day labor on the quayside. For the next several months, and as Xandra's belly swelled, their spirits filled with dreams and their hearts with hope.

In the cave, Xandra and Albano, lying on their straw mat and propped with feather pillows against the stone, spent hours practicing French. Every so often, Albano would place his head close to the warmth of Xandra's belly, hoping to feel the kick of the baby, a feeling that never ceased to fill him with wonderment. Already, Albano read and spoke French; now he enjoyed teaching it to Xandra, correcting her diction as she read from the newspaper, her eyebrows twisting in the effort.

They would adopt the ways of France, its language, its traditions, unquestioningly. They would apply for citizenship once there. In France, just as they did in the cave, they vowed to pray privately, and never to force their faith on each other. They also vowed never to blame each other for the choices they made together. They made plans for their child, and for future children. They would teach them about God but not impose a religion. They would teach them about their respective languages and cultures but not to fear people who were different from them. The future thrilled them. Leaving Smyrna would be hard, especially for Xandra, because it would be giving up entirely on the hope of ever connecting with her family again.

One day, after toiling all day under the hard sun loading bags of dried apricots into a boat for Aleppo, Albano went to the American Express office, which he used as a mailing address. Uncle Moshe had sent not a letter this time, but a parcel.

Albano brought it back to the cave that evening, and he and Xandra opened the small brown package excitedly. The box contained a letter, a beautiful shawl of the finest silk decorated with miniature Eiffel Towers, and a French dictionary thickly bound in black leather.

Dearest Albano and Xandra,

I certainly don't plan on waiting years for my new business partner! I took the liberty of sending you a few things. The dictionary might not thrill you, but this time, the adage that one should not judge a book by its cover will not apply. As to your boat expense, you will find within the pages of this book that one thing you said you have never encountered before.

Your Uncle Moshe

"What is he saying?" Xandra wondered, the beautiful silk shawl already wrapped around her shoulders. "Your Uncle Moshe is strange. I don't know what he means half the time."

Albano shook his head. "He's an imaginative person. He likes to tell stories." He shrugged, "This dictionary can only be helpful for our lessons," he said, turning the pages. Suddenly he stopped, widening his eyes.

"What?" Xandra asked as Albano was suddenly turning the dictionary in all directions, opening its pages, fiddling with the cover. "What are you doing, Albano?" Albano was now looking at the cover until his fingers met a slight bulging under the leather. He looked at Xandra, took his knife, and gently peeled off the glue around that area.

A small diamond fell into his lap.

They both gasped. Xandra brought her hands to her mouth. "Oh my God!"

Albano marveled. "That's the thing I said I had never seen before. I guessed what he was trying to tell us: a diamond! Uncle Moshe sent this to pay for the boat ride."

****

Thus, a month later, on a crisp early September morning of the year 1922, Albano was walking toward Smyrna's quayside dressed in his best clothes. In a secret fold of his pants pocket was the small diamond that never left his possession, the key to their safe passage out of Smyrna. Today, he would finalize his arrangement with a ship going to Marseille and pick up the stamped visas that awaited him at the French consulate. Then he would approach the many jewelers in Smyrna and see who would give him the best price for his diamond.

He had not sold the diamond right away because he found it much easier to conceal it than to hide the equivalent in currency. Albano also had a murkier reason: he found it difficult to part with such a wonderful thing. At night, he and Xandra delighted in watching it glisten in the light of the fire. During the day, when he was sure to be alone, Albano took it out of the small leather pouch Xandra had sewn for it and admired its luminescent beauty in the sun. To think that one little stone, carved just so, could hold such value and such beauty! To think that one little shiny rock could transform three lives!

It was early in the morning still, and the French consulate would not open for a little while. Albano decided he would wait for the consulate's opening by doing one of his favorite things, which was to buy a newspaper and sit on the terrace of a French bistro and order a coffee. When he was a child, Albano had admired those groomed, educated European men as they sat on the terraces before heading to work, taking their time to be served breakfast and peruse the news. They had then seemed to him the embodiment of poise and sophistication. He had known then, without believing it possible, that this was the life he wanted.

What a glorious September morning this was, he thought, as he descended toward the quays. He only wished Xandra could share this moment with him. She had not left Mount Pagus in over a year. She was even more prudent not to be seen, unmarried as she was, now that she had a large belly. In Paris, things would be different. The two of them would be able to share every moment, without hiding, without fear. In Paris, he decided, they would start every morning so: they would awaken just as the dawn broke and would walk together down the streets until they found a nice café. They would order breakfast and read the newspaper together. No one would look at them or judge them. They would be like any husband and wife, simply having their breakfast.

****

As Albano walked, the sky was bright blue, and a sea breeze ruffled the top of palm trees and caressed his skin. It was a shame to leave Smyrna now, he thought, just as the city had regained its cosmopolitan flair. The French, the British, and the Italians had returned to Smyrna. On the quayside, you could again sit on the terrace of restaurants, order a cassoulet or an eggplant parmigiana, and watch people from every corner of the earth go about their business. The Ottoman Empire had been on the losing side in 1919 and so large parts of it, including Smyrna, were now under Greek control. But the Greeks, who had taken the city without much bloodshed, ran it well. Preserving their commercial interests meant preserving everyone else's as well. For this reason, even the local Turks didn't object too loudly to the fact that their city had been taken from them.

As Albano made his way toward the pier, he averted his eyes when he passed groups of Armenians, Greek, or Turkish men. The sight of Europeans in their finest attire on their morning stroll by the water did not tell the whole story. Smyrna, open as it was to the sea and the rest of the world, was only a pocket of calm and prosperity, strangely exempt from the vicissitudes of the time. Nothing was serene in the Empire. The Greeks ran the city, but the war with the Turks still raged. Hatred was everywhere. The many years of war had turned peaceful men into soldiers and reasonable ones of all ethnicities into political extremists and religious fanatics. Every day, Albano questioned his decision to wait until their child was born to leave for Europe. Was it wise? Their situation was precarious. Everyone in the Armenian quarter was a danger to them, and they had few friends in the Jewish quarter. And then, there was Xandra who looked gloriously beautiful with her swollen belly. Her vulnerability had become a source of anguish to him. Since the early days of the war, men had reverted to their darkest instincts. Her beauty and the vulnerability of her pregnancy put her at risk. He did not tell her this, but it was something he worried about a great deal.

The moment he arrived on the quayside, Albano was startled to see not just one but several warships on the horizon. He made his way toward the row of cafés, restaurants, and brasseries, and like everyone he passed, looked out at the sea. People were agitated, exchanging speculations, wondering out loud about the presence of warships in the bay. Albano went to sit on the terrace of a French café he favored. "What is happening?" he asked the usual waiter.

"We don't know," the waiter said, setting a cup of coffee on his table. "They keep coming and coming, one warship after another. Here!" He pointed in the distance. "Another one coming! Over there!"

The arrival of a new warship sent everyone into a frenzy of extrapolations.

"Is it an attack?" someone asked.

"The Turks are here!" another shouted.

"Of course not," someone said. "This is the Greek fleet, can't you see? The Greeks aren't about to attack their own city." In the crowd, people laughed.

As more warships entered the bay, and as everyone peered at the horizon, trying to make sense of things, the flags on some of the ships became visible. A Levantine man pulled expensive binoculars out of their case and began to scrutinize the horizon. "What do you see?" people asked.

"It's not just the Greeks!" the Levantine man exclaimed. "I see a French flag. And this one is British!"

"And an Italian destroyer!" screamed another man who also had binoculars. "This makes no sense."

Soon there were about twenty European warships on the horizon as well as many Greek vessels. A post office employee came running in, red and sweaty and brandishing a printed cable.

"Kemal's army has won in Anatolia. The Greeks are defeated!"

Everyone in the café went silent. Cigarettes fell from lips. People stood up, dropped their newspapers and napkins.

Fear rocked Albano like a terrible earthquake, as though the ground had shaken beneath his feet. Everyone on the quay began to speak at once, all saying the same thing, in their language: "This was impossible. It had to be incorrect. How could the Greeks be defeated? They had the largest and strongest army. A much better army than Mustapha Kemal's."

"I heard the Greek army is bankrupt. They have no weapons, no shoes, no horses," someone said.

"The Greek newspapers have kept saying that everything was fine."

"They were only trying to raise our spirits."

"But why are there European warships in the bay?"

"Are they here to protect us against the Turks?"

The thought was both chilling and reassuring. It would make sense that the boats had been dispatched to intervene. There were too many Europeans living and working in Smyrna. The warships must have been sent here as a deterrent.

Things were happening fast. They watched, filled with dread and hope as an imposing Greek warship came close to the quay and dropped anchor. Soon, a dozen rafts approached, each holding just a few Greek sailors. They docked, and the sailors put down their oars, prepared their rifles, and waited. For what? The sight of rifles quieted everyone. The crowd, confused, waited as well. All eyes were on the Greek sailors and their weapons. Something would happen any instant now; the crowd sensed it.

Suddenly, there was a shift in people's attention. Café chairs were pushed in unison as men rose from their tables. Gazes shifted, and hundreds of disbelieving faces turned away from the boats and toward the crowd on the quayside. People parted, revealing a lone soldier who was making his way across the quay, limping toward the water. It was a Greek soldier, bare feet, weaponless. His uniform was in shreds and bloodied. There was a thick, dirty bandage over his head. His eyes were empty, and he looked at no one. People continued to part all around him as he labored toward the water on what seemed to be his last reserves of strength. Were the rafts waiting for him? Albano wondered if he was someone important in need of an escort.

"A retreating Greek soldier!" someone said out loud, voicing what everyone understood at once.

The soldier made his way to the dock. Once there, assisted by the Greek sailors, he clambered into one of the rafts. But the raft did not move; the sailors did not take their oars. They continued to wait. A heavy silence fell on the quayside as heads turned in unison toward a second Greek soldier, in just as bad shape, now appearing through the crowd. And now another. And another, and soon there were dozens of them. All were in a terrible condition. All seemed propelled to get to the water, and all climbed inside the rafts. One soldier dropped to his knees and then to the ground before he could reach the dock. Two soldiers not much better off than he was picked him up by his armpits and dragged him toward the boats.

In minutes, the mood on the quayside had shifted. There was a sense of urgency, of mounting panic among the patrons of the restaurants, the fishermen, the restaurant waiters. Albano felt it too, the sensation of doom, like a big wash of dread that hollowed out the belly: something terrible had happened, or was about to. One moment a dozen soldiers clambered toward the boats, the next there was a hundred of them, and the reality of the pathetic state of the Greek army was revealed. The soldiers were dirty, shoeless, bandaged, and bloodied. Many had lost their weapons. On each face was painted the carnage they had suffered. But as pathetic as it was to witness the collapse of an army, no one on the quay was prepared to face what happened next. In the trail of the soldiers appeared the first of the Greek refugees. Soon there were hundreds of them: children, old men, and women, women carrying babies. Judging from their exhaustion, they must have been walking for days. They carried few belongings. They were filthy and haggard. Many immediately started to beg for water and food. There were many injured among the civilians and many burnt victims dragged in stretchers or pushed in wheelbarrows. The cries and moans of pain iced the blood as much as the deadness in their eyes.

The rafts dispatched to rescue the fleeing army, now filled, began to make their way back to the Greek fleet. The incoming Greek soldiers who continued arriving down from inland in droves gathered on the dock, awaiting rescue.

"Who are these people?" someone asked.

"Did you see?" someone pointed out. "Not a single Greek refugee was allowed into the rescue boats."

"They will come back for them."

"What if they don't? How many more are there? What if they leave the refugees here? The city cannot absorb all these people."

Albano understood what everyone on the quay understood. If the Greek army was retreating, it meant that the Turks were advancing. In less than a day, Mustapha Kemal could be in Smyrna, eager to retake the city. There was no telling what would happen then. Throughout the Empire, it had been the same story. What a fool he had been to believe that Smyrna would be any different! There had been retaliation on civilian populations: the systematic destruction, the burning of villages, rapes, and murders had reached a paroxysm of madness everywhere. Why would Smyrna be exempt from all this? The state of those refugees, now advancing by the thousands, betrayed the devastation they must have suffered inland, a devastation which might soon befall the Christians of Smyrna.

"They will burn the city down!" someone cried out.

"Assuredly not," a voice said. "Mustapha Kemal would not allow the destruction of the Jewel of the Orient." There was a collective murmur of assent. The Turks would not want the city damaged. It had too much Islamic history, magnificent mosques, not to mention that Smyrna played an essential commercial role on an international scale.

"This is why the warships are here," someone said. "Every country wants to preserve its interests and its citizens. They are standing guard. Kemal will never dare create a diplomatic incident. After all, he is only at war with the Greeks, not with all of Europe." There was a collective sense of relief. People had found ways to convince themselves that they would be safe.

Albano thought differently.

He knew in an instant what he needed to do. He needed to head for the French consulate to get their stamped visas and run back up Mount Pagus to fetch Xandra. They would board the first French ship that would take them. The luxury of waiting until Xandra had safely given birth was a notion of the past. If this was true that the Turks were advancing, no Christian in the city was safe. Doubt came to his mind. Should he first pick up the visas? They were stamped at last and ready to use. Or should he not waste a moment in alerting Xandra? The Turkish army would want to take possession of the highest ground in the city, as was their symbolic way to claim it. What if they decided that Mount Pagus constituted the highest part of the city?

He needed to get Xandra first! The visas would have to wait.

Albano put money down next to his steaming coffee and abandoned the café. He rushed away from the esplanade as soldiers and refugees poured into the quay in increasing numbers. Many simply collapsed as close to the water as possible. Those who could immediately set up camp, laying claim to every nook they could find on the esplanade, against the walls of buildings, on porches and stoops, all around the fountain where he had met Hagop that first day, and under every bit of shade they could find. Women were crying out for food and water for their children as Good Samaritans came out of restaurants and cafés bringing glasses of water and bread. One thing was obvious: at the rate with which the refugees were arriving, those efforts would soon prove vastly insufficient.

****

Albano arrived in the cave two hours later. In the cave, Xandra was preparing a meal. She got up from the ground, her expansive belly weighing her down. "What is happening?" she asked the instant she saw the expression on his face, his red cheeks, and sweaty clothes.

"The Greeks have lost," Albano said. "The Turks are coming. Thousands of refugees are pouring into Smyrna in the trail of what's left of the Greek army. We need to go down to the city. Now."

He had expected Xandra to panic, but that wasn't her way. She only blanched and asked, "Why now?"

"There are European and American ships, even Japanese ones, in the bay to watch over the city. If there is looting or massacres, it will be in the mountains and inland where the rest of the world cannot see."

"Did you get the visas?"

At that moment, Albano sensed it: he had made a mistake. "I thought it best to get you first," he said.

"Why can't we stay in the cave? It has protected us this far."

"How long would we need to stay in hiding? Days? Months? How would we eat? And after that, what is to say that Kemal's Smyrna would let Christians and Muslims coexist?"

"What about Jews?"

"I think he might leave Jews alone."

"Then you can get food from your uncle, and I'll continue in the cave until the baby comes."

Albano shook his head. "I think we need to leave before the baby is born. We need to leave now. With all the sick refugees coming in I worry that you might be turned down at the hospital."

"The hospital would not turn down a pregnant woman."

Albano tried not to let his voice betray all he had seen. "I saw pregnant women and children in need of care in the streets today."

"The baby will come in the cave then," Xandra said, shaking her head stubbornly. "You will help me with the birth, and I will feed our child. We don't need the hospital."

"You have not seen what I saw," Albano implored. "I fear that a great tragedy is about to befall the city. We need to board the first French ship we can and leave. Immediately."

Xandra put her hand on her belly, protectively. She was quiet for a long while, thinking. "If you are certain this is what we must do," she said.

"I am certain of nothing," he admitted.

Xandra did not respond. In the darkness of the cave, she began gathering their belongings in silence. They packed clothes for the child, the ones she had sewn. Also food: cheese, olives, bread, and dried fruit. Albano filled their sheepskin with water. Xandra packed up their spare set of clothes and sandals. They concealed the finials in the folds of Xandra's wide skirt, in narrow pockets she had sewn especially for this purpose between layers of her petticoat.

Within thirty minutes, all was ready. From the crevice behind the boulders, they retrieved the money stashed away for the hospital birth fee.

****

They trekked slowly, hiding in bushes when they heard the galloping of a horse or the roar of an automobile. When they joined the main road, Xandra and Albano gasped. On his way to the cave, he had crossed paths with refugees by the hundreds who were going down the mountain and heading for the sea. Now, the road to the city was packed with thousands upon thousands of refugees and soldiers, perhaps a hundred thousand or more. Albano had never seen so many human beings in one place.

They joined the slowly moving crowd, felt their heat, their stench. They could not have gone any faster than the crawling pace at which this wave of sick, wounded, hungry, and thirsty humans moved. Albano stayed close to Xandra. They both carried their possessions on their back, with Albano bearing the heaviest load. Dozens of times Albano felt sick having to fend off children and mothers who were begging. How rapidly and easily a person could revert to caring only about his self-interest, even in the face of hungry children.

Already, it was dark. The slow procession of moonlit silhouettes slowed to a crawl when they finally arrived near the quayside. Xandra and Albano, pressed against many bodies, held hands and said nothing as they advanced ever so slowly, trying not to bump into those ahead of them. On the darkening horizon, one could still make out the reassuring presence of the dozen warships anchored in the harbor.

The glamorous esplanade of the morning had turned into an encampment, a lumpy mass composed of thousands of strewn bodies, parcels, goats, caged chickens, and whatever meager possessions with which the refugees had managed to escape. The smell of feces and urine was terrible, as were the moans that floated in the falling night.

On the docks, the Greek rescue boats worked relentlessly by the light of lanterns carrying soldiers to the destroyers and then rushing back to the quay for more.

Albano held Xandra's hand tightly as they walked across the esplanade in the darkness, stumbling on the limbs of sleeping children, and barely avoiding stepping in trash and excrement, until they found an open spot near an Armenian family, a mother, father, and their three small children. Xandra set blankets on the ground, and she and Albano discreetly shared a few almonds.

"As soon as it is morning," Albano whispered, "I'll go to the French consulate and retrieve the visas. I'll sell the diamond, send a cable to Uncle Moshe explaining the situation, and we will present ourselves at the first ship in the direction of France, newly purchased tickets in hand."

This optimistic plan, buoyed by Albano's falsely reassuring tone, allowed them to fall into an uneasy sleep.

****

With the call of the first caged rooster, the esplanade awakened and Albano took in the seriousness of the situation. The lighthearted atmosphere that had prevailed on the quay through both wars had made way to desperation. The entire quayside was nothing but a mass of wounded, sickly refugees, exhausted from their painful trek from inland to shore, and more of them were arriving every minute. They were Christians and, for the most part, Greek and Armenian women, children, and elderly folks. All had followed the retreating Greek army for protection. The only young men present were the crippled ones who had not been suited for war. One woman in ten appeared to be pregnant.

"Why did you come here?" Albano asked the Armenian mother and father near where they had settled.

"We followed the army to the water, and here we are," the husband answered with exhaustion. It was clear that he had no desire to converse. "We hope to escape by boat before Kemal's army enters Smyrna," he said wearily.

"But why did you leave?"

The man peered at him, dismayed by Albano's ignorance. "The Turks have destroyed our village, burned everything. They raped our women and girls. They even slaughtered children. Innocent children! From our village, we alone were able to bring our family intact. So many have lost everyone."

"This is the way of the Turks," the wife told Xandra, her face distorted with loathing and rage. "They are beasts, and they will want the blood of everyone here."

Xandra and Albano looked at each other, a current of terror passing between them. "But they won't need to kill anymore," Albano said almost pleadingly. "They have won."

"It is true what they say!" the husband said, disgusted. "You Smyrniots have suffered nothing of the wars." He spat on the ground and added angrily, "This is the way it has been. Each military victory is followed by rapes and massacres."

"But you are Armenian," Xandra said. "The Turks are at war with the Greeks."

"They are at war with anyone who is not Muslim, but they hate the Armenians the most. Jews and Muslims are in this together; they want to exterminate every single Christian in the Ottoman Empire."

Xandra seemed about to respond something in defense of the Jews, but Albano silenced her with a wary look.

"They say Kemal's army is well trained and honorable," Albano said with as much assurance as he could muster.

To this, the husband shook his head glumly. "Perhaps, but the Chettes have filled his army."

"What are those?"

"Irregulars and mercenaries. They are devoted to Kemal, but they are not soldiers. They do not follow discipline. And what of your local Turkish citizens? What will they do when Kemal arrives? They will celebrate and join in the looting, that's what they'll do. This is how it has been in every village, in every city." The man changed his tone to a whisper so that only Albano and Xandra could hear. "But if the Turkish army doesn't, the Greek army will. They know they have lost Smyrna and they will destroy everything so that Kemal won't be able to put his hands on it."

As though this conversation was spontaneously repeating itself from person to person, the population on the quay seemed gripped with collective panic. The Armenians and Greeks feared the Turkish army, but the Armenians feared the Greeks too. Everyone was terrified.

As the Greek soldiers continued being evacuated by the hundreds, everyone else was beginning to stand in lines awaiting a chance to board a ship, holding a spot for their families, clutching papers that proved their nationalities. It was clear that orders were not to evacuate. Tempers started to flare up.

"They are still not taking refugees! Soldiers first, they say," a Greek man growled upon returning from the dock.

On other docks further to the right, another kind of activity was building. Vehicles were unloading throngs of British, French, and Italian citizens who pressed themselves into lines. Levantines families were in line as well, dressed in their manner, a mix between styles of the Occident and the Orient. Their luggage was arranged in neat piles as Turkish servants fanned them and brought them refreshments from the nearby cafés. Nowhere had the divide between human circumstances been more striking: one group hopeless, famished, filthy, and the other radiating entitlement and self-importance. But there was a single emotion the wealthy and the downtrodden shared, and that was fear. No one knew for sure what was about to unfold, but all seemed clear on the urgent need to leave Smyrna.

"Why aren't the British and French warships sending rescue boats? What are they waiting for?" someone in the crowd said.

"Word is they won't take in refugees. In their minds, this is an issue between the Greeks and the Turks, and they want to remain neutral. Each warship will only take their own citizens."

Xandra looked at Albano, panic-stricken. Albano whispered to her reassuringly. "Our situation is different. We will have French visas. We won't be refugees in their eyes."

A small boat detached itself from the Italian destroyer and docked. Italian journalists and photographers clambered out noisily and proceeded to unload their equipment, still and movie cameras. The Italian journalists made their ways to the cafés and opened their briefcases to reveal encased typewriters. They immediately took out paper and carbon and began typing. Others unfurled their equipment and started taking photographs. Albano was reminded of the story of the human zoo, and of the people who found it entertaining to visit them. Whatever was about to happen, the world would be watching indeed.

In the harbor, refugees had to make way for Levantine automobiles. The cars stopped, and servants in white livery jumped out and stacked crates, boxes, and suitcases while others loaded them onto private boats. The Levantine women shielded their skin from the sun with lace umbrellas and put lavender-scented handkerchiefs over their noses to protect their senses from the stench. "The Levantines are sending their women and children away," Xandra said. "I recognize some of my customers."

"I recognize some of them as well."

"Could we ask them for help?"

"If it comes to that," Albano said.

Xandra looked at him intently. "When will we know if it has come to that?"

"Let me retrieve the French visas as soon as the consulate opens. Then we'll know more."

"Maybe we should go to the Armenian quarter," Xandra said. "Perhaps seeing the danger, someone I know will forgive us for what we did and offer us shelter for a day."

Albano hesitated before stating the harsh truth. "Xandra, I am not certain the Armenian quarter will be safe at all once Kemal's army arrives."

They decided that Xandra would stay next to the Armenian family while Albano picked up the visas. The French government building was only five minutes away. Albano walked across the quayside trying not to listen to his thoughts. For now, at least, things were relatively calm. The many warships floated in the bay and beyond, a sight that was both alarming and reassuring. The crowd of refugees had huddled on the quayside although the influx seemed to have slowed. But it was too many people in too close proximity. Albano sensed it; the slightest incident would trigger a chain reaction of panic. If that happened, things would deteriorate. Unrest would affect the functioning of the consulate, the banks, and the ocean liner traffic and derail his plans, plans that were very far off course already. He felt trapped. He sensed that they all were, trapped on the quayside with a single goal, a single thought: to find a boat out of Smyrna. That task, which would have been effortless just the day before, might soon become insurmountable. Why had they planned to wait for after the birth to leave? He should have known to leave as soon as the diamond arrived! Their attachment to Smyrna and to the way things were had been too strong. Xandra had asked him to stay until the birth, and he had agreed. Why had he trusted her instincts and ignored his own?

When he arrived at the French consulate, Albano's fear was confirmed. Already, there were several hundred men and women in line hoping for a visa. He joined the line and resigned himself to a long wait. At least, their visas were signed. It was only a matter of retrieving them.

He waited there, anxious about Xandra's well-being. It was safer for her out on the quayside, protected by the sheer mass of people stranded there and in full view of the European boats, than out on the streets where things felt uncertain. But the sun was fierce. At this time of the day, there would be no shade for Xandra or anyone on the quay.

There were about forty people ahead of him. People sat on the stairs and waited. The consulate opened. Everyone stood up. But when they saw that the guards only let in three people at a time, people returned to sitting on the stone steps. The long wait in the sun began. Every so often, the guards would open the door to let a few people in, and a few others would come out with relief on their faces.

Albano had been there for two hours, perhaps three, in the untenable heat of the day. Only about twenty people had entered and exited the building so far, and there were about twenty more ahead of him. He could not leave the line to see how Xandra was doing and risk losing his place. A few men had gone to urinate on the steps rather than lose their spot, and now it smelled wretched. Albano was standing in line and waiting. He felt bored and anxious, sleepy and impatient, drowsy and thirsty, but suddenly, all this was replaced by a sort of chill up his spine. He felt the chill in his body and the tingle of fear in his palms before he could even understand that something was happening. A sound, impossible to define a first, was breaking through the fabric of the day. It began as a sort of clamor; voices and shouts intermingled. Soon, it was as though the entire city were emitting a low moan.

Things happened fast. In an instant, the line Albano was in dispersed. Everyone ducked into corners, and he did as well, not knowing what was to fear or from where the threat came. An otherworldly silence fell upon the city. All sounds were sucked out of the air as though a hundred thousand people were holding their breath.

There was a tremendous vibration; he felt it. And then thunder broke. Drums and trumpets. The sound of thousands of hoofs beating the pavement. Gunshots. The terrified howls of women and children. Crowds parted only meters from where Albano stood, to reveal the phantasmagorical vision of the Turkish army entering Smyrna.

First came the cavalry mounted on majestic horses and moving in perfect military unison. The cavalrymen wore embroidered Circassian hats and gleaming curved scimitars and carried Turkish flags and banners. The cavalcade moved thunderously through the street, followed by a military band and finally a mass of soldiers on foot wearing black fezzes, long guns over their shoulders, and swords strapped around their waists.

The Muslim population of the city rushed into the street and stood at windows, erupting in jubilation, weeping with joy, and waving Turkish flags. Albano only felt dread.

At a command, the cavalry stopped, separated into two lines, and drew their swords. Albano, only meters away from all this, gasped in shock. The army's countenance was formidable. After witnessing what remained of the Greek army, there was no longer the shadow of a doubt as to who was victorious in the war.

All of Albano's expectations and rationale, everything he had thought would happen, everything he had planned, was shattered at once. All he could do was watch as the calls of trumpets and the rhythmic pounding of drums reached their climax, and Mustapha Kemal himself made his victorious entrance into Smyrna. Kemal, only feet from where Albano was, stood splendidly, very straight on his gorgeous horse. With his chiseled face and piercing eyes, he looked every bit the fearsome leader of his reputation. He did not stop, and neither did the procession. They were followed by exultant Turks, men, women, and children. All went up the streets, no doubt to reach the highest ground and thus officially claim the city.

Drenched in sweat, Albano slithered back deep into the crowd and out of sight. He walked up the deserted steps to the consulate. At the door, he knocked again and again, but no one opened. After ten minutes of this, Albano bolted in the direction of the quayside.

When he arrived, a heavy silence had seized the mass of refugees. The quayside was a zoo indeed. A terrible zoo. The refugees on the quayside had been ambushed like beasts between Kemal's army and the sea. They cowered, prayed, and cried just as the Turkish citizens of Smyrna were flocking into the streets, shooting their firearms in the air, laughing, waving flags, and shoving each other to catch a glimpse of the military procession. In the water, British, French, Italian, and American destroyers and cruisers stood guard, but the restaurants, the cafés, and the brasseries, so lively the day before, were not only closed but boarded up, the owners still in the process of hammering wood planks over windows. This struck Albano as a terrible omen. The optimism of the Smyrniots, their determination to go on living to the fullest despite the world's mayhem, their insistence that commerce could erase all differences between races ended when the restaurants and cafés that had remained defiantly open through many wars and invasions now boarded their doors. Suddenly, the boats in the bay did not reassure the way they had the day before. Albano nudged his way through the crowd in search of Xandra. The mass of people felt denser, more desperate. There were ripples of alarms, rumors, bits of sentences overheard. "The officers are in control," one Greek man said. "No one will go crazy while Kemal is here, and Kemal wants the respect of the Americans and Europeans, and they are watching from the boats." Albano prayed that was true.

Xandra was sitting on the blanket right where he had left her. Waiting for him, trusting him to fix everything. "The French consulate shut its doors when Kemal's army arrived," he had to tell her.

"What can we do?" she asked.

Albano noticed the strain on her face and wondered if she had slept at all the night before. "We can only wait for it to reopen," he said.

"Look at all these people," she whispered. "They all want to leave too."

"Their situation is very different from ours," he assured her. "They have nothing. We have money, we have visas awaiting us, and we have the diamond."

"Oh my God, Albano," Xandra exclaimed, suddenly realizing. "You have to go!"

He frowned. "Go where?"

"You have to go to Frank Street and sell the diamond. Without money, we will never get a boat, even if we get our visas."

Albano rushed in the direction of Frank Street as the sounds of Turkish celebration emanated from every corner of the city. There were rumors that looting had begun. He quickened his pace. People were in the streets, celebrating still, but the women and children were gone; only the men remained. They walked in groups, brandishing jugs of alcohol and swords, sometimes even a rifle. Albano saw a group of men coming out of a store, carrying things they had stolen. One by one, the shops and restaurants he passed closed, windows were shut, entrances to stores were boarded up. Albano began to run as fast as he could, powerlessly trying to beat the clock. But by the time he arrived on Frank Street, every jeweler had locked their front doors and closed their wooden shutters.

Crestfallen, Albano returned to the quayside and told Xandra what had happened. She only closed her eyes and did not speak. What could she have said? He spent the rest of the day going back and forth between Xandra and walking around the area to assess the situation. He walked along the quay listening to rumors, checked on the French consulate, bartered some of their food against fresh goat milk that he brought to Xandra, and back to the consulate. But the consulate never reopened that day. As the day progressed, Albano's dread grew. European citizens on the quay were filing into boats that carried them away into the ships of their respective countries. One by one, the Levantine families sailed away in their private boats.

By dusk, all that was left on the quay were the refugees. Albano no longer trusted that his and Xandra's situation was different from theirs.

As night fell, the sounds of gunshots and celebration receded into the distance. The people on the quay grew quiet, and many allowed themselves to hope that perhaps they would be safe after all. The army was elsewhere. The looting would occupy the rowdiest elements. Thus far, there had been no violence.

Albano lay close to Xandra. She sat upright, her back against a jute bag filled with millet, and he curled up on his side, his head on her lap. Periodically, there would be the sound of guns fired into the air. Still, he fell asleep as she softly caressed his hair and as the wind carried echoes of Turkish celebration.

****

Albano was awakened by Xandra's hand on his shoulder. She was wide awake. It was nearly morning.

"Did you sleep at all?" he asked.

Xandra did not respond. She looked pale; her eyes were red. "There are rumors of looting in the Armenian quarter," she murmured.

"Who says this?"

"How do we know that my family is safe?"

Albano rubbed his eyes. "I will go and inquire."

"It's too dangerous."

"I know the back alleys. I won't take the main streets."

"I know that my father wants to kill you!"

Albano took Xandra's hands and rubbed them soothingly between his. "I will look from the street. I will make sure everyone is safe, and I will come back."

Albano drank some tea that the Armenian family had made. Then he and Xandra ate the last of their bread. He got up and trudged across the quay through the multitude of refugees. Smells were getting worse. Greek and Armenian flags, which had been everywhere just the day before were conspicuously absent from sight. Turkish flags now dangled from every window.

Albano arrived at the edge of the Armenian quarter to find not a soul on either side of a crude barricade made of piled chairs and tables. Who had set this up, he wondered worriedly? Was it the Armenians to prevent the Turks from coming in, or the Turks to stop them from getting out? Yori and the rest of the Armenian men had no doubt prepared for the eventuality of a Turkish invasion. They must have had weapons stashed away to protect themselves, Albano hoped, ammunition, escape plans and routes figured out. From what he could see on his side of the barricade, the Armenian quarter looked deserted. Windows were boarded up, entrances to buildings bolted, streets empty. He waited for a while, pacing along the barricade, unsure what to do. He was about to move a few chairs to enter when two heavily armed Turk guards appeared before him and pushed their guns in his chest. The men did not dress like soldiers from Kemal's army.

"Are you Armenian?" they demanded to know.

"I'm Jewish," Albano mumbled.

"Do you have business in here?"

There was a muffled scream in the distance, the sounds of broken glass. "Only friends I, I meant to visit," he stuttered.

"Go back where you came from. We are under military instructions. No one can leave or enter the Armenian quarter."

As the exchange took place, both parties pretended to ignore the echoes of a woman's screams resonating in the streets.

"When will it open up again?" Albano asked, trying to appear nonchalant.

"It will open when it opens, Jew. Now go!"

Albano walked away. When he was out of sight, he leaned against a wall and tried to calm his breathing. For an hour, he went through back alleys and tried different streets, but everywhere was barricaded.

He returned to Xandra and told her what had taken place, although he mentioned none of the chilling sounds of violence and distress he had heard. Xandra swallowed her tears before they appeared. "There are rumors that they are killing people in there."

"I think that everyone is gone," he lied. "I saw no one on the streets except for Turks."

"Something is wrong, Albano. I know it. And there is looting taking place, to be sure. We can hear the gunshots from here."

"Looting, yes. But people must have run away."

"Please ask people as you wait in line for the visas," she implored.

Albano went. The line was even longer than the day before, but despite people tapping and pleading at the door, the French consulate did not open that day.

By noon, all knew what was taking place in the Armenian quarter. Smyrna's Turkish civilians, perhaps helped by Kemal's army's irregulars, and perhaps even under orders of Mustapha Kemal himself, had shut down the Armenian quarter street by street, making it impossible for anyone to see what was happening as they methodically looted stores and pillaged houses.

All through the following night came the distant echoes of the rampage taking place. Albano felt less than certain that everyone had evacuated. What if, instead of running, they had thought themselves safer inside their houses? And what if they were trapped now, with all exit routes blocked? What if behind each bolted door was a terrified family? Locked doors were no match for drunken looters. Xandra, imagining her mother, father, and little sisters cowering in terror in the cellar, cried all night long, and Albano was powerless to comfort her.

With daybreak came rumors of atrocities. The rumors spread like fire on parched land. Albano removed his caftan and the diamond it concealed and gave it to Xandra. "Keep this. It will be safer with you."

"What will you do," Xandra asked? Her eyes were red. She looked exhausted. "I will ask if anyone has any information about your family."

Once he was away from the crowd, Albano strategized. He could not pass as Turk; his accent would immediately betray him. To be mistaken for Greek or an Armenian might be life-threatening. Of all the minorities in Smyrna, Jews were, at the moment, the least threatened. So, for the first time in a long while, Albano retrieved his kippah from his pocket and placed it on his head.

When he arrived at the entrance of the Armenian quarter, the barricades seemed abandoned. He climbed over and around the mess of broken chairs and tables and slowly walked through the streets, staying close to buildings in case he needed to hide. The destruction took his breath away. The ground was a sea of broken glass, and not a single window stood. Every door was gone, reduced to splinters, every storefront turned to rubble.

Albano advanced inside the Armenian quarter, walking on the debris. The silence was heavy, painful. Where were the looters? Where were the people? Before he turned onto the main street, a smell unknown and horrendous grabbed his throat, but it came too late to prepare him for the devastation that lay before him. Dozens of bodies were strewn on the pavement. Men, women, and children; dead. Butchered. The smell of decaying flesh soon replaced every other smell. Flies circled in malefic clouds over the bodies. Drying blood ran down the length of the sloping street. Albano's legs folded under him, and he fell to his knees.

A tremendous sound of shattering glass broke the silence, and he only had seconds to get up and sprint into an open building. In the darkness, he watched as a group of men, about a dozen of them, brandishing guns, flags, swords, and bottles of alcohol, walked past without seeing him. They shouted drunkenly, laughed, stumbled on each other. Albano held his breath as they began to enter one building after another, each time exiting empty-handed. Finding nothing left to steal made them furious. They began to fire gunshots at façades and throw things at windows. Albano cowered. His kippah would hold no power against those bloodthirsty beasts. Eventually, the men stepped over the bodies as though they were logs, turned a corner down the street, and disappeared.

Albano stayed where he was, trying to gather his thoughts and breathe normally. Soon another group of men appeared, Turkish soldiers in uniform this time. They were drunk as well, disheveled, and with none of the exemplary discipline of the day before. They were dragging a young man by his arms. They stopped in the middle of the street and beat him mercilessly. Albano, his whole body shaking, closed his eyes and waited. When the young man went quiet, the soldiers left, and the street was silent again. Albano waited a few minutes, then ran to the man. He was dead.

He returned to his hiding spot and remained there for a long time. Layered with his fear for Xandra's family, Albano felt the rise of a terrible suspicion. These horrors were not only the work of drunken men turned murderers. If soldiers were doing it, they were all doomed. It meant that military discipline had broken down. And in the absence of military rules and restraint, every soldier could transform into a well-trained and well-armed savage.

If he stayed in the Armenian quarter, he might become the next man they beat to death, but a terrible urge told him to remain here. How could he leave until he knew that Xandra's family was safe? Nauseous with fear and dread, Albano moved from carriage entrances to cellar doors, inching closer to Xandra and Hagop's family house. The magnitude of the devastation stunned him. Every Armenian household had been invaded and pillaged. Belongings were sprawled into the streets. Everything was in pieces, defaced. The pavement was a sickening hue of red-brown from all the blood now dried up. The bodies were an intolerable sight. They had not just killed, those beasts, they had mutilated, dismembered, disfigured, and then killed. Men, women, or children, even tender babies; they had not cared. Everywhere, flies swarmed. The smell was relentless, suffocating, abject.

He had hoped at first that people were hiding in cellars and attics. He had pictured mothers, their hands on their children's mouths to quiet them. Daughters still hiding under floorboards. Entire families huddled in secret rooms with men at their doors, armed to defend them. But now Albano began to pray for the opposite. He hoped that no one had attempted to hide. To run away would have been the only option for survival.

He moved through the neighborhood slowly, ducking into dark doorsteps, hiding behind doors, and plunging into dark alleys the moment he heard footsteps or drunken laugher.

****

The door to Yori's bakery was open.

Inside, all that was made of glass was shattered, every chair and table overturned. The beautiful one-hundred-year-old fresco on the wall, the one Xandra's family was so proud of, had been defaced with excrement. The air and sticky surfaces were thick with flies. The smell of warm pastries, honey, and roasting nuts still hung in the air absurdly. Albano, his heart beating wildly with fear of what he might find, walked to the main living room. Everything that could be carried had been stolen, and everything that could not was destroyed. The furniture, the rugs, the tapestries on the walls, the dishes were gone. There was nothing left of Xandra's family's cherished belongings.

He stepped over shattered objects, and his heart stopped. On the floor, sticking out from a pile of rubble, was an inert arm. He rushed to it and came to his knees. It was Ina, Xandra's mother. There was a clean, small wound in her chest that reddened her blouse. Albano brought his shaking hand to feel her pulse and recoiled at the feel of her arm cold and stiff already. He got up, staggered away, stumbled around the room. He went down the steps, bumping into everything, to the underground cellar where Yori made his bread. He found no one downstairs, only rubble and exploded bags of flour that thinly coated everything. Albano breathed with relief. If Yori wasn't there, it meant that he had run away with his four young daughters. But why had Ina stayed behind?

He clambered up out of the cellar. Standing in the room were Ina lay, he felt something fall lightly on his head; feathers and straw bits floated in the air that seemed to be coming from the sky. He looked up. They were coming from spaces between the ceiling's board. Was there a room upstairs he had not known about? Gripped with the worst presentiment, he looked around and found, behind a curtain, a narrow staircase that led to the upper floor. He willed himself to climb up the stairs. After a few steps, he stopped. There was blood at his feet and many footprints in the blood. Hearing nothing but the pounding of his own heart, he climbed slowly. Before he reached the room, he saw Yori sprawled on the floor. His eyes were open and in the center of his forehead was a small bullet hole. Albano started to run madly down the stairs; he slipped on the blood and tumbled all the way down. But once there, he knew he had to return. He went back up the stairs, stepped over Yori's body, and walked to a door. He entered the room.

There, covered in feathers coming from a punctured mattress, were Xandra's little sisters. Clara, Agda, and Octavia, and even four-year-old Tessa, lay in their blood, their dresses torn to pieces, their throats slit.

Albano ran out of the room, down the stairs, and out the door of the destroyed bakery. Outside, he collapsed on the pavement and threw up bile.

****

As soon as he could stand on his feet again, he ran away from the Armenian quarter, passing soldiers and drunken Turks. Albano ran so fast that the men only laughed and shot drunkenly in his direction.

Albano did not stop running until he found himself on Frank Street.

He stopped in the middle of Frank Street and bent forward, his hand on his knees. His lungs felt ready to explode. When he had caught his breath, he looked around. Yesterday, Frank Street had been a lively marketplace. Now it was ghost-like. The shops and cafés were boarded up, and the silence was spine-chilling. He saw not a single person dead or alive. The façades, doors, and windows were intact. The terrible violence must, therefore, have had a system; the carnage had physical boundaries. It was clear to him that the Armenian quarter had been singled out as a playground for the devil.

At that moment, he made a pact with himself. He would never tell Xandra what he had seen. He would never tell anyone. If he told no one, perhaps one day he too would disbelieve it.

****

On the quay, Albano gasped in shock. While he was gone, a new form of anarchy had taken over the quayside. The day had been hot. Trash and excrement had piled up. The odor, compounded by the number of people and the growing heat of the sun, had reached an intolerable level. Refugees were continuing to trickle down in an endless stream. Albano guessed that there must now be at least one hundred thousand refugees huddled there.

He did not find Xandra sitting next to the Armenian family where he had left her, but standing a few feet away from them, her belongings packed at her feet. "Did you see my family?" she asked, her face taut with apprehension.

He looked straight into her eyes and lied. "They must have found shelter somewhere."

She closed her eyes with relief. "Is it true that everything was looted?" she asked.

Albano nodded. "Everything."

"Even my parents' house?"

Albano looked away so that she would not read the horror in his eyes. "Yes."

"Even the bakery?"

"The bakery was ransacked. There is nothing left."

"What about the oven? Is the oven still there? Surely they cannot destroy or steal an oven made of stone?"

"It seemed fine," he said. He had paid no attention to the oven.

"Then, they can rebuild," Xandra said resolutely. "Do you think my family is somewhere on the quay?" she added. "Look how many people are here. Do you think it's possible that Hagop returned and that he led them to the cave? He's the only one who knows the way to get there. He knows the cave is the only safe place."

He marveled at Xandra's capacity for hope. In his gut, he knew that Hagop had never returned to Smyrna. He or someone would have seen him on the quayside a long time ago. Was Hagop in a camp somewhere in Anatolia? Was he sick or starving? Was he dead? Wherever he was, it was preferable to bearing witness to what Albano had just seen.

A collective call of anger resonated from the docks. Everyone looked in that direction. A British rescue boat was leaving half full and refusing to let anyone else in.

"What is happening?" he asked.

"The foreign ships are still only taking the foreign nationals, even now that Kemal has arrived," one man explained.

"This will be a disaster if they do not start to evacuate," another man said. "People have no food or water, and there is nowhere they can go."

Nearby, a woman let out a moan that turned into a howl. She was on her back with several women by her side. Some began to make a tent around her with blankets and shawls to give her privacy. "She is having her baby," Xandra said in a tiny voice. Unconsciously, she placed her hand over her own massive belly. They looked at each other somberly. "We can't stay here," she said, pointing to the terrace of Brasserie de France. "People are dying."

Albano had not consciously registered it before: from everywhere on the quay, groups of men were carrying inert bodies and lining them up against the façade of the Brasserie. "I'll go to the Levantine quarter or the European quarter," he said. "I will come back to you as soon as I find a safe place."

"No, Albano," Xandra said, shaking her head forcefully. "This time, I will come with you."

"Please stay here, with the nice family."

"The family does not want me here anymore."

"But why?"

She looked at him with sadness. "They say I am with a Jew."

"Why would it bother them?" he asked angrily. "At a time like this!"

"I am not spending another minute away from you, wondering if you are alive or dead," she said. "Wherever you are going, we will be together."

"The streets are too dangerous."

"And this is not?" she asked.

Albano noticed how pale Xandra was. The hair around her face was wet with sweat. "You look unwell," he said.

"I just need to get away from the stench."

"At least here there are the ships, boats…."

Xandra only shook her head no. Albano knew that there was no point in insisting. "Come," he said and took her hand.

He hoisted their bag onto his back, and they trudged through the multitude, heading in the direction of the Levantine quarter. Moving through the crowd was difficult as more refugees poured in, dirtier and more terrified than the ones before. In truth, Albano did not know where to go next. He held Xandra's hand and walked in a fog, the imprint of what he had seen embedded in him. The vision of horror would ice his soul, he feared, for the rest of his life.

At some point, he became conscious that he was holding Xandra's hand in public. Nothing that had mattered two days ago had importance now. "Let's spend the night in front of the French consulate and decide in the morning," he said.

"Should we try to take refuge in the Jewish quarter?" Xandra wondered.

"It is too far, and I worry that Jews too could become a target. No, we must head in the direction of the European areas. They say that Kemal wants the European leaders to think well of him. It will be the safest area to be sure." Was Albano sure? He wasn't. But as he said this, he became convinced of it.

****

There was no line in front of the French consulate. A sign on the door said that the consulate was closed. About a hundred people had opted to camp out on the marble doorsteps regardless. Albano managed to find a spot for him and Xandra on the porch right next to the entrance.

It was a hard surface, but it would be in the shade at the hottest time of the day.

Night fell. They wrapped themselves in blankets. Albano refused to eat the last of their food. "There is nothing left after that," Xandra told him. He insisted she should eat it all, and when she protested, he told her if not for her, for the child.

He thought he would never fall asleep, but miraculously, he held Xandra tight and succumbed to a dark, nightmarish slumber for a few hours.

****

He awakened in the middle of the night. Xandra was asleep and sitting upright. He delicately moved her down to her side and covered her with the blanket. People were sound asleep on the steps.

His eyes got accustomed to the dark. He walked to the door of the consulate and placed his ear against it. What would happen if he knocked now? Perhaps someone who was also awake would open the door, if for no other reason than curiosity. He knocked for an hour, politely, patiently. When one of the sleepers on the marble step moved, he stopped. He varied his rhythm, made the knocking musical so that it would be apparent that he was doing this deliberately. He made sure to keep his knocking firm but unthreatening. He had seen how things were going. Banging violently at the door was the opposite of what would lead to its opening.

After half an hour of this, and just as he was about to give up, he heard someone fiddling with the lock. He held his breath. The door opened just enough for a man's face to appear. He wore nightclothes and even a night hat. "What do you want," the man whispered in French. He was perhaps forty years old, with black eyes and a thin mustache. He did not look angry or threatening, just worried. "The consulate is closed. You have to stop knocking." He added, "You are preventing us from sleeping."

"I will let you sleep but please listen," Albano said in his best French. "I am here to pick up my visas. It would only take a few minutes, and then I will be gone."

"We're not making visas anymore."

"I am not asking you to make a visa. I am asking you to give us the visas that already exist. I received a notice of it a few days ago. I was about to pick them up when Kemal arrived."

The man said nothing but shook his head no. "I have a letter of employment in Paris," Albano insisted, unfolding the crumpled paperwork that he always kept in his trouser pocket. "We are expected there." The man continued to shake his head adamantly. "Monsieur, my wife is Armenian," Albano said, desperately. "You know what has gone on in the Armenian quarter, do you not? That small piece of paper, which is already stamped on someone's desk, is all that remains in the way of us getting out of Smyrna." And seeing the man was still listening, he added, "She is pregnant and about to give birth. All you have to do to save three lives is look for the papers and hand them to me. I don't even need to come inside."

The man thought for a long moment. "Give me your names," he finally said to Albano's disbelief. "I'll see what I can find."

Ten minutes later, the door opened again, just a few centimeters. Albano peered into the French man's eyes wordlessly as he handed him an envelope. "I stamped them," the man said. And before Albano could thank him, the door closed. No one, not even Xandra, had seen what had taken place.

Albano opened the envelope and found the stamped visas. They were saved.

****

The next morning, they stood in line at the dock where the French rescue boats continued to shuttle between the quayside and the French destroyer moored in the distance. Albano and Xandra stood up straight. Their clothes showed signs of wear. Albano hoped that they did not look as downtrodden as the Greek and Armenian refugees.

"We have visas," Albano said in his strongly accented French when it was their turn to show their papers.

"We only take in French nationals," the sailor answered.

"We have visas. Stamped visas which we got from the French consulate," Albano declared, using his firmest tone.

"The consulate is closed," the French sailor said, not believing him.

"We were given our visas; they are stamped and in good order." Albano insisted. "We have letters of employment in Paris, and we have money."

The sailor looked at him dubiously. "Where is your money?"

Albano took the money from his pocket and showed it to him. The sailor looked at the Turkish currency. It was clear that he was incapable of knowing how much what Albano held in his hands was worth. And in truth, it wasn't enough for a boat ride to France. If only he had sold the diamond when he still had a chance! "I have more," Albano whispered. "Much more. I just don't have it with me quite yet."

The French sailor looked at him with mistrust. "Coming onboard is not a matter of money," he said. "We operate under strict orders of the French government. This is a rescue mission, not a commercial venture."

"But how else can we sail to France?" Albano asked. "We have work waiting for us there," he repeated. "We are expected."

"You will need to find a private boat." The sailor looked at him and smirked, "With all your money, it should not be difficult."

"What we need to do," Albano told Xandra later on, "is find someone who will buy the diamond. Someone rich. The sailor was right; we need to find a private boat. Our best chance is with the Levantines. Perhaps we should go the European quarter and knock at the doors of Levantines we know, old customers from the bakery."

"Are there still Levantines left? A great many took boats out of the city. You saw them."

"They can't all have left," Albano said. "The women and children are away, but the men would not leave their properties and businesses unattended: their banks, their factories, their warehouses. I will knock on every door until one opens. Just as I did to get the visas."

They set out toward the Levantine quarter. Going along the water was out of the question: there were so many souls huddled in masses that it would have taken hours just to step over parcels and bodies. They decided to walk through the streets instead.

At first, they struggled to walk across the esplanade full of refugees. But as they moved away from the quayside, streets were increasingly emptier. It was as though individuals had the instinct to huddle together, holding on to each other to make a single organism, like fire ants during a flood. He and Xandra were doing the exact opposite; they were separating from the solid mass, drifting into the unknown.

The farther they walked away from the esplanade, the quieter things became. There was no one in the streets; no one was at any of the windows. Stores were shut and boarded. People had either left or were staying inside. The silence and emptiness of the street were deeply unsettling. Smyrna had turned into a ghost city. Albano knew in his gut that if people were not there, it meant that the streets were not safe, even in the European quarter. He fought the urge to run back to the esplanade. He had to reason with himself. This was only fear taking hold of him after what he had seen; none of these horrors would happen where so many Europeans lived. He wished that Xandra could walk faster, but as it was, she struggled. Her feet and ankles were swollen. Her heavy belly made every step difficult. But to rush her would alarm her.

"Where is everyone?" she asked. "Are you sure we should not go to the Jewish quarter instead?"

"No one in the Jewish quarter would be able to afford the diamond," he said. He tried to make his voice confident, rather than terrified. He wanted Xandra to think that he was optimistic about their options, not that he had begun to fear for her life and the life of every Christian in Smyrna. The vision of Xandra's family haunted him every instant. Evil was here, pouring like black ink through the streets, up and down stairs, through every house and every bedroom. All they could do was try and run from it because if God could not stop it, there was nothing they could do. "We're almost there," he said.

"If they are not hurting the Jews, maybe we should look like Jews," Xandra suggested. Albano nodded and placed his kippah on his head. He wrapped his prayer shawl over his shoulders and let the fringes dangle. Xandra took the silk shawl with Eiffel Tower prints that Uncle Moshe had sent them and wrapped it around her hair.

They advanced carefully, along walls, hand in hand, their hearts beating too fast. Xandra abruptly stopped. "Oh, Albano, look!" she said in a strangled whisper. Albano looked. Out in the alley to their right was the body of a man. "Should we see if he needs help?" she asked.

Albano had no doubt the man was dead. "No," he said. "Let's go on."

They had not taken ten steps when a woman began to scream. The scream was unending, terrible and then, abruptly, it stopped.

Paralyzed, they waited. Xandra's face was white. "What is happening, Albano?"

"Shh!"

A deafening noise of hooves on the pavement was coming in their direction. They had only moments to take cover in one of the alleys. A group of ten men on horses rushed by.

From somewhere not too distant came another piercing scream. And then a single gunshot, followed by silence.

"We need to turn back," Albano muttered.

"But," Xandra said, "the men went in that direction."

Albano looked at Xandra as though he were seeing her for the first time. And at once he realized his terrible mistake. To remove Xandra from the quay where she could disappear in a crowd had been madness. Her beauty, her vulnerable belly, made her prey. How many mistakes had he made already, by not planning, by failing to act at the correct time? They should never have left the cave. "We can't continue walking in the street like this," he said. "We need to take cover. Wait for the night."

"If these men find us, they will rob us," Xandra said.

"I do not worry about the men pushed by greed," Albano said. "It is the men who are powered by hatred that we must watch for." He saw that she was not understanding. "They are killing Christians," he admitted.

"In the Armenian quarter?"

"Yes."

"Are you sure my family escaped?"

"They were … gone when I got there," he said without looking at her for fear that his eyes would betray him.

They began to knock at every door that was still unbroken. No one would open. Going from door to door, Albano and Xandra hid in corners when they heard throngs of men on horses. Xandra looked exhausted. She had had little to eat since they left the cave. "Do you have the strength to go on? Do you need to rest?" he asked.

"I can walk," she said. "If we reach the Levantine quarter someone will recognize us and shelter us, or at least help us with some food, whereas here there is nothing."

And suddenly, without warning, there was the sound of many footsteps. They had only time to hide in the recesses of a building's entryway. They held on to each other and held their breath.

The men were only a few meters away. Albano shrank further back into the shadow, protecting Xandra by pushing her against the wall.

A man's voice calmly said, "Stop hiding, Jew." This was said nonchalantly, as though the man who spoke did not doubt that Albano was cornered without the chance of escape.

Albano put his fingers gently over Xandra's mouth. With his eyes, he indicated what he was about to do. She tried to take hold of his hand to stop him, but he did not let her. He stepped out of the shadow and said, "I am not hiding."

There were three men. Mean-looking. One of them was on horseback, and the other two were on foot. They reeked of alcohol. Their clothes were stained with wine and blood. The man on the horse was so drunk he could barely stay up. His body kept leaning to the right. He would straighten up, then lean again.

"What are you doing, then, Jew?" the first man said. He seemed the least drunk of the three, and the most aggressive.

"I am here ... like you," Albano said.

"We are taking back what belongs to us," the man said.

"So am I," Albano answered, with no idea what the man meant.

"Nothing here belongs to you, Jew. You can only have what we have rejected. Are you going through trash, Jew? Cleaning the streets, like a rat?"

Albano decided to go along with the man's thinking. "I am," he said.

"After we have gotten rid of every Christian in town, we will get rid of your lot as well."

"Give us what you have," the second man said. "Give us your money."

Albano paused for only a second before retrieving the hospital birth money from his pocket and handing it to him. The men laughed and hollered at their good fortune and pocketed the money.

"And what is that?" The man on the horse said, pointing in the direction of the shadow within the building's entryway.

"Nothing."

"Is that your woman, Jew? Come see us, woman," he ordered.

Xandra bravely stepped out of the shadow, her eyes lowered. Her stillness broke Albano's heart. She still wore Uncle Moshe's Eiffel Tower silk shawl over her hair, but she had also tied the thin cloth that had contained their food over the lower half of her face. Albano understood what she was trying to do: covered this way, she could easily pass for a Muslim woman. Albano stopped her from going forward, putting his hand on her arm. "She is with child," he said.

The third man came down from his horse. He vacillated and came close to her, looking at her befuddled. "I like pregnant women. It is like raping two for the price of one." The two other men emitted riotous laughs, which pleased him. "I like your woman, Jew," he said slurring his words. Leering, he came near her and lifted his hand to touch her face.

"Don't!" Albano shouted. He moved his body directly in front of Xandra's. The first man pounced on him, struck him across the jaw. The second man kneed him in the groin with a savage laugh. Albano folded over. They went on hitting him, with their fists, and with the handles of their guns, blow by blow. He fell to the ground, and his forehead hit the pavement hard. In one instant, all three men had seized Xandra. Albano made a superhuman effort to rise, but each time, he collapsed. The men ripped Xandra's shawl off her face, and her beauty was revealed. There was silence, awe perhaps. Immediately after, the rage in their eyes transformed into a terrifying hunger.

Things happened fast. Albano watched helplessly, his face pressed against the ground, his body limp and unresponsive as his beloved received a violent push. She fell to the ground on her back. Now one of the men man was on top of her, slapping her, while the others hollered like mad beasts. Xandra made no noise. She did not moan or cry out. Albano came on all fours and tried to get up, blood pouring down his face from the cut on his forehead. "Stop!" he shouted.

The drunkest of the three men, the one who rode the horse and was the leader, was undoing his belt. "She's mine!" he told the two others. "You'll have her next." So the first man moved off her, and now the leader was on top of Xandra, tugging at her dress clumsily.

The other two men went to Albano and kicked him again and again. Through the kicks to his ribs and belly, Albano found within him a formidable power. He shouted, "She is Muslim! She could be your sister. Allah does not want you to rape your sister!"

The man on top of Xandra continued to struggle with his pants and her dress, but after a moment, he stopped moving. And a miracle happened: he lifted himself away from her and stumbled up. At first, the other two giggled and leered, but soon they stopped, careful not to humiliate their leader. Perhaps the man was too drunk to complete his act. Perhaps he saw her pregnant belly and had a change of heart. Perhaps Albano had put doubt in his mind. Perhaps he was just tired of perpetrating atrocities. Albano would never know. The man moved toward his horse. "Let's go," he said. The other two, their bloodlust not satisfied, turned to Albano and went back to kicking him in the ribs and head. But they grew tired of this too and eventually left.

When they were gone, Albano found the strength to crawl to Xandra and be conscious long enough to see that she was breathing. He managed to drag her into the shadow of the entryway before falling unconscious, next to her.

****

In his dream, he heard Xandra's plaintive voice. "Albano?" His head throbbed, but he thought he was in the cave, safe. "The baby is coming," said the voice in the dream.

"I am so happy," he answered through his haze of slumber.

"Albano…." He felt Xandra's grip on him, and the alarm in her voice awakened him this time. "The baby is coming, Albano…."

Albano opened his eyes. Xandra was sitting up, panic-stricken. Pain radiated throughout his body, in his ribs, in his groin, in his skull. How could he have slept through this? But he had not slept; he had passed out. "Are you hurt?" he asked. "How long did I sleep?"

Xandra looked at him with gaunt eyes. "Many hours. The cut on your head stopped bleeding. There is another cut on your arm. It is deep, but I was able to stop the blood."

"The baby? What did you say about the baby?"

"It is the fall, I think. At intervals, my belly is becoming hard as stone, and liquid came out of me." She looked at him gravely. "That is the sign that the baby wants to come out."

Albano rubbed the crust of blood that caked his face. "It is too early," he said.

"I have seen healthy babies born in the eighth month," she said. She took a bit of water from their gourd and used the bottom of her skirt to wash the blood from his face. "Can you see at all? Your left eye is nearly shut. Have they broken bones?"

Albano tried to sit up. Judging from the shooting pain in his torso, he was certain more than one of his ribs were broken. The wound on his forehead throbbed. The cut in his arm was deep enough to reveal the tendon and part of the bone, but he could move it. "We need a hospital for you," he told her. He looked in his pocket but found nothing there.

"The money is gone," Xandra reminded him. "The men took it, remember? Did they find the diamond?"

Albano felt the hem of his caftan. The tiny bulge was there, immensely reassuring. "They did not know to look."

"They did not find the finials," she told him.

"How could they not?"

"I had taken them out of my skirt and hid them near the wall. Now I have them again."

"The finials are not worth taking such risks."

Xandra helped him up, first to his knees, and then she helped him stand against a wall for support. She brought the gourd to his lips, and he drank. The pain was so intense throughout his body that he could not figure out what hurt most, but he could move. "Can you walk?" she asked. And suddenly, she turned pale, held her swollen belly, and moaned.

"You are in pain!" Albano exclaimed.

They hung on to each other and set out to walk alongside the buildings. They had to maneuver around piles of trash and broken furniture, bricks, glass, abandoned belongings, and, worst of all, corpses. They did not stop until Albano spotted something. He bent down and retrieved a French flag and wrapped Xandra in it. "I've seen people do this in the hope that the Turks will leave them alone."

Xandra stopped, doubled over with pain. She burst into tears. "I don't even know where we're going."

Albano took her face in his hands and kissed the tears from her eyes. Her face was hot and moist. "Anywhere that will give us asylum. The American Consulate, the American or French hospital."

"They are not opening for anyone," she wept.

"We have visas, my dearest. We have visas and our diamond, and you are pregnant. There are reasons for people to shelter us."

"But how do you know for sure?"

"Providence let us obtain visas. We were lucky enough to be given a diamond. These men let us go. You know what this means, don't you?"

"No."

"It means that God is on our side."

"Your God or mine?" she said with a small smile, drying her eyes with her sleeve.

Albano caressed her cheek. "They both are."

****

They hid when they needed to and walked when they could. They saw very few souls in the streets of the European quarter. Those who weren't here to destroy were hiding. An automobile zoomed past and abruptly stopped a few meters from them. Two men jumped out. Albano and Xandra recoiled in the shadow of a portico, but the men were not after them. They were carrying glass jars, which they thrashed against the walls of buildings. The men climbed back into the automobile, which drove a hundred more meters, and they got out again and threw more bottles through the broken windows of a building. There was the sound of broken glass. Then the automobile was gone.

"What are they doing?" Xandra asked.

"I don't know." They passed the broken bottles, and the pungent scent of kerosene filled their lungs. "Let's hurry," Albano urged.

When they arrived in the Levantine quarter, their hopes vanished. On every block the sprawling white villas and the treasures they hid lay open, disemboweled. Flower gardens were crushed, windows shattered, fountains desecrated, marble statuary tossed to the ground. Grand pianos, couches, beds: everything too heavy to be carried away had been defenestrated and laid in rubble down below. The poor servants who had pointlessly stood guard to protect the houses, likely at the command of their masters, lay among the ruins, their throats slit.

Albano and Xandra passed the residences in silence. On every street, they met the same wreckage. They encountered no one they knew, living or dead. "There is no sense in being here," Albano said. "The Levantines can't help us any more than they could help themselves. All those who could have been of assistance to us have fled. Let's go on Rose Street. There are hospices there, and maybe the Red Cross office has been spared."

"May God hear you," Xandra muttered.

"Will you be all right?"

She looked at him gravely. "I don't know how these things work, but the hardening of my belly is happening more often."

The narrow, beautiful Rose Street had been ransacked. The only people they saw were sprawled on the pavement, dead. They continued walking, with Xandra pausing every few minutes until her contraction passed. The rank smell of kerosene floated around them like a muted menace.

Albano remembered that very near the end of the Levantine quarter, near the place where he and Xandra would finish her delivery route, near their beach and their tree, was Hôpital Sainte Geneviève, a small hospital they had passed a hundred times without paying attention to it. He decided to head there. When they got near it, they heard clamoring and approached carefully. There was a group of about one hundred souls, the first gathering they had encountered since they left the quayside. They were Greek and Armenian refugees and terrified Smyrniots, most of them wounded, huddled at the foot of Hospital Sainte Geneviève's iron gate. They were calling and screaming in many languages, and shaking the gate, begging for refuge. Up in the window, Albano saw the shape of a woman dressed in white: a nun, or else a nurse.

"There are doctors in the hospital!" Albano exclaimed. "That's why those people are here."

They joined the voices, shouting and calling and shaking the gate, but no one opened. To be this close to help and get no help at all was enraging, unjust, pointless. They grabbed the wrought iron, shaking it, clinging to the last vestiges of hope, which had been shattered in so many ways in the last days, still believing that human decency was possible, that it existed still, just beyond the gate. The day was ending. To continue knocking and shaking the gate to no avail was nonsense. Albano did not think it was a good idea to join the group about to spend the night, vulnerable, out in the open.

"Let's find shelter in an abandoned house nearby," he told Xandra.

The sun was setting fast. Albano entered several buildings through open doors only to find dead bodies covered in flies. In the narrow streets, the sea wind had stopped flowing, and the air was saturated with the odor of decomposing corpses. As terrible as this was, an even more ominous feeling haunted Albano. It was unspecified. He could not name or express his fear. It was as though the consistency of the air was off somehow. Something felt wrong. And then it hit him: the wind! For the last few days, the wind had been blowing from the sea. But since sundown, it had begun blowing from inland. With the change of wind came the scent that sent chills down his spine. Xandra must have understood at the same time. "The wind has turned," she said.

"It smells like kerosene and smoke," he said.

"I think this is what these men were doing," Xandra said. "They were throwing bottles filled with kerosene through those windows."

Fire and earthquakes had destroyed Smyrna many times. Each time, it had been rebuilt faster and with lighter materials. Now built mostly out of wood, the city was more vulnerable than ever. "With the wind turning, if someone wanted to set the city on fire, it would be easy to do," Albano said somberly.

****

Albano and Xandra tried to get inside two houses near the hospital, but the smell of decomposing bodies deterred them. They tried a third house, which was located nearly across from the hospital. It had been ransacked and looted. Anything that could not be taken away had been vandalized; there was not a single chair left standing, not a curtain that had not been shredded, but there were no bodies. "This is where we'll spend the night," Albano said. He made a rudimental bed for Xandra out of the soft things he could gather, and he folded the French flag into a pillow. Despite the cramps that were coming now every few minutes, Xandra fell asleep. Albano sat on the wood floor next to her. After he was beaten and had fallen unconscious, she must have stayed awake to watch over him, and now she had no strength left. Albano caressed her hair. Her skin was hot to the touch, the hair around her face and neck soaked with sweat. In her exhaustion, she only moaned through the contractions.

He was unable to close his eyes to rest. He decided to go up to the rooftop. The house was three stories high. It had been a beautiful house, with exquisite mosaics and beautiful windows and doors. The walls were whitewashed, the floors made of expensive wood. Up on the rooftop, he stopped to take in the expansive view of the quayside, the bay, and, in the far distance, Mount Pagus. He leaned against the carved balustrade. How marvelous must the lives of the owners of this house have been. How many evenings must they have gathered here on summer nights, relishing the cooling breeze, the setting sun, and the echoes of the lively city below. How quickly and irrevocably had all their fates changed. He thought of himself and Xandra, of their future children. He pictured them at the balcony of their own house in Paris. He had imagined their future happiness so vividly that he could feel it. He had made Xandra a promise. Now was not the time to sink into despair.

Clouds hurried in the sky, and the rising moon shone brightly, revealing the outline of the many ships standing guard in the bay. From the balcony, he could see the distant mass of hundreds of thousands of refugees on the vast quayside. From where he was, he also had a good view of the hospital below and the many poor souls huddled at the gates. Inside the hospital, oil lamps were lit. Through the windows, he watched the hospital cots filled with sick and wounded people. A dozen nurses dressed in white worked tirelessly by their sides. This hospital, just out of reach, was where Xandra needed to be. What would become of them if they were not let in? Would he deliver the baby himself? What would he need? Would he need water? And where would he get food? When it came out, the baby surely would feed on Xandra's milk, which would come at some point although he did not know how to make sure it did. Xandra, too, needed to eat for strength. He had never seen her so weak, so sickly, so feverish.

A chill crept along his spine. Something was wrong with Xandra! The hot skin, the sweating, the paleness. She wasn't just giving birth; she was ill! He rushed down the stairs to her and touched her forehead, felt her pulse. Fever! He could see now, plain as day, that she was burning with it. Thoughts jumbled up through his brain. Could it be that the baby was dead inside? He knew this was possible. And when this happened, could a woman give birth to a dead child? Surely, they did. It must happen. He cursed his ignorance in women's matters. Xandra needed the proper care immediately. He spent the next hour going up and down the stairs to check on Xandra and back up to the rooftop where he stared across the street at the hospital's windows, thinking, praying, and spinning hopeless and optimistic thoughts together until he felt he was going mad.

One by one, the refugees at the gate curled into balls and went to sleep.

He was watching the hospital, mentally willing it into opening its gate for them, when something caught his attention. To the right of the hospital was a small, dark alley. Every so often the alley briefly lit up with a dim light. Peering and waiting for the next time the light would come on, he finally understood what was going on. There was a small side door to the hospital, with people secretly coming in and out of it.

He jumped to his feet, ran down to Xandra and whispered to her, "I think I found a way to get inside the hospital. I'll be right back."

Xandra only moaned.

Albano made a wide detour so that he could access the alley alongside the building and not walk past the gate where people were camped out. He found the door by touch and sat next to it in the darkness. He thought of knocking at first but decided his best chance was to wait until the door opened again, allowing him to speak to a person face to face.

After an hour, spent mad with anxiety about having left Xandra alone, he was about to rush back to her when he heard a slight click, and ever so slowly the door was pushed open. Two men came out carrying a body on a stretcher. Coming from the light and into darkness, they did not see him. What they were doing, he understood, was getting rid of their dead. The men with the stretcher walked away from the door, but before it could be shut again, Albano put his foot up and blocked it from closing. A person, having not seen Albano's foot, struggled to shut it.

"Please let me in," he whispered in English, unsure what language was likeliest to be spoken there. "My wife is about to give birth."

"Who are you?" a heavily accented voice in the dark whispered back anxiously.

"We have no water, no food. Her baby is coming any moment. Please shelter us. We will not tell anyone."

"We have many wounded," the man's voice said through his unsuccessful efforts to shut the door on Albano's foot. His accent sounded German. "We are well above capacity."

Albano instinctively realized that the man's insistence in arguing with him was a good sign. "I have seen bodies coming through," he said. "You must replace them with the living. Give us a chance. She will give birth in the street. She was struck by crazed men, and the baby is coming early, and now she burns with fever."

"Are you Armenian, or Greek?" the man asked. Albano's eyes had somewhat gotten used to the darkness, and he could see that this was an old man with furrows between his eyes and a deeply lined face. His collar and black habit revealed that he might be a priest or a vicar, or that he had a function in a Christian church.

"I am Jewish," Albano admitted.

"We cannot help Jews. We have enough of our people to tend to."

"Please, my wife is – well, she is not my wife. She is Armenian. She is Christian. I am only protecting her. Please do not let a Christian child be born in the streets with murderers running wild."

By now, the man had figured out that Albano's leg was what kept the door from closing and was kicking it as hard as he could, which was not very hard because he was an old man. "I am sorry, we're doing all that we can."

"I can pay you."

The man stopped kicking. "We have no beds."

"I have a diamond."

The eyes on the other side of the door lit up, and the old man looked at him as though for the first time. "Show me."

Albano wrestled with his caftan, tore at the lining. He opened his dirty palm and showed his diamond. For a moment, he and the man stared at the precious stone that gleamed intensely, its beauty almost ludicrous in Albano grimy hand.

"How do I know it is real?" the old man said.

"You won't know. You will have to take a chance. You have little to lose. All this gamble will cost you is to let my wife come inside."

The old man stopped wrestling with the door and seemed to be weighing this. "Come back with her," he finally said.

"Will you open?" Albano asked.

"Tap four times, and then once."

Albano ran back to Xandra and awakened her. Her clothes were drenched in sweat. "The hospital will take you!"

She looked at him with sickly eyes. "I don't know how I will walk."

Albano did not let her finish her sentence. He lifted her limp body in his arms and carried her down the stairs and into the street. His broken ribs felt as though they might pierce through his chest, but he did not care. "It smells like fire," she said dreamily.

"Let's go!"

Excruciating pain shooting through his body with every step, Albano carried Xandra down the stairs, out of the house, around the back of the hospital, and into the alley. Once there, he tapped as instructed.

The transaction took an instant. The door opened. The diamond was dropped into an open palm, and Xandra was let in. She burst into tears. "Albano! How will we pay for the boat now?"

"I will run to the quay and try to find someone we know."

"Let him inside too," Xandra begged through her tears.

"Impossible. He must wait outside," the old German man said.

"Xandra, I will run to the quay now. I will be back in a short time," Albano assured her.

"Take me with you!"

He looked into Xandra's beautiful, sickly eyes. "You and our child will be safe here. I will look for a boat, show them our visas, and secure our passage out of Smyrna. Then as soon as the baby is here, we will board the boat."

"No! Albano. Don't leave me here."

"Just think of Paris," he whispered to her, as a nurse's hand was on her arm, trying to move her away from the door. Xandra clutched her arms around his neck, sobbing. "Don't leave me!"

"You must be quiet!" The old man urged.

"Think of our dream," Albano murmured in her ear. "Remember my promise to you. You and I and our children will live in a beautiful house in Paris, remember? We will have a boy and a girl."

She tightened her grip, but a contraction engulfed her in pain, and she let go. A moment later, she was inside, and the door had shut. He heard her scream his name.

Xandra would be safe in the hospital. The gate was massive. It had resisted the looting and the madness and would continue to do so. Inside, there would be capable hands to help her give birth. Albano stood, numb with anguish at the thought of leaving any distance between them, but he had to find a boat if they were to have any chance at all of escaping. He sprinted toward the quayside, ignoring his pain.

****

He progressed slowly toward the quayside, moving from doorway to doorway and hiding when groups of men passed by brandishing swords and firearms. He was in a strange state of shock and confusion: moments of terror and despair, alternating with great pangs of numbness. Many times, he had to remember where he was and why he was there. The agonizing pain in his chest was nothing compared to the one in his arm. Xandra had wrapped it in a thin piece of cloth torn from her dress while he was unconscious. He lifted the bandage. The blood had dried up, but the flesh around the cut was red and swollen, oozing pus. He knew that all sort of terrible things could happen from such a wound. He had seen healthy men amputated after smaller skin lacerations began to fester.

He made his way to Frank Street, hoping for some semblance of normality. The day before, Frank Street had been eerily quiet but safe. Now it wasn't, or rather he was witnessing the aftermath of a terrible rampage. Bodies were strewn along the length of the street. Where there had been bustling international shops, brasseries, and restaurants, now there was only death. In the fountain-filled courtyards, beside door fronts, porches and verandas were the bodies of women, children, and men, many with bodies mutilated, ears or noses cut off, eyes gouged. The state of many of the young girls and women left no doubt as to their fate before being murdered. The smell of kerosene stung his eyes and nose. The stench of death clung to everything.

How could men do this to one another? Again and again, he had heard that these sorts of things had taken place elsewhere in the world, but those accounts had not felt real. They had felt like the fables in books. He had been incapable of imagining such hell could happen here.

Scattered ashes flew around, and a burning smell wafted through the streets. It was not the familiar scent of brush or chimney fires; it was the pungent odor of burning tar, burning oil. It was the smell of fire consuming houses.

On the quayside, it was chaos. The number of refugees seemed to have quadrupled overnight. And yet the many European, American, and even Japanese warships still stood immobile in the harbor. Could they possibly not know what was going on in the city? The presence of the foreign ships was preventing atrocities from spreading to the quayside, but for how long? If the killing and raping and robbing happened in plain view of the ships, would the French, the British, the Americans, or the Italians persist with their preposterous neutrality? Albano felt anger consume him.

Somewhere above, on the far edge of the city, a massive black cloud was rising.

He struggled from dock to dock, visa in hand, asking everyone, looking for familiar faces. Albano was conscious that his appearance worked against him. His eyelids were nearly shut, his nose and eyes were black and blue, and there was a deep gash on his forehead and dried up blood on his face and clothes. He felt his best chance would not be with the military boats: the soldiers were under strict orders not to take civilians, so he did not waste time with them. Instead, he went toward the docks where the Levantine boats moored. Greece, Italy, Palestine, Egypt, the boat's destination did not matter. From wherever they ended up, he would contact Uncle Moshe and beg him to help them with money for their passage. Now that Albano had neither money nor diamond, only his visa, all he could do was to make empty promises of reimbursement. But very few pleasure boats remained on the quay, and among the ones still leaving, he found no one willing to wait for him and Xandra. He thought of Hagop at that moment. Only a year ago, the quayside had belonged to them. Hagop would have known people and would have had the right words to convince them. He would have laughed with them, and insulted them in ten languages, and it would have worked.

He began noticing that people on the quay were turning and looking in the direction of the city. He looked up to see where fingers were pointing. The cloud of smoke that had been hovering far back, nearly outside the city limits, was now enormous. Not only that. There were several black clouds now, coming from different parts of the city. No one understood why so many fires had sprouted at once. Someone shouted, "I smelled petroleum. They are setting Smyrna on fire!" The word spread across the quay like a noxious wave. "The Christians are setting fires to their own quarters so that the Turks can't lay hands on their new properties."

"No, it is the Turks who are setting fires. They have received orders from Mustapha Kemal's headquarters."

"All the fire hoses have been cut; the firemen can do nothing!" someone screamed.

"Why would the Turks burn a city that is now under their control?"

"They want to decimate every Christian."

"They want to burn all the bodies so the Allies will not know of their crimes."

"They waited for the right wind, the one that blows away from the Turkish and Jewish quarters. See, the fire was set in several places at once. They are methodical."

"That's the work of the Jews!"

"The Jews and Turks would not want to burn Smyrna; they need Smyrna!"

"The foreign warships need to evacuate us! If the fire continues and the wind continues blowing toward the sea, it will soon reach the quay."

In a matter of minutes, panic set in. It was pandemonium. "We are trapped between the fire and the sea!" People began throwing themselves senselessly into the water and swimming to the boats, trying to get in them, hanging on to ropes and ladders. Those who had accepted the notion that foreign ships were not taking refugees, now refused that notion and screamed and begged for rescue. People jumped from docks into the water or tried to throw themselves into boats from above. Those already onboard boats pushed down those who were struggling to get in. Sailors threatened to fire their rifles, and many did. Quite a few people began swimming towards the ships far out in the harbor.

And then came a scream. "The European quarter is up in flames!"

The revelation came to him like a sharp blow to his solar plexus. Xandra!

He pivoted and began running countercurrent to the crowd, jumping over piles of trash, tripping over bodies, falling and getting up, again and again. The fire was becoming huge at a pace he could not have imagined. He ran, despite his throbbing arm and broken ribs, as the sky rapidly, ominously darkened and as smoke rose straight above what seemed to be the area where Hospital Sainte Geneviève lay. Everyone was crazy now. A huge mass of people who must have been hiding in cellars and attics were fleeing away from the fire and towards him. He tried pushing his way through the panicked crowd, but it was impossible. He kept falling and being stepped on, but he continued, and as he did, he too had to step on fallen bodies, small children, and women crushed in the stampede. As he got closer to the European quarter's fire, there were fewer people in the streets. He should have been able to move faster, but now there was another obstacle: the smoke.

He placed his caftan over his nose. Now, between the thick smoke and the falling ashes, he was walking blindly. But worse, the temperature was rising, and he could feel the heat of the fire on his skin, as though he were stepping into an oven. Still, he advanced as burning cinders and pieces of roofs fell on him. Soon, he could not breathe, and the heat was so great that the hair on his arms was singed. He bent down as he walked, trying to stay close to the ground until he was on all fours, crawling, trying to breathe in the air at ground level. He coughed, choked. He could no longer open his eyes and resorted to feeling his way by touching the stone edges of the buildings. And suddenly there was a strange silence. Albano had just enough time to register the silence before an enormous conflagration swept him up and threw him into the air. And everything went dark.

****

Albano returned to consciousness face down in humid dirt. It was dark, and he did not know where he was. The air was saturated with smoke and ashes, and he coughed for a long while. He slowly rose to his knees, propping himself with his elbows and hands. When his eyes got accustomed to the dark, he realized that he was in a stone cellar below ground level. A dim light came from above. He could not understand what he was doing here. His head throbbed. He was covered in mud, and something viscous stuck to his neck. He felt the back of his head with his fingers. There was a new, deep, bloody gash on the back of his head, but the blood was thick and dry, so he must have been unconscious for hours.

Suddenly the terrible understanding came. "Xandra!" he hollered. He found a ladder and went up it. When he was all the way up, he understood what must have happened: either he had managed to fall into the cellar at the moment of the explosion or it had propelled him there.

Outside it was gray, opaque, and suffocating. The sky was obscured by the air saturated with smoke and ashes, and it was hard to see more than a few steps ahead. Everywhere he walked, Albano stepped into many centimeters of soft ashes, and stirred-up ashes followed him, billowing in his trail. These ashes, what were they made from? Houses? Furniture? People? How long had he been unconscious?

Out in the street, the scene of devastation he could glimpse was complete. He came to the understanding that his landing inside a cellar below ground had saved his life. The fire must have leaped through the neighborhood, caught on every building made of wood, and moved through them in mere minutes. But he had been inside a humid stone cellar, and so the fire had gone elsewhere. The air below ground must have been breathable, which was why he had not suffocated.

In the street, there were too many burned bodies to count. He alone must not have been licked by the flames! The fact that he had not been burned or asphyxiated by this torrent of fire and smoke, the fact that he was standing at all, was a miracle.

He could not recognize any of the buildings now that they were charred, and without the sun or the moon to guide him, he did not know north from south or east from west. Burning cinders, leftover parts of buildings that must have burst into flames many hours ago, still produced an infernal heat. He clambered his way through the streets, or what might have been streets. The cafés, houses, restaurants, churches, banks, gardens could not be told apart from each other: all were blackened beams, cinder, and rubble. Ashes blanketed the fallen bodies and continued coming down from the sky like soft, gray snow. From the appearance of the cinders, the fire may have swept through the place twenty-four hours ago, perhaps more. That's how long he had been unconscious.

He needed to find Xandra. Xandra was in the hospital. Hospitals were the safest places to be.

He held the cloth of his caftan over his face to filter the air he was breathing and set out, avoiding falling embers, rubble, and bodies. The desolation was immense. But he was alive. He had escaped. Xandra must have escaped, too. Why would God bother with a single miracle?

Struggling to find a recognizable marker in the desolate graveyard that had been his city, he walked and muttered the same two words over and over: "Please, God. Please, God."

****

He walked in circles until finally the smoke cloud cleared up and patches of blue sky were visible, and through it, the light improved. He guided himself better.

When he finally arrived where Hospital Sainte Geneviève should have been, he let out a howling scream. There was nothing there. Only the gate remained standing, absurdly unscathed. Behind it were the ruins of two stone walls opened to the sky. Everything else was cinders and burned debris. He stepped over smoldering wood beams, metal bed frames melted into strange shapes, the carcass of a cradle, a filing cabinet, abandoned shoes. The whole time he shouted, "Xandra! Xandra!," his heart near explosion from terror.

"They are all dead," a man behind him said.

Albano turned. The man was sitting on the ashy ground, like a dark angel floating on a grey cloud. His hair and beard were burned in patches. He wore a torn, dirty black suit rolled up above the ankles. Tears streaked his face black with soot.

Albano shouted at the man, "They are not dead. They ran away! They ran for protection."

"There was no time," the man said in a vacant voice. "The conflagration happened in an instant. There was nowhere to run to."

"But you are here. You are alive!" He turned away from the man, ignoring him, and returned to calling, "Xandra! Xandra!"

The wind opened a gap in the smoke above that let in sunlight. He saw that he was standing in what must have been the hospital's food hall, now open to the air with crumbling walls on two sides. Two men and four nurses from the Red Cross, hair, clothes, and faces black with ashes, slowly moved through the debris, the men lifting bodies onto stretchers and lining them up against one of the walls. There were dozens of bodies lined up there, charred beyond recognition. He ran to a nurse. "There was a woman here," he asked frantically in French. "She was giving birth! She was Armenian. Do you remember her? I brought her here. I think it was yesterday. Or the day before. How long ago did the fire happen?"

The Red Cross woman shook her head in ignorance. "I just arrived by boat from the shore. I don't think anyone made it out of here." She turned away, but Albano saw her glimpse at the row of dead bodies. It was as though a knife had just been planted through his belly. He tottered toward the area where the nurse had looked. Numb with terror, he walked among the corpses. None of them recognizable as people, only as human shapes. Several were twisted in terrible ways, their bodies curled into the position where they had met their fate, as though they had thrashed while on fire. Others had their arms alongside their bodies, as though their bodies had burned in their sleep. He went from body to body, forcing himself to look when all he wanted to do was run.

He saw them. It was them; he knew this immediately. Her hair, her clothes, her face, her flesh were gone. Nothing about the woman was recognizable, but he knew this was Xandra because someone had placed a minuscule dead infant wrapped in a shawl on top of her, as though in a final embrace. The infant was not burned: someone must have kept it from the fire and then placed him back on top of his mother's charred remains. Albano knew the infant was his child, and the woman was Xandra, because of the shawl in which the baby was wrapped. It was the Parisian shawl from Uncle Moshe, the one with the small Eiffel Towers.

Albano fell to his knees, buried his face in the thick ashes that covered the ground, and began to howl.

****

Later, many hours later, numb, Albano took his baby in his arms. The child weighed nothing. In the sun that now pierced ferociously through the whitening smoke, he headed toward the water and along the beach. The pain above his elbow was excruciating, but he welcomed it.

All around, emerging from the rubble, were lone, haggard, disoriented silhouettes. Survivors like himself, people who would never be able to understand why they were still alive, or why they alone must live to endure the loss of everything they knew and everyone they loved. From every direction came the screams and sobs of the survivors. But Albano remained silent.

His dead infant in his arms, he stood on the beach and looked in the distance at the esplanade of the quayside. Now the smoke had parted, and he could witness the same events that had just happened where he now stood. The fire that had consumed the European quarter had reached the quay. There, hundreds of thousands of refugees, trapped between sea and fire, awaited their terrible death. From where he stood on the beach, he could see the European boats, now frantically evacuating the people on the quayside, but it was too late. The heat was such that the sailboats that tried to get close saw their sails catch fire. For each boat in the harbor, there were a hundred people, ant-like in size from where Albano stood, treading water around it, swimming among drowned bodies.

He carried his dead child's tiny body and crossed paths with people in as much despair as he was.

He finally reached the beach. Their beach.

He walked to their tree. The tree was now a dark carcass, standing on the ash-covered sand. He stood on the beach with his infant, where the shade of the tree should have been. He set the corpse on the sand at the base of the tree and began digging. He dug with his bare hands, and when the hole was deep enough, he set his child in it and gently covered him back with the Eiffel Tower shawl, and then with sand.

He did not say a prayer.

He returned to the ruins of the hospital, wrapped Xandra's charred remains in a piece of tarp, and carried her, now weightless, to the beach. The pain in his heart was so deep that the pain in his arm was nothing compared to it. There, he dug a new hole right next to their child's grave and buried his beloved.

He did not say a prayer for Xandra either. There was no prayer left in him.

When he was done, he walked into the flat sea. Trash of all sorts floated on the water, as ashes continued to fall softly on the surface. The water felt hot. The corpses of people who had drowned trying to escape the fire floated in the water by the hundreds. He realized now that the people he had seen walking around, specter-like, those who had survived, must have been the good swimmers, those able to tread water and swim far enough from the shore not to suffocate from the toxic air or be cooked by the heat. Those people had returned to shore and entered hell.

As he swam away from shore, salt stung the open wounds on his skull and arm, and his broken ribs stabbed his lungs. He was not a good swimmer. He kept going under and swallowing tepid water. He did not swim toward the pier or the quayside. He swam forward, out to sea. The water became colder and colder the farther he swam. He turned back to see Smyrna only once. The city was engulfed in flames. His family's burial ground would be the whole city, if not the entire Ottoman Empire.

As Albano swam further and further away from the coast, the floating corpses, innumerable at first, became scarce. Further out to sea, the screams on the shore became muffled and then disappeared. He felt the cold sea caress his body, the salt, excruciating on his wounds at first, now healing them perhaps. No matter how men built and destroyed cities and killed one another, the sea was deep and eternal, and soon he would be one with it.

Albano swam towards the horizon. He would go until the Aegean Sea took him. But his body did not want to die, and it took hours before, exhausted, he finally began sinking under and swallowing water. By then Smyrna was no longer on the horizon. The only indication that it had existed at all was the mass of black smoke that tarnished the blue of the sky. He thought of the finials and how they must have melted in Xandra's skirt folds.

When Albano's body finally broke down, his eyes and nostrils filled with water, he did not feel panicked, or fearful. A last thought came to him as he went under, the most peaceful thought: the bodies burned in the fire were fixed in death in the convulsions of trying to escape the flames. But Xandra and the baby had been burned in a position of repose, she on her back, her legs straight, her arms alongside her body, and the baby set there on top of her.

This meant that they were already dead when the fire consumed the hospital.

This meant that the baby and Xandra did not die in the fire, but in childbirth.

There was nothing he could have done to save them.

He felt gratitude that they were spared the unimaginable horror of being burnt alive.

The last thing Albano did before going under one final time was to thank God for giving him Xandra.

****

Many miles away, up on the hillside above the city, sitting in the shadow of the Red Cross truck that had carried him away from the hospital, the old German priest watched the terrible smoke blanket that covered Smyrna. He sponged the sweat off his brow and got up. In the medical truck, he took out a clean compress and poured water on it. With a hunched back, he walked to the olive orchard and the makeshift beds set in the shade of the trees where the Red Cross nurses were hard at work in the implacable heat of the sun. The old priest walked to the bed where the young woman moaned. He gently applied the compress to the side of her face.

"Albano," the young woman muttered through her fever and pain.

"Quiet, my child," the old man said. "You must rest now."

CHAPTER 11

Family Spy

"Do you know what made your father decide to leave Smyrna?" Cassie asked.

Marceline shook her head in ignorance. "Why does anyone become an expatriate? I would think that for most it's a combination of things. Better opportunities elsewhere? Who knows? He must have decided that there wasn't much for him there. And the city had burned down, so there was that." She thought for a moment, looking at the rivulets of rain against the window's glass pane. "To be honest, he never spoke about it."

"So my father is not the first man in our family who preferred not to speak about the past," Cassie noted.

"Well there had been some dark stuff to be sure," Marceline said. "Somehow along the way he had lost the use of an arm."

Cassie tried to remember if she had noticed that in the picture. "He was missing an arm?" she asked.

"No, it was there. But there was nerve damage below the elbow. His lower arm and hand were nearly useless."

"It must have been difficult for him."

"After the first world war, men missing limbs and covered in scars were the rule rather than the exception. But for my father, as for most men of the time, the invisible scars must have brought the most pain."

"I can't get over the fact that my grandfather was a Turkish Jew," Cassie said. "I had no idea that I had such exotic ancestry."

"My father did not see himself as Turk. The Republic of Turkey wasn't founded until after he left the region. So he wasn't Ottoman, since the Ottoman Empire did not exist anymore, and he wasn't Turk. One thing is for certain: my father wasn't French either, and the French people would not let him forget it."

Cassie eyed the album on the table. "Do you have photos of him?"

"Not from his childhood. My father grew up extremely poor."

"I thought he was wealthy."

"Not until he arrived in Paris when he was in his early twenties and his uncle took him under his wing. Uncle Moshe's business was quite successful already, but my father became a great asset. He was intelligent and spoke many languages. At home they spoke Ladino and Hebrew, and he had grown up with so many cultures living side by side that he had learned to speak Arabic and French and I think Armenian and some modern Greek. Languages were good for business."

"And your mother?" Cassie corrected herself, "My grandmother. She was French?"

"Her name was Lucienne. She came from an entirely different world from Father's. Their universes did not always happily intersect. Possibly the only thing they had in common was that they were both Jewish. My father did the best he could to keep up with her ways. He was a steadfast provider, a man of keen intellect, a loving father, but there was in him a reservoir of sadness, a secrecy that quite literally drove my mother mad."

"My grandmother? Mad as in crazy?" Cassie asked.

"Please do not rush ahead. I'm trying to be thorough. The main thing you must keep in mind is that your father was Jewish."

"Truthfully," Cassie said, "my father never spoke of religion. I don't think it mattered to him."

"Did not matter?" Marceline said, spitting out her words. "Of course, it mattered! My dear, Judaism, being a Jew, that was what mattered most!"

"But I —"

"Everything about your father, all his little secrets, and lies, they all spring from the fact that he is Jewish. Whether he liked it or not, his story is a tiny Marceline of the story of Jewish people."

Cassie felt that the comment was absurd and hyperbolic with nothing whatsoever to do with her reality. "I really don't think he felt that way at all and—"

Marceline raised her hand to stop her. "Darling, this is not a subjective matter. It is factual. Now please stop interrupting me." She unfolded her glasses with frail hands covered in heavy rings. There was something wonderful about being coquettish at eighty-seven, Cassie thought, when she, who in theory was on the market for a mate, could hardly be bothered to put on lipstick. "Would you like to see photographs of your dad as a child?" her aunt asked.

Did she *want* to see a photograph? Cassie would have given a kidney to get any information that would help her understand her father as a boy, or at any age.

Marceline opened the album and placed an index finger, covered almost entirely by an immense turquoise ring, on a black and white photograph of a baby dressed in his embroidered white gown and bonnet, his mouth wide open into a toothless scream. "I remember distinctly the day Gustave arrived," she said. "Possibly one of my earliest memories, since I was eighteen months old. I was precocious though. I am told that by that age I could speak in enough sentences to order the maids around."

Cassie scrutinized the photograph. "That's my dad? He seems from another area."

"1925 to be exact. Your father was a terribly unattractive newborn, I must say: scrawny and fussy, but I was passionate about him." She pointed to the picture of a little girl barely larger than the baby she held in her arms. "Here I am. My affection for baby Gustave was the nearest I ever got to maternal sentiments." Marceline pointed to another photograph where a baby sat upright in a massive black contraption perched up on thin wheels almost as tall as a little girl next to them. "This is me, pushing the pram," she said.

Marceline turned the album's page and pointed to a series of photographs of a fancy picnic by a lake where people in their finest attire posed for a camera. "This is us at the Bois de Boulogne. It must have been 1928 because I remember distinctly that there was a birthday cake for me and that I was turning five." In one of the photographs, a dozen women in fur-trimmed coats, beaded lace dresses, and cloche hats, sitting in folding chairs, seemed dressed for an episode of a wedding on some Victorian epoch TV series rather than a picnic by the lake. A few of the women in the group had short hair, Garçonne style. Marceline pointed to one of the women whose eyebrows appeared to have been plucked and redrawn and whose mouth was painted in that bee-stung shape that must have been the fashion. Around her neck was a long strand of pearls. Her dress, straight and loose and belted at the hip, emphasized her slenderness. Her nose and chin were a bit strong, and she was not the prettiest in the group, but she looked regal, much like Marceline did, and she had an air of confidence about her, if not superiority.

"That is Mother."

Cassie whistled softly in admiration. "Very elegant."

"Indeed," Marceline said, pointing to a toddler who sat on a blanket, wooden toys surrounding him. "This is Gustave at age three."

Cassie pointed to a stern, stiff woman by his side. "Who is this?"

"One of our British nannies at the time. I don't remember her name; they seemed to come and go interchangeably." She pointed to the photograph of a pretty little girl, pouting in a stiff white dress and curled hair tied with ribbons. "And this is me. Funny how vividly I remember that day. The adults strolling along the lake, the pretty ladies twirling their umbrellas, the mustachioed gentlemen who conversed with them. I remember that some of the men in the group were attempting to ride unicycles and kept falling, and the women laughed. Someone had set out a phonograph and was trying to make it play a tune. On the pond, they had made teams. Men and ladies clambered inside small wooden boats with much laughter. The men grabbed oars and began racing each other across the lake. The ladies, my mother included, applauded and cheered from the shore. Those were the années folles. After the sufferings and restrictions of the Great War, people wanted to behave lightheartedly. Adults dressed as they wished, drank liquor, danced the night away. Unfortunately for us, lightheartedness was not afforded to actual children who were expected to behave like miniature adults. I had been told to sit still and not dirty my dress. That is why I look so cross."

Marceline turned the page to a new photograph. A man in a suit held Gustave on his lap. Marceline had her arms around his neck. Cassie immediately recognized the man she had only once, as a child, seen in a picture. "That's him! My grandfather!"

"We called him Baba. I loved no one more."

"He looks like an actor, like a French Clark Gable or something."

"Baba was very handsome. It occurs to me now that he should have been rowing a boat and playing with the other adults. Instead, here he is in this photograph, sitting with us on that picnic blanket. I was too young to be aware that my father did not exactly fit in with this uppity Parisian crowd."

Cassie's grandfather, sitting in the dappled shade of a chestnut tree, was staring toward the lake, seemingly absorbed in some sorrowful vision. "He does look kind of sad," she said.

"Men have secret scars that they must bear alone. Whenever we asked Baba about his past, he would say that this life with us was all that mattered to him. He said he wanted to forget. This was a generation of adults who had greatly suffered from the war, and who worked, often maniacally, at distracting themselves from their suffering and loss. My father, too, might have wanted to forget, but it did not appear that he could. I would strive for his attention in the hope of bringing him back to joy. Had he not said it himself? That he was happy when he was with us?" Marceline looked at Cassie. "Did your father share any of this with you?"

Cassie shook her head. "Not a word."

"But did you not ask?"

"Here and there my sisters and I must have tried. As a child, you get rebuffed enough times, and you learn what the taboo subjects are."

"And this is how history is forgotten," Marceline said. "Forgotten and therefore repeated."

"Were you practicing Jews?"

"Sort of. We were Jewish, but we did not call ourselves that because this would have implied adhering to certain modes of behavior, and a certain devotion to the religion. We called ourselves Israelites. We were mildly observant. One of the few religious traditions Israelites upheld was to marry among themselves. For example, it had been important, when my mother was looking for a husband, that the husband be Jewish. As for the rest, it was interpreted loosely." Marceline flipped the pages of the album, "Look at this," she said. "I don't remember a single Passover, but this is us and our annual Easter egg hunt. The maids hid chocolate eggs wrapped in foil throughout the house, and Gustave and I ran up and down, basket in hand, looking for them."

"You did not celebrate Jewish holidays?"

"We regarded religious services as social events. We never thought of denying our Jewish identity; we were proud of it. But to me, being Jewish equated to little more than getting to wear my prettiest dresses and ribbons on High Holy Days. The chauffeur would drive us to the synagogue, and there was the amusing tradition of walking the last hundred yards on days when the rule was not to use cars. We celebrated Hanukah, but Mother always had a Christmas tree in a corner for reasons that were not explained to us. On Friday evenings, we were invited to Shabbat dinners at the home of the Parisian Jewish bourgeoisie, or we hosted them. We ate kosher only when we invited more observant Jews to our home, such as the occasional rabbi. Otherwise, it was not rare for pork roast to be served for Shabbat. My father refused to eat treif, but if there was boeuf bourguignon for dinner, he'd eat it, picking at the lardons and leaving them on the side of his plate while my mother rolled her eyes."

"But you said that everything that happened with my dad had to do with being Jewish."

"That is my whole point. For every Jew who wants to believe that he or she has integrated into society, there is a society intent on remembering that they are different. Post-World War I, most French Jews whose families had been French for multiple generations believed that they were French before they were Jewish. Our family and our Jewish friends' families were acutely aware that France not only protected our right to exist but was one of the very few countries in the world to impart us with equal rights. And so French Jews gave the République their unmitigated devotion. A devotion that would not be rewarded, as we all know how things turned out for the Jews during the second world war."

This gave Cassie pause. Her father was born in 1925, which meant that he was only fourteen years old when the war broke, sixteen when the Germans invaded France. As Marceline said, everyone knew how things had turned out. "How did your family make it out in one piece?"

"That is a long story, which I am about to tell you. But first, you might want to understand the setting. Within the Jewish community of the nineteen twenties, there was a strong sense of class. Mother felt secure in her knowledge that she stood proudly on the top echelon. By marrying my father, she had married below her milieu. Mother's ancestors had entertained Russian princes and Flemish countesses. She was quick to point out that she was also of Catholic descent – this might explain the Christmas tree. Some of her ancestors had gone astray, I suppose, making her, for all intents and purposes, Jewish, but she was heir to a long lineage of Christian nobility with a family tree going as far back as Saint Louis, ninth King of France and, ironically, a ferocious anti-Semite."

"I think I remember my father saying something about that," Cassie interrupted. "About some blue blood ancestry. I never paid it any attention."

Marceline looked at her mockingly. "Well, it's quite telling that he would remember this but conveniently forget the Jewish part, don't you think?"

"I don't know," Cassie said.

"Mother had class and elegance," Marceline continued, "but her father and brothers had perished in the Great War, and all that remained of their wealth was the house whose upkeep they could not afford. At twenty-five, Mother was still not married. The men, especially Jewish men who had come back from the Front in one piece, were few and far between. Concessions had to be made. Then my father arrived. He was Jewish, recently hired to work with his uncle, whose rug business was thriving. Yes, I know, the cliché of the Jewish carpet salesman. But it was noble enough commerce. Well, Mother must have had her moment of hesitation. Baba was a foreigner and a merchant without the slightest pedigree. But he was a charming and, as you saw, a very handsome man. Mother was finding herself an old maid with a family fortune dwindled to nothing and so must have been willing to overlook details of nationality, class, and upbringing. Meanwhile, marrying her would allow my father to integrate into French life in ways that would have been otherwise impossible." Marceline pointed to a photograph of her grandfather. "I wish you could see, too bad the photo is in black and white, but Baba had that golden eye color us three seem to share."

"Amber," Cassie said.

"Who wants amber eyes when they can be gold, wouldn't you agree?" Marceline said. Her haughtiness of earlier had been replaced with a certain youthfulness, as though in speaking about her childhood she were reverting to a younger version of herself. Her aunt's hair was thick and white as snow, but the beauty of her youth was still visible as the light of the day shone through the window on her face, revealing her fine features, her aquiline nose, her peach-colored skin, and the pale amber — or gold — of her eyes. "It was hard for people to place Baba's nationality," she said, "Italian, Persian, Greek. But no one could have mistaken him for French. He spoke every language with an indefinable accent, softly rolling his r's. Baba was likable. Everyone who met him, my mother included, fell under his spell. I adored my father. Gustave adored him too. And even though Mother could be dismissive at times, she was undoubtedly in love with him."

"What was your mother like?"

"She was educated, or at least as educated as the times had permitted a French woman to be. She read. She played the piano beautifully. She had a modern way of thinking about the role of women. She hated the notion that a woman was to be subservient to a man, and she may have resented men for the opportunities afforded to them. Now, of course, that changed the moment she had a daughter. When it came to my standing in the world, she was quite the traditionalist."

"How did your parents meet?"

"At a dinner party at Moshe's, my father's uncle. Like my father, Moshe came from the Ottoman Empire. He had made his fortune in Europe long before my father joined him in Paris. I often wondered what my mother was doing at Uncle Moshe's that evening. Those two did not belong to the same worlds. Uncle Moshe was boisterous, a large man with a booming voice who, when he could not be understood because of his broken French, just spoke louder. I've heard Mother refer to him as "the peacock." Mother valued restraint, decorum, and pedigree; Moshe had none of those. In any case, Moshe hosted a dinner, and Mother happened to be invited through shared friends."

"And so, they fell in love?"

"From the moment they met, my parents must have recognized in each other the answer to pressing needs. The benefits for a merger of sorts. Otherwise, they were an unlikely match. Mother was an assertive woman who did not tolerate contradiction, which might have been one of the reasons she had not found a husband earlier. She did not possess the demure qualities men of the time looked for in a woman. Mother wore the pants, so to speak. At least in the beginning. My father let her decide almost everything. He made money, increasing amounts as the years passed, but it was Mother who decided how to spend it, whom to invite to dinner, which salons to attend, where to go on holidays, and everything concerning the children's upbringing. Wearing the pants also meant she could be quick to anger and dismissive with Father. Perhaps his lack of social status became more difficult for Mother to overlook as the collective disposition of French citizens toward foreigners began to change during the ramp up to the Second World War. Or perhaps she became scared, and who would blame her? She might have perceived my father's gentle ways as weakness and felt it was up to her to display more traditionally masculine traits."

"Did they love each other?"

"Well, maybe not in the classic sense, but there was affection. Mother was possessive of Baba and jealous of every woman she perceived as prettier than she was. As for Baba, he put Lucienne on a pedestal, and he seemed aware that she was his social superior. As I mentioned, Mother's fortune had been lost, but there were nice remnants of her family's past glory. Mother's family could be traced back at least ten generations, and each generation left artifacts, jewelry, paintings, silver, and furniture to the generation that followed. Gustave and I grew up surrounded by it all. Today, little of this treasure remains. The bulk of it was stolen during the Second World War and never recovered. The few things we could salvage were pieces small enough to pack and take with us when the time came to flee the Nazis. And, of course, there was the house."

"This house? Where we are right now?"

"It has been in our family for over a hundred years and was built by my great-grandfather on Mother's side. The house has good bones, but it isn't as grand now as it was when your father and I were children. You should have seen it before the war. Our family lived in style. There was a chauffeur, a cook, maids. And an endless procession of nannies, which we called British nurses – the kind prized in society at the time – was dispatched to our care and education. The nannies lived with us. There was usually one for me and one for Gustave. If the nannies had a human nature, they made it a point of professionalism never to reveal it. It wasn't until much later, when my knowledge of English proved itself useful, that I could see any benefit to leaving small children to the care of such cold-hearted women."

"They were mean?"

"Only indifferent and strict, and expected to be that way. People did not indulge children the way they do now. In those days, they were to be seen and not heard. There was little crossover between the world of children and the world of grown-ups. We learned how to dress, behave, and speak to resemble miniature adults. Your father and I lived in fear of the British nannies. They punished us at the least perceived infraction; they took away our favorite toys and even chose if we deserved dessert or not. Our parents deferred to them for most matters concerning us."

"That's kind of hard to imagine these days."

"We did not know any different. Our parents were mostly absent when we were little. My father worked long hours. Moshe did most of the traveling and Baba stayed in the Paris office until late every day. Mother wasn't around much either. She was forever attending teas, and lunches, and the charity events of Paris's elite society. For this reason, Gustave and I found ourselves in the peculiar position of being the masters of the house, with the adult staff deferring to us. Our daily life was minutely scheduled by the nannies with lessons, restrictions, rules, and obligations. Interestingly, the British nannies had power over us, and Gustave and I had power over the maids, the cook, the chauffeur, and our tutors. It was unspoken, but we each knew our place. All Mother demanded of us was perfect behavior and dedication to our studies. She did not take an interest in us unless we accomplished something exceptional. Being groomed for the life of privilege that awaited us, that was our work. It came in the form of endless lessons and tutoring. Ballet, piano, drawing, etiquette, manners, school work. I excelled at all this. Lessons challenged my competitive nature. I've always wanted to be the best."

"Where did you go to school?"

"When we were small, we did not attend. Tutors, which we called précepteurs, came to the house for our lessons. We were sheltered but not indulged, and certainly never idle. Mother was always stressed and displeased, but our father was fabulous. Every evening he arrived from work bringing us treats, which he hid in his coat pockets. That was the bright moment of our day. At bedtime, we had a tradition of story-telling. Baba did not read to us from books, but instead, he sat on our beds and told us all kinds of magical stories from the Orient, stories of monkeys, and magic carpets caught at the tip of the Eiffel Tower, and magical grottos filled with gold crowns, and such."

Marceline took a breath, closed the photo album. "Our early childhood was carefree. But disconcerting events took place after 1929. I was too young to make sense of it. All I understood was that rich people were finding themselves in ruins overnight because something or other had crashed in a country called America. All we heard as children were bits of conversations, and our vivid imaginations took over. I imagined American skyscraper buildings, literally scraping the sky, and men in top hats and black coats soaring out of every window like crows, and into the clouds, and then crashing onto the ground. The world beyond the confines of my happy life was beginning to feel strangely precarious. Mother, who had always been fretful, became more nervous still. Gustave was a sensitive boy and absorbed it all. He began waking up at night with terrible nightmares. He was pale, too thin, and tense as a wound-up spring. He chewed on his sleeve constantly. The British nannies were blamed for this, and Mother kept hiring sterner ones."

"That seems counterintuitive."

"She was under the impression that Gustave was spoiled and self-indulgent, and that character in a child was something that required molding through brute strength."

Cassie looked at one of the photographs in which Marceline seemed to be about ten years old. Her chin was up, her body about to bounce out of the frame, her black curls barely tamed. She smiled, seemingly confident of her adorableness. Standing next to her, little Gustave looked imploringly at the camera. His body was scrawny in the suit, his collar too stiff for his neck. It was also apparent in all the photos that Gustave looked like his mother, whereas Marceline was the spitting image of her handsome father. "You were very pretty."

"Also, I looked gentile. This should have been of no consequence, but alas, as the century embraced anti-Semitism, this was no small matter. The fact was, Gustave looked Jewish, and I could pass for a non-Jew. Mother was quite thrilled about that." She paused and looked at Cassie, who must have looked confused. "You don't think your father looks Jewish?"

"I never thought of him looking like anything other than my dad. What does looking Jewish even mean? It would not occur to me to think of his physical appearance in those terms."

"Rest assured that others did," Marceline said. "The differences between Gustave and me were many and profound, but mostly I looked gentile and he did not. Also, he was a soft child, and I was admittedly a tough little thing."

Cassie felt a slight pinch in her heart. A sense of alarm. Her dad had hidden his Judaism to his own daughters. He had been raised in pre-war France. She did not like the math happening in her head. Her dad had been a selfish, neglectful dad as far as she was concerned. He had liked Odile and he had not liked her. A simple enough narrative. It had never occurred to her that he had been a child too. A child who had suffered.

Marceline looked absently around the room and out the window as she went inward, as if mentally dusting off fragments of memories, placing herself back in the same house but over half a century earlier.

"When I was seven and Gustave was five years old, and every night had turned into a sleepless mess for him, Baba insisted to Mother that Gustave needed a nurturing presence rather than a stern nanny. He wanted to hire someone gentle and motherly. Mother relented and interviewed new women. This possibly changed our lives. In fact, I remember the day of the interviews vividly. There were chairs lined up in the vestibule, and a dozen applicants, bearing reference letters, were made to sit and wait until Mother received them one by one. I was sitting in the garden by the gate and watching the women come in when I overheard our chauffeur gossip with our gardener, as they smoked on the other side of the gate. They did not see me and went on with their conversations. "Should we tell the pretty ones to turn back and not even bother?" the gardener said.

"She isn't foolish enough to hire help that might be a temptation," the driver responded.

They were talking about Mother.

"I would not worry about the boss. Surely, he has a mistress hidden away somewhere. Or perhaps more than one," said the gardener. "You'd know about it; aren't you the one driving him?"

The driver chuckled, "Haven't you seen who he works with? His uncle."

They both laughed, stepped on their cigarette butts, and went about their work. I did not know what they were talking about, but I was instinctively furious. I stomped into the house with the urge to tell Father and Mother that the staff had been gossiping behind their backs. But I was not halfway out of the garden when I had the hunch that telling on them might hurt my parents or at least mess with the order of things. Inside, I went to the library room and looked up the word mistress in a dictionary. As I suspected, the word in this context had nothing to do with a schoolmistress. I read the mystifying synonyms: kept woman; courtesan, concubine, paramour, and the even more perturbing word that gave me pause, lover.

Outside the library room, prospective nannies continued to line up, and Mother received them one by one in her study. Through the window, I saw my father walk out of the house and enter the car. The driver started the engine, and they left. A mistress? What would my father want with a mistress? Did he not love Mother?

That got me thinking. Indeed, the women on Mother's staff, the maids, the cook, the nannies, were homely, but I was convinced of Father's innocence. He did not show any interest for any of the fancy women who graced their dinner parties. He was generous with his time and attention, attentive and polite with all, but this behavior did not change when he was in the company of a beautiful woman. I felt that I needed to be more vigilant. How many more things went beyond the scope of my awareness? I decided to spy on my parents so as not to be caught off guard again. If there was something to know, I wanted to be the first one to find out about it.

Gustave was coming down the spiral staircase when he found me flat on my belly, spying on the group of aspiring nannies that sat on chairs in the vestibule down below.

"What is it?" he asked.

"Mother is hiring you a nanny," I told him. "I am spying on them."

"Why?"

"I'm a spy now."

"I'm a spy also then," Gustave said. He got down to his belly and looked down with me.

"There can only be one spy," I told him. "But you can be my acolyte."

We watched. There were twelve ladies, sitting with their backs straight, purses clutched on their laps, cheap hats planted firmly on their heads. They all dressed the same, narrow skirts, blazers, blouses all in variants of grey. Every fifteen minutes or so, the door to Mother's study opened, and one woman left and another entered. There were the thin ones and the large ones, but they otherwise looked so interchangeable to me that I wondered how Mother could tell them apart.

This went on for a while until the front bell rang. The maid opened the door to a new woman. From where we were, we could only see the bottom of the woman's long skirt, her thick, dark hose, and ugly shoes. A very unusual attire to say the least. The maid seemed to recoil at the sight of her and fumbled with her words, telling the arriving woman that the position had been filled, which was clearly a lie with all the other women still sitting in their chairs. The woman apologized in a heavily accented voice. She insisted that she had an appointment. "This won't do," the maid said sharply. "You must leave now." She began to close the door on the woman who said, "Wait! I have a letter."

This was the most captivating thing that had happened in the last hour of lying on our bellies at the top of the stairwell. Gustave and I twisted our necks to see the woman's face, but we were too high up the stairwell to see more than the bottom half of her. She handed an envelope to the maid, who took it reluctantly. From above we watched the maid open the envelope, read the note, and mumble, "In that case, if you would please take a seat."

The strange woman stepped forward and came into view below us. She did not wear the traditional outfit of nannies. She wore a shawl over her hair rather than a hat. Her profile revealed her as a beautiful young woman with dark eyes fringed with thick eyelashes, and a sensual mouth. She was pretty. And then, having sensed our presence, she turned to look up at us, and Gustave and I gasped. The entire right side of the woman's face, from her temple down the length of her cheek and covering her chin, was all a massive scar. It was as if her skin had been melted and set again. Burned. We had seen enough men return from the war with this kind of wound, but a woman, a nanny, never.

The woman looked at us and smiled, and her whole face blossomed into something kind and beautiful.

Her name was Sandra. I learned later that my mother had agreed to interview her only because of Uncle Moshe's pressure – he was after all my father's boss. It had been his signature and his recommendation on the letter she had shown the maid. Sandra was a refugee we soon learned. She had no family and, because of her disfigurement, could find no work.

The following day, she was hired.

Mother did put up a fight, but my father had the final word. I heard them argue behind closed doors. I had found an air vent on the floor of the library above the salon. If you leaned right on the vent and placed your ear tight against it, the conversations came out crystal clear. Baba made the case for the woman with the scar.

"But she is foreign," my mother said.

"Not any more foreign than the British ones," Father told her. "I think it is time we moved away from those women. They are not good for Gustave." This was news to me, as he had never criticized any of them in my presence.

"We know nothing about her," Mother said.

"Moshe vouches for her. Also, she can cook and bake the kinds of foods from my country. I am quite tired of French cuisine." That was news to me as well. I had no idea my father was displeased with anything at all.

Mother continued to argue, and Baba was calmly telling her why she would be good for the family. But at some point, Mother said that the woman was repulsive. Father became angry, he who never was angry. He raised his voice and said, "I have made a decision. The foreign woman is hired."

It was unlike him to contradict Mother, and I was shocked by this, but not as shocked as Mother was. At a loss for words, she stuttered, "But, Alban...."

"I will tell Moshe to send her at once," my father said. With this, he just left the room.

Thus, Sandra came to live with us.

At first, Gustave and I were horrified and fascinated by her scar, but within days, we did not see it anymore. The only times we were reminded of it was through the eyes of others who recoiled when they saw Sandra for the first time.

Father had been absolutely right. Sandra turned out to be the best thing that could have happened to Gustave and me. She spoke French hesitantly and never said one word more than she had to, but her quietness, her reluctance to speak up, were more than compensated by a genuinely loving heart. Although Sandra was officially Gustave's nanny, it was soon clear that my nanny was here for the teaching of manners and that Sandra was here to dispense the loving care to both of us. She had great empathy for us and cried along with us and laughed as well. Although she could barely read or write in French, she had an intelligence and pragmatism that commanded respect. She would listen to us, without judgment or advice. She would just sit and be with us. She soon became the one person I ran to when I was in trouble. When I felt ill, or worried, or mad, she was the person I counted on. With just a few words, she could turn drama into something manageable. Sandra came to love Gustave and me nearly as a mother would, caring for us deeply, and accepting us and loving us through our many flaws.

"How did she get burned," Cassie asked.

"Her burn covered the right side of her body, from her temple, cheek, and neck to her shoulder and arm and perhaps lower. We were embarrassed to ask how it had happened, and she did not volunteer the information. In all the time she lived with us, we never asked about her past. And she never offered to tell."

"Perhaps you were afraid to know?"

Marceline nodded. "Perhaps. Sandra's arrival in our lives, in 1931, coincided with Europe descending into madness. In the years that followed, she became our rock. We were lucky to have her."

"Anti-Semitism began, you mean?" Cassie asked.

Marceline was about to respond, but she was overtaken by one of her coughs. "Anti-Semitism has no beginning, and it has no end, my dear," she managed to say.

As on cue, Laure entered "Madame?" She said, pouring her a glass of water. "It's time for your rest."

Marceline looked at Casandra, dabbed at her eyes and sighed. "Being old is like being a baby all over again. They bathe you, diaper you, put you down for naps. The worst indignities."

"You have to go now?" Cassie said, disappointed. She had found out so much about her dad already, and yet there was so much more to learn.

"I am tired," Marceline admitted. "I can tell you more another time perhaps?"

"Of course, you should rest," Cassie said begrudgingly. "But I'm only here for a few short days. Would it be all right with you if I came back tomorrow?"

Marceline got up from her seat with Laure's help. "Not here," she said. "In neutral territory, away from Armelle and Jean-Bernard snooping into my business."

Cassie stood up. "Just tell me where and I'll be there."

"There's this place I like," Marceline said. "Le Valentin, Passage Jouffroy. You know where that is?"

"I'll find it," Cassie said.

"Please come at noon," Marceline said. She sighed unhappily. "That's the time between my morning nap and my afternoon nap."

"Thank you for speaking to me," Cassie said as Laure nudged her out of the room and toward the staircase. "It means a lot."

Marceline, who was at the door to her room, said, "Actually. I have not been entirely honest with you."

"How so?"

"I knew you were Gustave's daughter from the moment I looked through my window and saw you pass the gate."

Cassie was astounded. "How is that possible?"

"That coat you're wearing."

"It's my father's," Cassie said.

"To be precise, it is your grandfather's. I remember the coat being made by our tailor because I came to the fitting. This was in, let's see, I was about eight years old. It must have been 1931. It was during the Great Depression. Bad things were going on all around, soup kitchens, long lines. But we were still doing well. We could still afford tailored clothes. The treats I told you about, the ones my father used to bring us every evening," Marceline's voice almost broke. "They came out of those pockets." She looked away to hide her emotion.

Cassie stared at the coat. "My Jewish grandfather's coat? That sounds practically biblical."

"May I ask why you're wearing it?" Marceline asked. "It seems like an odd choice."

"It was in my dad's hospital room. I was freezing, so I took it. I did wonder why, of all the coats he owns, my dad had taken this one with him to the hospital."

"Your father's downfall was always sentimentalism," Marceline said.

CHAPTER 12

The Man on a Motorcycle

It was almost two in the afternoon by the time Cassie left Marceline's house. In that room smelling of pipe tobacco, perfume, and old papers, filled with books, knickknacks, and strange artifacts, with the rain falling hard against the window, Cassie had forgotten to look at her watch. Her mother and Odile were most likely at her dad's bedside, and she was late. She stood at the street corner hoping for a cab, her blood laced with caffeine, from all that Earl Grey tea. She hated Earl Grey, but she had been so impressed — intimidated was more like it — by old Marceline that she drank the brew stoically rather than admit her dislike for it. If there was a fitting metaphor for who she was, this was it.

After ten minutes, she gave up on the idea of a cab and began walking. She hurried back to the ninth arrondissement accompanied by the clapping sound of her cowboy boots on the pavement. Her mind was filled with visions of her father as a fragile little boy living in opulence in that Cité des Fleurs house, visions she needed to reconcile with the ailing old man in his hospital bed, so powerful that he could apparently hurt her while unconscious. She could not wait to tell her sisters all that she had learned. How much of it did her mother know already? Had her dad confided in her? Her mother always knew more than she let on. She walked down rue Marcadet, past cars, old buildings, neon signs, and people gazing at their cell phones amorously. Those buildings had been there when her grandfather, a young man from the Ottoman Empire, had first arrived in Paris in 1922. Albano had walked past the same buildings, along the same boulevards. Her father had strolled down these streets as a boy.

She walked along rue Joseph de Maistre. The rain had stopped. Children riding bicycles filled the playgrounds that had been empty earlier. Did her father and Marceline once play there? The wealth, the grand house, the nannies, the class-obsessed mother, the foreign father, the bratty big sister, none of it reconciled with the restrained man she knew. Her dad had a backstory now, pathos she could sink her teeth into. All Cassie had ever wanted was to break the code to her father's heart. Speaking to Marceline was like being handed the key. Or if not the key, a least a map to a key. Things revealed themselves as she walked. Why did her father own so many Persian rugs? Because rugs were the family business. Why did he know so much about furniture and architecture? Because he grew up with an eye for those things and the homeschooling to go with it. Who had stolen the second finial? Marceline had, obviously, since she had possession of it.

Marceline had abruptly ended her story in 1931. She had needed to regroup. She had been upset, that much was clear. It did not take a historian to know what came next. Her dad had grown up in a time and place when being Jewish could cost you your life. He had survived, somehow, and she was about to find out how. Marceline seemed surprised, contemptuous even, of the fact that he had chosen to hide his Judaism. He had wanted to erase the past, as Marceline had said? Or perhaps he had wanted to hide himself and his daughters from a time where history might repeat itself, as history always did.

****

When she arrived at the hospital, Odile was standing outside the dressing room waiting for her. "How come you're wearing Papa's coat?" she asked, sounding appalled by this.

"I was cold," Cassie said.

Odile looked down at Cassie's red cowboy boots. "And what in the Lord's name are those?"

"Long story," Cassie said, "an incredible story, in fact. I've had quite the exciting morning. That's why I'm late. I can't wait to tell you all about it. How is Papa today?"

"Maman's with him," Odile said. "We spoke to his doctor already." Odile appeared to hesitate. "The doctor says his condition is stable, but … well, they feel he needs a lot of rest and—"

"Let's go see him."

"I could use a break," Odile said tensely. "Let's go the cafeteria."

This was not what Cassie wanted to do, but she could not afford to pass on a rare offer to do something normal and sisterly with Odile. "Sure," she said.

In the cafeteria, a janitor was mopping the floor. The room smelled of synthetic lemon detergent. Unnerving French pop music played in the background. Cassie and Odile put coins in a machine and waited for their espressos as they were noisily expelled into plastic cups. They sat at one of the tables. Odile stirred sugar into her coffee, looking ill. "Are you all right?" Cassie asked.

"My stomach's acting out. Something I ate." Odile's stomach had always been a barometer for her moods.

"Well, I met Marceline," Cassie said excitedly.

Odile seemed very surprised. "You did?"

"I even went to her house."

"Is she really Papa's sister?"

"Unbelievably, yes. They could not be more different, though. She's eighty-nine years old, two years older than Papa. But they have opposite personalities. She is sharp as can be. And she seems ... I don't know ... fearless."

Odile pinched her lips. "Unlike Papa, you mean."

"No, I mean ... she's a character. She's eccentric. She told me interesting things about our grandfather. Do you know that he was from Smyrna? In the Ottoman Empire?"

"No," Odile said, excited. "I didn't know that. Wait, the Ottoman Empire? Wasn't that centuries ago?"

"I know, it sounds ancient, but apparently, it only ended in the nineteen twenties. About the time the Sacré-Coeur opened its doors."

"That has to be incorrect," Odile said.

"No, really, I went there yesterday and read it on a plaque."

Odile rolled her eyes. "Well then, if you read it on a *plaque*."

"And believe it or not, Papa was Jewish."

Odile squinted, shook her head. "Of course not."

"He had two Jewish parents." Odile was looking at her blankly, waiting for the punchline. "Amazing, isn't it?"

"I don't see how that's possible," Odile said. "Papa is Catholic. Everyone knows that."

"Apparently not by birth."

"If you say so," Odile said, shrugging with impatience.

"And that makes us half Jewish!"

"Whoopee," Odile said flatly.

"You're not amazed?"

"I frankly don't care one way or another." The way Odile said this, it was apparent she cared a whole lot. It was apparent, in fact, that she was seething.

"Why did he not tell us?"

"Maybe he forgot."

Cassie looked at Odile in disbelief. "Seriously?"

"Who cares. If Papa didn't want to be Jewish, that was up to him."

"I'm not so sure one can decide not to be Jewish."

"It's not a race," Odile said. "It's a religion. You can convert to it."

"It's both, I think. I'm not sure how it works."

"Well, we're not Jewish."

"I don't know," Cassie said. "*I* might be. I'm open to it."

"Why am I not surprised?" Odile snapped. "You never met a part of your upbringing you didn't want to reject."

Cassie stiffened in her chair, "Here it comes...."

"One day you're French, and the next you're American. One day you're Catholic, and now you've turned Jewish."

"Oh please, it's not like you're some devout Catholic. When was the last time you set foot in a church?"

"The point is, you grew up in France and were raised Catholic. Is that so terrible? Is that so disgusting to you?" Odile's voice quivered, "Are *we* so disgusting to you?"

"What scares you so much about the idea of Papa being Jewish? Or you being a Jew for that matter."

Odile snapped, "Don't say that word!"

"That *word?*" Cassie's was suddenly furious. "Do you mean the JEW word? For your information it's not a disparaging term, Odile, it's what Jewish people are called." Cassie controlled her breathing the best she could. She could have said so much more. The urge to verbally crush Odile was nearly irresistible, and the urge to crush her physically was not far behind. She could easily have reached across the table and slapped her, and Odile would have slapped her back, or pulled her hair, just as they had done throughout their childhood, with the two of them transforming into a four-arms-four-legs shrieking monster right there on the cafeteria's linoleum floor. Tempting. "Marceline will tell you about Papa if you're too frigging stubborn to hear it from me," she said between clenched teeth. "I'm seeing her tomorrow. She wants to meet you. You can come along."

Odile pinched her lips. "Not interested," she said without an instant of reflection.

"But ... why not?"

"My loyalty is to Papa."

Cassie was dumbstruck. "Why are we even discussing loyalty?"

"Here is a woman Papa didn't want to have anything to do with, and you're all chummy with her. I'm sorry, but no thank you."

Cassie raised her voice despite herself. "You don't get it at all! This is not betraying Papa; this is trying to understand him."

"You have your way of understanding him, and I have mine." Odile was even paler now. "Let's agree to disagree."

"Oh, bullshit, Odile!"

"Actually," Odile said, looking at the floor of the cafeteria, "there is something I need to talk to you about. Yesterday, this whole explosion, and screaming at you the way he did, that was hard on Papa."

Cassie rolled her eyes. "Not just on him."

"He's the one in a hospital bed, not you, last I checked," Odile snapped.

"True, true," Cassie said. "You think I don't know that?"

"We're so focused on fighting the lung infection right now that we tend to forget that he had heart surgery a few days ago. The last thing he needs is more strain on his heart."

"I could not agree more."

"The way he became emotional yesterday, that can't be good for his heart," Odile said softly.

"Probably not."

"Maman and I discussed this, and well … we think that it's better we do what we can to avoid any stress for him."

Cassie nodded in agreement. "We're on the same page."

Odile looked relieved. "Oh, good."

"Great," Cassie said, still nodding. She was happy that the argument had died down rather than escalate the way it invariably did. Maybe they were both mature enough to communicate without the usual drama. Maybe they could start a new chapter. Perhaps her father's illness could bring them closer. She smiled.

"Do you see what I'm trying to say?" Odile asked, suddenly worried.

"I – I'm not sure. Are you trying to say something?"

"Well," Odile said in a small voice and without looking at her, "We think you need to stay away."

"Away from what?"

"From Papa's room."

Cassie's stomach dropped. "What?"

"We decided … for the time being."

"Are you telling me I can't see Papa?"

"You said we were on the same page," Odile whimpered.

"*We* decided?" Cassie exclaimed. She tried to gather her jumbled thoughts through the wave of emotion: sadness, anger, a sense of betrayal and rejection. "Who's we? The doctors? You and Maman?"

Odile hesitated. "All of us, including the doctors."

"What doctors? Which doctor?"

"Doctor Dumant. We met with him this morning and—"

"Papa was on drugs. It was a freak thing! And I did nothing wrong. I just stood there, and he verbally attacked me!"

"No one said you did anything wrong," Odile said in a calm, paternalistic tone. "You don't have to take this personally."

"My own sister is asking me not to see my own father," Cassie cried out. "No, worse: my own sister is telling me not to see my own father because she believes I am harming him. And I shouldn't take it personally?"

"This is not about you."

"It is!"

"We're trying to give Papa the best possible chance at recovery."

"Unlike me, who's trying to *kill* him?" Cassie pushed her chair back and got to her feet. There was the anger and there was the caffeine, and she wasn't sure which of the two had taken over her brain. "Well, screw that! Nobody's going to dictate if I can see my own father. Like it or not, I'm going into that room."

"You can't!" Odile said, snapping at attention and jumping up from her chair.

"Who'll stop me?"

Cassie stormed out of the cafeteria, Odile running after her. "Cassandra, stop! Don't make a spectacle! Stop right now! Please listen to me. Stop!"

Cassie headed toward the room, but just before the door, she veered left and entered the first hallway, and then the next until Odile's calls and the sound of her shoes clip-clopping behind her stopped.

For ten minutes, Cassie walked through the hospital hallways in a fog, her chest heavy, her feet heavy, a painful lump stuck in her throat. She sat on a bench in a deserted hallway, a thousand-pound weight on her shoulders, defeated.

The image of Marceline came to her. Marceline in her multicolored dress, her posture, her pride. A spy for the OSS. How would Marceline handle this? Would she dissolve in a pool of tears? Cassie had a sense that she would not. Marceline did not strike her as the kind of woman who let other people affect the way she felt about herself.

She got up from the bench and stomped toward the intensive care unit. The reception area was crowded with patients, visitors, nurses, doctors, and staff. She made a beeline for the desk. Behind the desk, she recognized the frizzy-haired clerk she had badgered the day before. She gave the woman her name and avoided eye contact.

The frizzy clerk looked uneasy. She said, "The list of visitors has been restricted."

Cassie felt in her stomach the return of that hollow feeling. "Meaning?" she asked.

"Your name was crossed off the list of approved visitors," the clerk said, trying hard to appear detached from her victory.

Cassie was either going to burst into tears in front of all those people or attack. "That is my father in there. I flew all the way from the United States just to see him!"

"Yes, Madame, we are all well aware that you came from America." Cassie could hear the eye roll implied in the comment.

It was a small miracle that she didn't hurl herself at the woman's throat. "Yes, that's right! I am a proud citizen of the US of A!" she shouted. Around them, conversations suspended in mid-sentence, bodies froze in position. Everyone in the ICU, those who were ill and those who were well, the nurses and the aids, the visitors and the cleaning staff – everyone was watching. Cassie fought the urge to get louder. She said to the clerk in a controlled voice, "Why has the Chief of Services not seen me yet?"

"I told you, he does not see people."

"Let him decide if he will see me or not. Did you or did you not give him the message?"

"He was made aware of it."

"I sure hope so for your sake, because I'm ready to go right over your head. Tell him that if he doesn't see me, I will go over his head. All the way to the top! I will fight this with legal means. I will write letters to every journalist, every blogger, every politician and expose how this hospital treats its clients."

Doctor Dumant appeared at the desk, his stethoscope planted on either side of his neck. "What is ... this?" he asked dispassionately.

The clerk fumbled with her words. "Docteur Dumant. This person is ... she wants us to ... she demands...."

Cassie turned to the doctor, "And you! What gives you the right to separate me from my father? This whole thing has been mishandled by your hospital from the start. You botched the surgery; you exposed him to an infection; you did not give him the correct antibiotic. You drugged him into oblivion, which made him delusional enough to go batshit crazy. And now you're stopping me from seeing him? I'm not the one harming him. You are! The instant he set foot in this hospital you proceeded to kill him by any means possible."

"What is it you ... want from me," the doctor said in an exhausted voice.

"I want to speak to the Chief of Services!" She pointed at the clerk. "And this person here won't let me."

The doctor turned to the desk. "Did you forward the message, Mademoiselle Pinçon?"

"I think so," the clerk, who now had a name, said as she fumbled with papers. It was obvious from Mademoiselle Pinçon's demeanor that she was as flustered with people who were above her as she was intent on making people like Cassie feel two inches tall.

"She *thinks* so!" Cassie said, childish victory in her voice. "You never gave him the message, did you?"

The doctor sighed and turned to a nearby nurse, bypassing Pinçon entirely. "S'il vous plaît, Florence, could you ... make sure that the Chief of ... Services is aware that this lady wants to speak to him?"

"Oui, Docteur."

Without further words, Doctor Dumant walked away, looking at his clipboard. He put his hand on the door to the surgery unit, stopped, and turned toward Cassie. "By the way," he said. "So that we are ... clear, I am not the one keeping you away ... from the room."

"They told me you did."

"I only recommended that your ... father should be kept calm. Your mother and sister ... are the ones who made that decision. They took you off the list, and they ... have the power to do so." With this, he left.

Odile had lied. This was essentially a restraining order against her. This was nuts. This was deranged! Cassie drifted through the hallways like a somnambulist. All kinds of hurt flooded in. All the hurt she had so carefully pushed away was pushing back, about to swallow her whole. Her heart ached, and the lump in her throat seemed made of lead. She was in enemy territory here. She was under attack. Her sister hated her. Her mother hated her. Her father hated her. He always had! She was unloved because they were hateful, hateful people!

And also, because she was unlovable.

She stepped out into the courtyard and sat on an empty bench and stayed there, not even feeling the cold, humid air.

She did not know how much time had passed before Sabine sat next to her on the bench. "I had nothing to do with this; I want you to know," Sabine said. "No one consulted me. You're not missing much; Dad's not awake. And going into that room is like stepping through the gates of hell anyway."

Cassie wiped her eyes, rubbed her cheeks, felt her blood flow return. She looked at Sabine, who was wrapped in a thin coat. Her face was drawn. "How could they kick me out?" she asked her.

"They're afraid of you," Sabine said.

"King Kong and Godzilla are afraid of me?"

"They're more scared of you than you are of them."

Cassie shook her head in incomprehension. "But why?"

Sabine hesitated, looking for an accurate answer. She spoke without passion, looking at the ground. "You challenge their way of looking at the world and themselves. You need to be wrong, or else the whole castle of cards collapses."

"I'm not trying to be right. I'm trying to be ... I don't know ... not exactly appreciated ... I've resigned myself to the idea that that is not going to happen. Not approved of even. Forget about that. Accepted. That's the word. I just want to be accepted." She shook her head. "Right now, I'd settle for being tolerated."

"They've made you into this formidable enemy over the years. It's a story they tell themselves."

"I'm not even sure what that means."

Sabine moved her hair away from her face; she was trying to say something difficult. "When you left France, you were eighteen and I was eight. I looked up to you."

"You did?"

"You were just how I wanted to be when I grew up."

"I bet you've made some serious adjustments to your thinking since," Cassie said. Sabine did not answer. "I remember you too, of course. You were adorable." This was a lie. She had little recollection of Sabine as a child. It was the age difference. And she had been much too preoccupied with her teenage self to notice that she had an eight-year-old sister.

"After you left home I kept waiting for you to come back," Sabine said. She let her hair fall across her face as though she wanted to hide it. "And Papa and Maman hated Peter and the US. And little by little it got worse. Every time they spoke about you, it was to say that you had done or said this horrible thing. And then the letter ... I guess even I started to believe that you were this ... devil."

"I hope you don't mean that you've hated me for the last twenty years."

"Not hate, no. You're unpredictable. You shake things up. You're like a big wrench in the status quo. When you're here, it's impossible to go on looking at things quite in the same way. For all of us, it's damage control the minute you're involved."

"I'm Attila the Hun."

"But I think we need this," Sabine said. "Our family can use that kind of brain-shake."

"Attila the Hun, but in a fun way. You know, my kids consider me a complete bore. I consider myself a complete bore."

"You're certainly not boring."

"So, if I want their approval, all I need to do is to shut my mouth?"

"That's what I do, and I still don't get their approval." Sabine had meant this as a joke, but even her humor had an aftertaste of hopelessness.

Cassie looked at her sister and suddenly felt a terrible pang of guilt. Here she was, talking about herself when, clearly, she ought to be asking about Sabine. "Will you tell me what's going on with you for heaven's sake?"

Sabine was quiet for a minute, as though she was deciding if she should open up, or perhaps she just didn't know where to start. "Paul met someone," she said finally. "The full cliché."

From her own breakup experience, Cassie knew that platitudes only served to make oneself feel better. "I'm sorry," she said.

"I was two months pregnant."

"Did Paul know that?"

"Yes," Sabine said.

"Jeez," Cassie whistled, "what an asshole."

"I could not imagine raising children without him. Or sharing them with him and that woman. I had an abortion." She paused, looked away. "It was awful."

"I didn't know. No one called me."

"I was afraid you'd try to talk me out of it, the abortion."

"Me? I would have been supportive." Cassie reflected on this. "Actually, I'm pretty sure I would have tried to talk you out of it."

"One day, I'm happy, expecting twins –"

"Twins?" Cassie exclaimed.

"And the next, I'm –" Sabine shook her head. "I couldn't do this alone, be a mother, I mean. If it had been just one baby, maybe ... but Paul had just broken my heart. I was sinking. It was all too much." She took a deep breath, shook away whatever emotion rose in her. "I thought if I didn't do it then, I would never do it. And so, I did. It's done. It's over. The babies are gone."

"Sabine ... I don't know what to say. I wish I had been there for you."

"Since that, everything feels ... flat."

"How could it not? Have you seen someone about that? They have great medications nowadays."

"No."

"And therapy. What about therapy? Peter always said I needed therapy."

"For what?"

"Anger. Blaming. For not knowing myself. Not knowing what I want."

"You're describing everyone in our family."

"You don't seem to have anger, the way we do."

"I just redirect it."

"Where?"

Sabine pointed at herself, "Here."

In the hospital garden, a young father was walking behind his daughter. The little girl was learning how to walk. She was dressed in a navy coat, white wool stockings, and tiny Mary Jane shoes on her feet, like a child out of another century. Each time she almost toppled, the father lurched forward, but then he let her fall so that she could get a feel for it. Cassie smiled at the little girl and at the dad who smiled back. She realized that Sabine was looking right past them, not even seeing them.

"You're still young," she told her sister, knowing full well this was beside the point, but what can you say to someone who is grieving. "You have your whole life ahead of you. And you are beautiful."

"Thank you. I wish I could enjoy it. My youth, my life; I don't think I've ever felt carefree or young."

"Is there anything I can do to help?"

"This helps. The killer in this family is the feeling that you can't talk, that everything emotional is off limits. Speaking up is like stepping on land mines."

"Yep. Since I got here, they've been blowing up all over the place."

"And yet you're still standing."

"I am," Cassie said in surprise. "I *am* still standing."

****

They said goodbye, and Cassie left the hospital. She felt wiped out. All she wanted now was food in her belly followed by a long bath in that fantastic tub and then bed.

She entered La Jument Bleue at 7:10 p.m. Like clockwork, Indiana Jones was putting the lock on his motorcycle. Cassie hurried her step and rushed to the table they both coveted. Two could play this petty game. She zoomed inside and got to the table first. She folded her coat over the chair to claim it and was about to sit down when she sensed that Indiana was right behind her. She pivoted on her feet, ready to flash him a gloating smile. But she was faced with his expression of puzzlement and felt suddenly disarmed. "You wanted this table?" she asked.

"I did," he admitted. He was standing awkwardly, his helmet in one hand.

"Is that why you've been looking at me angrily?" she said. "Because I have your favorite table?"

Indiana blinked. "Not angrily," he said. "It's just that we all have our little habits."

Cassie sighed. She did not have another battle in her. "You can have your table." She grabbed her coat and moved it to the chair facing the only other empty table, which happened to be the table next to his.

"Merci," he said. "I like to be next to the window, to watch my bike. You have no idea how fast you can find yourself without a tire or a wheel." He removed his leather satchel, his jacket, his wool scarf and sat down.

Cassie settled in her chair. She was glad she had not been ridiculous about the table. It was a refreshing feeling to be the bigger person. "No explanation necessary," she said.

"When you park on the street, you can end up missing a rearview mirror; it's an antique. The parts are so hard to find. That's why I like to keep an eye."

"Hmm … hmm," she said.

They were now sitting next to one another at their respective tables, almost shoulder to shoulder, their backs to the mirrored wall, which was beyond awkward. "I've had lunch here every day for the last year," Indiana said.

"You like it that much?" she asked. They were talking, something she did not want to do, but because they sat side by side, they did not look at each other.

"Force of habit," he said. "As of late, I've been having dinner here as well."

He was trying to make conversation, she realized. He was being *nice*. Why had she assumed this would turn into a fight? When had fighting become her default mode? With her mother and father, with Peter, and now with the entire staff of a Parisian hospital that she wasn't so convinced deserved it. What was *wrong* with her? She was at her worst with Odile. Was there ever a time when she and her sister had not been at war? Odile was no better. She was always on the attack too. They reacted to each other, fed off each other's lunacy. But the thing was, it was the same pattern with her twins, always at each other's throat. Why? Could everybody else be to blame, and more important, could she be blameless when the only common denominator between all these fighting people was herself?

Indiana frowned and said. "You look mad. Are you're angry with me? Would you like the table back?"

She was surprised to see the intent look on his face as he waited for her answer. "Of course not," she said. His eyes were the palest of blue and his face nicely rugged, the face of a man who spends a lot of time outdoors. "I am angry," she admitted. "Furious, in fact. But not at you, and not about the table." And seeing that he seemed upset, she added, "I promise."

The waiter came to inform them that the dessert on special was profiteroles au chocolat. He set their tables and left. "The patronne usually reserves the table for me," Indiana said. "She did for years, and now I think I've fallen out of grace. At any rate, either you're doing something right, or I'm doing something wrong."

"We can't be still talking about the table?" Cassie said. "You did nothing wrong with the patronne. It's just that by the time you arrive in the morning, I've usually been sitting here for a while."

"Writing on placemats," he said.

"Well … I guess, yes," she answered, flustered that he had noticed. "I assume she doesn't have the heart to kick me out."

He feigned terror. "Are we speaking of the same patronne?"

She laughed. "I don't just write on placemats, you know. I order food, too."

"Steak au poivre and frites?"

She felt herself blush. "You're quite observant."

"With ketchup?"

"The way you said ketchup sounds like a reproach."

"That's not what people usually eat with a steak with pepper and cream sauce."

"What do they eat with it?"

"Well, pepper and cream sauce."

She tapped her hand to her skull. "So that's why they put it there!"

"The sauce is there to *enhance* flavor, you see," he said. "So that people won't have to resort to ketchup."

"It has nothing to do with flavor. I use ketchup strictly for comfort."

Indiana mimicked head to toe chills at the prospect. He then dug into his well-worn leather satchel. "I have something for you," he said.

"For me?" Cassie said, astonished.

"I hope you won't mind." He handed her a thin, flat package wrapped in brown paper. "I took the liberty of assuming that you could use this."

She stared at the package, then at him. "Do you always carry gifts around to give to perfect strangers?"

"Not until today."

She hesitated, but because he looked so earnest, she took the package from his hands. She stared at it. "This is weird," she said, not knowing exactly how to feel or why she even went along with this. She opened the package. In it was a single five-by-eight Moleskine notebook with a bright pink cover.

"Better than writing on placemats, no?" he said. "Do you like the color? I can trade it for any other color. It took me a while to decide. Women like pink. Some of them do, at least."

"Thank you," Cassie said. She felt helplessly moved by the gesture. When was the last time someone cared one bit what color she liked? Perhaps no one ever had. It was her first time being the object of random kindness, and it was coming at a vulnerable moment. She was usually the one anticipating the wants and needs of others, and to care for them was enough to fill her with love. But in the last years, those she loved had become self-sufficient, or they had moved on, and there was no one left to care for. Cassie steadied herself not to betray her emotion. "Did you plan on giving me this so that I would relinquish your table?"

"It was going to be either a bribe or a gift, and since you so generously gave me the table, it's definitely a gift. You should use a laptop, you know. Although I didn't feel that giving you a laptop would be appropriate at this juncture in our relationship."

She burst out laughing. "You and I are in a relationship?"

"We do share custody of a table."

Cassie shook her head, still laughing. "This is the most thoughtful gift I've received in a long time," she admitted.

"Oh, great, I'm glad."

This had been one seriously bizarre day. This morning she was learning about her ancestors from an aunt she didn't know existed. This afternoon she was being treated like a leper by her family. And here she was now, engaged in a shoulder-to-shoulder conversation with a handsome stranger over the ownership of a bistro table. "I thank you for your kindness," she told him. "The table is now yours without any grudge from me whatsoever. And for the record, I do own a laptop."

"Then it must be an invisible laptop," he said. "I'm Hervé," he added, extending his hand.

"Cassandra," she said shaking his hand. "Cassie."

"Ha!"

"Ha?"

"Cassandra," he said. "Daughter of King Priam and Queen Hecuba of Troy."

"Not that one, sorry to disappoint."

"She was given the gift of prophecy by the gods, but Apollo cursed her for not returning his love."

"What kind of curse?"

"He made it so that no one would believe her prophecies."

Cassie smiled, charmed against her will. "Well, that serves her right. What fool turns down Apollo?"

"You are new in the neighborhood?"

Cassie was not going to get into the big mess of the last few days with a stranger. "Sort of new," she said. "Returning."

"You come to La Jument Bleue every day," Hervé said. "But I had never seen you before three days ago."

"It's convenient for me," she said evasively. "What about you. You seem to live here."

"I work nearby, and since my home life has...." He searched for the appropriate word. "Well, deteriorated, I'm here a lot. It's close to work, and the food is good."

"Divorce?" she said, fishing for information.

"We were never married," he said. "What about you? I hear you're staying at Hôtel Petite Seine?" To her surprised expression, he eyed the old manager who was sitting at the bar. "I have my spies."

"So much for customer privacy."

"That's all he would tell me. So? How come you're staying there?" he asked. "A deteriorated home life too?"

Cassie thought about it. No, she didn't want to open up to this stranger. Not when stupid tears threatened to burst out of her at the slightest provocation. "It's kind of silly, carrying on a conversation while eating at separate tables," she noted.

"I was just thinking the same thing," Hervé said, and with this, he picked up his plate, knife, and fork and set them on her table, got up, and sat across from her. "Here we go," he said, reaching for his glass and setting it in front of his plate. "Have you tried the house wine?" he asked, peering at her with lagoon-colored eyes. "It's not bad at all."

Cassie's face burned. This she had not expected. To hide her surprise, she made a joke of it. "But what about the table?" she whispered, darting a worried look at the table Hervé had abandoned. "What about its feelings?"

Hervé spoke to the table as though it were a child, "If you remain very still we will come to you for dessert."

"You work in this neighborhood, huh? What kind of work do you do?" she asked, masking her growing self-consciousness by taking a large gulp of her water.

He shrugged. "I'm an administrator."

"That's vague."

"A bureaucrat," he said with a slight grimace. "I was forced to take this lousy administrative job. I'm wretched at it, and I hate every moment of it."

"You were *forced*?" she asked. She was flustered and was having trouble looking him in the eyes.

Hervé shrugged again, apparently one of his favorite things to do, and he looked pretty cute doing it. "I made a mistake," he said. "Well, it was not a mistake. Let's say I played with fire, I was burned – caught, I mean, and my boss sent me to purgatory for a few years. In actuality, it feels more like a pact with the devil. But I should not complain. They pay me well enough, and it allows me to pursue other interests."

"Such as Greek mythology?"

"For example, yes. I have many hobbies. What about you?"

"My latest hobby involves getting into arguments with anyone who comes within ten feet of me."

"I'll consider myself warned."

"As for work…." She thought about it. "I too made a pact with the devil. Although I'm pretty good at what I do."

"What do you do?"

"I'm a writer. Perhaps more of a ghostwriter of sorts."

"Ah, now it all makes sense!"

"What?"

"It explains the ghost laptop."

She laughed. "My laptop and my cell phone both just broke down. Mercury must be in retrograde."

"Oh no, it isn't," Hervé assured her. "Quite the contrary. Venus is in Mars. This is a time for action, and for love."

"I take it that astrology is another hobby of yours? Maybe you'll be able to tell me what's going to happen to me next."

"You're Cassandra," he said. "You're the one with the gift of prophecy."

"You know my gift is useless since I'm cursed. No one believes me anyway."

He raised a finger. "I *predict*," he said in a cavernous, prophetic-sounding voice, "that for dessert you'll have profiteroles au chocolat."

"You're cheating. That's not prophecy; it's mind reading."

"All right," Hervé said, and returning to his prophetic voice, added, "I *predict* that tomorrow you will not eat steak with ketchup."

"Now that's interesting. How do you know that?"

"Because you and I are going to eat in a place where they do not serve either."

"Are we?" Cassie felt herself blush to her roots. Was he asking her out? He *was* asking her out!

"I will pick you up right here tomorrow," he said. "And I will take you to a fantastic fish restaurant I know."

Evidently, she needed to say no. But what reason would she give? Looking out the window, she contemplated the deluge outside and Hervé's motorcycle that glistened in the rain. "I'm not climbing on that thing if that's what you have in mind."

"You might need to wear something insulating."

She pointed to her clothes. "Jeans and this coat are all I have."

"I'll bring a jacket and helmet. And a scarf." As he said this, and just as the waiter came in to take their orders, the patronne called from behind the counter.

"Hervé, phone call for you."

"Ha," he told Cassie. "If you'll excuse me." He got up from the table and walked to the counter.

"I am tired of being your secretary," the patronne grumbled as she handed him the receiver across the bar. "Get yourself a cell phone. Comme un homme normal," she said. Like a normal person.

He got up, listened to the person on the line. After a few minutes, he returned to the table. "I'm sorry, I can't stay. I must dash. An emergency at work." He hurried, putting on his jacket. "So, we're all set? 7:10 pm tomorrow? At your hotel?" he said, hoisting the satchel over his shoulder.

"I don't even know why, but I'm going to say … yes."

"Excellent. See you then."

He left money on the table for her dinner and left her sitting at La Jument Bleue, stunned and speechless.

****

After dinner, in her hotel, Cassie removed her boots and coat and sat in bed. She thought of Hervé and smiled. Did she really just accept a date with a handsome stranger? She giggled to herself, feeling like a teenage girl. Here she was in Paris with no computer and no phone. The last time this had happened, she was eighteen years old. She had been about to meet Peter, but unaware of it, about to leave everything behind and move to the United States, a country where she did not even speak the language. What had she been like at eighteen? She had been angry with her family, confused, rebellious. She had only known herself through the eyes of others: her secretive, passive-aggressive mother, her resentful sister, her indifferent, if not hostile, father. She had wanted an adventure. She had wanted another life. She had wanted a romance, something sweeping and wild. She had even dared wish she could shine one day, learn to be herself, whatever that meant.

Cassie closed her eyes. Marceline. That's the kind of woman she had wanted to become. But her life had taken a different turn, a twenty-year bifurcation away from the person she had hoped to be.

She went to stand by the window. Outside, the city sparkled, beautiful even in the rain. In Paris, there was a strange alchemy in the air. The moment you got there, forgotten yearnings emerged. Maybe the last twenty years had just been a detour. Maybe she could still become the person she wanted to be and live the life she had dreamed of. Maybe it wasn't too late.

The end of The Curator of Broken Things BOOK 1.

Book 2 and 3 of *THE CURATOR OF BROKEN THINGS* trilogy are available now as e-books and paperbacks.

Thank you for reading this book. If you enjoyed it, I hope you will consider reviewing it online.

I write for my readers and it is always a wonderful thing for me to receive emails and feedback, so don't be shy. Also, to receive bonus material such as historical details, prequels, characters' back stories, side stories, fun extended dialogues, and other insight into the Curator of Broken Things world, head over to my website www.corinegantz.com and sign up for the newsletter. I love to keep in touch and have a lot of material that didn't make it into the books.

Take care,

Corine.

ACKNOWLEDGEMENTS

Thank you to my first readers, Joanna Kamburoff, Katherine Kohler, Catie Jarvis, Peggy Schmouder, and Betsey Parlatore, for kindly and carefully sifting through versions of the books when they were still a mess. I am incredibly thankful to Donald Berman, a man with the soul of a writer, for his precision in English *and* French, and for his support for the novels. A great thank you to Lisa Yoo for her creative talent and expertise in design. Most of all, thank you to my husband Joe for his tireless editing, his honesty, his intuition, his kindness, his ebullient optimism, and for not wavering in his belief in me in the past 30 years.

ABOUT THE AUTHOR

Corine Gantz was born in France where she spent the first twenty years of her life. She studied Contemporary Art at the Sorbonne and worked in advertising and marketing in Paris, San Francisco, and Los Angeles. Her first novel, *Hidden in Paris*, was published in 2011 and has been translated in nine languages. She is the mother of two sons and lives near Los Angeles with her husband.

Email her:
corinegantz@live.com

Visit her website:
www.corinegantz.com

For information, email:
corinegantz@live.com
www.corinegantz.com

Carpenter Hill Publishing

ISBN-13: 978-0-9834366-5-2
ISBN-10: 0-9834366-5-7

Proofreading and copyediting by Donald Berman
donaldberman@hotmail.com

COVER ART

Cover illustration by David Navas
www.davidnavas.com

Cover design by Lisa Yoo
www.yisaloo.info

Made in the USA
Monee, IL
18 July 2021

73858858R10154